RANDOM
HOUSE

LARGE
PRINT

Saint Maybe

ANNE TYLER

Saint Maybe

Published by Random House Large Print
in Association with Alfred A. Knopf
New York   1991

25569945

CONTENTS

Saint Maybe

1

THE AIRMAIL
BOWLING BALL

On Waverly Street, everybody knew everybody else. It was only one short block, after all—a narrow strip of patched and repatched pavement, bracketed between a high stone cemetery wall at one end and the commercial clutter of Govans Road at the other. The trees were elderly maples with lumpy, bulbous trunks. The squat clapboard houses seemed mostly front porch.

And each house had its own particular role to play. Number Nine, for instance, was foreign. A constantly shifting assortment of Middle Eastern graduate students came and went, attending classes at Johns Hopkins, and the scent of exotic spices drifted from their kitchen every evening at suppertime. Number Six was referred to as the newlyweds', although the Crains had been married two years now and were beginning to look a bit worn around the edges. And Number Eight was the Bedloe family. They were never just the Bedloes, but the Bedloe *family*, Waverly Street's version of the ideal, apple-pie household: two amiable parents, three good-looking children, a dog, a cat, a scattering of goldfish.

In fact, the oldest of those children had long ago married and left—moved out to Baltimore County and started a family of her own—and the second-born was nearing thirty. But somehow the Bedloes were stuck in people's minds at a stage from a dozen years back, when Claudia was a college girl in bobby socks and Danny was captain of his high-school football team and Ian, the baby (his parents' big surprise), was still tearing down the sidewalk on his tricycle with a miniature license plate from a cereal box wired to the handlebar.

Now Ian was seventeen and, like the rest of his family, large-boned and handsome and easygoing, quick to make friends, fond of a good time. He had the Bedloe golden-brown hair, golden skin, and sleepy-looking brown eyes, although his mouth was his mother's, a pale beige mouth quirking upward at the corners. He liked to wear ragged jeans and plaid shirts—cotton broadcloth in summer, flannel in winter—unbuttoned all the way to expose a stretched-out T-shirt underneath. His shoes were high-top sneakers held together with electrical tape. This was in 1965, when Poe High School still maintained at least a vestige of a dress code, and his teachers were forever sending him home to put on something more presentable. (But his mother was likely to greet him in baggy, lint-covered slacks and one of his own shirts, her fading blond curls pinned scrappily back with a granddaughter's pink plastic hairbow. *She* would not have passed the dress code either.) Also, there were complaints about the quality of Ian's schoolwork. He was bright, his teachers said, but lazy. Content to slide through with low B's or even C's. It was the spring of his junior year and if he didn't soon mend his ways, no self-respecting college would have him.

Ian listened to all this with a tolerant, bemused expression. Things would turn out fine, he felt. Hadn't they always? (None of the Bedloes was a worrier.) Crowds of loyal friends had surrounded him since kindergarten. His sweetheart, Cicely Brown, was the prettiest girl in the junior class. His mother doted on him and his father—Poe's combination algebra teacher and baseball coach—let him pitch in nearly every game, and not just because they were related, either. His father claimed Ian had talent. In fact sometimes Ian daydreamed about pitching for the Orioles, but he knew he didn't have *that* much talent. He was a medium kind of guy, all in all.

Even so, there were moments when he believed that someday, somehow, he was going to end up famous. Famous for what, he couldn't quite say; but he'd be walking up the back steps or something and all at once he would imagine a camera zooming in on him, filming his life story. He imagined the level, cultured voice of his biographer saying, "Ian climbed the steps. He opened the door. He entered the kitchen."

"Have a good day, hon?" his mother asked, passing through with a laundry basket.

"Oh," he said, "the usual run of scholastic triumphs and athletic glories." And he set his books on the table.

His biographer said, "He set his books on the table."

That was the spring that Ian's brother fell in love. Up till then Danny had had his share of girl-friends—various decorative Peggies or Debbies to hang upon his arm—but somehow nothing had come of them. He was always getting dumped, it seemed, or sadly disillusioned. His mother had started fretting that he'd passed the point of no return and would wind up a seedy bachelor type. Now here was Lucy, slender and pretty and dressed in red, standing in the Bed-loes' front hall with her back so straight, her purse held so firmly in both hands, that she seemed even smaller than she was. She seemed childlike, in fact, although Danny described her as a "woman" when he introduced her. "Mom, Dad, Ian, I'd like you to meet the woman who's changed my life." Then Danny turned to Mrs. Jordan, who had chosen this inopportune moment to step across the street and borrow the pinking shears. "Mrs. Jordan: Lucy Dean."

His mother, skipping several stages of acquaintanceship, swept Lucy into a hug. (Clearly more was called for than a handshake.) His father said, "Well, now! What do you know!" The dog gave Lucy's crotch a friendly sniff, while Mrs. Jordan—an older lady, the soul of tact—hastily murmured something or other and backed out the door. And Ian clamped his palms in his armpits and grinned at no one in particular.

They moved to the living room, Ian bringing up the rear. Lucy perched in an easy chair and Danny settled on its arm, with one hand resting protectively behind her loose knot of black hair. To Ian, Lucy resembled some brightly feathered bird held captive by his brown plaid family. Her face was very small, a cameo face. Her dress was scoop-necked and slim-waisted and full-skirted. She wore extremely red lipstick that seemed not gaudy, for some reason, but brave. Ian was entranced.

"Tell us everything," Bee Bedloe ordered. "Where you met, how you got to know each other—everything."

She and Ian's father had seated themselves on the sofa. (Ian's father, who had a baseball player's mild, sloping build, was pulling in his stomach.) Ian himself remained slouched against the door frame.

"We met at the post office," Danny said. He beamed down at Lucy, who smiled back at him trustfully.

Bee said, "Oh? You two work together?"

"No, no," Lucy said, in a surprisingly croaky little drawl. "I went in to mail a package and Danny was the one who waited on me."

Danny told them, "She was mailing a package to Cheyenne, Wyoming, by air. I told her it would cost twenty dollars and twenty-seven cents. You could see it was more than she'd planned on—"

"I said, 'Twenty twenty-seven! Great God Almighty!' " Lucy squawked, startling everyone.

"So I told her, 'It's cheaper by parcel post, you know. That would be four sixty-three.' 'Let me think,' she says, and moves on out of the way. Gives up her place at the counter. Stands a few feet down from me, frowning at the wall."

"I had to take a minute to decide," Lucy explained.

"Frowns at the wall for the *longest* time. Three

customers go ahead of her. Finally I say, 'Miss? You ready?' But she just goes on frowning.''

"I was mailing some odds and ends to my ex-husband and I wanted to be shed of them as fast as possible," Lucy said.

A little jolt passed through the room.

Bee said, "Ex-husband?"

"Half of me wanted him to get that box tomorrow, even yesterday if it could be arranged, but the other half was counting pennies. 'That's fifteen-and-some dollars' difference,' this other half was saying. 'Think of all the groceries fifteen dollars could buy. Or shoes and stuff for the children.' "

"Children?"

"What got to me," Danny said, "was how she wouldn't be hurried. How it didn't bother her what other people made of her. I mean she just stood there pondering, little bit of a person. Then finally she said, 'Well,' and straightened her shoulders and chose to spring for airmail."

"It mattered just enough, I decided," Lucy said. "It was worth it just for the satisfaction."

"If she had said parcel post I might have let her go," Danny said. "But airmail! I admired that. I asked if she'd like to have dinner."

"He was the best-looking thing I'd seen in ages," Lucy told the Bedloes. "I said I'd be thrilled to have dinner."

Bee and Doug Bedloe sat side by side, smiling

extra hard as if someone had just informed them that they were being photographed.

There was this about the Bedloes: They believed that every part of their lives was absolutely wonderful. It wasn't just an act, either. They really did believe it. Or at least Ian's mother did, and she was the one who set the tone. Her marriage was a great joy to her, her house made her happy every time she walked into it, and her children were attractive and kind and universally liked. When bad things happened—the usual accidents, illnesses, jogs in the established pattern—Bee treated them with eye-rolling good humor, as if they were the stuff of situation comedy. They would form new chapters in the lighthearted ongoing saga she entertained the neighbors with: How Claudia Totaled the Car. How Ian Got Suspended from First Grade.

As for Ian, he believed it too but only after a kind of hitch, a moment of hesitation. For instance, from time to time he had the feeling that his father was something of a joke at Poe High— ineffectual at discipline, and muddled in his explanation of the more complicated algebraic functions. But Bee said he was the most popular teacher Poe had ever employed, and in fact that was true. Yes, certainly it was true. Ian knew she was right.

Or look at Claudia. The family's one scholar,

she had dropped out of college her senior year to get married, and then the babies started coming so thick and so fast that they had to be named alphabetically: Abbie, Barney, Cindy, Davey . . . Where would it all end? some cynical voice inquired from the depths of Ian's mind. Xavier? Zelda? But his mother said she hoped they would progress to *double* letters—Aaron Abel and Bonnie Belinda—like items on a crowded catalog page. Then Ian saw Claudia's children as a tumbling hodgepodge heaped in a basket, and he was forced to smile.

Or Danny. Wasn't it sort of a comedown that Danny had gone to work at the post office straight out of high school, when both sides of the family as far back as anyone could remember had been teachers? ("Educators," Bee called them.) But Bee pointed out how lucky he was, knowing so early in life what he wanted and settling in so contentedly. Then Ian readjusted; he shifted gears or something and *whir!* he was rolling along with the others, impressed by Danny's good fortune.

He had always assumed he was the only one who experienced that hitch in his thoughts. He assumed it until the day Lucy arrived, when he felt his parents' hidden start at the word "exhusband." Wait. The girl of Danny's dreams had chosen someone else before him? And was saddling him with someone else's children besides?

His father looked confused. His mother's broad face developed a brittle, tight surface, like something easily broken.

Ian himself absorbed the notion with no trouble. Of course, he wanted only the best for Danny. He had worshiped Danny since infancy—the family's all-round athlete, talented in every known sport but not the least stuck up about it, unfailingly sunny-natured and patient with his little brother. But as Ian saw it, Lucy *was* the best. The ex-husband was only a minor drawback; same for the children. What mattered was that pile of black hair and those long black lashes. None of Danny's previous girls could begin to compare with this one.

But he saw how steadily his parents smiled—stony, glazed smiles as they murmured chitchat. His mother said it certainly was an unusual way for a couple to meet. His father said he'd have opted for parcel post, himself; so *he* would never have been asked to dinner, would he, heh-heh. His mother said that speaking of dinner, Lucy must stay for spaghetti. Danny said she couldn't; he was taking her to Haussner's Restaurant to celebrate their engagement. The word "engagement" sent another shock through the room; for now it was plain that, yes, Danny really was set on this. Bee said maybe later in the week, then. Lucy thanked her in her foggy, fascinating voice. They all stood up. Ian stepped away from the door frame and received his first direct glance from Lucy. She had pure gray eyes, almost silver, and up close her little nose revealed a sprinkling of freckles.

After Danny and Lucy had left, his parents returned to the living room and sat back down on the couch. Supper was more than ready, but no one mentioned eating. Ian wandered over to the upright piano in the corner. Dozens of family photos, framed in dull brass or varnished wood, stood on an ivory lace runner. Other, larger photos hung behind, nearly obscuring the flowered wallpaper that had darkened over the years to the color of a manila envelope. He studied those: his grandmother standing grimly erect beside his seated grandfather, his Great-Aunt Bess trying to master a hula hoop, Danny in a satin track uniform with a first-place ribbon hung around his neck. Whenever Danny did something he enjoyed, his face would shine with a fine sweat. Even eating made him sweat, or listening to music. And in this photograph—where he'd recently been sprinting under hot sunshine, after all, and then had the pleasure of winning besides—he gleamed; he seemed metallic. You could imagine he was a statue. Ian lightly touched the frame. (Dust felted his finger. For all her great clattery housecleaning, Bee tended to let the little things slide.) Behind him, his mother said, "Well, we've been wishing for years he'd get married."

"That's true, we have," his father said.

"And now that the draft's stepping up . . ."

"Oh, yes, the draft," his father said faintly.

"Did she mention how many children she had?"

"Not that I can recall."

"If she has lots," Bee told him, "we can mix them in with Claudia's and form our own base-ball team."

She laughed. Ian turned to look at her, but he was too late. Already she had passed smoothly over to unquestioning delight, and he had missed his chance to see how she did it.

Lucy did not have lots of children after all; just two. A girl aged six and a boy aged three. She lived a couple of miles away, Danny said, in a rented apartment above a Hampden pharmacy; and she left the children with the pharmacist's wife when she went to work every day. He told Ian this later that night, when he stopped by Ian's room on his way to bed. He said she worked as a waitress at the Fill 'Er Up Café—the only job she could find that allowed her to arrange her hours around her children's. But he would soon put an end to *that*, Danny said. No working wife for Danny.

He said she had mailed that package at the request of her ex-husband. Her ex-husband was getting remarried and he wanted her to send him his things. Lucy had packed up every trace of him: the geisha girl figurine he'd won tossing darts at the fair, for instance, and the bowling ball in the red-and-white canvas bag that matched her own. Danny listed these objects in a detailed and lingering way, as if even they had fallen within the circle of his love. The bowling ball, he said, had accounted for much of the package's weight (a total of twenty-eight pounds). Lucy had also mentioned a trophy cup, which couldn't have been so very light either.

Ian tried to imagine Lucy bowling. Illogically, he pictured her in the shoes she had worn to the house—little red pumps with red cloth roses at the toes. The high heels would make tiny dimples in the glossy wood of the runway.

"She's a wonderful cook," Danny said. "Whenever I come to dinner she fixes a special meal for me and she lights new candles. Lucy feels people should always eat by candlelight. And sometimes she makes her own holders; last night it was two red apples. Wasn't that smart? She has the smartest ideas. She's good with napkins, too; she folds them into these different shapes, accordions or butterflies or wigwams, because Lucy says . . . ."

Lucy says, Lucy feels, Lucy believes. She

seemed almost present in the room with them. Danny lounged in the doorway with his hands in his trouser pockets, his eyes slanting slightly the way they did when something fired him up. The knot of his tie hung loose on his chest, which made him look tipsy even though he wasn't.

How did their evenings *end?* Ian wanted to ask. Did the two of them make out on her couch? Or maybe even go all the way?

Danny spoke of Lucy's knack for interior decorating, her concern for her children, her difficult past life. "Both her parents died in a car crash when she was still in her teens," he said, "and that husband of hers must not have been much, considering how far he's fallen behind on the child support. Not that she complains. She never says a word against anyone; that's not her style. I tell you, Ian, I've been looking for a woman like Lucy all my life, but I'd started to think I'd never find her. I almost thought there was something wrong with me. I'd meet these girls who seemed so pretty and so nice and then it would turn out I'd been hoodwinked; they were flirts or users or constitutional liars and everyone knew it but me. Shouldn't there be some sort of training course in how to judge a woman? How are guys supposed to figure these things out? Well, some just do; it's some kind of gift, I guess. But I was starting to worry I was jinxed. Then along comes Lucy. Two weeks ago she was a total stranger, can you believe it? And yet I'm certain she's the one. She makes her own curtains and she cuts her children's hair herself. She can plant a snipped-off twig in a pot and it will turn green and start growing. When I circle her waist with my hands, my fingertips almost meet."

Ian somehow knew exactly how that would feel: her body narrowing between his palms like a slender, graceful vase.

Danny and Lucy were married a week later, in the Presbyterian church on Dober Street that the Bedloes sporadically attended. Lucy wore a rose-colored suit and a white pillbox hat with a bow. She stood in front of the minister with her arm linked through Danny's, and her feet were placed primly together so that Ian's eyes were riveted to the seams on the backs of her stockings. He had never seen seams on stockings before, if you didn't count old black-and-white movies. He wondered how she got them so straight. They looked like two fountain-pen lines drawn with the aid of a ruler.

Pathetically few guests dotted the bride's side of the church. The first pew held a couple of waitresses from the Fill 'Er Up Café, both wearing cone-shaped hairdos that made them seem the tallest people present. Behind them sat the pharmacist and his wife, with Lucy's two children huddled against the wife. Ian had met the children at a family dinner the night before, and he hadn't thought much of them. Agatha was as cloddish as her name—plain and thick, pasty-faced. Thomas was thin and dark and nimble but no more responsive to grownups. During the wedding they both gazed elsewhere—up at the vaulted ceiling, around at the pebbly pink windows—till Mrs. Myrdal leaned over and whispered sharply. Agatha was the kind of child who breathed through her mouth.

But the groom's side! First came the parents, Doug Bedloe belted in and slicked down in an unfamiliar way and Bee wearing a new striped dress from Hutzler's. Then in the second pew, a row of Daleys—Claudia and her husband, Macy, and all five of their rustling, fidgeting children, even little Ellen, although a sitter had been hired to lurk at the rear of the church just in case. Ian sat in the third pew with Cicely, holding hands. And if he turned around, he could see Danny's friends from high school and his co-workers from the post office and just about the whole neighborhood as well: the Cahns, the Crains, the Mercers, Cicely's parents and her brother Stevie, Mrs. Jordan in her bald fur stole even on this warm May day, and every last one of the foreigners—a row of tan young men wearing identical shiny black suits. The foreigners never missed a chance to attend a celebration.

The minister spoke at some length about the

institution of marriage. Danny shifted his weight a few times but Lucy stayed dutifully motionless. Ian wondered why a hat like hers was called a pillbox. It looked more like a pill than a box, he thought—a big white aspirin.

Cicely squeezed his hand and Ian squeezed back, but not as hard. (She was wearing his class ring, bulky as a brass knuckle.) Distantly, he registered the bridal couple's "I do's"—Danny's so emphatic that the younger Daleys giggled, Lucy's throaty and endearing. Then Dr. Prescott pronounced them man and wife, and they kissed. It wasn't one of those show-off kisses you sometimes see at weddings. Lucy just turned and looked up into Danny's eyes, and Danny set both hands on her shoulders and bent to press his lips against hers very gently. After that they stepped back and smiled at the guests, and everyone rose and came forward to offer congratulations.

The reception was held at the Bedloes', with fancy little cakes that Bee and Claudia had been baking for days, and Doug's famous spiked punch in a plastic garbage can reserved only for that purpose, and bottled soft drinks for the children. There were more than enough children. Claudia's brood chased each other through a forest of grownups' legs. Rafe Hamnett's sexy twin ten-year-old daughters stood over by the piano, each slinging out a hip and brandishing a paper straw like a cigarette. Only Lucy's two seemed not to be enjoying themselves. They sat on a windowsill, almost hidden by the curtains on either side. At one point Cicely dragged Ian over to try and make friends with them—she was known at school for being "considerate"—but it wasn't a success. Thomas shrank against his sister and picked at a Band-Aid wrapped around his thumb. Agatha kept her arms folded and stared past them at her mother, who was offering a small hand to each guest as Danny introduced her. ("Honey, this is Melvin Cahn, who lives next door. Melvin, like you to meet the woman who's changed my life.")

Cicely asked Agatha, "Isn't it nice that you have a new uncle? Think of it: Uncle Ian."

Agatha shifted her gaze to Cicely as if it took real effort.

"Isn't that nice?" Cicely said.

Agatha finally nodded.

"She's overcome with joy," Ian told Cicely.

Cicely made a face at him. She was a pert, sweet, round-eyed girl with a bubbly head of blond curls. Today she wore a yellow shift that turned her breasts into two little upturned tea-cups. Ian laced his fingers through hers and said, "Let's go to your place."

"Go? I haven't said hello to your folks yet."

But she let him lead her away, past Doug Bedloe with his punch dipper poised, past her little brother with his six-gun, past the foreigners practicing their English on the front porch. "Is it not fine day," one of them said—Joe or Jim or Jack; they all had these super-American names shortened from who-knows-what. They stood back respectfully and followed Cicely with their eyes (how they admired blondes!) as Ian guided her down the steps.

Next to the curb, Danny's blue Chevy stood waiting. The bride and groom were driving to Williamsburg for their honeymoon—just a three-day trip because that was the longest Lucy felt comfortable leaving the children. Some of the neighborhood teenagers had tied tin cans to the rear bumper and chalked JUST MARRIED across the trunk. *Married!* Ian thought, and he realized, all at once, that Danny really had gone through with it. He was a husband now and would never again stop by Ian's bedroom door at night, his suit coat hooked over his thumb, to talk about the Baltimore Colts. Ian felt a rush of sorrow. But Cicely's parents wouldn't stay at the reception forever, so he said, "Let's go," and they started walking toward her house.

That summer, Ian got a job with Sid 'n' Ed's A-1 Movers—a very local sort of company consisting of a single van. Each morning he reported to a garage on Greenmount, and then he and two lean, black, jokey men drove to some shabby house where they heaved liquor cartons and furniture into the van for a couple of hours. Then they drove to some other house, often even shabbier, and heaved it all out again. Ian managed to enjoy the work because he thought of it as weight lifting. He had always been very conscious of muscles. As a small boy, admiring Danny and his friends at sports, he had focused upon their forearms—the braiding beneath the skin as they swung a bat or punched a volleyball. There, he thought, was the telling difference, more than whiskers or deep voices. And he had examined his own reedy arms and wondered if they would ever change. But when it happened he must have been asleep, for all at once two summers ago he had noticed as he was mowing the lawn—why, look at that! The ropy muscles from wrist to elbow, the distinct blue cords of his veins. He had flexed a fist and gazed down, hypnotized, till his mother hallooed from the porch and asked how long he planned to stand there.

Well, like a lot of other things, muscles had turned out to be no big deal after all. (Now he thought it might be sleeping with a girl that made the difference.) But even so, he continued to work at building himself up. He deliberately chose the heaviest pieces of furniture, pushing ahead of Lou and LeDon, who were happy to lag behind with the bric-a-brac. Then in the evenings he came home hot and sweaty and swaggery, and his mother would say, "Phew! Go take a shower before you do another thing." He stood under the shower till the water ran cold, after which he dressed in fresh jeans and a T-shirt and went off to eat dinner at Cicely's. His mother hardly cooked at all that summer. Claudia was sick as a dog with her latest pregnancy, so often as not Bee would have spent the day baby-sitting. Sometimes she said, "What, you're eating at the Browns' *again?*" But he could tell she was just as glad. She and his father would have a sandwich in front of the TV, or they'd walk over to Lipton's. She said, "Mind you don't wear out your welcome, now." Then she forgot about him.

He and Cicely twined their feet together under the table while her mother served him double portions of everything. Cicely slid a hand secretly up his thigh, and Ian rearranged his napkin and swallowed and told Mrs. Brown how much he liked her cooking. Mr. Brown was usually absent, out selling insurance to homeowners who could be reached only in the evenings, but Cicely's little brother was there—a pest and a nuisance. He would tag along after dinner, boring Ian to death with baseball questions. He hung around the two of them on the screened back porch. "*Stee*-vie!" Cicely would say, and Stevie would ask, "What? What am I doing?"

"Don't you have any friends of your own?"

"I'm not doing anything."

"Ma, Stevie's being a brat again."

"Stevie, come along inside, now," Mrs. Brown would call.

Then Stevie would leave, kicking the glider as he passed and lowering his prickly, white-blond head so no one could see his face.

Ian and Cicely had been going together since ninth grade. They were planning to get married after college, although sometimes Cicely teased him and said she'd have to see who else asked her, first. "Change the name and not the letter, change for worse and not for better," she said. But then she would move over into Ian's lap and wrap her arms around his neck. She smelled of baby powder, warm and pink. She wore pink underwear, too—a slippery pink bra with lace edges. Sometimes when they had been kissing a while she would let him unfasten the hook at the back, but he had to be careful not to tickle. She was the most ticklish person he had ever met. Things would just be getting interesting when all at once she would pull away and fall into peals of helpless laughter. Ian felt like a fool when that happened. "Oh, great. Just great," he would say, and she would say, "It's not *my* fault if your hands are cold."

"Cold? It's ninety-eight degrees out."

"That's not *my* fault."

Did other girls behave like this? He would bet

they didn't. He wished she were, oh, more womanly, sometimes. More experienced. He said, "This is supposed to be a moment of romantic passion, must I remind you." He said, "We're not in kindergarten, here." Once he said, "Have you ever considered wearing stockings that have seams?" But when Cicely started laughing she just couldn't seem to stop, and all she did was shake her head and wipe the tears from her eyes.

One August afternoon, he came home from work to find a note on the hall table: *Claudia in hospital, Dad and I staying with kids*. At first he didn't think much about this. Claudia was nearly always in the hospital, it seemed to him, giving birth to one baby or another. He dropped the note in the wastebasket and climbed the stairs, with the dog panting hopefully behind him. But then while he was showering, it occurred to him that Claudia couldn't be having her baby yet. She didn't even look very pregnant yet. He'd better call his mother and find out what was wrong.

As soon as he was dressed, he bounded back downstairs to use the phone. But on the next-to-last step he heard somebody crossing the dining room. Beastie, following close on his heels, uttered a low growl. Then Lucy appeared in the doorway. "Ian?" she said.

"Oh," he said.

She wore a big white shirt of Danny's and a pair of red pedal pushers, and her hair was tied back in a red bandanna. She looked about twelve years old. "Have you talked with your mom yet?" she asked him.

"No, but she left a note. What's the matter with Claudia?"

"Oh, nothing all that serious. Just, you know, a little bleeding . . ."

Ian began studying an area slightly above her head.

"So anyway," she said, "I thought I'd fix you some supper. Ordinarily I'd invite you to our place, but we're going out so I brought something over. There's potato salad, and ham, and I've put some peas on the stove to warm up."

He didn't tell her he usually ate at Cicely's. All summer the family had tactfully left her and Danny alone, allowing them to get past the honeymoon stage, so they met only on special occasions like Bee's birthday and the Fourth of July. Lucy must not have any notion about their day-to-day lives.

He followed her through the dining room to the kitchen, where he found Thomas and Agatha sitting in two straight-backed chairs. There was something eerie about children who kept so quiet you didn't realize they were in the house. Thomas held a large, naked doll with a matted wig. Agatha's hands were folded tidily on the table in front of her. They looked at Ian with no more expression than the doll wore. Ian said, "Well, hi, gang," but neither of them answered.

He leaned against the sink and watched Lucy flitting around the kitchen. Her hair billowed halfway down her back, longer than he would have expected. She wore white sandals and her toenails were painted fire-engine red. None of the girls at school painted their nails anymore. Everyone was striving for the natural look, which all at once struck Ian as homely.

He realized she must have spoken to him. She was facing him with her head cocked. "Pardon?" he asked.

"Do you want your ham cold, or heated up?"

"Oh, um, cold is fine."

"It won't be real fancy," she said, opening the refrigerator. "Tomorrow if your mom's still busy we'll ask you to dinner. Why, you haven't been over since I painted the living room!"

"No, I guess not," Ian said.

She and Danny were renting a one-story house just north of Cold Spring Lane. So far they had hardly any furniture, but everything they did have was modern, modern, modern—black plastic and aluminum and glass. Bee claimed it would take some getting used to, but Ian loved it.

"Next week I start on the children's room,"

Lucy said. "I found this magazine with the best ideas! Sit down, why don't you."

He pulled out a chair and sat across from the children. A place had already been laid for him with the company silver and his mother's best china. Two candlesticks from the dining room flanked a bowl of pansies. He began to feel ridiculous, like one of those rich people in cartoons who banquet all alone while a butler stands at the ready. He asked Thomas and Agatha, "Am I the only one eating?"

They gazed at him. Their eyes were a mournful shade of brown.

"How about you?" he asked Thomas's doll. "Won't you join me in a little collation?"

He caught Thomas's lips twitching—a victory. A chink of a giggle escaped him. But Agatha remained unamused. "Her name is Dulcimer," she said reprovingly.

"Dulcimer?"

"Ian doesn't care about all that," Lucy told them.

"She used to have clothes," Agatha said, "but Thomas went and ruined them."

"I did not!" Thomas shouted.

Lucy said, "Ssh," and lit the candles.

"She used to have a dress with two pockets, but he put it in the washer and it came out bits and pieces."

"That was the washer did that, not me!"

"Now she has to go bare, because his other dolls' clothes are too little."

Ian forked up a slice of ham and looked again at Dulcimer. Her body was cloth, soiled to dark gray. Her head was pink vinyl and so were her arms and her legs, which had a wide-set, spraddled appearance. "Maybe she could wear real baby clothes," he suggested.

"Mama won't—"

"That's what I say, too!" Thomas burst out.

"Mama won't let her," Agatha continued stubbornly. There was something unswerving about her. She reminded Ian of certain grade-school teachers he had known. "Mama's got all these baby clothes she buys at Hochschild's, nightgowns and diapers and stuff Dulcimer would *love*, but Mama won't lend them out."

"Have some peas," Lucy told Ian.

"Oh, thanks, I'll just—"

"Today she bought a teeny-weeny baby hat with blue ribbons but she says if Thomas plays with it he'll get it dirty," Agatha said.

Ian looked over at Lucy, and Lucy looked back at him ruefully. She said, "Don't tell the others, will you?"

"Okay."

"I want to wait till Claudia gets out of the hospital."

"My lips are sealed," he said.

It was a pleasurable moment, sharing a secret

with Lucy. The secret itself, though, he wasn't so sure of. He thought of Danny circling her waist with his hands, his fingertips nearly meeting. Couldn't he have let her stay as she was? Did everything have to keep marching forward all the time?

She said, "We ought to get going, kids."

"Well, thanks for the food," Ian told her.

"You're very welcome."

After they left he could have stopped eating— he was already late for supper at Cicely's—but he worried Lucy would find out somehow and feel hurt. So he made his way through everything, sweating in the candlelight, which was, to tell the truth, sort of uncomfortable for August. She had laid out the ham slices in a careful, scalloped design that reminded him of the patterns etched alongside the ocean. And although it would have saddened him to let the ham go to waste, it saddened him too to finish it and end up with just the empty plate.

Claudia did manage to keep her baby. In fact, she went way past her due date. Her doctor had predicted the first week in December, but things dragged on so long that Ian started betting the baby would arrive on his birthday, January 2. "Oh, please," Claudia said. "Let's hope to God you're wrong." She was big as a house and her ankles were swollen and she'd had to have her rings cut off with a hacksaw. At Christmas she was still lumbering around, and Christmas dinner was a spectacle, with Claudia and Lucy sitting elbow to elbow in their ballooning maternity smocks. Lucy turned out to be the type who carried her baby a great distance in front of her (something to do with her small frame, perhaps), so that even though she had two months to go, she looked nearly as pregnant as Claudia. She was officially a member of the family now—the honeymoon joyfully over and done with, in the Bedloes' eyes, the moment she announced her good news. Now they felt free to stop by her house more often and to invite her and Danny for potluck. Ian had almost reached the point where he could take her for granted. Although still when she turned her silvery gaze upon him he had an arrested feeling, a sense of a skipped beat in the atmosphere of the room.

One of the Bedloe traditions was that important dinners, on holidays and such, were not the usual boring assortment of meats and vegetables. Instead, Bee served their favorite course: hors d'oeuvres. Oh, there'd be a turkey at Thanksgiving, cakes for birthdays, but those were just a nod to convention. What mattered were the stuffed mushrooms, the runny cheeses, the spreads and dips and pâtés and shrimps on toothpicks. The family was secretly proud of this practice; they enjoyed watching guests' reactions. Nothing humdrum about the Bedloes! That Christmas they had oysters on the half shell, and the look of horror on Lucy's children's faces made everybody laugh. "Never mind," Danny told them. "You don't have to eat them if you don't want to."

Danny was exuberant these days. He had re-searched pregnancy and childbirth as if he ex-pected to deliver the baby himself, and he kept a long scroll of possible names scrunched in his pocket. For some strange reason, he seemed very fond of Thomas and Agatha. Well, Thomas was all right, Ian supposed. He looked kind of cute in his dapper little sailor outfit. But Agatha! Really there was only so much you could do with such a child. Her frilly pink dress made her face appear all the more wooden, and her hair stood out at her jaw in a monolithic wedge. Sometimes Ian caught her giving him one of her flat stares, reminding him of that doll that Thomas was so attached to. Dulcimer. Same numb, blank face, same unseeing eyes.

They moved to the living room and settled themselves, groaning. The cat threw up an oys-ter behind the couch. Barney fed cracker crumbs to the goldfish, Abbie played "The First Noel" on the piano with a rhythm as ponderous as army boots, and Doug brought out his Polaroid Land camera and took pictures of them all— each photo after the first one showing somebody

holding a previous photo, admiring it or grimac-
ing or industriously coating it with fixative. Then
little Cindy, who had fallen asleep in front of the
fire, woke up cranky, and the dog accidentally
stepped on her and made her cry. Claudia said,
"That's our cue! Time to go!" and she heaved
herself to her feet. They all departed at once—
Claudia's family and Danny's—leaving behind a
litter of torn gift wrap and mismatched mittens
and oyster shells. "This was our best Christmas
ever, wasn't it?" Bee asked Doug. But she always said that.

Claudia's baby came two days later—a girl.
Frances, they named her. Ian said, "Well, I was
almost right. It's almost my birthday."

"Cheer up," Bee told him. "There's always the
next one."

"Next one! Good grief."

The next one of Claudia's, they both meant.
It never occurred to them that *Lucy's* baby might
arrive on his birthday. But that was what
happened.

He had spent the evening at Cicely's, where
she and his friends threw him a party. When he
got home he found his mother waiting up for
him. "Guess what!" she said. "Lucy had her
baby."

"What, so soon?"

"A little girl: Daphne. She's small but healthy,

breathing on her own . . . Danny called about an hour ago and he was so excited he could hardly talk."

"After this he won't be fit to live with," Ian said gloomily.

"And Lucy's doing fine. Oh, won't the neighbors tease us? They'll be counting on their fingers, except in this case it's obvious that . . . you want to go with me to the hospital tomorrow?"

"I have school tomorrow," Ian said.

Besides, he had never been much interested in infants.

He didn't see the new baby for a week, in fact, what with one thing and another. Neither did Claudia, who was stuck at home with her own baby. So on Sunday, when everyone gathered at the Bedloes' for dinner, Danny made a big production of introducing his daughter. "Ta-da!" he trumpeted, and he entered the house bearing her high in both hands—a tiny cluster of crochet work. "Here she is, folks! Miss Daphne Bedloe." Lucy looked paler than usual, but she laughed as she bent to unbutton Thomas's jacket.

"Let's see her," Claudia commanded from the couch. She had constructed a kind of nest there and was nursing Franny. Ian had retreated to the other side of the room as soon as he saw Claudia fumbling under her blouse, and he made no move now to come closer. All newborns looked more or less alike, he figured. And this one might still be sort of . . . fetus-shaped. He hung back and dug his hands in his pockets and traced an arc in the rug with one sneaker.

But Danny said, "Don't you want to see too, Ian?" and he sounded so hurt that Ian had to say, "Huh? Oh. Sure." He took his hands from his pockets and approached.

Danny set her on the couch next to Claudia and started peeling off layers. First the crocheted blanket, then an inner blanket, then a bonnet. His fingers seemed too thick for the task, but finally he said, "There!" and straightened up, grinning.

What was that fairy tale? "Sleeping Beauty," maybe, or "Snow White." Skin as white as snow and hair as black as coal and lips as red as roses. So she was prettier than most other babies, yes, but still not all that interesting. Until she opened her eyes.

She opened her eyes and fixed Ian with a thoughtful, considering stare, and Ian felt a sudden loosening in his chest. It seemed she had reached out and pulled a string from somewhere deep inside him. It seemed she *knew* him. He blinked.

"Your birthday-mate," Danny was saying. "Or

birthmate, or whatever they call it. Isn't she something?"

To regain his distance, Ian let his eyes slide over to Claudia. He found her looking directly into his face, meaningfully, narrowly. He couldn't think what she wanted to convey; he didn't understand her intensity. Then it came to him, as clearly as if she had spoken.

This is not a premature baby.

He was so astonished that he let his eyes slide back again, forgetting why he had glanced away in the first place. And it was true: she might be small but her cheeks were round, and her little fists were dimpled. She looked nothing like those "Life Before Birth" photos in *Life* magazine.

"Isn't she a love?" Bee asked. "Two loves," she added, blowing a kiss toward Franny. And Claudia said, "She's a beauty, Lucy."

Ian turned to study Claudia. She was smiling now. Her face—a younger, smoother version of Bee's—seemed relaxed and peaceful. The hitch had been smoothed over. Not a trace of it remained. Here was their newest member, born early but in perfect health, thank God, and everything in the Bedloe family was as wonderful as always.

Well, hold on (Ian told himself). Don't be too hasty. Daphne was no longer brand-new, after all. She'd had six whole days to catch up before he laid eyes on her. Best to put the subject right out of his mind.

But over the next few weeks it kept sidling back, somehow.

If Danny and Lucy had been going together forever, why, a seven-months baby (quote, unquote) would have been something to wink at. But they hadn't been going together forever. Nine months ago they hadn't even known each other. Lucy had not yet walked into the post office to plunk her famous package on Danny's counter. She might have been dating someone else entirely.

In school last year a senior had had to get married to a girl he swore he hardly knew. Or rather, he swore *everybody* knew her. It was Ian's first intimation of the fix a man could find himself in. Women were the ones who held the reins, it emerged. Women were up close to things. Men stood off at one remove and were forced to accept women's reading of whatever happened. Probably this was what Ian's father had been trying to tell him in that talk they'd had a few years ago, but Ian hadn't fully understood it at the time.

One night he asked Cicely, "What do you think of Lucy?"

"Oh, I just love her," Cicely said.

"Yes, but—"

"She's always so easy to talk to; she always asks me these questions that show she's been listening. Real questions, I mean. Not those who-cares questions most other grownups ask."

"Yes . . ." Ian said, because he had noticed the same thing himself. Lucy had a grave, focused manner of looking at him. He could imagine she had been reflecting upon him seriously ever since their last meeting.

"I just think Danny is lucky to have her," Cicely said, and Ian said, "Well, yes, he is. Yes, he is lucky."

Ian had quit his job with Sid 'n' Ed's when school reopened; his mother made him. This was his senior year and she wanted him to concentrate on getting into a halfway decent college. The last thing he needed was to waste his time hauling other people's mattresses, she said.

But what she didn't seem to realize was that a person his age had to have a social life, and a social life took money. By February, he was broke. So when Lucy called and asked if he would baby-sit—a job he hated, and one he was ill equipped for besides, as youngest in his family—he didn't immediately refuse. "Well," he said, stalling, "but I don't even know how to change a diaper."

"You wouldn't have to," Lucy told him. "I

would change her just before I left. And most likely she'd be sleeping; this would be after-noons."

"Oh. Afternoons."

"Just a couple of hours after school now and then. Please, Ian? I'm about to lose my mind cooped up all day. And I can't keep imposing on your mother, and Mrs. Myrdal won't come any-more and Cicely's got cheerleading practice. I just want to get out on my own a while—go shopping or take a walk with nobody hanging onto me. I'd pay you a dollar an hour."

"You would?" he said.

On the rare occasions Claudia had talked him into sitting, the pay had been fifty cents.

"And Thomas and Agatha have taken such a shine to you. They're the ones who suggested you."

"Oh, well, in that case," Ian said. "If it's a matter of popular demand . . ."

So he started walking over from school one or two afternoons a week and staying till dusk. It wasn't a job that required much work, but somehow he found it far more tiring than Sid 'n' Ed's. No wonder Lucy wanted a break! This was the coldest, grayest time of year, and the stark modern furniture that had seemed so elegant in the summer had a bleak feel in the winter. Toys and picture books covered the white vinyl couch. Sheaves of Agatha's pulpy first-grade papers lay scattered across the rug. Thomas and Agatha had the used, slightly tarnished look that even the best-tended children take on late in the day, and they pressed in upon him too closely, drilling him with questions. Was Ian ever going to play in the World Series? Did he know how to drive a car? A motorcycle? An airplane? Did he and Cicely go to many balls? (This last from Agatha, who had a big crush on Cicely.) Gradually he forgot that they had once been tongue-tied in his presence.

They clung to the belief that Ian felt a special affection for Dulcimer, and they always made a point of displaying what she was wearing that day—one or another infant outfit handed down from Daphne. "Why, Miss Dulcimer!" Ian would say. "I do believe fuzzy pink flannel is your most becoming fabric." They thought it was hilarious when he spoke to her directly. Then they might play Parcheesi—Ian's idea; all the Bedloes loved any kind of game—or he read to them, his throat aching tightly with held-back yawns as he imitated various squeaky animals.

Daphne was usually an invisible, slumbering presence, but if Lucy stayed out too long Ian might hear a tentative cry from the children's room. He would find her lying in her crib, sucking her fist and watching the door so his first impression was always that considering stare. She was the only person he knew of with navy blue eyes.

He would lift her awkwardly, in a bunch, pretending not to notice the dampness seeping around the legs of her terry-cloth pajamas. He would carry her to the kitchen and set a bottle in the electric warmer. Waiting for it to heat, he breathed her smell of warm urine and something vanilla-ish—maybe just her skin. Thomas tugged at one of her terry-cloth feet. "Hey there, Daffy. Daffy-doo." Daphne squirmed and murmured into the curve of Ian's neck.

When Lucy returned, she brought a burst of cold air through the door with her. The cold seemed to lie on her surface in a sparkling film. And she was always lit up and laughing, excited by her expedition. She would hold out her arms to the children. "Were you good?" she would ask. "Did you miss me?" and she'd take the baby from Ian and nuzzle her face, nose to nose. "Guess what: I felt a couple of snowflakes. I bet we're going to have snow tonight." Balancing Daphne on her hip, she would fish in her big shoulder bag for Ian's pay—generously rounding off to the nearest dollar, sometimes even adding a tip and telling him to take Cicely someplace nice. Ian knew that she and Danny weren't rich, and he would protest but she always insisted. "Well, thanks," he'd say lamely, and she would say, "Thank *you!* You don't know how you saved my life." Her money smelled of her cologne, a tingly scent that clung to the bills for hours afterward and hung in his room when he emptied his pockets at bedtime.

One afternoon when she returned there was something distracted about her. She greeted the children absently and failed to inquire after Daphne, who was still asleep. "Ian," she said right away, "can I ask you something?"

"Sure."

"Can I ask what you think of this dress?"

She slipped her coat off, revealing a different dress from the one she had left the house in. Holding her arms out at her sides, she spun like a fashion model. Thomas and Agatha gazed at her raptly. So did Ian.

It was the most beautiful piece of clothing he had ever seen in his life. The material was a luminous ivory knit, very soft and drapey, but over her breasts and her hips it was perfectly smooth. What would you call such material? He could imagine its silkiness against his fingertips.

"Do you think Danny will mind?" Lucy asked. "I don't want him to feel I'm a spendthrift. Do you think I should take it back?"

"Oh, well, I wouldn't," Ian said. "Now that you've gone to the bother of lugging it home."

She looked down at it, doubtfully.

He told her, "That, um, what-do-you-call . . ."

That V neckline, he wanted to say, *plunging so low in the middle. And that skirt that whisks around your legs and makes that shimmery sound.*

But what he said was, "That cloth is not bad at all."

"But would you think it cost a lot?"

"Oh, only about a million," he said. "Give or take a few thousand."

"No, don't say that! That's what I was afraid of. But it didn't cost hardly anything, I promise. You want to know what it cost? Nineteen ninety-five. Can you believe it? Can you believe that's all it cost?"

Well, she did want his answer, after all. So he reached out to touch the fabric at her waist. It was so fine-spun it made his fingers feel as rough as rope. He curved his palm to cup her rib cage and he felt the warmth of her skin underneath. Then Lucy took a sharp step backward and he dropped his hand to his side.

"Oh, ah, nineteen ninety-five sounds . . . very reasonable," he said. His voice seemed to be coming from somewhere else.

There was a moment of silence. All he heard was Agatha's snuffling breath.

"But anyhow!" Lucy said, and she laughed too gaily, artificially, and lifted her bag from the table. "Thanks for your opinion!" she said. Was she being sarcastic? She owed him two dollars but she paid him five. A hundred-and-fifty-percent tip. He said, "I'll bring your change next time I see you," and she said, "No, keep it. Really."

He felt mortified by that.

Walking home through the twilight, he kicked at clumps of old snow and muttered to himself. Once or twice he groaned out loud. When he entered the front hall Bee said, "Hi, hon! How was our little Daffodil?" But Ian merely brushed past her and climbed the stairs to his room.

Over the next few days—a Friday and a weekend—he didn't baby-sit; nor would he have ordinarily. He and Cicely went to a movie; he and his two best friends, Pig and Andrew, went bowling. Striding toward the foul line with the bowling ball suspended from his fingers, he thought of Lucy mailing that package to Wyoming. What kind of woman owns her own bowling ball? Not to mention the geisha girl figurine.

Really there was a great deal about Lucy that was, oh, a little bit tacky, when you came right down to it. (What a relief, to discover she wasn't flawless!) Now he recalled the grammatical slips, *It won't be real fancy* and *It didn't cost hardly anything*; the way she sometimes wore her hair down even with high heels; the fact that she had no people. He knew it wasn't her fault her parents had died, but still you'd expect a few family connections—brothers and sisters, aunts, at least cousins. And how about friends? He didn't count those two waitresses; they were just workmates. No, Lucy kept to herself, and when she went out in the afternoons she went alone and she returned alone. He envisioned her rushing in from one of her shopping trips, her cheeks flushed pink with excitement.

Funny how she never brought any parcels back.

Why, even last Thursday she'd brought no parcel, the day she came home with that dress.

She hadn't bought that dress at all. Someone had given it to her.

She wasn't out shopping. She was meeting someone.

She had asked if the dress looked expensive. Not *Do you think I paid too much?* but *Could I get away with saying I paid next to nothing?* "Can you believe it?" she had asked. (Insistently, it seemed to him now.) What she'd meant was, *Will DANNY believe it, if I tell him I bought it myself?*

He watched the bowling ball crash into the pins with a hollow, splintery sound, and a thrill of malicious satisfaction zinged through him like an electrical current.

When she phoned Monday night to ask if he could baby-sit the following afternoon, he felt confused by the realness of her. He had somehow forgotten the confiding effect of that gravelly little voice. But he was busy, he told her. He had to study for a test. She said, "Then how about Wednesday?"

He said he couldn't come Wednesday either. "Besides," he said, "baseball practice is starting soon, so I guess after this I won't be free anymore."

Lucy said, "Oh."

"Pressing athletic obligations, and all that," he said.

There was a pause. He forced himself not to speak. Instead he conjured up a picture of Danny, for whose sake he was doing this. His only brother! His dearest relative, who trusted everyone completely and believed whatever you told him.

"Well, thanks anyway," Lucy said sadly, and then she said goodbye. Ian was suddenly not so certain. He wondered if he had misjudged her. He stood gripping the receiver and he noticed how his heart ached, as if it were he, not Lucy, who had been wounded.

For Doug's birthday, Bee made his favorite hors d'oeuvres—smoked oyster log and spinach balls and Chesapeake crab spread. Claudia made a coconut cake that looked like a white shag bathmat. She and her family were the first to arrive. She had Ian come out to the kitchen with her to help put on the candles—fifty-nine of them, this year. Ian wasn't in a very good mood, but Claudia kept joshing him so finally he had to smile. You couldn't stay glum around Claudia for long; she was so funny and slapdash and comfortable, in her boxy tan plaid shirt the same color as her skin and the maternity slacks she was wearing till she got her figure back. They ran out of birthday candles and started using other kinds—three tall white tapers and several of those stubby votive lights their mother kept for power failures. By now they had the giggles. It was almost like the old days, when Claudia wasn't married yet and still belonged completely to the family.

So Ian said, "Hey. Claude."

"Hmm?"

"You know Lucy."

"What about her?" she asked, still teary with laughter.

"*You* don't think she had that baby early. Do you?"

Her smile faded.

"Do you," he persisted.

"Oh, Ian, who am I to say?"

"I'm wondering if somebody ought to tell Danny," he said.

"Tell him?" she said. "No, wait. You mean, talk about it? You can't do that!"

"But he looks like a dummy, Claude. He looks so . . . fooled!"

He was louder than he'd meant to be. Claudia

glanced toward the door. Then she set a hand on his arm and spoke hurriedly, in an undertone. "Ian," she said. "Lots of times, people have, oh, understandings, you might say, that outsiders can't even guess at."

"Understandings! What kind of understandings? And then also—"

But he was too late. The swinging door burst open and the children rushed in, crying, "Mom!" and "Danny and them are here, Mom." Claudia said, "What do you think of our cake?" She held it up, all spiky and falling apart. She was laughing again. Ian pushed past her and left the kitchen.

In the dining room, Lucy bounced the baby on her shoulder while she talked with Bee. She still had her coat on; she looked fresh and happy, and she smiled at Ian without a trace of guilt. His mother said, "Ian, hon, could you fetch the booster seats?" She was laying a notched silver fish knife next to each plate. The Bedloes owned the most specialized utensils—sugar shells and butter-pat spears and a toothy, comblike instrument for slicing angel food cake. Ian marveled that people could consider such things important. "Also we'll need those bibs in the linen drawer," his mother said, but he passed on through without speaking. From the living room he heard the TV set blaring a basketball game. "Notice that young fellow on the right," his father

was saying. "What's-his-name. Total concentration. What's that fellow's name?"

Ian climbed the stairs while his family's voices
filled the house below him like water—just that
murmury and chuckly, gliding through the rooms
to form one single, level surface.

On Saturday Cicely's parents were taking a trip
to Cumberland, leaving Cicely in charge of her
little brother. They were planning to be gone
overnight. This meant that after her brother went
to bed, Cicely and Ian would be just like married
people, all alone downstairs or maybe even upstairs in her bedroom with the door locked. They
didn't discuss the possibilities in so many words,
but Ian got the feeling that Cicely was aware of
them. She said maybe he'd like to come over
about eight thirty or so. (Stevie's bedtime was
eight.) She wanted to cook him a really elegant
dinner, she said. They would have candles, just
like Lucy. Maybe Ian could dress up a little.
Maybe get hold of a bottle of wine.

He preferred the taste of beer himself, but he
would certainly bring wine, and also flowers. He
wasn't so keen on dressing up but he would do
that too, if she wanted. Anything. Anything.
Would she let him stay the whole night? It didn't
seem the right moment to ask. They were sitting
in the school cafeteria with accordion-pleated

drinking-straw wrappers whizzing around their heads.

Saturday morning he slept till noon, and as soon as he woke he phoned Cicely to see what color wine she wanted. "What *color*?" she said, sounding hurried. "Any color; I don't care."

"But aren't you supposed to—?"

"I have to go," she said. "Something's boiling over."

After he'd hung up he realized he should have asked about the flowers, too—what color flowers. Or was it only with corsages that the color mattered? This was a meal, not a prom dress. Oh, everything was all so new to him, all on a larger scale than he was used to. He worried he wouldn't know precisely what to do with her. He wished Danny were around. The only person in the house was his mother, and she was in one of her cleaning frenzies. She didn't even offer him lunch. He had to make his own—three peanut butter sandwiches and a quart of milk, which he drank directly from the carton when his mother wasn't looking.

In the afternoon he and Andrew went over to Pig Benson's house and played Ping-Pong. *Tick-tock, tick-tock*, the ball went, while Ian considered dropping a hint about tonight. Or would that be bragging? Danny had once told him that girls hate boys who kiss and tell. Also, it was possible that Pig and Andrew might do something juvenile like shine flashlights in Cicely's windows or lean on the doorbell and then run. It was *very* possible. Look at them: scuffling around the Ping-Pong table all gawky and unkempt and wild, acting years and years younger than Ian.

Although at the same time, there was something enviable about them.

When he reached home, his mother was standing in front of the hall mirror in her best dress, screwing on her earrings. "Oh! Ian!" she said. "I thought you'd never get here."

"What's up?"

"You're supposed to head over to Lucy's right away. She needs you to baby-sit."

"Baby-sit? I can't baby-sit! I've got a date."

"Well, I'm sure she won't be long; she's just meeting a friend for a drink, she says. Danny's at a stag party. Goodness, look at the time, and your father's not even—"

"Mom," Ian said, following her into the living room, "you had no business volunteering me to baby-sit. I've got plans of my own, and besides I think I might spend the night at Pig's. You have way, way overstepped, Mom. And another thing. This Lucy, calling up the minute Danny's back is turned—"

"Back is turned! What are you talking about? It's Bucky Hargrove's stag party; Bucky's getting married next week."

She was plumping cushions and collecting sections of the evening paper. Her high heels gave her an unaccustomed, stalking gait, and Ian could tell she was wearing her girdle; she inhabited her dress in such a condensed manner. She stooped stiffly for a dog bone and said, "Not that I approve of such things: bunch of grown men telling dirty jokes together. So that's why I said to Lucy, 'Why, of course you should get out! Ian would be glad to sit!' I said. And don't you let on you feel otherwise, young man, or you'll be grounded for life and I mean it."

The front door opened and she spun around. "Doug?" she called.

"Here, sweetheart."

"Well, thank the Lord! You've got fifteen minutes to dress. Did you forget we were invited to the Finches'?"

When Ian passed through the hall on his way out, he sent his father a commiserating look.

It was near the end of March, that period when spring approaches jerkily and then backs off a bit. The light was hanging on longer than it had a week ago, but a raw, damp wind was moving in from the north. Ian zipped his jacket and turned up the collar. He circled a group of Waverly Street children playing hopscotch—bulkily wrapped little girls planting their feet in a no-nonsense, authoritative way down a ladder of chalked squares. He performed a polite minuet with one of the foreigners, dodging right, then dodging left, till the foreigner said, "Please to excuse me," and laughed and stepped aside. Ian nodded but he didn't stop to talk. Talking with the foreigners could tie up half the evening, what with that habit they had of meticulously inquiring after every possible relative.

By the time he reached Jeffers Street, dusk had fallen. The windows of Danny's house glowed mistily, veiled by sheer white curtains. Ian rang the doorbell and then knocked, to show he was a man in a hurry. The sooner Lucy got going the sooner she would be back, he figured.

He had expected her to look shamefaced at the sight of him. (Surely she knew she hadn't played straight, going behind his back to his mother.) But when she opened the door, she just said, "Oh, Ian! Come in. I really do appreciate this." Then Thomas and Agatha hurtled toward him from the living room, both wearing footed pajamas. "Ian!" they shouted. "Did you bring Cicely? Where's Cicely? Mama said maybe—"

"Let him catch his breath," Lucy told them. She was putting on her coat. She wore a red turtleneck and long, loose woolen pants that gave the effect of a skirt. It seemed unjust that she should be so pretty. "My friend Dot phoned at the very last minute," she said. "I know it's a Saturday night, but I thought maybe if you invited Cicely over—"

"She has to stay with her brother," Ian said bluntly. He stood in front of her with his fists in his jacket pockets. "I'm supposed to go to *her* house. I promised I'd be there at eight thirty."

"Oh, well, that's no problem. Right now it's—" She slid back a sleeve and checked her watch. "Six forty. I'll tell Dot I have to be in early. Remember Dot? From the Fill 'Er Up Café?"

"Yeah, sure," Ian said heavily.

But she didn't seem to catch it. She was looking for something. "Now, where . . ." she said. "Has anyone seen my keys? Well, never mind. You be good, kids, hear? and you can stay up till I get back." Then she left, shutting the door behind her so neatly that Ian didn't even hear the latch click.

In the living room, Daphne sat propped in her infant seat in front of the TV. "Hey there, Daph," Ian said, shucking off his jacket. The sound of his voice sent her little terry-cloth arms and legs into unsynchronized wheeling motions. She craned around till she was looking up into his face and she gave him a lopsided smile. It was sort of flattering, really. Ian squatted to pick her up. He felt as surprised as ever by the fight in her—the wiry combativeness of such a small body. Even through the terry cloth, the heat from her tiny armpits warmed his fingers.

"Ian," Thomas said, "*why* don't you come over anymore?"

"Now we got no one," Agatha said, "and Mama called Mrs. Myrdal and begged and pleaded but Mrs. Myrdal hung up on her."

"Are you mad on account of I beat you at Parcheesi last time?" Thomas asked.

"Beat me!" Ian said. "That was just a fluke. The merest coincidence. Bring on the board and I'll prove it, you young upstart."

Thomas tittered and went off for the Parcheesi board.

While the two children were setting up the game on the rug, Ian phoned Cicely. "Hello?" she said, out of breath.

"Hi," he said. He shifted Daphne to his hip.

"Oh, Ian. Hi."

"I'm over baby-sitting at Lucy's. Just thought I'd let you know, in case you find yourself desperate for the sound of my voice or something."

"Baby-sitting! When will you be done?"

"It shouldn't take long. Lucy promised—"

"I have to go," Cicely broke in. "I'm following this recipe that says *Simmer covered, stirring constantly*. Can you figure that out? I mean, am I supposed to keep popping the cover off and popping it back on, or what? Do you suppose—"

She hung up, perhaps still talking. Ian sat down on the rug and settled Daphne on his knee.

It was true he liked all games, but Thomas and Agatha were not very challenging opponents. They employed a strategy of avoidance, fearfully clinging to the safety squares and deliberating whole minutes before venturing into open territory. Also, Thomas couldn't add. Each toss of the dice remained two separate numbers, laboriously counted out one by one. "A two and a four. One, two. One, two, three—"

"Six," Ian said impatiently. He scooped up the dice and flung them so they skittered across the board. "Eight," he said. "Ha!" Eight was what he needed to capture Agatha's man.

"No fair," she told him. "One douse went on the carpet."

"Die," he said.

Her jaw dropped.

"One *die* went on the carpet," he said. He picked up his own man.

"No fair if they don't land on the board!" she said. "You have to take your turn over."

"I should worry, I should care, only babies cry no fair," Ian singsonged. He pounded his man down the board triumphantly. "Five, six, seven—"

The phone rang.

"—eight," he said, nudging aside Agatha's man. He hoisted Daphne to his shoulder and reached up for the phone on the plastic cube table. "Hello?"

"Ian?"

"Hi, Cicely."

"On your way over, could you pick up some butter? My white sauce didn't thicken and I had to throw it out and start again, and now I don't have enough butter for the rolls."

"Sure thing," Ian said. "So how's our friend Stevie?"

"Stevie?"

"Is he getting ready for bed yet?"

"Not *now*; it's a quarter past seven."

"Oh. Right."

"Oops!" she said.

She hung up.

Ian hoped she wasn't losing sight of the important issues here. White sauce, rolls, what did he care? He just wanted to get that brother of hers out of the picture.

Daphne breathed damply into his left ear. He boosted her higher on his shoulder and turned back to the game.

They finished Parcheesi and started Old Maid. Old Maid was sort of pointless, though, because Thomas couldn't bluff. He had that sallow kind of skin that reveals every emotion; whenever he grew anxious, bruiselike shadows deepened beneath his eyes.

The game went on forever and Daphne

started fussing. "She wants her bottle," Agatha said, not lifting her gaze from her cards. Ian went out to the kitchen to take her bottle from the refrigerator, and while he waited for it to warm he jounced Daphne up and down. It didn't do any good, though; he seemed to have lost his charm. All she did was fuss harder and climb higher on his shoulder, working her nosy, sharp little toes irritatingly between his ribs.

When he returned to the living room, the other two had abandoned the card game and were watching TV. He sat between them on the couch and fed Daphne while a barefoot woman sang a folk song about hammering in railroad ties. Thomas sucked his thumb. Agatha wound a strand of hair around her index finger. Daphne fell asleep halfway through her bottle and Ian rose cautiously and carried her to her crib.

At 8:15, he started getting angry. How was he supposed to make it to Cicely's by 8:30? Also he had to stop off at home beforehand—change clothes, filch some wine from the pantry. Damn, he should have seen to all that before he came here. He jiggled a foot across his knee and watched a housewife in high heels explaining that bacteria cause odors.

At 8:35, the phone rang. He sprang for it, already preparing his response. (*No*, you can't stay out longer.) "Ian?" Cicely asked. "When you come, could you bring some gravy mix?"

"Gravy mix."

"I just can't understand where I went wrong."

Ian said, "Did Stevie get to bed all right?"

"I'm going to see to that in a minute, but first this gravy! I pick up the spoon and everything in the pan comes with it, all in a clump."

"Well, don't worry about it," Ian told her. "I'll bring the mix. Meanwhile, you get Stevie into bed."

"Well . . ." Cicely said, trailing off.

"Dad's old rocker dull and gray?" two girls sang on TV. "Stain it, wax it, the Wood-Witch way!"

After he'd hung up, Ian turned to the children and asked, "Did your mother say where she was going?"

"No," Agatha said.

"Was it someplace she could walk to?"

"I don't know."

He rose and went to the front window. Beyond the gauzy curtains he saw street lamps glinting faintly and squares of soft yellow light from the neighboring houses.

There was a wet, uncorking sound behind him—Thomas's thumb popping out of his mouth. "She went in a car," Thomas said distinctly.

Ian turned.

"She went in a car with Dot," Thomas told

him. "Dot lives down the block a ways and Mama went over to her house and got herself a ride." He replaced his thumb.

A wail floated from the children's room. Ian glanced at Agatha. A second wail, more assured.

"You didn't burp her," Agatha said serenely.

Thomas merely sent him the drugged, veiled gaze of a dedicated thumb-sucker.

From 8:40 to 9:15 Ian walked Daphne around and around the living room. Thomas and Agatha quarreled over the afghan. Thomas kicked Agatha in the shin and she started crying—unconvincingly, it seemed to Ian. She rolled her knee sock down to her thick white ankle and pointed out, "See? See there what he did?"

Ian patted the baby more rapidly and revised his plans. He would not go home first after all; they would do without the wine and butter and whatever. He would simply explain to Cicely when he got there. "I don't care about dinner," he would say, drawing her into his arms. "I care about *you*." And they would climb the stairs together, tiptoeing past her brother's door and into—

Oh-oh.

The one thing he could not do without—the three things, in their linked foil packets—lay in the toe of his left gym shoe at the very back of his closet. There was no way he could avoid going by his house.

The phone rang again and Ian picked up the receiver and barked, "What!"

Cicely said, "Ian, where *are* you?"

"This goddamn Lucy," he said, not caring if the children heard. "I've a good mind to just walk on out of here."

Agatha looked up from her shin and said, "You wouldn't!"

"Everything's stone cold," Cicely said.

"Well, don't worry. The dinner's not impor-tant—"

"Not important! I've been slaving all day over this dinner! We're having flank steak stuffed with mushrooms, and baked potatoes stuffed with cheese, and green peppers stuffed with—"

"But how about Stevie? Did Stevie get to bed all right?"

"He got to bed hours ago."

Ian groaned.

"Is that all you care about?" Cicely asked. "Don't you care about my cooking?"

"Oh! Yes! Your cooking," Ian said. "I've been looking forward to it all day."

"No, don't say that! I'm afraid you'll be dis-appointed."

"Cicely," Ian said. "Listen. I'll be over soon no matter what. Just wait for me."

He hung up to find Thomas and Agatha eyeing him reproachfully. "What're you going to do? Leave us on our own?" Thomas asked.

"You're not babies anymore," Ian said. "You can take care of yourselves."

"*Mama* never lets us. She worries we'd get into the matches."

"Well, would you?" Ian asked him.

Thomas considered awhile. Finally he said, "We might."

Ian sighed and went back to walking Daphne.

For the next half hour or so, they played I Spy. That was the most Ian could manage with Daphne fretting in his arms. Agatha said, "I spy, with my little eye . . ." and her gaze roamed the room. Ian was conscious all at once of the mess that had grown up around them—the playing cards, the twisted afghan, the strewn Parcheesi pieces.

". . . with my little eye, as clear as the sky . . ." Agatha said, drawing it out.

"Will you just for God's sake get on with it?" Ian snapped.

"Well, I'm trying, Ian, if you wouldn't keep interrupting."

Then she had to start over again. "I spy, with my little eye . . ."

Ian thought of Lucy's gray eyes and her perfect, lipsticked mouth. The red of her lipstick was a *bitter* red, with something burnt in it. She had had things her own way every minute of her life, he suspected. Women who looked like that never needed to consider other people.

Daphne finally unknotted and fell asleep, and Ian carried her to the children's room. He lowered her into the crib by inches and then waited, holding his breath. At that moment he heard the front door open.

His first concern was that the noise would disturb Daphne. That was how thoroughly he'd been sidetracked. Then he realized he was free to go, and he headed out to tell Lucy what he thought of her.

But it wasn't Lucy; it was Danny, standing just inside the living room door and screwing up his face against the light. Ian could tell he'd had a couple of beers. He wore a loose, goofy smile that was familiar from past occasions. "Ian, fellow!" he said. "What're *you* doing here?"

"I'm going out of my mind," Ian told him.

"Ah."

"Your wife was due back ages ago, and anyhow I didn't want to come in the first place."

"Thomas!" Danny said fervently, peering toward the couch. "And Agatha!" He seemed surprised to see them, too. He told Ian, "You sure did miss a great party. Good old Bucky Hargrove!"

"Look," Ian said. "I am running late as hell and I need you to give me a lift to Cicely's house."

"Huh? Oh. Why, sure," Danny said. "Sure, Ian. Except—" He pondered. "Except how about the kids?" he asked finally.

"How about them?"

"We can't just leave them."

"Take them along, then," Ian said, exasperated. "Let's just *go*."

"Take Daphne, too? Where's Daphne?"

Ian gritted his teeth. The Kent cigarette song sailed out from the TV, mindless and jaunty. He turned to Agatha and said, "Agatha, you and Thomas will have to stay here and baby-sit."

She stared at him.

"Seven minutes, tops," Ian said. "Don't open the front door no matter who knocks, and don't answer the phone. Understand?"

She nodded. Thomas's eyes were ringed like a raccoon's.

"Let's go," Ian told Danny.

Danny was swaying slightly on his feet and watching Ian with mild, detached interest. "Well . . ." he said.

"Come *on*, Danny!"

Ian snatched up his jacket and gave Danny a push in the right direction. As they walked out he felt a weight slipping blessedly from his shoulders. He wondered how people endured children on a long-term basis—the monotony and irritation and confinement of them.

Outside it was much colder than before, and wonderfully quiet.

Danny bumped his head getting into the car, and he had some trouble determining which key to use. After that, though, he started the engine easily, checked sensibly for traffic, and pulled into the street. "So!" he said. "Cicely lives on Lang Avenue, right?"

"Right," Ian said. "Stop by home first, though."

"Stop by home first," Danny repeated meekly.

Ian tapped a foot against the floorboards. He felt commanding and energetic, charged up by righteous anger.

Dimly lit houses slid past them, and a dog chased the car a block or so before giving up. Danny started whistling a tune, something sort of jazzy and hootchy-kootchy. Probably they'd had a stripper at Bucky Hargrove's party, and waitresses in fishnet stockings and girls popping out of cakes and such. And Ian, meanwhile, had been warming baby bottles. He swung toward Danny sharply and said, "I might as well inform you right now that you have lost your favorite sitter for all eternity."

"Huh? What say?" Danny asked.

"I had a huge, important engagement at eight thirty. I'm talking crucial. Lucy knew that. She swore on a stack of Bibles she'd be back in time."

"Where is she, anyhow?" Danny asked, flicking his turn signal.

"Drinking with a girlfriend. So she says."

"I didn't even know she was planning to go out."

"Her waitress friend, Dot. Is what she *claims*."

"Dot from the Fill 'Er Up Café," Danny agreed.

"Goddamnit, Danny, are you blind?" Ian shouted.

Danny's eyes widened and he looked frantically in all directions. "Blind?" he asked. "What?"

"She's out more often than she's in! Don't you ever wonder who she's with?"

"Why, no, I . . ."

"And how about that baby?"

"Baby?"

"Premature baby? Get serious. Premature baby with dimples?"

Danny opened his mouth.

"Two months early and breathing on her own, no incubator, no problems?"

"She was—"

"She was somebody else's," Ian said.

"Come again?"

"I just want to know how long you intend to be a fall guy," Ian said.

Danny turned onto Waverly and drew up in

front of the house. He cut the engine and looked over at Ian. He seemed entirely sober now. He said, "What are you trying to tell me, Ian?"

"She's out all afternoon any time she can get a sitter," Ian said. "She comes back perfumed and laughing and wearing clothes she can't afford. That white knit dress. Haven't you ever seen her white dress? Where'd she get it? How'd she pay for it? How come she married you quick as a flash and then had a baby just seven months later?"

"You're talking about that dress with the kind of like crisscrossed middle," Danny said.

"That's the one."

Danny started rubbing his right temple with his fingertips. When it didn't seem he meant to say anything further, Ian got out of the car.

Inside the house, only the hall lamp was lit. His parents must still be at the Finches'. Beastie rose from the rug, yawning, and followed him up the stairs, which he climbed two steps at a time. He went directly to his room, fell to his knees in front of the closet, and rooted through the clutter for his gym shoes. Once he'd located the foil strip, he slid it into his rear pocket and stood up. Then he ducked into the bathroom. The biggest night of his life and he couldn't even stop to shower. He wet his fingers at the sink and ran them through his hair. He bared his teeth to the mirror and debated whether to brush them.

In the street below, an engine roared up. What on earth? He drew aside the curtain and peered out. It was Danny's Chevy, all right. The headlights were two yellow ribbons swinging away from the curb. The car took off abruptly, peeling rubber. Ian dropped the curtain. He turned to confront his own stunned face in the mirror.

Near the stone wall at the end of the block the brakes should have squealed, but instead the roaring sound grew louder. It grew until something had to happen, and then there was a gigantic, explosive, complicated crash and then a delicate tinkle and then silence. Ian went on staring into his own eyes. He couldn't seem to look away. He couldn't even blink, couldn't move, because once he moved then time would start rolling forward again, and he already knew that nothing in his life would ever be the same.

2

THE DEPARTMENT
OF REALITY

When the baby woke from her afternoon nap, she made a noise like singing. "La!" she called. But the only ones who heard were Thomas and Agatha. They were coloring at the kitchen table. Their crayons slowed and they looked at each other. Then they looked toward their mother's room. Nowadays their mother took naps too. She said it was the heat. She said if they would just let her be she would stay in bed from spring till fall, sleeping away this whole hot, muggy summer.

"La!" Daphne called again.

They couldn't pick her up themselves because last week Thomas had dropped her. He'd been trying to feed her a bottle and she had somehow tumbled to the floor and bumped her head. After that their mother said neither one of them could hold her anymore, which wasn't at all fair to Agatha. Agatha had turned seven this past April and she was big for her age besides. She would never have allowed Daphne to wiggle away like that.

Now Daphne was talking to herself in a questioning tone of voice, like, Where *is* everybody? Have they all gone off and left me?

Agatha's page of the coloring book had an outline of an undressed man full of veins and arteries. You were supposed to color the veins blue and the arteries red. A tiny B and R started you off and from then on you were on your own, boy. Tough luck if you slipped over onto the wrong branch accidentally and started coloring the red parts blue. It was just about the most boring picture in the world but Agatha kept at it, even when the veins narrowed to black threads and she didn't have a hope of staying inside the lines.

Thomas's page was boring too, but at least there were more shapes to it. His undressed man had different organs—pipes and beans and balloony things. He got to do that page because the coloring book was his, but then he pretended the organs didn't exist. He smeared over them every which way with a purple crayon, giving the man a suit that ended jaggedly at his wrists and bare ankles. "Now you've gone and ruined it," Agatha told him.

"I did not. I made it better."

"You're bearing down too hard, too. Look at what you did to your crayon."

He looked. Earlier he'd peeled the paper off and now the crayon curved sideways in the heat from his hand, like their mother's poor bent candles in the napkin drawer.

"I don't care," he said.

"Your last purple crayon!"

"I didn't like it anyhow," he said, "and this coloring book is stupid. Who gave me this stupid coloring book?"

"Danny gave it to you," Agatha said.

He clapped a hand over his mouth.

Danny hadn't given him the coloring book; it was Grandma Bedloe. She'd picked it up at the Pantry Pride one day when she went to buy their mother some food. But Thomas always worried that Danny was listening to them up in heaven, so Agatha said, "He bought it as a special, special present, and he hoped very much you would like it."

Thomas removed his hand and said loudly, "I do like it."

"Then why'd you mess all over it?"

"I made a mistake."

Daphne said, "Oho! Oho!"—not laughing, as you might imagine, but starting to complain. The next step would be real wailing, all sad and lost and lonely. Thomas and Agatha *hated* that. Thomas said, "Go tell Mama."

"You go."

"You're the oldest."

"I'm not in the mood."

"Last time I went, she cried," Thomas said.

"She was having a difficult day."

"Maybe this day is difficult too."

"If you go," Agatha said, "I'll give you my patent leather purse."

"I don't use a purse."

"My plastic camera?"

"Your camera's broken."

Daphne had reached the wailing stage. Agatha started feeling desperate. She said, "We could stand next to the crib, maybe. Just talk and smile and stuff."

"Okay."

They got up and went down the hall, past the closed door of their mother's room and into the children's room. It smelled of dirty diapers. Daphne was sitting in that superstraight way she had with her fingers wrapped around the crib bars, and when they came in she grew quiet and pressed her face to the bars so her little nose stuck out. She had been crying so hard that her upper lip was glassed over. She blinked and stared at them and then gave a big sloppy grin.

"Now, what is this nonsense I'm hearing?" Agatha said sternly.

She was trying to sound like Grandma Bedloe. Grownups had these voices they saved just for babies. If she'd wanted, she could have put on her mother's voice. "Sweetheart!" Or Danny's. "How's my princess?" he would ask. Used to ask. In the olden days asked.

Best to stick with Grandma Bedloe. "Who's this making such a hullabaloo?"

Daphne grinned wider, with her four new crinkle-edged teeth shining forth and her lashes all wet and sticking to her cheeks. She wore just a little undershirt, and her diaper was a brownish color—what their uncle Ian would call Not a Pretty Sight.

"Give her her pacifier," Thomas suggested.

"She gets mad if you give her a pacifier when she wants a bottle."

"Maybe she's not hungry yet."

"After her nap, she's always hungry."

Daphne looked back and forth between the two of them. It seemed to be dawning on her that they weren't going to be much help.

"Just *try* her pacifier," Thomas said.

"Well, where'd it go?"

They reached in between the bars and patted the sheet, hunting. Some places the sheet was damp, but that might have been the heat, or tears. The smell was terrible.

"Found it!" Thomas crowed. He poked the pacifier between Daphne's lips, but she spat it out again. Her chin began quivering and her eyebrows turned bright pink.

"Phooey," Thomas said. He picked up the pacifier and jammed it in his own mouth, and then he backed off till he was sitting on the edge of his bed with his arms folded tight across his chest.

"Maybe we could feed her in her crib," Agatha said.

Thomas made noisy sucking sounds.

Agatha went to the kitchen and dragged a gallon jug of milk from the refrigerator. She set the jug on the table and took a cloudy nursing bottle from the jumble of unwashed dishes next to the sink.

Daphne was back to "Oho! Oho!"

First Agatha tried pouring very, very slowly, but milk got all over the table and soaked Thomas's page of the coloring book. When she speeded up she did better. She replaced the nipple and carried the bottle down the hall, de-chilling it in her hands as she walked. Outside her mother's door she paused and listened but she didn't hear a sound. It must be a two-pill nap, or even three-pill. She went on into the children's room.

Daphne's mouth was an ugly shouting square

now and she was red-faced and snotty and sweaty. Thomas had his eyes squeezed shut. "Wake up," Agatha told him roughly as she passed. She fitted the bottle between the crib bars and held it toward Daphne. "Here."

Daphne flailed out and the bottle went flying. Off popped the nipple. Milk splashed the decal of the rabbit in pink overalls on the headboard. "Stupid!" Agatha shouted. "Stupid fat old *baby*!"

Daphne cried harder. "Help me reach this bottle," Agatha told Thomas, but Thomas had pulled his bedspread up over his head. She turned back to the bottle. It lay on its side toward the rear of the crib, and every time Daphne bounced another glug of milk would spill out onto the sheet. Finally Agatha pressed the two clamps on the railing to lower it. There was Daphne, no longer fenced in, quieting slightly and hiccuping and looking interested. There was the bottle, within easy reach. Agatha found the nipple in a fold of wet sheet and put it back on, and then she tipped the bottle toward Daphne. This time, Daphne accepted it. She drank sitting up, blinking at the first cold swallow but after that making do. One hand clutched over and over on Agatha's wrist. "Mm," she said at each gulp. "Mm. Mm." Agatha suddenly felt the most enormous thirst.

Behind her, she heard the slithering sound of

Thomas coming out of his bedspread. She heard the smack as he pulled the pacifier from his mouth. "She sure does stink," he said.

She didn't answer.

"You going to change her, Agatha?"

She stood firm, cupping her elbow with her free hand. She did know how to change a diaper. She had often helped her mother—fetched the powder or the washcloth. Yes, she thought she could do it on her own. But still she didn't answer. She tossed her head to flick her hair off her face. She felt Thomas come up cautiously to stand next to her. He was twiddling the pacifier between his fingers. Just as Daphne let go of the nipple after her last gulp (*Squirrel*-oh! the nipple said), he reached over and plugged her mouth with the pacifier. Daphne went on sucking. Thomas and Agatha took a step back, but Daphne stayed quiet.

"Soose," Thomas said happily.

That was what their mother called a pacifier: soose.

Agatha took a clean diaper from the stack on the bureau. She tipped Daphne onto her back and slid the diaper beneath her. The pins were no trouble. This was going to be easy. But the poo was disgusting. She wrinkled her nose and folded the dirty diaper inward. Thomas said, "Yuck!" and went back to his bed.

She carried the diaper down the hall to the

bathroom, holding it in a clump far out in front of her. She lowered it into the toilet and swished it around. All the ick started crumbling away. She flushed the toilet and swished again in clearer water, back and forth, dreamily.

Sometimes their mother said "soose" and sometimes she said "soother." Maybe they were both the same word. People here in Baltimore said "pacifier," and so did Thomas and Agatha, trying to fit in; but their mother was not from Baltimore. She was from out in the country where they used to live with their father in a metal-colored trailer. Then they all got divorced. This was when Thomas was just a baby. He couldn't even remember. And then later they moved to Baltimore in Mr. Belling's long black car. Everything was going to be wonderful, wonderful, their mother said. She got so many new clothes! Their apartment sat over a drugstore that stocked every kind of candy, and when Mr. Belling visited he sent Thomas and Agatha downstairs with a dollar bill each and they could take as long as they liked deciding. Thomas did remember Mr. Belling. He didn't like him much, though. When Mr. Belling stopped coming, Thomas asked if he could have the Baltimore Colts mug Mr. Belling used to drink his beer from, and their mother started crying. She snatched the mug from the dish drainer and slammed it against the sink until it broke in a million pieces. Thomas said, "I'm sorry! I'm sorry! I didn't *really* want it!" After that their mother had to get a job and leave them with Mrs. Myrdal, but then she met Danny. She acted more like her old self once she met Danny. On her wedding day she said it was *all* of them's wedding day. She gave Agatha a little pink rose from her bridal bouquet.

Thomas said Danny was probably their real father. Agatha knew he wasn't, though. She told Thomas their real father was nicer. In fact Danny was the nicest man she had ever known—nicer than their father, who had never had much to do with them, and certainly a whole lot nicer than Mr. Belling, with his two fat diamond rings and his puckered eyes the color of new dungarees. But she wanted Thomas to feel jealous over what she could still remember. Thomas had a terrible memory. Agatha's memory was letter-perfect; she never forgot a thing.

Thomas forgot three separate times, for instance, three different days in a row, that Danny had gone and died. Three mornings in a row he got up and said, "Do you think Danny will fix apple pancakes for breakfast?" The first day she could understand, because the news was still so fresh and neither one of them was used to it yet. So she just said, "No, did you forget? He went and died." But the second day! And the third! And those were weekdays, too. Danny would never have fixed apple pancakes on a weekday. "What's the matter with you?" she asked Thomas. "Can't you get it into your head? He had a car crash and he died." Thomas just took on a kind of closed look. He didn't seem to miss Danny as much as he missed the pancakes. It made her furious. Why did she have to be the only one who remembered? She said, "He gave Ian a ride home and we had to stay by ourselves. Not answer the phone, not open the door—"

Thomas clamped his hands over his ears.

"So when the phone rang we didn't pick it up," Agatha said. "And when the door banged we didn't unlock it."

Thomas said, "Nee-nee-nee-nee-nee!" but she rode over it. "Mama had to crawl in a window," she went on, "and she tore her sleeve and she was crying; she was worried we'd been murdered, and then the phone rang again and—"

"Shut up! Shut up! Shut up!"

She just had these urges to be evil to him. She couldn't say exactly why.

The water in the toilet was so yellow now she could hardly see the diaper, so she flushed once more. Then it felt like someone bossy and selfish reached up and grabbed the diaper away from her. She gave a little gasp and let it go. The water rose calmly higher and higher; it reached the rim. She had never guessed what a scary thing a toilet was. Thick yellow water slopped over the edge and spilled across the floor while she stood watching, horrified.

"Mama!" she shrieked finally.

Silence.

The water in the toilet slid down again.

Agatha stepped out into the hall, shaking, and went to her mother's bedroom door. She gave a tiny tap with her knuckles and then placed her ear to the door and listened.

They used to go straight in without a thought. They used to play among her bedclothes till she woke. But lately they'd stopped doing that.

(You could almost think, sometimes, that their mother wasn't there behind her face anymore.)

Agatha went on down the hall to the children's room. As she walked in, she saw Daphne roll onto her stomach and drop like a stone out of the crib. Agatha flung herself forward in a silent rush and caught her—an armload of bare-bottomed, clammy baby. She sank weak-kneed to the floor. Still busily sucking her pacifier, Daphne crawled away to a jack-in-the-box. Thomas sang to his doll, "My aunt gave me a nickel, to buy a pickle . . ."

All of a sudden, Agatha seemed to see things so clearly. Daphne's bottom was stained yellow. Thomas's shirt was splotched with food. The floor was covered with toys and dirty clothes and a cantaloupe rind on a plate beneath a cloud of fruit flies. Milk was dripping down the wall behind the crib.

She stood up and collected Daphne and staggered over to the crib with her and plopped her down. She wrestled Daphne's diaper around her, being very, very careful with the safety pins, and then she raised the railing and locked it. "Stay there," she told Daphne. "Put on a different shirt," she told Thomas.

"What shirt?"

"I don't care. Just different."

He laid Dulcimer aside, grumbling, and slid off his bed. While he was rummaging in bureau drawers, Agatha returned to the bathroom and stirred a towel through the puddle around the toilet. Then she hid the towel in the hamper. She went out to the kitchen and put the milk back into the fridge. "Chew, chew, chew, chew, chew, chewing gum," Thomas sang, while Agatha spread his coloring book on the windowsill to dry. One by one she plucked his crayons from the pool of milk on the table. They were beginning to dye the milk all different shades, lavender and pink and blue. She dumped them into the waste can under the sink.

"What are you *doing*?" Thomas asked, coming up behind her. He was wearing a green shirt now that clashed with his blue shorts, and it was buttoned wrong besides.

"Button your buttons over from scratch," Agatha told him. She unfolded a cloth and started wiping off the table.

"What did you do with my crayons?"

"They were all wet and runny."

"You can't just throw them away!"

He started rooting through the waste can. Agatha said, "Stop that! I just got everything nice again!"

"You better give me back my crayons, Agatha."

Their mother said, "Is it still daytime?"

She was standing in the doorway in her slip. Her pillow had made a mark across one cheek and she didn't have any makeup on. "I thought it was night," she said. "Is that Daphne I hear?"

"Make Agatha give me back my crayons, Mama!"

But their mother was drifting down the hall, heading toward Daphne's "Oho! Oho!"

"Stealer!" Thomas hissed at Agatha. "Crayon stealer!"

She put the wet cloth in the sink. "Sticks and stones will break my bones," she said, "but names will never—"

"You can go to jail for stealing!"

"Is this my little Daphne?" their mother said, back again with Daphne in her arms. "Is this my sweetheart?"

She sat in a kitchen chair and settled Daphne

on her lap. Daphne's diaper was dry but it was so loose it pouched in front of her stomach. The table was clean but it was damp where Agatha had wiped it. Everything looked fine but just barely, like a room where you walk in and get the feeling something was rustling and whispering till half a second ago. But their mother didn't seem to notice. She stared down at Daphne with her face bare-naked and erased and pale. "Is this my Daphne?" she kept saying, "Is this my baby Daphne?" so it began to sound as if she really did wonder. "Is this her?" she asked. "Is it her? Is it?" And she looked up at Thomas and Agatha and waited for them to answer.

When the hottest part of the day was over, they got ready for their walk to the typewriter store. This was something they'd started doing just in the past few weeks, but already there was a pattern to it. Agatha liked patterns. So did Thomas. Together they hauled Daphne's stroller out of the coat closet and unfolded it. Daphne watched from the rug, flapping her arms up and down when she heard the wheels squeak. Maybe she liked patterns, too.

They went to see if their mother was ready, but she was shut up in her bathroom. When she came out, she wore her white blouse that wrapped and tied at the side and her watery flowing India skirt. She blotted her lipstick on a tissue and asked, "How do I look?"

"You look nice," they both told her.

From the living room, Daphne made a fussy sound. Their mother sighed and picked up her bag. "Let's go," she said.

The air outdoors felt heavy and warm, but at least the sun wasn't beating down so hard anymore. Their mother walked in front, wheeling Daphne in her stroller, and Thomas and Agatha followed. Thomas's shirt was still buttoned wrong. Agatha's playsuit bunched at the crotch. She thought she and Thomas should have been dressed up too, if they were trying to make friends with the typewriter man, but that didn't seem to have crossed their mother's mind. Sometimes lately there were these holes in the way she did things, places she just fell apart. Like last night, when she got lost in the middle of what she was saying and couldn't find her way out again. "Do you believe this?" she had been saying. "That I'm back to . . . back to . . ." Then she'd just stared. It had frightened them. Thomas started crying and he flew at her with both fists. "Back to nothing," she had said finally. She was like a record player you had to jostle when it hit a crack. Then she'd said, "I think I'll go to bed," although it wasn't even dark outside and Daphne hadn't been put down for the night yet.

They passed the house with all the statues in the yard—elves and baby deer and a row of ducks. Agatha wished their own yard had statues, but her mother said statues were common. "Right now," she said, "the last thing I can afford is looking common." She talked a lot these days about what she couldn't afford. Danny hadn't left them well provided for.

They passed the house that said MRS. GOODE, PALMIST—FORTUNES CHEERFULLY TOLD, but their mother didn't stop. Agatha was glad. Mrs. Goode was gray all over and her parlor smelled of mothballs. They came to where the shops began, shoe repairs and laundromats. At Luckman's Pharmacy Thomas and Agatha slowed hopefully, but their mother said, "We'll go to Joyner's this time." She rotated her drugstores because she didn't want people thinking she bought too many pills. It was a pity, though. Luckman's had one of those gumball machines with plastic charms intermingled. Thomas and Agatha let their feet drag and sent a longing gaze backward.

Traffic in this area was busier, and the bus exhausts made the heat seem worse. Thomas wore a smudgy mustache of sweat. Each click of their mother's heels shot something like a little sharp paring knife straight through Agatha's head.

On Govans Road the long, low front of Rumford & Son's Office Equipment took up nearly half a block. They stood facing it across the street, waiting for the light to change. Thomas said, "Wouldn't it be nice if typewriter stores had gumball machines?"

"Well, they don't, and I don't want you asking," their mother said.

"I wasn't going to ask!"

"Just be very, very quiet, so I won't be sorry I brought you."

In the olden days, she didn't have to bring them places. She'd say, "Oh! I'm going stir-crazy, I tell you." Or, "I'm getting cabin fever." She would ask Ian or Mrs. Myrdal to baby-sit, because back then she could afford it. She would go out all afternoon and come home happy and show the children what she had picked up for them—candy bars and lollipops, sometimes even toys if they were small enough to fit in her bag. But now she had to take the three of them everywhere. She took them to her doctor, even, and when she was called inside Agatha had to watch the other two. "Can't we go back to having sitters?" Agatha would ask, already knowing the answer. The answer was, "No, we can't. Face the facts, sweetheart: we're in the Department of Reality now." Their mother's favorite thing to say. Agatha hated hearing that and she would cover her ears like Thomas, but when she took her hands away her mother would still be talking. "You think I like having you with me every single second? Think I wouldn't rather just leave on my own any time I get the notion?"

Their mother loved them, but they kept trying to make her *not* love them. That was what she told them. "You want me to walk out on you," she told them, "but I refuse to do it."

Whenever she said that, Thomas would take hold of some little part of her clothing, down near the hemline where she didn't notice.

The light turned green and they crossed the street. Their mother's heels sounded daintier now. When they stepped inside the store, cold air washed over them—lovely, cold, blowing air—and Daphne said, "Ah," which made their mother laugh. Wasn't it wonderful how quickly she could change! To laugh like that, her best little husky-throated laugh, the instant she walked through the door! And the typewriter man wasn't even listening yet, although he came over soon enough. He said, "Why, look who's here!" You could see how pleased he was. He was a blond, pale man with skin that flushed when he smiled. "What brings you out on such a hot afternoon?" he asked their mother.

"Oh, we were just taking a stroll," she said. All of a sudden she seemed bashful. "We were passing by and I said, 'Shouldn't we visit my typewriter, kids?' "

"Absolutely. You don't want it feeling neglected," he said.

He beamed down at Agatha. She gave him her biggest smile back, all teeth.

The showroom was filled with desks, and a typewriter sat on each one. Some were big complicated electrics and some were little low-slung manuals. If it were up to Agatha, they'd have a manual. Those looked easier. But her mother's was electric, with keys that chattered loudly almost before you touched them.

They had first come to this store in the spring, shortly after Danny died. Their mother had decided to be a secretary. "I have endured my very last of the Fill 'Er Up Café," she told them. "This time I want an office job." So one afternoon they had walked to Rumford's, where their mother asked a lady with squiggly hair if she could use a machine to learn to type. "Do what?" the lady said. Their mother had explained that she wanted to sit at a desk for just exactly twelve days and teach herself out of a book called *Touch Typing in Twelve Easy Lessons*, and she promised that all three children would be as quiet as mice. "Hon," the lady said, "this is not a secretarial college."

"Well, don't you think I know that?" their mother cried. "But how do you suppose I could manage a *real* secretarial college? How do you expect me to pay? Who would watch my children?"

"Hon—"

"This is all I've got to go on, don't you understand? I need to find a job of some kind, I need to find employment!"

Then the typewriter man came over. "What seems to be the trouble here?" he asked, and the lady looked relieved and said, "This is Mr. Rumford, the owner. *He* can tell you," and she walked away. Mr. Rumford had been much more sympathetic. Not that he let their mother carry out her plan (he was really just the owner's *son*, he said, and his father would have a conniption), but he admired her spunk and he suggested that she rent, instead. She could rent from this very store and practice in the privacy of her home. Their mother said, "Oh! I never thought of that," and she took a Kleenex from her pocket and blew her nose.

"Know what I recommend?" the man had said. "An electric. Look at those pretty fingernails! You don't want to ruin your nails, now, do you?"

Their mother tried to smile.

"A manual, you have to pound down hard," he told her. "That's why you see those professional stenographers with their squared-off, ugly, short fingernails."

Agatha hid her own hands behind her back. Her mother looked up into the typewriter man's eyes. She said, "But wouldn't an electric be more expensive?"

"Pennies a day! Just pennies."

"And heavy, too. I mean an electric must weigh a lot more. And I'm not . . . I'm all on my own. I don't have anyone to carry things."

"Tell you what," he said. "I'll bring it by myself, after work."

"You would do that?"

"It'll be my pleasure," he told her. "Let me show you the machine I have in mind." And off he went, leading them through the rows of desks.

The machine he had in mind was a blue metal hulk with a cord so thick that when he brought it that evening, the only outlet they could plug it into was the one behind the refrigerator. He had to move the refrigerator and pull the kitchen table over so the cord would reach, and then he was red in the face and their mother made him sit down and have a beer. While he was drinking his beer, he showed her the special features— the electric return and the keys that would re- peat. "This is just so nice of you," their mother told him. "I know *Mrs.* Rumford must be having to keep your supper warm."

"I'd be mighty surprised if she was," he said. "We're in the process of a divorce." Then he placed her fingers in the right position on the keys—what he called "home base"—and taught her to type *a sad mad lad*, which made her laugh. When he left he gave her his card so she could call him with any questions.

That night she whizzed through the first five lessons in a single sitting. Agatha woke in the dark to hear the clacking of the keys, and when she came out to the kitchen her mother said, "See how far I've gone! At this rate I'll be an expert in no time." Agatha went back to bed and slept better than she had in weeks.

The next morning the kitchen table was covered with sheets of typing—*pat rat sat hat* and *pop had a top*. Agatha poured Coca-Cola into a glass and added a spoonful of instant coffee (her mother's favorite way to get herself going) and carried it into the bedroom. Her mother was asleep in her slip with an arm hanging over the edge of the mattress, so it looked like one of those times when she would have trouble waking. But she opened her eyes at just the clink of the glass on the nightstand and she thanked Agatha very clearly. She spent that morning on Lessons Six through Eleven while Agatha, who this once was allowed to skip school, watched over Thomas and Daphne. Lesson Twelve was not important, their mother decided. That was only numerals, which she could go on doing hunt-and-peck unless she had to work for an accountant or something, which she certainly wasn't planning on. She was planning to work for one of the downtown law firms, something at a nice front desk with flowers in a vase, she said, where she would answer the phone in a la-de-da voice and type letters clickety-click while the clients sat in the waiting room waiting. She demonstrated how she would look—nose raised snootily in the air and fingers tripping smartly as if the keys were burning hot. She was still in her bathrobe but you could see she was going to be perfect.

Around lunchtime that day they walked to Cold Spring Lane and bought a newspaper. They used to have home delivery but now they couldn't afford it. Once she was hired, their mother said, they'd have home delivery again and they would sit around the breakfast table reading their horoscopes before she went to her office. Agatha had a thought. She said, "But Mama, who's going to *stay* with us?"

"We'll work that out when we come to it," her mother said, tipping the stroller up onto a curb.

"Work it out how?"

"We'll manage, Agatha. All right?"

"You wouldn't just leave us on our own, would you?"

"Have I ever, ever left you on your own?"

Agatha opened her mouth but then closed it.

Thomas looked over at her. His eyes filled with tears.

"Stop it," Agatha told him.

He stood in the middle of the sidewalk and his face crumpled up.

"What in the world?" their mother asked. She turned to stare at him.

"He's just . . . feeling sad," Agatha explained. She didn't want to remind her about Danny.

At home, their mother had spread the paper across the coffee table and circled every secretarial ad—dozens of them. The problem, she said, was not finding a job but choosing which one. "If I'd known how easy this was I'd have done it years ago," she said. Then during Daphne's nap she took the paper off to the bedroom telephone. For a while her voice murmured: "Da-dah? Da-da-dah? Da-de-*dah*-da . . ." Finally a long quiet spell. Thomas and Agatha looked at each other. They were watching soap operas with the sound turned off. Thomas took his thumb out of his mouth and said, "Go see."

So Agatha went to tap at the door. No answer. She turned the knob and peered through the crack. Her mother was sitting against the headboard with the telephone on her lap. She was staring into space.

"Mama?" Agatha said.

"Hmm?"

"Did you find a job?"

"Agatha, do you have to keep pestering me? Isn't there any place in this house where I can be private?"

"Maybe there'll be something tomorrow," Agatha said.

"Well, even if there is," her mother said, "I'll lose out the minute I tell them the truth. These people just *want* you to lie. They practically *beg* you to lie. 'I've got thirty years' experience,' they want me to say. Even though I'm not but twenty-five."

"Should I bring you a Coke, Mama?"

"No, just let me get on with this. I'm going to try a couple more."

Now what they heard from the living room was louder and firmer, though still no easier to make out. "*Dah*-da. *Dah*-da-da." And when she came to stand in the doorway, she was smiling. "Well," she said, "I've set up an interview."

They could tell it was something they should hug her for.

That evening she practiced her typing—little rushes of clacks separated by pauses when she had to make capital letters. She let Agatha phone Passenger Pizza even though they couldn't afford it. And the next morning she took them to stay at Grandma Bedloe's while she went to her interview. Grandma Bedloe said, "Doesn't Agatha have school today?" but their mother said, "Her head was hurting." She gave Agatha one of her secret looks—not a wink but more of a twinkle, without a single muscle moving. Then off she went to the bus stop, wearing the rose-colored suit she had married Danny in. Grandma Bedloe said, "She is way overdressed." This worried Thomas, you could tell. His thumb homed in to his mouth and he glanced at Agatha. But Agatha had seen how perky their mother looked spiking down the front steps with her hair flouncing over her shoulders, so she wasn't concerned. Anyhow, of all people to talk! Grandma Bedloe in her slacks and a man's plaid shirt, with the skin beneath her eyes grown so loose and droopy and pleated since Danny died.

When their mother came back, she was walking more slowly. "How'd it go, dear?" Grandma Bedloe asked.

"Fine," their mother said.

"You got the job?"

"We'll have to see."

"When will they let you know?"

"It may be a while," their mother said, and she didn't seem to move her lips as she spoke.

She wouldn't stay for lunch. She said she had to get Daphne home for her bottle. "This is why I think your Aunt Claudia's so smart to breastfeed," Grandma Bedloe told the children, and their mother spun around from settling Daphne in her stroller and said, "Well, I *don't* breastfeed. All right? I never breast-fed a one of them and I don't intend to start now!"

Grandma Bedloe said, "Why! Lucy? All I meant was—"

"*Some* people can let themselves get saggy and baggy but I don't have that luxury. I can't afford to take anything for granted in this life, I've learned. If there's one thing I've learned, it's that. You think I enjoy this? Watching my weight and painting my nails, never letting my guard down, always on the lookout for split ends?"

"Split ends?"

"Oh, forget it. Thanks for keeping the children," their mother said, and she took hold of the stroller and pushed it through the door.

On the way home, she wouldn't talk. Or she talked, but only to herself. "Snob!" she whispered once. She stalked behind the stroller a while and then whispered, "Conceited!" Agatha thought at first she meant Grandma Bedloe (who had never acted like a snob that she knew of and was not a bit conceited). But then their mother said, "Just tell me what *words per minute* have to do with anything!" So Agatha knew it must be someone at the interview.

At home, their mother left Daphne in her stroller in the middle of the kitchen while she phoned the typewriter man. "You can come and fetch this machine of yours," she started right in. "Pick it up and haul it back, I'll be glad to see the last of it. What? This is Lucy Bedloe. You brought me a Smith-Corona day before yesterday."

He must have said something. She paused. Unsmiling, she made a short laughing sound. "Oh, really. What a thing to say," she said.

Another pause.

Another laugh, this time a real one.

"You surely know how to brighten up a person's mood," she said.

Then she sat down on a kitchen chair and told him about her awful morning, this woman in charge of hiring who'd acted so uppity and hoity-toity . . . So anyhow, she said. Would he please come and get his machine? She should have realized she wasn't the type for an office.

He came after work and he stayed for supper. She made him an omelet. She set two of the least bent candles in the center of the table. "This is delicious," he said after his first mouthful.

She said, "Oh, no, really, you caught me without any groceries. You should see what I usually fix."

What she usually fixed was Kellogg's Corn Flakes, but Agatha knew she didn't mean it as a lie. It was more like a politeness. Trying to help her out, Thomas and Agatha kept their eyes on their plates and ate extra neatly.

He took the typewriter away with him when

he left, but he told their mother not to feel dis-
couraged. "Want to know what I think?" he
asked. "I think someone's going to jump at the
chance to hire a gal like you. All you got to do
is bide your time—that and keep your skills up.
Sure you don't want to hang on to this machine?"

"I can't afford it," she said.

"Tell you what: I'll hold it for you. You liked
this model, didn't you? I'll hold it in the showroom
a while in case you change your mind."

"Well, that's very thoughtful," she said.

So now she had her own machine at Rumford
& Son's, which they went regularly to visit. And
at first she really did type on it. She sat down at
the desk and showed the man she still remembered her *pat rat sat hat*. But then she started
just *talking* about her typewriter. She asked how
it was getting along without her and he said it
looked mighty lonesome and she laughed and
changed the subject. Today, for instance, she
discussed the weather. She said how some people had all the luck, working in an air-conditioned
building; how at home she slept with nothing to
cool her off but a fan; how she had to slide out
of her negligee halfway through every night on
account of the heat. She scooted the stroller a
few inches forward, a few inches backward, forward, backward, over and over, speaking in her
slow, scrapy voice and every so often laughing

when the typewriter man said something funny.

Thomas crawled under a desk and told Agatha it was his house. The typewriter on top was so little and cute that Agatha started punching the keys. She had to punch really hard because it wasn't electric, and Thomas complained about the noise. He said, "This is *my* house. You go somewhere else." Agatha pretended not to hear. She typed *agatha dean 7 years old baltimore md usa.* Thomas shouted, "Stop that racket on my roof!" and reared up and bumped his head. When their mother heard him crying she broke off her conversation and turned. "Oh, Thomas," she said, "now what?" But the typewriter man didn't seem cross. He said, "Why, what's this? Two customers in need of my assistance," and he helped Thomas out from under the desk. "Something I can show you, sir? Some question I can answer?"

Thomas stopped crying and rubbed the top of his head. "Well," he said. He thought a moment. He said, "You know how people have those blood veins one in each arm?"

"Blood veins, ah . . ."

"So how come any place you prick will bleed? Wouldn't you think there'd be places that don't?"

"Ah, well . . ."

"I apologize for this," their mother said. "They promised they'd behave. Come on, children, I'm taking you home."

"No, Mama! *I* behaved!" Agatha said. She didn't want to leave the air-conditioning.

But her mother said, "Nice talking with you, Murray."

"Hurry back, okay?" the man said, and he walked them to the door. Agatha could tell he was sorry to see them go.

Out on the sidewalk their mother started humming. She hummed "Ramblin' Rose" while they waited for the traffic light, and she took them to Joyner's Drugstore for Life Savers. Just trailed her fingers across the candy counter, brush-brush, nothing to it, and dropped the two rolls in her bag. Then she twinkled her eyes at Thomas and Agatha. They giggled and she instantly looked elsewhere as if she'd never met them.

While she collected her prescription, Agatha rocked the stroller because Daphne was starting to fuss. Thomas dawdled up and down the aisles, hunting dropped coins. At Luckman's he'd once found a nickel and put it in the gumball machine, but all he got back was gum. He'd been hoping for a set of silver plastic handcuffs the size of finger rings.

The pharmacist saw them to the door, saying, "Still hot out there?" Thomas and Agatha smiled up at him, remembering to look attractive— Thomas not sucking his thumb, Agatha not letting her mouth flop open—but their mother said, "Mmhmm," and wheeled the stroller on through without a glance. You never could be sure, with her, who you had to be nice to and who you didn't.

Standing at the front window and holding back the curtain, Agatha watched for the first star. In the summertime she had to be alert, because the sky stayed light for so long that the stars would more or less *melt* into view. Agatha knew all about it. She waited at this window every night. Sometimes Thomas waited too, but he wasn't nearly so faithful. Also he said his wishes aloud, no matter how often she warned him not to. And he wished for definite objects—toys and candy and such—as if the sky were one big Sears, Roebuck Christmas catalog. "Star light, star bright, first star I see tonight . . . I wish for a front-end loader with real rubber treads on it."

Agatha, on the other hand, wished silently, and not even in words. She wished in a strong wash of feeling, instead. *Let everything turn out all right*, was the closest she could put it. Or, no, *Let us be safe*. But that was not exactly it either.

She looked from the sky to the street and saw Ian and Grandma Bedloe coming up the sidewalk. Ian carried a picnic basket covered with a red-checked cloth, and Grandma Bedloe carried a cake tin. Agatha loved Grandma Bedloe's cakes. She made one last sweeping search for her star and then gave up and ran to answer the doorbell.

"Hello, dearies," Grandma Bedloe said, and she kissed Agatha first and then Thomas. It was just since Danny died that she'd started kissing them. It was just since Danny died that she'd dried out so and shortened, and begun to move so stiffly. But the stiffness was rheumatism, she said: her knees acting up. A matter of humidity.

"See what we brought you!" she told them. "Devil's food cake and fried chicken. Where's your mother?"

"She's having a nap."

"A nap?"

She glanced over at Ian. He wore his most faded jeans and a plain white T-shirt; he must have just got off work. Agatha thought he resembled those handsome teenaged hoodlums on TV. She wished the girls at school could see her once in his company, but it never seemed to happen.

"I hope you haven't had supper yet," Grandma Bedloe said. "Has your mother started anything cooking? How long has she been in her nap? Does she usually nap at this hour?"

Each question brought her further into the house. She pressed forward, passing Thomas and Agatha, heading for the kitchen, where she set the cake tin on the table and turned to look around her. "Oh, my, I'd say she *hasn't* started cooking," she said. "Goodness. Well. Try and make space for that basket on the counter, Ian. Agatha, dear, shall I put a few of these dishes to soak while you wake your mother?"

"Or we could eat without her," Agatha said. "We could let her rest."

"No, no, I'm sure she'd want—where's Daphne?"

"In her crib," Agatha said.

"She's napping too?"

"No, she's just . . . Mama just set her there a while."

"Well, let's go get her!" Grandma Bedloe said. "We can't leave our Daphne all alone, now!" And off she went, with Thomas and Agatha following.

In the children's room, Daphne poked her nose between the crib bars and cooed. "Hello, sweetness," Grandma Bedloe told her. She picked her up and said, "Somebody's sopping." Then she looked at the supplies lined against the footboard—a filled nursing bottle, a plate of darkening banana slices, and one of the bread-sticks Daphne liked to teethe on. "What *is* all this?" Grandma Bedloe asked. "Her lunch? Her supper? How long has she been in here?"

"Just a teensy while," Agatha said. "Honest. She just did get put down."

"Well, I'm going to change her diaper and dress her in some nicer little clothes," Grandma Bedloe said. (It was true that Daphne's undershirt didn't seem very fresh.) "You and Thomas go start your suppers."

So they went back to the kitchen, where Ian was unpacking the basket. He didn't ask what parts of the chicken they preferred. Agatha had been going to say the keel, a word she'd heard last week at a fast-food place. "I'll have the keel, please." Whatever that was. She figured it might make Ian stop and notice her. But he served each of them a drumstick without a word and went to the refrigerator for milk. He filled two glasses and thought a minute and then bent forward and sniffed. Then he took both glasses to the sink and poured them out. Agatha pinched a piece of crust off her drumstick and placed it in her mouth, meanwhile waiting to see what other drink he would offer. But he didn't offer anything. He just pulled out a chair and sank down onto it.

"Aren't you going to eat too?" Thomas asked him.

But he must not have been listening.

"Ian? You can have our mama's share. I bet she won't be hungry."

"Thanks," Ian said after a pause. But he didn't reach into the basket.

Grandma Bedloe was talking to Daphne. "Now, doesn't that feel better?" she was saying. "Let's go show Mommy." She knocked on their mother's bedroom door. They heard her turn the knob and walk in. "Oh, Mom-mee! Look who's come to see you, Mommy."

Their mother gave one of her sleep-moans.

"Lucy?" Grandma Bedloe said. "Are you all right, dear?"

Poor Grandma Bedloe. She didn't know their mother had to wake on her own. Finally she came back to the kitchen, carrying Daphne in a white knit romper that showed off her curly black hair. "Does your mother tend to sleep like that till morning?" she asked.

Agatha said, "Oh, no." She was glad to be able to tell the truth. "She'll get up again! Don't worry! She wakes up after dark and then she's awake all night, just about."

Grandma Bedloe settled Daphne on her hip. She said, "I certainly hope . . ." Then she said, "I wouldn't blame her a bit, understand . . ." Finally she said, "Tell me, Agatha, do you think she might be taking a little too much to drink?"

"Drink?"

"I mean, alcohol? A beer or two, or wine?"

"No," Agatha said.

"I hope you don't mind my asking. And you know I wouldn't blame her. We all like a little cocktail now and then!"

"Mama doesn't," Agatha said.

"Well, that's something," Grandma Bedloe said with a sigh.

Then she started pestering Thomas to eat his

chicken. She claimed he was skinny as a sparrow. Come to think of it, he *was* kind of skinny. But she was wrong about the cocktails. Their mother never drank at all. She said drinking made her say things.

She also said that dead people don't really leave us; they just stop weighing anything. But Agatha didn't know who was right there, her mother or Grandma Bedloe, because when she'd asked Grandma Bedloe why they had needed six people to carry Danny's coffin, Grandma Bedloe said, "What do you mean?" Agatha said, "Couldn't just one person do it? With just the tips of his fingers?" Grandma Bedloe said, "Why, Agatha, he was a full-grown man. He weighed a hundred and seventy pounds." Then she had turned all teary and Grandpa Bedloe told her, "There, hon. There, hon."

"He used to say he was getting a paunch, and he'd have to start watching what he ate," Grandma Bedloe wept. "He never dreamed how little time he had! He could have eaten anything he wanted!"

"There, honeybee."

Now it occurred to Agatha that what had weighed so much was the coffin itself. Maybe that was why they'd needed six people.

After supper Grandma Bedloe tidied the kitchen while Ian played Parcheesi with Thomas and Agatha. He held Daphne on his knee and gazed down at the board with a sort of puzzled expression. When Thomas miscounted on purpose, he didn't even notice. "Cheater!" Agatha told Thomas. "He's cheating, Ian."

"Really?" Ian said.

"He should be up in front of you where you could take him off next move."

"Really," Ian said.

He had been a lot more fun in the olden days.

When Grandma Bedloe had finished the dishes she came to stand in the doorway, wearing a flowered apron of their mother's that Agatha had forgotten about. "Ian," she said, "I cannot in all good conscience walk out and leave these children on their own like this."

Ian shook the dice in one cupped hand and spilled them across the board: a four and a six. "You hear me, Ian?" his mother asked.

Agatha watched their faces, hoping. They could stay, she wanted to tell them. Or they could take the three of them home with them. But then what about their mother?

"Maybe you could bring her too," she suggested to Grandma Bedloe.

"Bring who, dear?"

"Maybe you could bring us all to your house. Mama too."

Ian moved one man four spaces. Then he reached toward another man.

"If you wrap her in a blanket, she can walk pretty good," Agatha said. "Stir coffee into her Co-Cola and make her drink it and then hold her hand; she can walk anywhere you want her to."

Ian's fingers stopped in midair. He and Grandma Bedloe looked at each other.

Just at that moment, footsteps creaked in the hall and here came their mother, tying the sash of her kimono. It was the shiny gray kimono she hardly ever wore, not her usual bathrobe, so she must have known there were visitors. Also her hair was brushed. It puffed around her shoulders and down her back, dark and cloud-shaped, so her face stood out brightly. She gave them all her best smile. "Oh! Mother Bedloe. And Ian," she said. "This is so embarrassing! Caught napping in the shank of the evening! But I took the children on a long, long walk this afternoon and I guess I must have worn myself out."

Grandma Bedloe and Ian studied her. Thomas and Agatha held very still.

Then Grandma Bedloe said, "Why, my heavens! Pushing a stroller, on a day like today! Of course you're worn out. You just sit yourself down and let me bring you some supper."

Agatha let go of her breath. Thomas was smiling too, now. He had a smile like their mother's, sort of dipping at the center, and he looked relieved. And Grandma Bedloe was moving toward the kitchen, and Ian reached again for his Parcheesi piece. *Everyone* was relieved.

So why did Agatha suddenly feel so anxious?

It was past their bedtime but their mother hadn't noticed yet. She was perched on a stool in the kitchen, reading a cookbook and munching one of the drumsticks Grandma Bedloe had left on the counter. "Beef Goulash," she read out. "Beef with Pearl Onions. Beef Crescents. Agatha, what was that beef dish Grandma Bedloe told us about?"

"I don't remember," Agatha said, switching to a yellow crayon.

"It was rolled up in Bisquick dough."

"I remember she talked about it but I don't remember the name."

"Bisquick dough sprinkled with herbs of some kind. She had it at their neighbors'."

"Maybe you could call and ask her."

"I can't do that. She'd want to know who I was making it for."

Her mother set down the drumstick and wiped her fingers on a paper towel before turning another page. "Beef à la Oriental," she read out.

"Couldn't you just say you were making it for the typewriter man?"

"These things are touchy," her mother said. "You wouldn't understand."

That hurt Agatha's feelings a little. She scowled and kicked her feet out. By mistake, she kicked Thomas. He was drowsing over a plastic cup of grapefruit juice. He opened his eyes and said, "Stop."

"Always serve a man red meat," her mother told Agatha. "Remember that for the future."

"Red meat," Agatha repeated dutifully.

"It shows you think of them as strong."

"What if you served them fish?"

"Men don't like fish."

"They like chicken, though."

"Well, yes."

"If you served them chicken, would they think you thought they were scared?"

"Hmm?" her mother said.

Thomas said, "Mama, Agatha kicked me." But his eyes were closing again.

"Well, here goes," their mother said, and she reached for the phone.

"You're calling Grandma Bedloe?" Agatha asked.

"No, silly, I'm calling Mr. Rumford."

She dialed in that special way she had, very fast and zippy. She must know the number by heart. She had called two earlier times that Agatha was aware of—one morning while he was at work, just to make sure he didn't have anyone else; and then one evening, hanging up when he answered. Also they'd gone in person to see where he lived. They'd ridden the bus out to Ruxton in the company of nothing but colored maids; they'd peered through the window at his red brick house. "Deserted," their mother had said in a pleased, flat voice. "And no one has tended those shrubs in ages." Then they rattled back to town all by themselves, having left the maids behind.

"Hello?" their mother said into the receiver.

Her forehead was suddenly creased.

"Hello, is this . . . who is this?"

She listened. She said, "You mean the, um, the *wife* Mrs. Rumford?"

Then she said, "Sorry." And hung up.

Thomas said, "Agatha kicked me, Mama."

Their mother closed the cookbook and stared down at it. She stroked the cover, the golden letters stamped into the cloth.

"Mama?"

"We'd better go to bed," Agatha told Thomas.

"You're not the boss of me!"

"It's time, Thomas," she said, and she made her voice very hard.

He slid off his chair and followed her out of the kitchen.

In the children's room, Daphne was asleep. They undressed in the dark, using the light from the hallway. Thomas wanted his cowboy pajamas but Agatha couldn't find them. She said he'd have to wear his airplane pajamas instead. He climbed into them without an argument, staggering around the room as he tried to fit his feet through. Then he said he had to pee. "Use Mama's bathroom," Agatha told him.

"What for?"

"Just do."

She'd kept him away from the other one all evening. She worried the toilet would flood again.

She lay down in bed and pulled the covers up and listened to her mother moving around the house. Every sound meant something: the TV clicking on and then off, a drawer in the living room opening and then closing, the clang of a metal ashtray on the coffee table. Their mother smoked only when she was upset, holding the cigarette in some wrong-looking way with her fingers sticking out too straight. Agatha heard the scrape of a match, the pushed, tired sound of her breath whooshing forth.

Where were the pills? The popping of the lid off the pill bottle?

At least when she took pills she didn't fidget around like this.

Thomas appeared in the doorway—a black-and-gray shape against the yellow light. He crossed not to his own bed but to Agatha's. She had more or less expected that. She grumbled but she slid over to make room. His hair smelled like sugar browning in a saucepan. He said, "She didn't come kiss us good night."

"Later she'll come."

"I want her to come now."

"*Later*," Agatha said.

"She didn't read us a story, either."

"I'll tell you one."

"Reading's better."

"Well, Thomas! I can't read in the dark, can I?"

Sometimes she noticed how much she sounded like her mother. Same sure tone, same exasperated answers. Although she failed to resemble her in any other way. At a family dinner last winter Grandma Bedloe had said, "What a pity Agatha didn't inherit Lucy's bone structure."

"Once upon a time," she told Thomas, "there was a poor servant girl named Cinderella."

"Not that one."

"Once upon a time a rich merchant had three daughters."

"Not that one either. I want 'Hansel and Gretel.'"

This was no surprise to Agatha. (He liked things that rhymed. *Nibble, nibble, like a mouse, who is nibbling at my house?*) But Agatha hated "Hansel and Gretel." There wasn't any magic to it—no fairy godmothers, or frogs turning into princes. "How about 'Snow White'?" she asked. "That's got *Mirror, mirror, on the wall . . .*"

"I want 'Hansel and Gretel.' "

She sighed and resettled her pillow. "All right, have it your way," she said. "Once upon a time Hansel and Gretel were taking a walk—"

"That's not how it starts!"

"Who's telling this: you or me?"

"First there's their parents! And dropping breadcrumbs on the path! And the birds eat all the crumbs and Hansel and Gretel get lost!"

"Keep your voice down!" Agatha hissed.

Daphne slept on, though. And in the living room their mother's footsteps continued. Pace, pace. Swish of kimono. Pace, pace.

The night after Danny's funeral, she had paced till morning. (Back then she didn't have her pills yet.) The next day when Agatha got up she found the ashtray heaped with nasty-smelling butts and her mother asleep on the couch. Danny's picture stood on the coffee table nearby—the one she usually kept on her bureau. He was laughing under a beach umbrella. His eyes were dark and curly and full of kindness.

Agatha never thought about Danny anymore.

"I have to pee," Thomas whispered.

"What, again?"

He slid out of bed and hitched up his pajama bottoms. "It was too much grapefruit juice," he said.

Agatha leaned against her pillow and folded

her arms and watched him go. The cigarette smoke from the living room made her nose feel crinkly inside. Wasn't it strange how dead butts smelled so dirty, but lighted cigarettes smelled exciting and promising.

Something nagged at her mind, a bothersome thought she couldn't quite get hold of. Then she noticed what she was hearing: the flushing of the toilet. Oh, no. She threw back her covers and started out of bed.

Too late, though. Thomas shrieked, "Mama! Mama!" and their mother cried, "Thomas?" Her bare feet came rushing down the hall. Her kimono made a crackling sound like fire.

Agatha decided to stay where she was.

"Oh, my God," her mother said. "Oh, my Lord in heaven."

She must be standing in the bathroom doorway. Her voice echoed off the tiles.

"What did you put down that toilet?" she asked.

"Nothing! I promise! I just flushed and the water poured everywhere!"

"Oh, my Lord above."

Agatha wondered if the toilet was still running. She couldn't hear it. She imagined the house flooding silently with the murky yellow water from Daphne's diaper.

"Just *go*, will you?" their mother said. "Go back to bed and stay there. And don't you dare use this toilet again till I can get hold of a plumber, hear?"

The word "plumber" sounded so knowledgeable. Yes, of course: there was a regular, normal person to take charge of this situation, and that meant it must happen to other people too. Agatha pulled her covers up. She watched Thomas enter the room and trudge to his own bed. He walked like an old man, huddled together across the back of his neck. He lay down and reached for Dulcimer and hugged her to his chest.

It wasn't like him to be so quiet. Maybe he had guessed the toilet was Agatha's fault.

She said, "Thomas?"

No answer.

"Thomas, is the water still spilling over?"

"Doe," he said, and the stopped-up sound of his voice told her he was crying.

"You want to come sleep in my bed?"

"Doe."

In the hall she heard their mother's bare feet heading toward her bedroom, and then a pause and then hard shoes clopping out again—or maybe boots. Something big and heavy. Clop-clop toward the kitchen, clop-clop back down the hall. The swabbing of a mop across the bathroom floor. Well, so. It would all be taken care of.

Agatha relaxed and let her eyes fall shut. She might even have slept a few minutes. She saw sleep-pictures floating behind her lids—a black cat hissing and then Ian rattling his dice and all at once flinging them into her face and causing her to start. Her eyes flew open. The lights were still on, and the radio was playing a Beatles song. Ice cubes clinked in a glass. The cloppy footsteps came down the hall, and there was her mother outlined in the doorway. From the ankles up she was thin and fragile, but on her feet she wore two huge shoes from Danny's closet. She came over to Agatha's bed, shuffling slightly so the shoes wouldn't fall off. "Are you awake?" she whispered.

Agatha said, "Yes."

She realized that Thomas must not be. His breathing had grown very slow.

Her mother sat on the edge of the bed. In one hand she held a glass of Coke and in the other her brown plastic pill bottle, uncapped. Probably that was what had rattled in the dream; not Ian's dice after all. She tipped the bottle to her mouth and swallowed a pill and then took a sip of Coke. She said, "Do you believe this? Do you believe a person would just have to fend for herself in this world?"

"Won't the plumber come help?" Agatha asked.

"Everything is resting on my shoulders."

"Maybe Grandma Bedloe knows a plumber."

"It's Howard Belling all over again," her

mother said, which was confusing because, for a second, Agatha thought she meant that the plumber was Howard Belling. "It's the same old story. Unattached, they tell you. Separated, they tell you—or soon about to be. And then one fine morning they're all lovey-dovey with their wives again. How come other people manage to have things so permanent? Is it something I'm doing wrong?"

"No, Mama, *you* didn't do anything wrong," Agatha said.

Her mother tipped another pill into her mouth and took another swallow of Coke. The ice cubes sounded like wind chimes. She raised one foot, her ankle just a stem above the clumsy shoe. Agatha thought of "Clementine." *Herring boxes without topses, sandals were for . . .*

"No wonder men aren't afraid of things!" her mother said. "Would *you* be afraid, if you got to wear gigantic shoes like these?"

Yes, even then she would be, Agatha thought. But she didn't want to say so.

Her mother bent to kiss her good night, brushing her face with the soft weight of her hair, and then she rose and left. Her shoes clopped more and more faintly and her ice cubes tinkled more distantly. Agatha closed her eyes again.

She tried to ride away on the beat of rhymed words—*herring boxes without topses* and *Johnny over the ocean, Johnny over the sea,*

Johnny broke a milk bottle, blamed it on me.

Nibble, nibble, like a mouse, she thought. *Who is nibbling at my house?*

She kept repeating it, concentrating. *Nibble, nibble . . .* She fixed all her thoughts upon it. *Like a mouse . . .* But no matter how hard she tried, she couldn't push back the picture that kept forming behind her lids. Hansel and Gretel were wandering through the woods alone and lost, holding hands, looking all around them. The trees loomed so tall overhead that you couldn't see their tops, and Hansel and Gretel were two tiny specks beneath the great dark ceiling of the forest.

3

THE MAN WHO FORGOT HOW TO FLY

In his ninth-grade biology class, Ian had watched through a microscope while an amoeba shaped like a splash approached a dot of food and gradually surrounded it. Then it had moved on, wider now and blunter, distorted to accommodate the dot of food within.

As Ian accommodated, over and over, absorbing the fact of Danny's death.

He would see it looming in his path—something dark and stony that got in the way of every happy moment. He'd be splitting a pizza with Pig and Andrew or listening to records with Cicely and all at once it would rise up in front of him: *Danny is dead. He died. Died.*

And then a thought that was even worse: *He died on purpose. He killed himself.*

And finally the most horrible thought of all: *Because of what I told him.*

He learned to deal with these thoughts in order, first things first. *All right, he's dead. I will never see him again. He's in Pleasant Memory Cemetery underneath a lilac bush. He won't be helping me with my fast ball. He hasn't heard I got accepted at Sumner College. Trees that were bare when he last saw them have bloomed and leafed without him.*

It felt like swallowing, to take in such a hard set of truths all at one time.

And then he would tackle the next thought. But that was more of a struggle. *Maybe it was an accident,* he always argued.

He smashes headlong into a wall by ACCI-DENT? A wall he knew perfectly well was there, a wall that's stood at the end of that street since before he was born?

Well, he'd been drinking.

He wasn't drunk, though.

Yes, but, you know how it is . . .

Face it. He really did kill himself.

And then finally the last thought.

No, never the last thought.

Sometimes he tried to believe that everyone on earth walked around with at least one unbearable guilty secret hidden away inside.

Maybe it was part of growing up. Maybe if he
went and confessed to his mother she would
say, "Why, sweetheart! Is that all that's bothering you? Listen, every last one of us has
caused *somebody's* suicide."

Well, no.

But if he told her anyway, and let her get as
angry as she liked. If he said, "Mom, you decide
what to do with me. Kick me out of the house,
if you want. Or disown me. Or call the police."

In fact, he wished she *would* call the police.
He wished it were something he could go to
prison for.

But if he told his mother she would learn it
was a suicide, and everyone assumed it was an
accident. Driving under the influence. Too much
stag party. That was the trouble with confessing:
it would make him feel better, all right, but it
would make the others feel worse. And if his
mother felt any worse than she did already, he
thought it would kill her. His father too, probably.
This whole summer, all his father had done was
sit in his recliner chair.

Once his mother asked, "Ian, you don't suppose Danny was depressed or anything, do
you?"

"Depressed?"

"Oh, but what am I saying? He had a new
baby! And a lovely new wife, and a whole new
ready-made family!"

"Right," Ian said.

"Of course, there could have been *little* problems. Some minor snag at work, maybe, or a rocky patch in his marriage. But nothing out of the ordinary, don't you agree?"

"Well, sure," Ian told her.

Was that all it had been? A rocky patch? Had Ian overreacted?

He saw how young he was, how inexperienced, what a shallow, ignorant *boy* he was. He really had no idea what would be considered out of the ordinary in a marriage.

On Sundays when the family gathered, he sent Lucy sidelong glances. He noticed she was growing steadily paler, like one of his father's old Polaroid photos. He wanted to believe Danny's death hadn't touched her, but there she sat with something still and stricken in her face. Her children quarreled shrilly with Claudia's children, but Lucy just sat straight-backed, not appearing to hear, and smoothed her skirt over and over across her lap.

Privately Bee told the others, "I wish she had someone to go to. Relatives, I mean. Of course we'd miss her but . . . if she had someone to tend the children so she could get a job, for instance! I know *I* ought to offer—"

Doug said, "Don't even consider it."

"Well, I'm their grandma! Or one of them's grandma. But lately I've been so tired and my knees are acting up and I don't see how I could handle it. I know I ought to, though."

"Don't give it a moment's consideration."

Did Lucy ever think, *If only I hadn't gone out with Dot that night?* Did she think, *If only Dot's car hadn't broken down?*

For it *was* Dot she'd gone out with. And the car *had* broken down, someplace on Ritchie Highway. That much emerged at the funeral, which Dot had attended all weepy and disbelieving.

Did Lucy ever think, *If only I had been a faithful wife?*

No, probably not, for Ian couldn't shake off the feeling that he was the one she blamed. (At the very least, he'd made Danny drive him home that night.) He was almost positive that she slid her eyes reproachfully in his direction as she smoothed her skirt across her lap. But Ian looked elsewhere. He made a point of looking elsewhere.

Only Cicely knew the whole story. He had told her after the first time they ever made love. Lying next to her in her bed (her parents had gone to a Memorial Day picnic, taking her little brother with them), he had thought, *Danny will never know I've finally slept with a girl.* His eyes had blurred with tears and he had turned abruptly and pressed his hot, wet face into Cicely's neck. "I'm the one who caused Danny's accident," he blurted out. But the thing was, she wouldn't accept it. It was like some physical object that she kept batting away. "Oh, no," she kept saying. "No, that's silly. You didn't do anything. Lucy didn't do anything. Lucy was a *perfect* wife. Danny knew you didn't mean it."

He should have said, "Listen. You have to believe this." But her skin was so soft, and her neck smelled of baby powder, and instead of speaking he had started making love again. He had felt ashamed even then at how easily he was diverted.

Or here was something more shameful than that: In the emergency room that awful night, when the doctors said there was no hope, Ian had thought, *At least now Cicely can't stay mad at me for missing our dinner date*.

Despicable. Despicable. He ground his teeth together any time he recalled it.

That summer he worked again for Sid 'n' Ed's A-1 Movers. Lou had been fired for bleeding all over some lady's sofa after he sat on his own whiskey flask; but LeDon was still there, along with a new man named Brewster, a rough-and-tough, prune-colored type who didn't have two words to say from one day to the next. That was fine with Ian. He felt grateful just for someplace to escape to, some hard labor to throw himself into.

One move he helped with was obviously upward, from a tiny house in Govans to a much
nicer one in Cedarcroft. Workers were swarming
around the new place, patching the roof and
resodding the lawn and measuring for window
screens. In the kitchen he found a man installing
wooden cabinets, and he stood watching as one
was fitted precisely into place. The man plucked
nails out of nowhere. (Maybe he had a mouthful,
like Bee with her sewing pins. His back was
turned so Ian couldn't tell.) He hammered them
in with quick rat-a-tats. And he didn't act the least
self-conscious, not even when Ian said, "Looks
good." In fact, he didn't bother answering. Or
maybe he hadn't heard. Ian said, loudly, "Nice
piece of work."

Then he understood that the man was deaf.
It was something about his head—the way he
held it so steady, not troubling to keep alert for
any sounds. Ian stepped forward and the man
glanced over at him. He had a square-jawed,
deeply lined face and a bristly gray crewcut.
"Looks good," Ian repeated, and the man nodded briefly and returned to his hammering.

Ian felt a twist of envy. It wasn't just the work
he envied, although that was part of it—the all-
consuming task that left no room for extraneous
thoughts. It was the notion of a sealed-off world.
A world where no one traded speech, and where
even dreams, he supposed, were soundless.

He dreamed Danny stood in the doorway jingling a pocketful of change. "I nearly forgot," he told Ian. "I owe you."

Ian caught his breath. He said, "Owe me?"

"I never paid you for baby-sitting that evening. What was it—three dollars? Five?"

Ian said, "No, please," and backed away, holding up his palms. He woke to hear his own voice saying, "No. No. Please."

His parents drove him to school on a hot day in September. Cicely had already left for her own school, near Philadelphia, but since that was just an hour from Sumner College there had not been any big farewell scene. In fact, they were planning on meeting that weekend. And Andrew was close by too, at Temple. But none of Ian's friends were attending Sumner, and he was glad. He liked the idea of making a new beginning. His mother said, "Oh, I hope you won't be lonesome!" but Ian almost hoped he would be. He saw himself striding unaccompanied across the campus, a mysterious figure dressed all in black. "Who *is* that person?" girls would ask. Although he didn't actually own anything black, come to think of it. Still, he had his plans.

They dropped his belongings at the freshman dorm, where the only sign of his roommate was a khaki duffel bag and a canvas butterfly chair printed to resemble a gigantic hand. (At least

Ian assumed the chair was his roommate's. All the other furniture was blond oak.) Then they walked over to the Parents' Reception. Ian was in favor of skipping the reception and so was his father, but his mother insisted.

At the college president's house they were given three paper cups of 7-Up with orange sherbet floating foamily on top, and they stood in a clump by a blond oak table trying to make conversation with each other. "Quite a crowd," his father said, and his mother said, "Yes, isn't it!" Ian started eating spice cookies from a plate on the table. He ate one after the other, frowning and chewing intently as if he could have made many interesting comments if only his mouth weren't full. "Are these all parents of freshmen, do you suppose?" his father asked. "Well, maybe some are transfers' parents," his mother said.

She stood among these ruffly people in her ordinary navy dress, and her shoes were plain flat pumps because of her knees. Without high heels she seemed downtrodden, Ian noticed, like somebody's maid. And his father's suit was rucked up around his calves with static cling or something. He had the crazy appearance of a formally attired man standing shin-deep in ocean breakers. Ian swallowed a sharp piece of cookie and felt it hurting all the way down his throat, all the way to his chest where it lodged and wouldn't go away. He wanted to say, "Take me back to Baltimore! I'll never complain again, I promise." But instead he joined in the small talk, and he noticed that his voice had the same determined upward slant as his mother's.

They left the reception without having spoken to another soul, and they walked together to the parking lot. The family car looked dusty and humble. Ian opened the door for his mother, but she was used to opening her own door and so she got in his way and he stepped on her foot. "Sorry," he said. "Well . . ." She kissed his cheek and slid hurriedly inside, not looking at him. His father gave him a wave across the roof of the car. "Take care of yourself, son."

"Sure thing," Ian said.

He stood with his palms clamped in his armpits and watched them drive off.

His roommate was a zany, hooting, clownish boy named Winston Mills. Not only was the hand-shaped chair his, but also a bedspread made from an American flag, and a beer stein that tinkled out "How Dry I Am" when you lifted it, and a poster for a movie called *Teenage Robots*. The other boys thought he was weird, but Ian liked him. He liked the fact that Winston never had a serious discussion or asked a serious question. Instead he told the entire plots of movies Ian had never heard of—werewolf movies and Japanese westerns and monster

movies where the zippers showed clearly between the scales—or he read aloud in a falsetto
voice from a collection of syrupy "love comics"
he'd found at a garage sale, meanwhile lolling
in his butterfly chair with the huge pink fingers
curving up behind him.

Ian dreamed Danny drove onto the quad in
his Chevy, which didn't have so much as a
dented fender. He leaned out his window and
asked Ian, "Don't you think I knew? Don't you
think I knew all along?" And Ian woke and
thought maybe Danny *had* known. Sometimes
people just chose not to admit a thing, not even
to themselves. But then he realized that was
immaterial. So what if he'd known? It wasn't till
he'd been told point-blank that he'd felt the need
to take action.

As far as Ian could see, college was not much
different from high school. Same old roots of
Western civilization, same old single-cell orga-
nisms. He squinted through a microscope and
watched an amoeba turn thin and branchy,
curve two branches around a black dot, thicken
to a blob and drift on. His lab partner was a girl
and he could tell she liked him, but she seemed
too foreign. She came from someplace rural and
said "ditten" instead of "didn't." Also "cooten":
"I cooten find my notebook anywhere." He lived
for the weekends, when Cicely rode out to Sumner on a tiny, rattling train and they hung around

his dorm in the hope that Winston might leave for one of his movies at some point. Supposedly Cicely was bunking with the older sister of a girl she knew from home, but in fact she shared Ian's narrow bed where late at night—silently, almost motionlessly, all but holding their breaths—they made love over and over again across the room from Winston's snoring shape.

He called home collect every weekend; that was easier than his parents' trying to call him. But the Wednesday before Halloween his mother phoned, reaching him purely by chance as he was passing through the dorm between classes. "I hate to bother you," she said, "but I thought you'd want to know. Honey, it's Lucy."

"Lucy?"

"She died."

He noticed that a sort of whirring silence seemed to be traveling down the corridor. He said, "She what?"

"We think it was pills."

He swallowed.

"Ian?"

Oh, God, he thought, *how long will I have to pay for just a handful of tossed-off words?*

"Are you all right, Ian?"

"Sure," he said.

"We got a call from Agatha last night. She told us, 'Mama keeps sleeping and won't wake up.'

Well, you know that could have meant anything. Of course I made plans to get right over there but I did say, 'Oh, sweetie, I bet she's just tuckered out,' and that's when Agatha said, 'She wouldn't even wake for breakfast.' I said, 'Breakfast?' I said, 'This morning?' Ian, would you believe it, those children had been on their own since the night before when she put them to bed. Then she went to bed herself and just, I don't know, I mean there's no sign she did it on purpose but when we walked in she was flat on her back and breathing so slowly, just a breath here and another breath there, and this pill bottle sat on her nightstand totally empty. There wasn't any letter though or anything like that. So it *couldn't* have been on purpose, right? But why would she take even one of those pills? Our family's never held with sleeping pills. I always say, get up and scrub the floors if you can't sleep! Do some reading! Improve your mind! Anyhow, we called the ambulance and they took her to Union Memorial. She had gone on too long, though. If they'd got to her right away, well, maybe; but she'd been lying there a whole night and a day and there wasn't much they could do. She died this noon without ever regaining consciousness."

Can't we just back up and start over? Couldn't I have one more chance?

"Ian?" his mother was saying. "Listen, don't breathe a word to the children."

He found his voice from somewhere. He said, "They don't know yet?"

"No, and we're not ever going to tell them."

Maybe the shock had sent her around the bend. He said, "They're going to have to find out sometime. How will you explain it when she doesn't come home from the hospital?"

Or when she fails to show up for Thomas's high-school graduation or Agatha's wedding, he thought wildly, and he almost laughed.

"I mean we're not going to tell them they might have saved her," his mother said. "If they'd phoned earlier, I mean. They'd feel so guilty."

He leaned against the wall and briefly closed his eyes.

"So we've set the funeral for Friday," his mother said, "assuming her people agree to it. Did she ever happen to tell you who her people were?"

"She didn't have any. *You* know that."

"Well, distant relatives, though. Isn't it odd? I don't believe she once mentioned her maiden name."

"Lucy . . . Dean," Ian said. "Dean was her name."

"No, Dean would have been her first husband's name."

"Oh."

"There must be cousins or something, but the children couldn't think who. We said where could we reach their daddy, then? They didn't have the slightest idea."

"He lives in Cheyenne, Wyoming," Ian said. As clearly as if he'd been present, he saw Lucy heaving her package onto the post office counter. She looked up into Danny's face and asked in her little cracked voice how much it would cost to airmail a bowling ball to Wyoming.

"Your father has already called every Dean in the Cheyenne directory," his mother said, "but he came up empty. Now all we have to rely on is someone maybe seeing the obituary."

Two boys were walking down the corridor. Ian turned so he was facing the other way.

"Ian? Are you there?"

"I'm here."

"I told your father I wasn't going to phone you. I said, why interrupt your studies? But he thought maybe you could come on account of the children. Well, goodness, *I* can handle the children but they're so . . . the baby hasn't slept since she got here. And Thomas just sits around hugging that doll of his, and Agatha's being, oh, Agatha; you know how she is. Somehow I just never have felt like those two's grandma. Isn't that awful? They can't help it! But somehow . . . and your sister's all tied up with Davey's measles . . ."

Ian could guess what this was leading to. He felt suddenly burdened.

"So your father said maybe you could come help out a few days."

"I'll catch the next Greyhound," he said.

He rode to Baltimore that evening on a nearly empty bus, staring at his own reflection in the window. His eyes were deep black hollows and he appeared to have sharper cheekbones than he really did. He looked stark and angular, bitterly experienced. He wondered if there was any event, any at all, so tragic that it could jolt him out of this odious habit of observing his own reaction to it.

His father met him at the terminal. Neither of them knew yet how they were supposed to greet each other after long separations. Hug? Shake hands? His father settled for clapping him on the arm. "How was the trip?" he asked.

"Pretty good."

Ian hoisted his knapsack higher on his shoulder and they walked through the crowd, dodging people who seemed to have set up house-keeping there. They threaded between stuffed laundry bags and take-out food cartons; they stepped over the legs of a soldier asleep on the floor. Outside, Howard Street looked very bustling and citified after Sumner.

"So," his father said, once they were seated in the car. "I guess you heard the news."

"Right."

"Terrible thing. Terrible."

"How're the kids?" Ian asked him.

"Oh, they're okay. Kind of quiet, though."

They entered the stream of traffic and drove north. The evening was still warm enough for car windows to be open, and scraps of songs sailed past—"Monday, Monday" and "Winchester Cathedral" and "Send Me the Pillow That You Dream On." Ian's father said, "Your mom put me to work this afternoon hunting Lucy's relatives. I don't know if she told you."

"She told me you tried calling Cheyenne."

"Yes, well. No luck. And I stopped by the Fill 'Er Up Café—remember the Fill 'Er Up? Where Lucy used to work? I was hoping to find those two waitresses from the wedding. But the owner said one had walked out on him and the other moved south a couple of months ago. So then I went through Lucy's drawers, thinking there'd be, oh, an address book, say, or some letters. Didn't find a thing. Hard to figure, isn't it? This is what we've come to, now that people phone instead of writing."

"Maybe there just *aren't* any relatives," Ian told him.

"Well, in that case, what'll we do with the children?"

"Children."

"The older two have their father, of course. Soon as we track him down. But I suppose it's expecting too much that he would raise the little one as well."

"Well, naturally," Ian said. "She isn't even kin!"

"No, I guess not," his father said. He sighed.

"He doesn't even keep in touch with the two that are!"

"No."

"Couldn't you and Mom, maybe . . ."

"We're too old," his father said. He turned up Charles Street.

"You're not old!"

"We've just reached that time in our lives, Ian, when I think we deserve a rest. And your mother's not getting around so good lately; I don't know if you've noticed. Doc Plumm says this thing in her knees is arthritis. Can't exactly picture her chasing after a toddler."

"Yes, but—"

"Never mind, I'm sure we'll come up with someone or other," his father said, "once we find that ex-husband."

Then he went back to deploring how no one wrote letters these days. Pretty soon, he said, this country's mail service would be canceled for lack of interest. Turn all the post offices into planters, he said, and his lips twisted into one of his wry smiles before he recollected himself and grew serious again.

At home, Beastie nosed Ian's palm joyfully and lumbered after him into the living room, where his mother was walking Daphne up and down. She kissed him hello and then handed him the baby, who was too near sleep to do more than murmur. "Oh, my legs!" Bee said, sinking onto the couch. "That child has kept me on my feet all evening."

Thomas sat at the other end of the couch with his doll clutched to his chest, her yellow wig flaring beneath his chin like a bedraggled sunflower. Agatha sat in an armchair. She surveyed Ian levelly and then returned to her picture book. Both of them wore pajamas. They had the moist, pale, chastened look of children fresh from their baths.

"Have you eaten yet?" Ian's mother asked him. "I fed the children early because I didn't know."

"I can find something."

"Oh. Well, all right."

Daphne had gained weight, or maybe it was her sleepiness that made her feel so heavy. She drooped over Ian's shoulder, giving off a strong smell of apple juice.

"Your father's been through . . . various drawers," his mother said. She glanced toward Agatha. Evidently Lucy's name was not supposed to be spoken. "He didn't find a thing."

"Yes, he told me."

Agatha turned a page of her book. Ian's father crossed to the barometer on the wall and tapped the glass.

"Ian, dear," his mother said, "would you mind very much if I toddled off to bed?"

"No, go ahead," Ian said, although he did feel a bit hurt. After all, this was his first visit home.

"It's been such a long day, I'm just beat. The older two are sleeping in Danny's room, and I've set up the Port-a-Crib in your room. I hope Daphne won't disturb you."

"I'll be okay."

"He looks downright domestic, in fact," his father said, and he gave a snort of laughter. Doug belonged to an era when the sight of a man holding a baby was considered humorous. He liked to say he'd changed a diaper only once in all his life, back when Bee had the flu and Claudia was an infant. The experience had made him throw up. Everyone always chuckled when he told this story, but now Ian wondered why. He felt irked to see his father drift behind Bee toward the stairs, although *his* knees were not arthritic and he might easily have stayed to help. "Night, son," he said, lifting an arm.

"Good night," Ian said shortly.

He sat on the couch next to Thomas. Daphne instantly made a chipped sound of protest, and he stood up and started walking again.

"Ian," Agatha said, "will you read us a story?"

"I can't right now. Daphne won't let me sit down."

"She will if you sit in a rocking chair," Agatha said.

He tried it. Daphne stirred, but as soon as he began rocking she went limp again. He wondered why his mother hadn't thought of this—or why Agatha hadn't informed her.

Agatha was pulling up a footstool so she could sit next to him. Her eyes were lowered and her plain white disk of a face seemed complete in itself, ungiving. "Get a chair, Thomas," she ordered. Thomas slid off the couch and dragged over the miniature rocker from the hearth. It took him a while because he never let go of Dulcimer.

The book Agatha placed on Ian's lap dated from his childhood. *The Sad Little Bunny*, it was called. It told about a rabbit who got lost on a picnic and couldn't find his mother. Ian wondered about reading this story under these particular circumstances, but both children listened stolidly—Thomas sucking his thumb, Agatha turning the pages without comment. First the rabbit went home with a friendly robin and tried to live in a tree, but he got dizzy. Then he went home with a beaver and tried to live in a dam, but he got wet. Ian had never realized what a repetitive book this was. He swallowed a yawn. Tears of boredom filled his eyes. The effort of reading while rocking made him slightly motion-sick.

On the last page, the little rabbit said, "Oh, Mama, I'm so glad to be back in my own home!" The picture showed him in a cozy, chintz-lined burrow, hugging an aproned mother rabbit. Reading out the words, Ian noticed how loud they sounded—like something tactless dropped into a shocked silence. But Agatha said, "Again."

"It's bedtime."

"No, it's not! What time is it?"

"Tell you what," he said. "You get into your beds, and then I'll read it once more."

"Twice," Agatha said.

"Once."

What did this remind him of? The boredom, the yawns . . . It was the evening of Danny's death, revisited. He felt he was traveling a tread-mill, stuck with these querulous children night after night after night.

In the morning the minister came to discuss the funeral service. He was an elderly, stiff, formal man, and Bee seemed flustered when Ian led him into the kitchen. "Oh, don't look at all this mess!" she said, untying her apron. "Let's go into the living room. Ian can feed the children."

But Dr. Prescott said, "Nonsense," and sat down in a kitchen chair. "Where's *Mr*. Bedloe?" he asked.

Bee said, "Well, I know it sounds heartless, but he had to take the day off yesterday and of course tomorrow's the funeral so . . . he went to work."

"Is that good?" Dr. Prescott asked Daphne. She was squirting a piece of banana between her fingers and then smearing it across her high-chair tray.

"It's not that he doesn't mourn her. Really, he feels just dreadful," Bee said. "Ian, could you fetch a cloth, please? But substitute teachers are so hard to get hold of—"

"Yes, life must go on," Dr. Prescott said. "Isn't that right, young Abigail."

"Agatha," Bee corrected him. "It's Claudia's girl who's named Abigail."

"And will the children be attending the service?"

"Oh, no."

"Sometimes it's valuable, I've learned."

"We think they'll have a *fine* time staying here with Mrs. Myrdal," Bee said. "Mrs. Myrdal used to sit with them when they lived above the drug-store and she knows all their favorite story-books."

She beamed across the table at Agatha. Agatha gazed back at her without a trace of a smile.

Dr. Prescott said, "Agatha, Thomas, I realize all that's happened must be difficult to understand. Perhaps you'd like to ask me some questions."

Agatha remained expressionless. Thomas shook his head.

Ian thought, *I would! I would!* But it wasn't Ian Dr. Prescott had been addressing.

He'd remembered to bring his suit but he had forgotten a tie, so he had to borrow one of his father's for the funeral. Standing in front of his mirror, he slid the knot into place and smoothed his collar. When the doorbell rang, he waited for someone to answer. It rang again and Beastie gave a worried yap. "Coming!" Ian called. He crossed the hall and sprinted downstairs.

Mrs. Myrdal had already opened the front door a few inches and poked her head in. Her hat looked like a gray felt potty turned upside down. Ian said, "Hi. Come on in."

"I worried I was late."

"No, we're just getting ready."

He showed her into the living room, where she settled on the sofa. She was one of those women who grow quilted in old age—her face a collection of pouches, her body a series of squashed mounds. "My, it's finally getting to be fall," she said, removing her sweater. "Real nip in the air today."

"Is that so," Ian said. He was hanging about in the doorway, wondering whether it was rude to leave.

"And how are those poor children bearing up?" she asked him.

"They're okay."

"I couldn't get over it when your mother called and told me. Those poor little tots! And I understand your parents won't be keeping them."

"No, we're trying to find some relatives," Ian said.

"Well, it's a shame," Mrs. Myrdal said.

"I don't guess *you* know of any relatives."

"No, dear, your mother already asked me. I told her, I said, 'I'm sorry, but I wouldn't have an inkling.' Although just between you and me, I'm pretty near positive that Lucy was, well, not from Baltimore."

"Ah."

"You could sort of tell, you know," she said. "I always sensed it, even before we had our falling out. You heard we'd fallen out, I suppose."

"Not in so many words," Ian said.

"Well!" Mrs. Myrdal said. She folded her sweater caressingly. "One time we went downtown together and I caught her shoplifting."

"Shoplifting?"

"Bold as you please. Swiped a pure silk blouse off a rack and tucked it into the stroller where her innocent baby girl lay sleeping. I was so astounded I just didn't do a thing. I thought I must have misunderstood; I thought there must be *some* explanation. I followed along behind her thinking, 'Now, Ruby, don't go jumping to conclusions.' On we march, past the scarf counter. Whisk! Red-and-tan Italian scarf scampers into her bag. I know I should have spoken but I was too amazed. My heart was racing so I thought it had riz up in my throat some way, and I worried we'd be arrested. We could have been, you know! We could have been hauled off to jail like common criminals. Well, luckily we weren't. But next time she phoned I said, 'Lucy, I'm busy.' She said, 'I just wanted to ask if you could baby-sit.' 'Oh,' I said, 'I don't believe I care to, thank you.' She knew why, too. She didn't let on but she had to know. Couple of times she asked again, and each time I turned her down."

Ian ducked his head and busied himself patting Beastie.

"Not that I wished her ill, understand. I was sorry as the next person to hear about her passing."

From the stairs came the sound of footsteps and his mother's voice saying, ". . . juice in that round glass pitcher and—" She arrived in the doorway with the baby propped on her hip. Thomas and Agatha were shadowing her. "Oh! Mrs. Myrdal," she said. "I didn't hear you come in."

Mrs. Myrdal rose and reached out in that fumble-fingered, greedy manner that old ladies take on around babies. "Would you look at how this child has grown!" she said. "Remember Mrs. Moo-doe, darlin'?" She accepted Daphne in a rumpled bunch and cocked her head at the other two. "Thomas and Agatha, I'd never have known you!"

"Now, we shouldn't be long," Bee told her. "It's going to be a very simple . . . Ian, where's your father got to?"

Ian said, "Um . . . ."

"Isn't this just like him! Check the basement, will you? Mrs. Myrdal, the tea bags are in the . . ."

Ian went out to the kitchen. He thought, *She was only shoplifting.* He crossed the pantry and started down the basement steps. *She wasn't meeting some man, she was shoplifting.* He called, "Dad?"

"Down here."

That dress was not a present from her lover after all.

His father was tinkering at his workbench. Wearing his good dark suit, his hair still showing the comb lines, he bent over the lamp from the attic bedroom. "Are we set to go?" he asked without turning.

Why, even I have been known to shoplift. Me and Pig and Andrew, back in fifth grade. It's nothing. Or next to nothing.

"Ian?"

He looked at his father.

"Are we set to go?"

"Yes," Ian said after a moment.

"Well, then."

His father switched off the light above the bench. He started toward the stairs. He halted next to Ian and said, "Coming?"

"Yes."

They climbed the stairs.

Oh, God, this is the one last little dark dot I can't possibly absorb.

In the hall, his mother was putting on her hat. "Why is it," she asked his father, "that the minute everyone's ready, you choose to disappear?"

"I was just looking at that lamp, sweetheart."

The three of them left the house and walked to the car. Ian felt bruised all down the front of his body, as if he'd been kicked.

The last time he'd been in this church was for Danny's funeral—and before that, for Danny's wedding. When he stood on the sidewalk looking up at Dober Street Presbyterian, all his thoughts were gathered toward his brother. He could almost believe that Danny had been left behind here, in this peaked stone building with the louvered steeple.

Inside, his parents stopped to greet Mrs. Jordan while Ian continued down the aisle. He passed Aunt Bev and her husband, and Cousin Amy, and a couple of the foreigners from the neighborhood. He caught sight of Cicely's blond curls gleaming like fresh pine shavings, and he slid in next to her and took hold of her hand, which turned out to contain a knob of damp Kleenex. Her lashes and her cheeks were damp too, he saw when she smiled at him. She had told him when he telephoned that she wouldn't think of not coming to this, even though it meant a two-hour train ride. She just needed to say goodbye, she told him. She had always thought Lucy was special.

The organ started playing softly, and Dr. Prescott entered through a side door and took a seat behind the pulpit. Below the pulpit lay the casket, pearly gray, decorated with a spray of white flowers. The sight of it made Ian feel cold. Something like a cold blade entered his chest and he looked away.

Now the others were filing down the aisle— his father solemn and sheepish, his mother wearing an expression that seemed less griefstricken than disappointed. "I'm not angry; just disappointed," she used to tell Ian when he misbehaved. (What would she say now, if she knew what he had done?) Behind came Claudia and Macy with Abbie, who was evidently considered old enough now for funerals. She had on her first high heels and wobbled slightly as she followed the others into a pew. This wasn't the front pew but the one just behind. Maybe the front pew was reserved for Lucy's blood relations, if any showed up.

But none did. The organ music dwindled away, Dr. Prescott rose and announced a prayer, and still no one arrived to fill that empty pew.

The prayer was for the living. "We know Thy daughter Lucy is safely by Thy side," Dr. Prescott intoned, "but we ask Thee to console those left behind. Comfort them, we pray, and ease their pain. Let Thy mercy pour like a healing balm upon their hearts."

Like a healing balm. Ian pictured something white and semiliquid—the bottle of lotion his mother kept by the kitchen sink, say—pleasantly scented with almonds. Could the balm soothe not just grief but guilt? Not just guilt but racking anguish over something impulsively done that could not be undone?

Ordinarily indifferent to prayers (or to anything else even vaguely religious), Ian listened to this one yearningly. He leaned forward in his seat as if he could ride the words all the way to heaven. He kept his eyes tightly shut. He thought, *Please. Please. Please.*

In the pews around him he heard a rustling and a creaking, and he opened his eyes and found the congregation rising. Struggling to his feet, he peered at the hymnbook Cicely held in front of him. ". . . with me," he joined in belatedly, "fast falls the eventide . . ." His voice was a creak. He fell silent and listened to the others— to Cicely's clear soprano, Mrs. Jordan's plain, true alto, Dr. Prescott's rich bass. "The darkness deepens," they sang, "Lord, with me abide!" The voices ceased to be separate. They plaited themselves into a multistranded chord, and now it seemed the congregation was a single person—someone of great kindness and compassion, someone gentle and wise and forgiving. "In life, in death, O Lord," they finished, "abide with me." And then came the long, sighed "Amen." They sat down. Ian sat too. His knees were trembling. He felt that everything had been drained away from him, all the grief and self-blame. He was limp and pure and pliant as an infant. He was, in fact, born again.

Through the burial in Pleasant Memory Cemetery and the car trip home, through the flurry of reclaiming the children, setting up the coffeepot, and greeting the guests who stopped by afterward, Ian wandered in a dreamlike state of mind. He traveled around the living room with a plate of butterscotch brownies, failing to notice it was empty till his brother-in-law pointed it out. "Earth to Ian," Macy said, guffawing, and then Mrs. Jordan relieved Ian of the plate. Cicely came up from behind and slipped a hand into his. "Are you all right?" she asked him.

"Yes, fine," he said.

Her fingertips were soft little nubbins because she bit her nails. Her breath gave off the metallic scent of Coca-Cola. Mrs. Jordan's craggy face had a hinged and plated look, like an armadillo hide. Everything seemed very distinct, but also far away.

"It's been too much," Mrs. Jordan told Cicely. "Just too much to take in all at once. First Danny, and now Lucy!" She turned to draw one of the foreigners into the conversation; he was hovering hopefully nearby. "Why, I remember the day they announced their engagement!" she said. "Remember, Jim?"

"Jack," the foreigner said.

"Jack, I was there when he brought her home. I'd come over to borrow the pinking shears and in they walked. Well, I knew right away what was what. Pretty little thing like that, who *wouldn't* want to marry her?"

"Woe betide you," Jack told Ian.

"Um . . ."

"O lud lud! Please to accept my lamentations."

This must be the foreigner who was so devoted to *Roget's Thesaurus*. Bee was always quoting choice remarks. Mrs. Jordan gave him a speculative stare. "I suppose in your culture, Lucy wouldn't have lasted even this long," she said. "Don't they throw themselves on their husband's pyre or something?"

"Pyre?"

"And now I reckon Doug and Bee will have to take on those poor children," she told Ian.

Ian said, "Well, actually—"

"Just look at that little one. Did you ever see anything so precious?"

Ian followed her gaze. In the doorway to the hall, Daphne stood rocking unsteadily. Her dazzling white shoes—hard-soled and ankle-high—no doubt helped to keep her upright; but still, standing alone at ten months was quite an accomplishment, Ian suspected. Was this the first time she'd tried it? He thought of all the fuss that would have been made ordinarily—the applause and the calls for a camera. But Daphne went unnoticed, a frail, wispy waif in an oversized dress, looking anxiously from face to face.

Then she spotted Ian. Her eyes widened. She grinned. She dropped to the floor and scuttled toward him, expertly weaving between the grownups' legs and pausing every now and then to wrench herself free from the hem of her dress. She arrived at his feet, took hold of his trousers and hauled herself to a standing position. When she beamed up at him, she had to tip her head so far back she nearly fell over.

Ian bent and lifted her into his arms. She nestled against his shoulder. "Oh, the darling," Mrs. Jordan said. "Why, she's crazy about you! Isn't she, Ian? Isn't she? Ian?"

He couldn't explain why the radiance left over from church fell away so suddenly. The air in the room seemed dull and brownish. Mrs. Jordan's voice sounded hollow. This child was far too heavy.

Back in school, he kept trying to recapture that feeling he'd had at the funeral. He hummed "Abide with Me" under his breath. He closed his eyes in hopes of summoning up the congregation's single, melting voice, the soft light from the pebbled windows, the sense of mercy and forgiveness. But nothing came. The bland brick atmosphere of Sumner College prevailed. Biology 101 progressed from nematodes to frogs, and King John repudiated the Magna Carta, and Ian's roommate dragged him to see *Devil-Women from Outer Space*.

At night, Danny stood at the blackboard in front of Ian's English class. "This is a dream," he announced. "The word 'dream' comes from the Latin word *dorimus*, meaning 'game of chance.' " Ian awoke convinced that there had been some message in this, but the harder he worked to decipher it, the farther away it drifted.

He phoned home Saturday afternoon and learned that Mrs. Jordan, of all people, had cleverly uncovered the name of Lucy's ex-husband. "What she did," Bee told Ian, "was sit Agatha down beside her and run through a lot of everyday, wife-ish remarks. She said, 'Don't forget the garbage,' and, 'Suppertime!' and, 'You're late.' Her theory was, the name would sort of swim into Agatha's memory. She thought Thomas was too young to try it on. But all at once Thomas pipes up, 'You're late with the check again, Tom!' he said. Just out of nowhere!"

"Well, that would make sense," Ian said. "So Thomas must be Tom Junior."

"I said to Jessie Jordan, I said, 'Jessie,' I said, 'you're amazing.' Really I don't know what I'd have done without her, these past few days. Or *any* of the neighbors. They've all been so helpful, running errands for me and taking the children when my legs are bad . . ."

What she was saying, it seemed to Ian, was, "See what you've gone and done? See how you've ruined our lives?" Although of course she didn't mean that at all. She went on to say the

Cahns, next door, had lent her their sitter, and the foreigners had brought over a pot of noodle soup with an aftertaste resembling throw-up. "People have been just lovely," she said, "and Cicely's mother called to say—"

"But what about Thomas Senior?" Ian broke in.

"What about him?"

"Did you look for him in the Cheyenne phone book?"

"Oh, we'd already called all the Deans in Cheyenne, but now we have a name to give the officials. They ought to be able to track *something* down—driver's license, marriage license . . . I remember Lucy said once he'd remarried."

That night Ian dreamed that Lucy sat in her living room among bushel baskets of mail—letters and fliers and magazines. Then Danny walked in and said, "Lucy? What is this?"

"Oh," she said, "I just can't open them anymore. Since you died it seems I haven't had the heart."

"But this is terrible!" he cried. "Your bulks and your flats I could understand, but first-class, Lucy! First-class envelopes lying untouched!"

"Then talk to Ian," she said in a wiry, tight voice.

"Ian?"

"Ian says I'm not a bit first-class," she said, and her mouth turned down at the corners, petulant and spiteful looking.

Ian awoke and blinked at the crack of light beneath the door. Winston was snoring. Someone's radio was playing. He heard the scrape of a chair down the hall and carefree, unthinking laughter.

Sunday morning he rode into town on the college's little blue church bus. Most of the passengers were students he'd never laid eyes on before, although he did recognize his lab partner, dressed in a hard-surfaced, voluminous gray coat. He pretended not to see her and proceeded toward the long seat at the rear, where he settled between two boys with haircuts so short and suits so tidy that they might have stepped out of the 1950s. Really this was a sort of *losers'* bus, he realized, and he had an impulse to jump off while he still could. But then the senior class secretary boarded—a poised, attractive girl—and he felt reassured. He rode through the stubbled farmlands with his eyes fixed straight ahead, while the boy on his left fingered a rosary and the boy on his right whispered over a Bible.

At the courthouse square in Sumner, the bus stopped and everyone disembarked. Ian chose to follow the largest group of students, which included the senior class secretary and also a relatively normal-looking freshman named Eddie something whom he'd seen around the dorm. He and Eddie fell into step together, and Eddie said, "You on your way to Leeds Memorial?"

"Well, yeah, I guess so."

Eddie nodded. "It's not too bad," he said. "I go every week on account of my grandmother's paying me."

"Paying you?"

"If I don't miss a Sunday all year I get a check for a hundred bucks."

"Gosh," Ian said.

Leeds Memorial was a stately brick building with a white interior and dark, varnished pews. The choir sounded professional, and they sang the opening hymn on their own while the congregation stayed seated. Maybe that was why Ian didn't have much feeling about it. It was only music, that was all—something unfamiliar, classical-sounding, flawlessly performed. Maybe the whole church had to be singing along.

The theme of the day was harvest, because they were drawing close to Thanksgiving. The Bible reading referred to the reaping of grain, and the sermon had to do with resting after one's labors. The pastor—a slouching, easygoing, just-one-of-the-guys type with a sweater vest showing beneath his suit coat—counseled his listeners to be kind to themselves, to take time for themselves in the midst of the hurly-burly. Ian felt enormous yawns hollowing the back of his throat. Finally the organist began thrumming out a series of chords, and the sermon came to an end and everyone rose. The hymn was "Bringing in the Sheaves." It was a simple-minded, seesawing sort of tune, Ian felt, and the collective voice of the congregation had a note of fluty gentility, as if dominated by the dressed-up old ladies lining the pews.

Walking back to the bus, Eddie asked if he'd be coming every Sunday.

Ian said he doubted it.

His Thanksgiving vacation was fractious and disorganized; Lucy's children had still not been claimed. By now they had moved in upon the household in full force. Their toys littered the living room, their boats and ducks crowd-ed the bathroom, and Daphne's real crib—much larger than the Port-a-Crib—cramped his bed-room. He was alarmed at how haggard his mother looked, and how heavy and big-bellied. The waistband of her slacks was extended with one of those oversized safety pins women once decorated their kilts with. And the holiday dinner she served was halfhearted—no hors d'oeuvres, not even beforehand, and the turkey unstuffed and the pies store-bought. Even the company seemed lacking. Claudia snapped at her children, Macy kept drifting away from the table to watch a football game on TV, and the foreigners had to leave before dessert in order to meet the plane of a new arrival. All in all, it was a relief to have the meal over with.

He tried to help with the children as much as possible. He played endless games of Parcheesi; he read and reread *The Sad Little Bunny*. And he rose at least once each night to rock Daphne back to sleep, sometimes nodding off himself in the process. Often he had the feeling that she was rocking *him*. He would wake to find her coolly studying his face in the dark, or even prying up one of his lids with her chubby, sticky fingers.

Ironically, it was during this vacation that Cicely told him she might be pregnant. In the middle of a movie called *Georgy Girl*, which concerned a young woman who was tiresomely, tediously fond of infants, she clutched a handful of his sleeve and whispered that she was two weeks late. "Late for what?" he asked, which for some reason made her start crying. Then he understood.

They walked out on the movie and drove around the city. Ian kept inventing other possibilities. She was tense about her exams, maybe, or it was all that traveling back and forth on the train, or—"I don't know! How would I know?

Some damn reason!" he said, and she said, "You don't have to shout! It was your fault as much as it was mine! Or more, even; way more. You're the one who talked me into it."

This wasn't entirely accurate. Still, on some deeper level it seemed he deserved every word she hurled at him. He saw himself as a plotter and a predator, sex-obsessed; Lord, there were days when thoughts of sex with anyone—it didn't have to be Cicely—never left his mind for a moment. And now look: here was his rightful penance, marriage at eighteen and a job bagging groceries in the A&P. He drew a breath. He said, "Don't worry, Ciss. I'll take care of you."

They were supposed to stop by Andrew's after the movie, but instead he drove her home. "I'll call you tomorrow," he said, and then he went on to his own house and climbed the stairs to his room, where he found Daphne sitting upright and holding out her arms.

By the time he returned to school on Sunday evening, he had almost persuaded Cicely to see a doctor. What he hoped for (although he didn't say it) was a doctor who could offer her a magic pill or something. There must be such a pill. Surely there was. Maybe it was some common cold remedy or headache tablet, available on open shelves, with NOT TO BE TAKEN DURING PREGNANCY imprinted on the label—a message in code for those who needed it. But if he mentioned this to Cicely she might think he didn't want to marry her or something, when of course he did want to and had always planned to. Just not yet, please, God. Not when he'd never even slept with a *dark*-haired girl yet.

He flinched at the wickedness of this thought, which had glided so smoothly into his mind that it might have been there all along.

In Biology 101 on Tuesday, his lab partner said she'd noticed him on the church bus. She wondered if he'd like to attend the Wednesday Night Youth Group at her place of worship. "Oh, I'm sorry, I can't," he said instantly. "I've got a paper due."

"Well, maybe another time, then," she said. "We always have such fun! Usually they show a movie, something nice and clean with no language."

"It does sound like fun," he said.

He meant that sincerely. He ached, all at once, for a blameless life. He decided that if Cicely turned out not to be pregnant, *they* would start living like that. Their outings would become as wholesome as those pictures in the cigarette ads: healthy young people laughing toothily in large, impersonal groups, popping popcorn, taking sleigh rides.

But on Thursday, when Cicely phoned to tell him she'd got her period, what did he do? He said, "Listen. You have to go on the pill now.

You know that." And she said, "Yes, I've already made an appointment." And that weekend they picked up where they had left off, although Cicely still had her period and really it was sort of complicated. He had to rinse all the bed-clothes the following morning, and as he stood barefoot in the dormitory bathroom watching the basin fill with pink water, he felt weary and jaded and disgusted with himself, a hopeless sinner.

Christmas fell on a Sunday that year. Ian didn't get home till Friday evening; so Saturday was a hectic rush of shopping for gifts. Only on Christmas Eve did he have a chance to look around and realize the state of the household. He saw that although a good-sized tree had been erected in the living room, no one had trimmed it; the box of decorations sat unopened on the piano. The swags of evergreen were missing from the banister, the front door bore no wreath, and the house had a general air of neglect. It wasn't just relaxed, or folksy, or happy-go-lucky; it was dirty. The kitchen smelled of garbage and cat box. The last two remaining goldfish floated dead in their scummy bowl. None of the gifts had been wrapped yet, and when the children asked to hang their stockings it emerged that all the socks were in the laundry.

"Well, I'm sorry," Bee said, "but one person or another has been sick the last two weeks running and I just haven't had a minute. So I'm sorry. Hang something else, instead. Hang grocery bags. Hang pillowcases."

"Pillowcases!" Thomas said dolefully.

"Don't worry," Ian told him. "I'll do a wash tonight. You go on to bed and I'll hang your stockings later."

So that evening was spent in the basement, more or less. Ian found the hampers so overstuffed and moldy that he guessed the laundry had not been seen to in some time, and he decided to take care of the whole lot. Also he put himself in charge of gift wrapping. While his mother sat at the dining room table sipping the sherry he'd poured her, he swaddled everything ineptly in plain tissue. (She had not thought to buy Christmas paper.) He wrapped even the gifts meant for him—a couple of shirts, a ski jacket—pretending to pay them no heed. Periodically he left his work to run downstairs to the basement and start another load of laundry. The scent of detergent and fresh linens gradually filled the house. It wasn't such a bad Christmas Eve after all.

"Remember Christmas in the old days?" his mother asked. "When we got everything ready so far ahead? Presents sat under the tree for weeks! Homemade, most of them. Lord, you children made enough clay ashtrays to cover every surface, and none of us even smokes. But this year I just couldn't get up the spirit. Seems like ever since this happened with your brother I've been so . . . unenthusiastic."

Ian didn't know what to say to that. He made a big business of tying a bow on a package.

"And remember all the hors d'oeuvres at Christmas dinner?" she asked. "This year I'll be doing well to throw a piece of meat in the oven."

"Maybe we should go to a restaurant," Ian said.

"A restaurant!"

"Why not?"

"Let's hope we haven't come to *that*," his mother said.

In the living room they heard a sharp grunt— his father, asleep in his recliner chair.

But as it turned out, Christmas Day was not so different that year from any other. Mrs. Jordan came, along with the foreigners. The children contributed their share of excitement (Claudia's six and Lucy's three, combined), and Doug's Polaroid Land camera flashed, and the cat made choking sounds behind the couch. It was disconcerting, in a way. Last Christmas Daphne hadn't been born yet; nor had Franny. Now here sat Daphne chewing a wad of blue tissue while Franny stirred her fists through Agatha's jigsaw puzzle. They both seemed so accustomed to being here. And Danny and Lucy had completely vanished. Something was wrong with a world where people came and went so easily.

The day after Christmas, Sid at the movers' phoned to see if Ian could help out over vacation. Their man Brewster had left them in the lurch, he said. Ian told him he'd be glad to help. School would not reopen till mid-January and he could use the extra cash. So Tuesday morning, he reported to the garage on Greenmount.

LeDon was delighted to see him. That Brewster fellow, he said, had just up and walked away in the middle of a job. "He say, 'See you round, LeDon.' I say, 'Hey, man, you ain't *ditching* me.' He say, 'All day long I'm ditching you,' and off he go. Well, he won't never what you call real friendly."

They were moving an old lady from a house to an apartment—lots of old-lady belongings, bowlegged furniture and mothballed dresses and more than enough china to stock a good-sized restaurant. Her son, who was overseeing the move, had some kind of fixation about the china. "Careful, now! That's Spode," he would say as they lifted a crate. And, "Watch out for the Haviland!" LeDon rolled his eyes at Ian.

Then at the new place, they found out the kitchen was being remodeled and they had to set the china crates in the living room. "What the hell?" the son said. "This was supposed to be finished three days ago." He was talking to the cabinetmaker—the deaf man Ian had come across last summer, as it happened. "How much longer?" the son asked him. Any fool could see it would be *way* longer; the kitchen was nothing but a shell. The cabinetmaker, not looking around, measured the depth of a counter with a steel measuring tape. The son laid a hand on the man's forearm. The man turned slowly, gazed a moment at the son's hand, and then lifted his eyes to his face. "HOW . . . LONG!" the son shouted, exaggerating his lip movements.

The cabinetmaker considered, and then he said, "Two weeks."

"Two weeks!" the son said. He dropped his hand. "What are you building here, Noah's ark? All we need is a few lousy cupboards!"

The cabinetmaker went on about his business, measuring the counter's length now and the height of the empty space above it. Surely he must have known the son was speaking to him, but he seemed totally absorbed in what he was doing. Once again, Ian envied the man his insular, impervious life.

On New Year's Eve Pig Benson threw a big, rowdy party, but Ian didn't go. Cicely was babysitting her brother and it was her last night home. (Her college worked on a different schedule from

Ian's.) So they set all the clocks an hour ahead and tricked Stevie into going to bed early, and then they snuck upstairs to her room, where Ian unintentionally dozed off. He was awakened by church bells ringing in the New Year, which meant her parents could be expected at any moment. As soon as he'd dressed, he slipped downstairs and into the frosty, bitter night. He walked home half asleep while bells pealed and firecrackers popped and rockets lit the sky. What optimism! he found himself thinking. Why did people have such high hopes for every New Year?

He practiced saying the date aloud: "Nineteen sixty-seven. January first, nineteen sixty-seven." Monday was his birthday; he'd be nineteen years old. Daphne would be one. He shivered and pulled his collar up.

That night he dreamed Danny came driving down Waverly Street in Sumner College's blue church bus. He stopped in front of home and told Ian, "They've given me a new route and now I get to go anywhere I like."

"Can I ride along?" Ian asked from the sidewalk.

"You can ride along after you learn Chinese," Danny told him.

"Oh," Ian said. Then he said, "Chinese?"

"Well, I like to call it Chinese."

"Call what Chinese?"

"You understand, Chinese is not what I really mean."

"Then what *do* you mean?" Ian asked.

"Why, I'm talking about . . . let us say . . . Chinese," Danny said, and he winked at Ian and laughed and drove away.

When Ian woke, Daphne was crying, and the room seemed moist as a greenhouse from her tears.

Agatha's school reopened Tuesday, and Thomas's nursery school Wednesday. This should have lightened Bee's load, but still she looked exhausted every evening. She said she must have a touch of the flu. "Ordinarily I'm strong as a horse!" she said. "This is only temporary, I'm positive."

Ian asked, "What's the word on Tom Dean, Senior? Any sign of him?"

"Oh," his mother said, "I guess we'll have to give up on Tom Dean. It doesn't seem he exists."

"Then what'll you do with the children?"

"Well, your father has some ideas. He's pretty sure from something Lucy once mentioned that she came from Pennsylvania. Maybe her first marriage was recorded there, he says, in which case—"

"You're stuck with them, aren't you," Ian said.

"Pardon?"

"You're stuck with those children for good."

"Oh, no," she told him. "I'm certain we'll find

somebody sooner or later. We'll just have to. We'll have to!"

"But what if you don't?" Ian asked her.

Her face took on a flown-apart, panicked look.

Two of the children weren't even Bedloes, and he wondered if it occurred to his parents that those two could simply be made wards of the state, or whatever—popped into some kind of foster home or orphanage. But he suspected that with Daphne, they wouldn't feel free to do that. Daphne was their dead son's child, and an infant besides. She wasn't already formed, as the other two were. She hadn't yet reached the knobby-kneed, scabby stage that only a mother could love; she was still full of dimples, still tiny and beguiling.

Thomas, on the other hand, could cause a serious puncture wound if he accidentally poked you with his elbow. Holding him on your lap was like holding a bunch of coat hangers. Which didn't prevent his trying to climb up there, heaven knows. He had the nuzzling, desperate manner of a small dog starved for attention, which unfortunately lessened his appeal; while Agatha, who managed to act both sullen and ingratiating, came across as sly. Ian had seen how grownups (even his mother, even his earth-mother sister) turned narrow-eyed in Agatha's presence. It seemed that only Ian knew how these children felt: how scary they found every waking minute.

Why, being a child at all was scary! Wasn't that what grownups' nightmares so often reflected—the nightmare of running but getting nowhere, the nightmare of the test you hadn't studied for or the play you hadn't rehearsed? Powerlessness, outsiderness. Murmurs over your head about something everyone knows but you.

He finished moving a family into a row house on York Road and went home from there on foot, passing a series of shabby stores. The job had run unusually late. It was after seven on a dismal January evening, and most places had closed. One window, though, glowed yellow—a wide expanse of plate glass with CHURCH OF THE SECOND CHANCE arching across it in block letters. Ian couldn't see inside because the paper shade was lowered. He walked on by. Behind him a hymn began. "Something something something lead us . . ." He missed most of the words, but the voices were strong and joyful, overlaid by a single tenor that rose above the rest.

He paused at the intersection, the arches of his sneakers teetering on the curb. He peered at the DON'T WALK sign for a moment. Then he turned and headed back to the church.

A shopkeeper's bell jingled when he opened

the door. The singers looked around—some fifteen or twenty people, standing in rows with their backs to him—and smiled before they looked away again. They were facing a tall, black-haired man in a tieless white shirt and black trousers. The pulpit was an ordinary store counter. The floor was green linoleum. The lights overhead were long fluorescent tubes and one tube flickered rapidly, giving Ian the impression that he had a twitch in his eyelid.

"Blessed Jesus! Blessed Jesus!" the congregation sang. It was a tender, affectionate cry that sounded personally welcoming. Ian found his way to an empty spot beside a woman in a white uniform, a nurse or a waitress. Although she didn't look at him, she moved closer and angled her hymnal so he could follow the words. The hymnal was one of those pocket-sized pamphlets handed out free at public sing-alongs. There wasn't any accompaniment, not even a piano. And the pews—as Ian realized when the hymn came to an end and everyone sat down—were plain gray metal folding chairs, the kind you'd see at a bridge game.

"Friends," the minister said, in a sensible, almost conversational tone. "And guests," he added, nodding at Ian. All over again, the others turned and smiled. Ian smiled back, maybe a little too broadly. He had the feeling he was their first and only visitor.

"We have reached that point in the service," the minister said, "when any person here is invited to step forward and ask for our prayers. No request is too great, no request is trivial in the eyes of God our Father."

Ian thought of the plasterer who'd repaired his parents' bathroom ceiling. NO JOB TOO LARGE OR TOO SMALL, his panel truck had read. He brushed the thought away. He watched a very fat young woman heave herself to her feet just in front of him. The width of her sprigged, summer-weight skirt, when she finally reached a standing position, completely blocked his view of the minister. "Well, Clarice as you may have heard is down real bad with her blood," she said breathily. "We had thought that was all behind her but now it's come on back, and I asked what I could do for her and she says, 'Lynn,' says, 'take it to Wednesday Night Prayer Meeting, Lynn, and ask them for their prayers.' So that's just what I'm doing."

There was a silence, during which she sat down. As soon as she left Ian's line of vision, he realized the silence was part of the program. The minister stood with both palms raised, his face tipped skyward and his eyelids closed and gleaming. In his shirtsleeves, he seemed amateurish. His cuffs had slipped down his forearms, and his collar, Ian saw, was buttoned all the way to the neck, in the fashion of those misfits who

used to walk around high school with slide rules
dangling from their belts. He wasn't so very old,
either. His frame was lanky as a marionette's
and his wrist bones boyishly knobby.

Ian was the only one sitting erect. He bowed
his head and squinted at the billow of sprigged
skirt puffing out the back of the fat woman's
chair.

"For our sister Clarice," the minister said
finally.

"Amen," the congregation murmured, and
they straightened.

"Any other prayers, any other prayers," the
minister said. "No request is beyond Him."

On the other side of Ian's neighbor, a gray-
haired woman rose and placed her purse on her
seat. Then she faced forward, gripping the chair
in front of her. "You all know my son Chuckie
was fighting in Vietnam," she said.

There were nods, and several people turned
to look at her.

"Well, now they tell me he's been killed," she
said.

Soft sounds of dismay traveled down the
rows.

"Tell me he got killed jumping out of a plane,"
she said. "You know he was a paratrooper."

More nods.

"Monday night these two soldiers came, all
dressed up."

"Ah, no," they said.

"I told them I had thought he'd be safe. I said he'd been jumping so *long* now, looked to me like he'd learned how to stay alive up there. Soldier says, 'Yes, ma'am,' he says. 'These things happen,' he says. Says Chuckie was a, what do you call, fluke accident. Forgot to put his parachute on."

Ian blinked.

"Forgot!" his neighbor marveled in a voice like a dove.

" 'Forgot!' I said. 'How could that be?' This soldier tells me, it's the army's considered opinion that Chuckie had just jumped so often, he'd stopped thinking about it. So up he comes to that whatever, that door where they jump out of, the whole time making smart remarks so everybody's laughing—you remember what a card he was—and gives a little kind of like salute and steps into empty air. It's not till then the fellow behind him says, 'Wait!' Says, 'Wait, you forgot your—' "

"Parachute," Ian's neighbor finished sadly.

"So I don't ask your prayers for Chuckie after this; I ask for me," the woman said. For the first time, her voice was unsteady. "I'm just about sick with grief, I tell you. Pray for me to find some deliverance."

She sat down, fumbling behind her for her

purse. The minister lifted his palms and the room fell silent.

Could you really forget your parachute?

Well, maybe so. Ian could see how it might have come about. A man to whom jumping was habit might imagine that floating in space was all his own doing, like flying. Maybe it had slipped his mind he *couldn't* fly, so in the first startled instant of his descent he supposed he had simply forgotten how. He may have felt insulted, betrayed by all he'd taken for granted. *What's the big idea here?* he must have asked.

Ian pictured one of those animated films where a character strolls off a cliff without noticing and continues strolling in midair, perfectly safe until he happens to look down and then his legs start wheeling madly and he plummets.

He gave a short bark of laughter.

The congregation swiveled and stared at him.

He bowed his head, cheeks burning. The minister said, "For our sister Lula."

"Amen," the others said, mercifully facing forward again.

"Any other prayers, any other prayers . . ."

Ian studied the sprigged skirt while shame slammed into him in waves. He had said and done heedless things before but this was something new: to laugh out loud at a mother's bereavement. He wished he could disappear. He wanted to perform some violent and decisive act, like leaping into space himself.

"No prayer is unworthy in the eyes of our Creator."

He stood up.

Heads swiveled once again.

"I used to be—" he said.

Frog in his throat. He gave a dry, fake-sounding cough.

"I used to be good," he said. "Or I used to be not bad, at least. Not evil. I just *assumed* I wasn't evil, but lately, I don't know what's happened. Everything I touch goes wrong. I didn't mean to laugh just now. I'm sorry I laughed, Mrs. . . . ."

He looked over at the woman. Her face was lowered and she seemed unaware of him. But the others were watching closely. He had the sense they were weighing his words; they were taking him seriously.

"Pray for me to be good again," he told them. "Pray for me to be forgiven."

He sat down.

The minister raised his palms.

The silence that followed was so deep that Ian felt bathed in it. He unfolded in it; he gave in to it. He floated on a fluid rush of prayers, and all the prayers were for his pardon. How could God not listen, then?

When Ian was three or four years old, his

mother had read him a Bible story for children. The illustration had showed a Roman soldier in full armor accosting a bearded old man. "Is that God?" Ian had asked, pointing to the soldier; for he associated God with power. But his mother had said, "No, no," and continued reading. What Ian had gathered from this was that God was the other figure, therefore—the bearded old man. Even after he knew better, he couldn't shake that notion, and now he imagined the congregation's prayers streaming toward someone with long gray hair and a floor-length, Swedish-blue robe and sturdy bare feet in leather sandals. He felt a flood of gratitude to this man, as if God were, in literal truth, his father.

"For our guest," the minister said.

"Amen."

It was over too suddenly. It hadn't lasted long enough. Already the minister was saying, "Any other prayers, any other prayers . . ."

There weren't any.

"Hymn sixteen, then," the minister said, and everyone stirred and rustled pages and stood up. They were so matter-of-fact; they were smoothing skirts, patting hairdos. Ian's neighbor, a stocky, round-faced woman, beamed at him and tilted her hymnal in his direction. The hymn was "Leaning on the Everlasting Arms." The minister started it off in his soaring tenor:

"What a fellowship, what a joy divine,
Leaning on the everlasting arms . . ."

This time Ian sang too, although really it was more of a drone.

When the hymn was finished, the minister raised his palms again and recited a benediction. "Go ye now into the world and bear witness to His teachings," he said. "In Jesus' name, amen."

"Amen," the others echoed.

Was that *it*?

They started collecting coats and purses, buttoning buttons, winding scarves. "Welcome!" Ian's neighbor told him. "How did you find out about us?"

"Oh, I was just walking by . . ."

"So many young people nowadays don't give half enough thought to their spiritual salvation."

"No, I guess not," Ian said.

All at once he felt he was traveling under false pretense. Spiritual salvation! The language these places used made him itch with embarrassment. (Blood of the Lamb, Died for Your Sins . . .) He looked yearningly behind him, where the first people to leave were already sending a slap of cold air into the room. But his neighbor was waving to the minister. "Yoo-hoo! Reverend Emmett! Come and meet our young person!"

The minister, already choosing a path between the knots of worshipers, seemed discon-
certingly jubilant. His smile was so wide that his
teeth looked too big for his mouth. He arrived in
front of Ian and shook his hand over and over.
"Wonderful to have you!" he said. (His long,
bony fingers felt like dried beanpods.) "I'm Reverend Emmett. This is Sister Nell, have you introduced yourselves?"

"How do you do," Ian said, and the other two
waited so expectantly that he had to add, "I'm
Ian Bedloe."

"We use only first names in our place of worship," Reverend Emmett told him. "Last names
remind us of the superficial—the world of wealth
and connections and who came over on the
Mayflower."

"Really," Ian said. "Ah. Okay."

His neighbor laid a hand on his arm and said,
"Reverend Emmett will tell you *all about it*. Nice
meeting you, Brother Ian. Good night, Reverend
Emmett."

"Night," Reverend Emmett said. He watched
as she swirled a navy cape around her shoulders
(so she was, after all, a nurse) and sidled out
the other end of the row. Then he turned back
to Ian and said, "I hope your prayer was answered this evening."

"Thanks," Ian said. "It was a really . . . interesting service."

Reverend Emmett studied him. (His skin was an unhealthy shade of white, although that could have been the fluorescent lighting.) "But your prayer," he said finally. "Was there any response?"

"Response."

"Did you get a reply?"

"Well, not exactly."

"I see," Reverend Emmett said. He watched an aged couple assist each other through the door—the very last to leave. Then he said, "What was it that you needed forgiven?"

Ian couldn't believe his ears. Was this even legal, inquiring into a person's private prayers? He ought to spin on his heel and walk out. But instead his heart began hammering as if he were about to do something brave. In a voice not quite his own, he said, "I caused my brother to, um, kill himself."

Reverend Emmett gazed at him thoughtfully.

"I told him his wife was cheating on him," Ian said in a rush, "and now I'm not even sure she was. I mean I'm pretty sure she did in the past, I know I wasn't *totally* wrong, but . . . So he drove into a wall. And then his wife died of sleeping pills and I guess you could say I caused that too, more or less . . ."

He paused, because Reverend Emmett might want to disagree here. (Really Lucy's death was just indirectly caused by Ian, and maybe not even that. It might have been accidental.) But Reverend Emmett only rocked from heel to toe.

"So it looks as if my parents are going to have to raise the children," Ian said. Had he mentioned there were children? "Everything's been dumped on my mom and I don't think she's up to it—her or my dad, either one. I don't think they'll ever be the same, after this. And my sister's busy with her own kids and I'm away at college most of the time . . ."

In the light of Reverend Emmett's blue eyes—which had the clean transparency of those marbles that Ian used to call ginger-ales—he began to relax. "So anyhow," he said, "that's why I asked for that prayer. And I honestly believe it might have worked. Oh, it's not like I got an answer in plain English, of course, but . . . don't you think? Don't you think I'm forgiven?"

"Goodness, no," Reverend Emmett said briskly.

Ian's mouth fell open. He wondered if he'd misunderstood. He said, "I'm *not* forgiven?"

"Oh, no."

"But . . . I thought that was kind of the point," Ian said. "I thought God forgives everything."

"He does," Reverend Emmett said. "But you can't just say, 'I'm sorry, God.' Why, anyone could do that much! You have to offer reparation—concrete, practical reparation, according to the rules of our church."

"But what if there isn't any reparation? What if it's something nothing will fix?"

"Well, that's where Jesus comes in, of course."

Another itchy word: Jesus. Ian averted his eyes.

"Jesus remembers how difficult life on earth can be," Reverend Emmett told him. "He helps with what you can't undo. But only after you've *tried* to undo it."

"Tried? Tried how?" Ian asked. "What would it take?"

Reverend Emmett started collecting hymnals from the chair seats. Apparently he was so certain of the answer, he didn't even have to think about it. "Well, first you'll need to see to those children," he said.

"Okay. But . . . see to them in what way, exactly?"

"Why, raise them, I suppose."

"Huh?" Ian said. "But I'm only a freshman!"

Reverend Emmett turned to face him, hugging the stack of hymnals against his concave shirt front.

"I'm away in Pennsylvania most of the time!" Ian told him.

"Then maybe you should drop out."

"Drop out?"

"Right."

"Drop out of college?"

"Right."

Ian stared at him.

"This is some kind of test, isn't it?" he said finally.

Reverend Emmett nodded, smiling. Ian sagged with relief.

"It's God's test," Reverend Emmett told him.

"So . . ."

"God wants to know how far you'll go to undo the harm you've done."

"But He wouldn't really make me follow through with it," Ian said.

"How else would He know, then?"

"Wait," Ian said. "You're saying God would want me to give up my education. Change all my parents' plans for me and give up my education."

"Yes, if that's what's required," Reverend Emmett said.

"But that's crazy! I'd have to be crazy!"

" 'Let us not love in word, neither in tongue,' " Reverend Emmett said, " 'but in deed and in truth.' First John three, eighteen."

"I can't take on a bunch of kids! Who do you think I am? I'm nineteen years old!" Ian said. "What kind of a cockeyed religion *is* this?"

"It's the religion of atonement and complete forgiveness," Reverend Emmett said. "It's the religion of the Second Chance."

Then he set the hymnals on the counter and

turned to offer Ian a beatific smile. Ian thought he had never seen anyone so absolutely at peace.

"I don't understand," his mother said.

"What's to understand? It's simple," Ian told her. "What you mean is, you don't approve."

"Well, of course she doesn't approve," his father said. "Neither one of us approves. No one in his right mind would approve. Here you are, attending a perfectly decent college which you barely got into by the skin of your teeth, incidentally; you've had no complaints about the place that your mother or I are aware of; you're due back this Sunday evening to begin your second semester and what do you up and tell us? You're dropping out."

"I'm taking a leave of absence," Ian said.

They were sitting in the dining room late Friday night—much too late to have only then finished supper, but Daphne had developed an earache and what with one thing and another it had somehow got to be nine p.m. before they'd put the children in bed. Now Bee, having risen to clear the table, sank back into her chair. Doug shoved his plate away and leaned his elbows on the table. "Just tell me this," he said to Ian. "How long do you expect this leave of absence to last?"

"Oh, maybe till Daphne's in first grade. Or kindergarten, at least," Ian said.

"Daphne? What's Daphne got to do with it?"

"The reason I'm taking a leave is to help Mom raise the kids."

"Me?" his mother cried. "I'm not raising those children! We're looking for a guardian! First we'll find Lucy's people and then I know there'll be someone, some young couple maybe who would just love to—"

"Mom," Ian said. "You know the chances of that are getting slimmer all the time."

"I know nothing of the sort! Or an aunt, maybe, or—"

Doug said, "Well, he's got a point, Bee. You've been running yourself ragged with those kids."

Contrarily, Ian felt a pinch of alarm. Would his father really let him go through with this?

His mother said, "And anyway, how about the draft? You'll be drafted the minute you leave school."

"If I am, I am," Ian told her, "but I don't think I will be. I think God will take care of that."

"Who?"

"And I do plan to pay my own way," he said. "I've already found a job."

"Doing what?" his father asked. "Moving poor folks' furniture?"

"*Building* furniture."

They peered at him.

"I've made arrangements with this cabinet-maker," Ian said. "I've seen him at work and I asked if I could be his apprentice."

Student, was the way he'd finally put it. Having sought out the cabinetmaker in that apartment full of china crates and mothballs, he had plunged into the subject of apprenticeship only to be met with a baffled stare. The man had sat back on his heels and studied Ian's lips. "Apprentice," Ian had repeated, enunciating carefully. "Pupil."

"People?" the man had asked. Two furrows stitched themselves across his leathery forehead.

"I already have some experience," Ian said. "I used to help my father in the basement. I know I could build a kitchen cabinet."

"I dislike kitchens," the man said harshly.

For a moment, Ian thought he still hadn't made himself clear. But the man went on: "They're junk. See this hinge." He pointed to it—an ornately curlicued piece of black metal, dimpled all over with artificial hammer marks. "My real work is furniture," he said.

"Fine," Ian told him. What did he care? Kitchen cabinets, furniture, it was all the same to him: inanimate objects. Something he could deal with that he couldn't mess up. Or if he did mess up, it was possible to repair the damage.

"I have a workshop. I make things I like," the man said. He spoke like anyone else except for a certain insistence of tone, a thickness in the consonants, as if he had a cold. "These kitchens, they're just for the money."

"That's okay! That's fine! And as for money," Ian said, "you could pay me minimum wage. Or lower, to start with, because I'm just an apprentice. Student," he added, for he saw now that it was the uncommon word "apprentice" that had given trouble. "And any time you have to do a kitchen, you could send me instead."

He knew he had a hope, then. He could tell by the wistful, visionary look that slowly dawned in the man's gray eyes.

But were his parents impressed with Ian's initiative? No. They just sat there blankly. "It's not brute labor, after all," he told them. "It's a craft! It's like an art."

"Ian," his father said, "if you're busy learning this . . . art, how will you help with the kids?"

"I'll work out a schedule with my boss," Ian said. "Also there's this church that's going to pitch in."

"This what?"

"Church."

They tilted their heads.

"There's this . . . it's kind of hard to explain," he said. "This church sort of place on York Road, see, that believes you have to really do something practical to atone for your, shall we call them, sins. And if you agree to that, they'll pitch in. You can sign up on a bulletin board—the hours you need help, the hours you've got free to help others—"

"What in the name of God . . . ?" Bee asked.

"Well, that's just it," Ian said. "I mean, I don't want to sound corny or anything but it *is* in the name of God. 'Let us not love in—' what—'in just words or in tongue, but in—' "

"Ian, have you fallen into the hands of some *sect?*" his father asked.

"No, I haven't," Ian said. "I have merely discovered a church that makes sense to me, the same as Dober Street Presbyterian makes sense to you and Mom."

"Dober Street didn't ask us to abandon our educations," his mother told him. "Of course we have nothing against religion; we raised all of you children to be Christians. But *our* church never asked us to abandon our entire way of life."

"Well, maybe it should have," Ian said.

His parents looked at each other.

His mother said, "I don't believe this. I do not believe it. No matter how long I've been a mother, it seems my children can still come up with something new and unexpected to do to me."

"I'm not doing this to *you!* Why does everything have to relate to *you* all the time? It's for me, can't you get that into your head? It's something I have to do for myself, to be forgiven."

"Forgiven what, Ian?" his father asked.

Ian swallowed.

"You're nineteen years old, son. You're a fine, considerate, upstanding human being. What sin could you possibly be guilty of that would require you to uproot your whole existence?"

Reverend Emmett had said Ian would have to tell them. He'd said that was the only way. Ian had tried to explain how much it would hurt them, but Reverend Emmett had held firm. Sometimes a wound must be scraped out before it can heal, he had said.

Ian said, "I'm the one who caused Danny to die. He drove into that wall on purpose."

Nobody spoke. His mother's face was white, almost flinty.

"I told him Lucy was, um, not faithful," he said.

He had thought there would be questions. He had assumed they would ask for details, pull the single strand he'd handed them till the whole ugly story came tumbling out. But they just sat silent, staring at him.

"I'm sorry!" he cried. "I'm *really* sorry!"

His mother moved her lips, which seemed unusually wrinkled. No sound emerged.

After a while, he rose awkwardly and left the table. He paused in the dining room doorway, just in case they wanted to call him back. But they didn't. He crossed the hall and started up the stairs.

For the first time it occurred to him that there was something steely and inhuman to this religion business. Had Reverend Emmett taken fully into account the lonely thud of his sneakers on the steps, the shattered, splintered air he left behind him?

The little lamp on his desk gave off just enough light so it wouldn't wake Daphne. He leaned over the crib to check on her. She had a feverish smell that reminded him of a sour dishcloth. He straightened her blanket, and then he crossed to the bureau and looked in the mirror that hung above it. Back-lit, he was nothing but a silhouette. He saw himself suddenly as the figure he had feared in his childhood, the intruder who lurked beneath his bed so he had to take a running leap from the doorway every night. He turned aside sharply and picked up the mail his mother had set out for him: a *Playboy* magazine, an advertisement for a record club, a postcard from his roommate. The magazine and the ad he dropped into the wastebasket. The postcard showed a wild-haired woman barely covered by a white fur dress that hung in strategic zigzags around her thighs. (*SHE-WOLVES OF ANT-ARCTICA! In ViviColor!* the legend read.) *Dear Ian, How do you like my Christmas card? Better late than never. Kind of boring here at home, no Ian and Cicely across the room oh-so-silently hanky-pankying . . .* He winced and dropped the card on top of the magazine. It made a whiskery sound as it landed.

He saw that he was beginning from scratch, from the very ground level, as low as he could get. It was a satisfaction, really.

That night he dreamed he was carrying a cardboard moving carton for Sid 'n' Ed. It held books or something; it weighed a ton. "Here," Danny said, "let me help you," and he took one end and started backing down the steps with it. And all the while he and Ian smiled into each other's eyes.

It was the last such dream Ian would ever have of Danny, although of course he didn't know that at the time. At the time he woke clenched and anxious, and all he could think of for comfort was the hymn they had sung in the Church of the Second Chance. "Leaning," they sang, "leaning, leaning on the everlasting arms . . ." Gradually he drifted loose, giving himself over to God. He rested all his weight on God, trustfully, serenely, the way his roommate used to rest in his chair that resembled the palm of a hand.

4

FAMOUS RAINBOWS

Holy Roller, their grandma called it. Holy Roller Bible Camp. She shut a cupboard door and told Thomas, "If you all went to *real* camp instead of Holy Roller, you wouldn't have to get up at the crack of dawn every day. And I wouldn't be standing here half asleep trying to fix you some breakfast."

But it wasn't the crack of dawn. Hot yellow bands of sunshine stretched across the linoleum. And she didn't look half asleep, either. She already had her hair combed, fluffed around her face in a curly gray shower-cap shape. She was wearing the blouse Thomas liked best, the one printed like a newspaper page, and brown knit slacks stretched out in front by the cozy ball of her stomach.

One of the words on her blouse was VICTORY. Another was DISASTER. Thomas hadn't even started second grade yet but he was able to read nearly every word you showed him.

"If you all went to Camp Cottontail like the Parker children you wouldn't have to leave till nine a.m.," his grandma said, inching around the table with a stack of cereal bowls. "An air-conditioned bus would pick you up at the doorstep. But oh, no. *Oh*, no. That's too simple for your uncle Ian. Let's not do it the easy way, your uncle Ian says."

What Ian had really said was, "Camp Cottontail costs eighty dollars for a two-week session." Thomas had heard the whole argument. "Eighty dollars per child! Do you realize what that comes to?"

"Maybe Dad could make a bit extra teaching summer school," their grandma had told him.

"Dream on, Mom. You really think I'd let him do that? Also, Camp Cottontail doesn't take three-year-olds. Daphne would be home all day with little old *you*."

That was what had settled it. Their grandma had the arthritis in her knees and hips and sometimes now in her hands, and chasing after Daphne was too much for her. Daphne just did her in, Grandma always said. Dearly though she loved her.

She shook Cheerios into Thomas's bowl and then turned toward the stairs. "Agatha!" she called. "Agatha, are you up?"

No answer. She sighed and poured milk on top of the Cheerios. "You get started on these and I'll go give her a nudge," she told Thomas. She walked stiffly out of the kitchen, calling, "Rise and shine, Agatha!"

Thomas laid his spoon flat on top of his cereal and watched it fill with milk and then sink.

Now here came his grandpa and Ian, with Daphne just behind. Ian wore his work clothes—faded jeans and a T-shirt, his white cloth carpenter cap turned around backwards like a baseball catcher's. (Grandma just despaired when her men kept their hats on in the house.) He'd dressed Daphne in her new pink shorts set, and she was pulling the toy plastic lawn mower that made colored balls pop up when the wheels turned.

"The way I figure it," Ian was saying, "we'd be better off moving the whole operation to someplace where the lumber could be stored in the same building. But Mr. Brant likes the shop where it is. So I'm going to need the car all day unless you . . ."

Thomas stopped listening and took a mouthful of cereal. He watched Daphne walk around and around Ian's legs, with the lawn mower bobbling behind her. "This is what I'm bringing to Sharing Hour," she announced, but Thomas was the only one who heard her. "Ian? This is what I'm—"

"You should bring something fancier," Thomas told her.

"No! I'm bringing this!"

"Remember yesterday, what Mindy brought?"

Mindy had brought an Egyptian beetle from about a million years ago, pale blue-green like old rain spouts. But Daphne said, "I don't care."

"*Lots* of people have plastic lawn mowers," Thomas told her.

She pretended not to hear and walked in tighter and tighter circles around Ian's blue denim legs.

Once Daphne had her mind made up, nothing could change it. Everyone always joked about that. But Thomas worried she would look dumb in front of Bible camp. It was such a small camp that all the children were jumbled together, the three-year-olds in with the seven-year-olds like Thomas and even Agatha's age, the ten-year-olds; even ten-year-old Dermott Kyle. Dermott Kyle would be sure to laugh at her. Thomas watched her round-nosed white sandals taking tiny steps and he started getting angry at her just thinking about it.

Then Ian bent over and scooped her up, lawn

mower and all. He said, "What's your breakfast order, Miss Daph?" and she giggled and told him, "Cinnamon toast."

That Daphne was too ignorant to worry.

When Agatha came downstairs she looked puffy-eyed and dazed. She never woke up easily. Their grandma hobbled around her, trying to get her going—pushing the Cheerios box across the table to her and offering other kinds when Agatha shook her head. "Cornflakes? Raisin bran?" she said. Agatha rested her chin on her fist and her eyes started slowly, slowly drooping shut. "Agatha, *don't* go back to sleep."

"She'll be fine once she hits fresh air," Ian said. He was standing by the toaster, waiting for Daphne's toast to pop up. He'd set Daphne on the counter next to him where she swung her feet and banged her heels against the cupboard doors beneath her.

"She'd be even finer if she could sleep till a decent hour," their grandma told him. "Why, they're having to get up earlier in summer than in winter! Poor child can barely keep her eyes propped open."

"She ought to be in Camp Cottontail," their grandpa said suddenly. Everyone had forgotten about him. He was scrambling himself some eggs at the stove. "Camp Cottontail comes to the house for them about nine o'clock or so; I've seen the bus in the neighborhood."

"Wasn't I just saying that? While Holy Roller, on the other hand—"

"It's not Holy Roller, Mom. Please," Ian told her. "It's Camp Second Chance. And it's sponsored by my church and it's free of charge. Not to mention it offers the kids a little grounding for their lives."

Their grandma looked up at the ceiling and let out a long, noisy breath.

"When I was seventeen," their grandpa said from the stove, "I volunteered to be a counselor at my church's camp out in western Maryland. That's because I was in love with this girl who taught archery there. Marie, her name was. I can see her still. She wore this leather cuff on her wrist so the bowstring wouldn't thwack her. Every night I prayed and prayed for her to love me back. I said, 'God, if you'll do this one thing for me I'll believe in you forever and I'll never ask another favor.' But she preferred the lifeguard and they started going out together. After that, why, me and God just never have been that chummy."

"God and I," Grandma murmured automatically.

"I mean I still go to church on holidays and such, but I don't feel quite the same way about it."

Ian said, "Well, what does that prove? Good grief! You act as if it proves something. But all it proves is, you didn't know what was best for you. You were asking for a girl who wasn't right for you."

Their grandpa just shrugged, but their grandma said, "Oh, Lord, it's too early in the day for this," and she dropped heavily into a chair.

Agatha's eyes were closed now and Daphne had stopped swinging her feet. The dog lay next to the sink like a rumpled floor mat. Only Ian seemed to have any pep. He plucked the toast from the toaster, flipping it a couple of times so it wouldn't burn his fingers. As he turned to bring it to the breakfast table, he gave Thomas a quick little wink and a smile.

While Ian was driving them to camp he said, "You mustn't take it too seriously when your grandma and grandpa talk that way. They've had some disappointments in their lives. It doesn't mean they don't believe deep down."

"I know that," Thomas said, but Agatha just stared out the side window. She always got grumpy and embarrassed when talk of religion came up. Thomas suspected she was not a true Christian. He knew for a fact that she hated going to Camp Second Chance. Even the name, she said, made it seem they were settling for something; and what sort of camp has just a backyard, above-ground, corrugated plastic pool you have to fill with a garden hose? But she said this privately, only to Thomas. Neither one of them would have hurt Ian's feelings for the world.

Ian dropped them off at Sister Myra's house in a rush; he was running late. "Morning, Brother Ian!" Sister Myra called from her front door, and he said, "Morning, Sister Myra. Sorry I can't stop to talk." Then he drove away, leaving them on the sidewalk. Sister Myra lived in a development called Lullaby Acres where no trees grew, and it was hotter than at home. Thomas could feel a trickle of sweat starting down between his shoulder blades.

"My, don't you three look spiffy," Sister Myra said, opening the screen door for them. She was a plump, smiley-faced woman with a frizz of sand-colored curls. "What's that you got with you, sweetheart?" she asked Daphne.

"This here is my lawn mower."

"Well, bring it on in where it's cool."

It wasn't just cool; it was cold. Sister Myra's house was air-conditioned. Thomas thought air-conditioning was wonderful, even if it did mean they tended to stay inside as much as possible. Today, for instance, no one at all was playing in the brownish backyard around the swimming pool. Everybody was down in the basement rec room, which felt like a huge refrigerator. Dermott Kyle and Jason were lining up dinky plastic Bible figures in two rows across the indoor-outdoor carpet, making believe one row was ranchers and the other was cattle rustlers. Three girls were dressing dolls in a corner, and the Nielsen twins were helping Sister Myra's daughter Beth put today's memory verse on the flannelboard: *As the hart . . .* and then a word that Thomas couldn't figure out. He hoped the verse was a short one. Dermott Kyle had asked yesterday for *Jesus wept*, and it made the other campers laugh till Sister Myra pointed out how sad He must have been for our sins.

"We have three more people to wait for," Sister Myra said. "Mindy and the Larsons. Then we can begin. You all stay here with Sister Audrey while I go up and watch for the others."

Sister Audrey was sitting on a child's stool way too small for her. She was a big, soft, pale teenager in tight cutoffs and a tank top that showed her bra straps. When she heard her name she smiled around the room and hugged her potato-looking bare knees, but nobody smiled back. They were scared to death of Sister Audrey. She was helping out at Bible camp because she'd had a baby when she wasn't married and put it in a Dempster Dumpster and now she was atoning for her sin. They weren't supposed to know that, but they did. They discussed the details amongst themselves in whispers: how the baby had been wrapped in a towel (or Dermott said a grocery bag), how a janitor heard it peeping, how a police car took it where somebody grown could adopt it. Sister Audrey smiled at them hopefully while they clustered in the doll corner and rehashed this information. "Doesn't anybody want me to read them a story?" she called, but they weren't about to get that close to her; no, sirree.

Sister Myra came back downstairs with Mindy and one of the Larsons, Johnny. Kenny was home with the earache, she said. "Something for us to mention in our prayers," she told them, and she clapped her hands. "All right, campers! Gather round! Everybody pull up a chair!"

Some of the chairs were little wooden ones, painted in nursery-school colors. Others were regular folding chairs, and all the boys fought for those so they wouldn't look sissy. Especially Thomas. He couldn't bear to have Dermott Kyle mistake him for one of the babies.

"Our Lord in Heaven," Sister Myra said, "we thank You for another beautiful day. We thank You for these innocent, unsullied souls gathered in Your name, and we ask for Kenny Larson's recovery if it be Thy will. Now we're going to offer up our sentence prayers as we do every morning at this time."

That last part was spoken more to the campers than to God, Thomas felt. Surely God knew by now they offered up sentence prayers every morning. He must know what they were going to say, even, since most of them just repeated what they'd said on other mornings. The girls said thank-yous—"Thank You for the trees and flowers," and such. (With Agatha, it was, "Thanks for the family," in a mumbling, furry tone of voice.) The boys were more likely to make requests. "Let the Orioles win tonight" was commonest. ("If it be Thy will," Sister Myra always added in a hurry.) The only exception was Dermott Kyle, who said, "Thank You for air-conditioning." That always got a laugh. Thomas usually asked for good swimming weather, but today he prayed for Kenny Larson's earache to go away. For one thing, Kenny was his best friend. Also Thomas liked to come up with some different sentence now and then, and this one made Sister Myra nod approvingly.

Sister Audrey offered the closing sentence. "Dear God," she said, "look down upon us and understand us, we humbly beg in Jesus' name. Amen."

Some of the boys nudged each other at that, because she probably meant He should understand about the Dempster Dumpster. But then they caught Sister Myra's frown and so they put on their blankest faces and started gazing around the room and humming.

After Devotions came Sharing Hour. In school they called it Show and Tell. You didn't have to bring anything to Sharing Hour if you didn't want to, and most of the boys didn't. Also what you brought didn't have to be religious, although of course it was always nice if it was. It could be just some belonging you'd been blessed with that you wanted others to share the joy of. Sister Myra's daughter Beth, for instance, brought a beautiful silver whistle that used to be her Cousin Rob's from Boy Scout camp. But when it came time to let others share the joy of it, she refused. She said she didn't want people blowing it and passing on their germs. "Well, honestly, Beth," Sister Myra said, looking cross, but Beth said, "I got a right! I don't have to put up with all and sundry's summer colds!" She was a skinny stick of a girl who never seemed that healthy anyway. Her nose was always red, and her braids were the pale, pinkish color of transparent eyeglass frames. Sister Myra sighed and said, "Anybody else?"

Daphne stood up so hard that her chair fell over backwards. (You were supposed to raise your hand.) "Well, I have this," she announced, and she held the toy lawn mower over her head. All the girls said, "Aw!" They thought she was cute. Then the boys, Dermott and the nine-year-olds, said, "Awww," making fun of the girls, but you could tell they didn't mean any harm. They were smiling, and Daphne smiled back at them. Then she showed how the colored balls popped up when she pushed the lawn mower across the carpet. She *was* cute, Thomas realized. She was darling, with her springy black curls as thick as the wig on a doll and her face very small and lively. He felt suddenly proud of her, and also, for some reason, a little bit sad.

"Thank you, sweetheart," Sister Myra said. "Any other sharers?"

Agatha raised her hand. Thomas looked over at her; she hadn't mentioned she was bringing something. She stood up and rooted through her front pocket, knotting her mouth because she was kind of fat for her shorts and it was hard to get her fist around whatever it was. Finally she pulled out something round and clear. "A mustard seed," she said.

Sister Myra said, "A what, hon?"

"A mustard seed in a plastic ball, like what Reverend Emmett talked about yesterday at Juice Time."

"Oh, yes: 'If ye have faith as a grain of mustard . . .'" Sister Myra said. She held out her hand, and Agatha let the object drop into her palm. "Why, I remember these! We wore them on chains back in high school. We bought them at Woolworth's jewelry counter."

"It used to be my mother's," Agatha said.

Thomas's mouth fell open.

"My mother's dead now, and I don't know what church she belonged to. But when Reverend Emmett showed us those mustard seeds at

Juice Time I thought, '*That's* what that is! That round ball in my mother's box.' "

Their mother's jewelry box, she meant, the cloth-covered box Agatha kept her barrettes in; and she was evil, evil to show other people something from the mysterious bottom drawer. Hadn't she made Thomas cross his heart and hope to die if he told anyone their mother's things were hidden there? She wouldn't even let him tell Daphne, because Daphne might tell the grownups and then the grownups would go through their mother's papers and figure out a way to ship Thomas and Agatha off to strangers, keeping Daphne for themselves since Daphne was the only true Bedloe. Agatha had warned him a dozen times, and now look: here she was, speaking of "my" mother, of how "I" don't know what church she belonged to, while their mother's private mustard seed traveled from hand to hand like something ordinary. From Sister Myra's cushiony palm to Beth's wiry, freckled claw to Dermott Kyle's not-very-clean fist, and by the time it reached Thomas he believed he caught the smell of sweat. He held it up by its tiny gold ring and studied it at eye level. (He was no more familiar with it than the others were, since Agatha guarded that box so jealously.) Had the plastic been this scratched and clouded even before the others handled it? If so, then it was because of his mother's touch; her actual fingers had rubbed off the shine. Her actual eyes had looked upon that white glint of a seed.

He didn't really remember their mother, to tell the truth. When he tried to picture her, he had the vaguest recollection of following some red high-heeled shoes down a sidewalk and then looking up to discover they belonged to the wrong lady. "Mama!" he had cried in a panic, and there'd been a flurry of footsteps, a low, soft laugh . . . but he couldn't put together what she'd looked like. It seemed that whenever he tried he came up with a sort of *general* mother, the kind you imagine when someone reads out the word "mother" in a storybook. He'd asked Agatha once, "Did she used to have a station wagon, maybe? I think I remember a car pool, a lady in the car pool at my nursery school—"

But Agatha said, "What are you talking about? She didn't even know how to drive!"

"I must've mixed her up with someone else," he said.

But the car-pool lady stayed on in his mind— someone like other children had, waiting for him in a brown station wagon with wood-grained panels on the sides and a rear compartment full of tennis-ball cans and lacrosse sticks.

"The best thing is, Agatha's brought us something having to do with our faith," Sister Myra said. "She listened to what Reverend Emmett talked about at Juice Time and then she brought something related to that. Very nice, Agatha."

Agatha nodded and sat down in her chair. When Thomas passed the mustard seed to Jason, he felt he was parting with a piece of himself, like an arm.

The Bible verse for the day came from the Forty-second Psalm: *As the hart panteth after the water brooks . . .* First Sister Myra explained what it meant. "Does everyone know what a hart is? Anyone? Anyone at all?" Then she helped them memorize it, breaking the verse into phrases that they repeated after her. This was all in preparation for the Bible Bee, which was a kind of spelldown that happened every Friday. Sometimes they competed against other camps—last week, Lamb of God from Cockeysville. Lamb of God had won.

After Bible Verse it was time for Morning Swim. The girls changed upstairs in Beth's room and the boys changed in the workshop off the rec room. They met in the backyard. At first the sun felt wonderful, soaking into Thomas's chilled skin, and then all at once it felt too hot, *way* too hot, so that he was glad to race the others to the pool and clamber up the three wooden steps and drop into the lukewarm water. Sister Myra was the lifeguard. She stood hip-deep with her swimsuit skirt floating out around her and tried to make the boys stop splashing the girls. Sister

Audrey watched the baby pool, which was an inflatable rubber dish nearby. She wore her same tank top and cutoffs and didn't even remove her flip-flops but sat high and dry in a folding chair she'd dragged out, smiling or else squinting at the little ones as they sailed their toy boats and poured water from their tin buckets.

Jason said the Dumpster had been parked behind the stadium, but Dermott said Mondawmin Mall.

After their swim they sat down for lunch at two redwood picnic tables on the patio. That way they didn't drip across Sister Myra's floors; they'd be dry before they'd finished eating. It was Mindy's turn to ask the blessing (not a chance Dermott Kyle would get another turn, not after last time!), and then they had bologna sandwiches and milk. Dessert was little foil packets of salted peanuts because Sister Myra's husband worked for a company that made airplane meals and he got a special discount. By now they'd used up all their energy and they were quieter. Daphne fell asleep with her head on the table halfway through her sandwich. Thomas pumped a mouthful of milk from one cheek to the other to hear the swishing sound. Dermott asked, dreamily, "Does *everybody* see flashes of white light while they're chewing tinfoil?"

Still in their swimsuits, they were herded

downstairs (Daphne sagging over Sister Myra's shoulder), where they unrolled their blankets from home and stretched out on the floor for their naps. Sister Myra sat in a chair above them and read aloud from the Bible-story book with its queerly lightweight paper and orange drawings: "The Boy Jesus in the Temple," today. (How rude He was to His parents! But there must be some excuse for it that Thomas was still too young to understand.) The idea was, the little ones would sleep and the older ones would just rest and listen to the story. Thomas always meant to just rest, but Sister Myra's low voice mingled with the creaks overhead where Sister Audrey was clearing away lunch, and next thing he knew the others were rolling their blankets and Reverend Emmett had arrived for Juice Time.

Reverend Emmett was tall and thin and he never seemed to get hot, not even in his stiff white shirt and black trousers. All the children loved him. Well, all except Agatha. Agatha said his Adam's apple was too big. But the others loved him because he acted so bashful with them. A grownup, scared of children! He said, "How are our campers today? Enjoying this beautiful weather?" and when somebody (Mindy) finally said, "Yup," he practically fell apart. "Oh! Wonderful!" he said, all flustered and delighted. Then he sat down on one of the nursery-school chairs so his knees jutted nearly to his chin, and the others settled on the floor in a circle while Sister Myra and Sister Audrey passed out paper cups of apple juice. Reverend Emmett took a cup himself. (In his long, bony fingers, it looked like a thimble.) He said, "Thank you, Sister Audrey," and he smiled so happily into her face you would think he'd never heard of the Dempster Dumpster. Sister Audrey blushed and backed away and stepped on one of the Nielsen twins' hands, but since she was wearing her flip-flops it must not have hurt much. The twin only blinked and went on staring at Reverend Emmett.

Sometimes Reverend Emmett talked about Jesus and sometimes about modern days. Thomas liked modern days best. He liked hearing about the Church of the Second Chance: how it had started out meeting in Reverend Emmett's garage where the floor was still marked with oil stains from Reverend Emmett's Volkswagen. Or even before that: how Reverend Emmett, an Episcopal seminarian and the son of an Episcopal minister, had gradually come to question the sham and the idolatry—for what was kneeling before a crucifix but idolatry?—and determined to found a church without symbols, a church without baptism or communion where only the *real* things mattered and where the atonement must be as real as the sin itself, where for instance if you broke a playmate's toy in anger you must go home immediately and fetch a toy of your own, of as good or better quality, and give it to that playmate for keeps and then announce your error at Public Amending on Sunday. Or how Reverend Emmett's fiancée had dumped him and his father had called him a crackpot although his mother, the smart one in the family, had seen the light at once and could even now be observed attending Second Chance every Sunday in her superficial Episcopal finery, her white gloves and netted hat. But that was all right, Reverend Emmett said. To condemn a person for fancy dress was every bit as vain as condemning her for humble dress. It's only the inside that counts.

Today he talked about how meaningful it was that he should come for these chats of theirs at Juice Time. "This way," he told them, "it's a period of spiritual nourishment as well as physical." Then he put it more simply for the little ones. "You don't get just apple juice, you get the juice of heavenly knowledge besides." He said, "How lucky you are, to have both at once! Most children have to choose one at a time— either nourishment for the soul or nourishment for the body."

"Isn't there anything else?" Agatha wanted to know.

"Excuse me?"

But she shrugged and picked at a cuticle.

"And even young as you are, you can still bear witness," Reverend Emmett said. "You can live in such a way that people will ask, 'Who *are* those children? And what is the secret of their joy?' That's what 'bearing witness' means, in our faith—not empty words or proselytizing. Those cigarette smokers and coffee addicts and sugar fiends in their big expensive churches, contributing to the Carpet Fund and sipping their communion wine which we all know is an artificial stimulant—'Why are those children so *blessed?*' they'll ask. For you are blessed, my little ones. Someday you'll appreciate that. You're luckier than you realize, growing up in a church that cares for you so."

Then he took a small brown bottle out of his trouser pocket and said it came from Kenny Larson's doctor. He said all the campers had to have eardrops before they went in Sister Myra's pool again.

Next came Crafts, where they made framed scripture plaques from drinking straws. And after that, Song Time, where they sang, "I've got the peace-that-passeth-understanding down in my heart, down in my heart . . ." as fast as possible in hopes that someone's tongue would get twisted, but nobody's did. And then Afternoon Swim, the longest single period of the day.

Thomas thought maybe Sister Myra had lost all her zip by then and just let them go on swimming because it was easiest. During their nap she had changed back into her skirt and blouse (probably for Reverend Emmett's visit, even though clothes were not supposed to matter), and she didn't bother getting into her swimsuit again but sat on a chair next to the pool with her skirt pulled up above her knees and her face tipped back to catch the sun. Still, you couldn't put a thing past her. "No dunking allowed, Dermott Kyle!" she called, although Dermott was barely beginning to move in Mindy's direction and Sister Myra's eyes were closed. Her face was so freckled that it had a spattered look, as if someone had thrown handfuls of beige spangles at her.

Thomas knew how to swim—Ian had taught him last summer—but he hated getting his head wet. He swam straining out of the water, his arms flailing wildly and splashing too much. Agatha swam a slow, steady breast stroke like an old person. Her gaze was fixed and her chin stayed just under the surface, so that she looked obstinate. Dermott Kyle, naturally, was wonderful at every stroke there was and also claimed to be able to dive, although he couldn't prove it because Sister Myra didn't have a diving board.

In the baby pool, Sister Audrey stood ankle-deep and bent over with her hands in the water.

Johnny Larson was emptying a sprinkling can on top of Percy's head. Daphne was . . . Thomas couldn't see Daphne. He waded toward the edge of his own pool to check, and that's when he realized that the thing in Sister Audrey's hands was Daphne's little blue-flowered body.

Later, he couldn't remember how he got out of the water so fast. It almost seemed he was lifted straight up. Then he was running, with the sharp, stubbly grass pricking his bare feet, and then he was flying through the air as level as a Frisbee and belly flopping into the baby pool where Daphne lay on her stomach, smiling, making splashy little pretend-swim motions while Sister Audrey supported her.

He grabbed hold of Daphne anyway. (It seemed he'd been wound with a key and had to follow through with this.) He struggled to his feet, staggering a bit, hanging on to her even though she squirmed and protested. "You leave her alone," he told Sister Audrey. Sister Audrey stared at him; her mouth was partway open. Thomas hauled Daphne out of the pool, dumped her in a heap, brushed off his hands all businesslike, and then strode back to the big pool.

As soon as he was in the water, the others crowded around him asking, "What'd she do? What happened?" Sister Myra looked confused. (For once, she had missed something.) Thomas said, "I just don't like her messing with my little sister, is all." He set his jaw and gazed beyond them, over toward the baby pool. Sister Audrey was standing on dry ground now. She was concentrating on stepping back into her flip-flops, and something about her lowered head and her meek, blind smile made Thomas's stomach all at once start hurting. He turned away. "Boy, you were *out* of here," Dermott Kyle said admiringly.

"Oh, well, you do what you got to do," Thomas told him.

Toweled dry and dressed, their swimsuits hanging on the line outdoors and their hair still damp, they gathered for Devotions. Sister Myra said, "Dear Lord, thank you for this day of fellowship and listen now to our silent prayers," and then she left a long, long space afterwards. Silent prayers were sort of like Afternoon Swim; you had the feeling she was too worn out to make the effort anymore. *Everyone* was worn out. Still, Thomas tried. He bowed his head and closed his eyes and prayed for his mother in heaven. He knew she was up there, watching over him. And he knew his prayers were being heard. Hadn't he prayed for Ian not to go to Vietnam that time? And the draft notice came anyhow and Thomas had blamed God, but then the doctors found out Ian had an extra heartbeat that had never been heard before and never given a moment's trouble since, and Thomas knew his prayer had been answered. He'd stood up at Public Amending the following Sunday and confessed how he had doubted, but everyone was so happy about Ian that they just smiled at him while he spoke. He had felt he was surrounded by loving feelings. Afterwards, Reverend Emmett said he thought Thomas had not really sinned, just shown his ignorance; and he was confident it would never happen again. And sure enough, it hadn't.

"In Jesus' name, we pray. Amen," Sister Myra said.

They all rustled and jostled and pushed each other, glad to be moving again.

It was Agatha's turn to sit in front, but Ian said they should all three sit in back because he was picking up Cicely on the way home. "She's coming for supper," he told them. "It's a state occasion: Aunt Claudia's birthday. Remember?"

No, they hadn't remembered, even though they'd spent last evening making a birthday card. Daphne said, "Oh, goody," because that meant all the cousins would be there. Thomas and Agatha were glad, too—especially on account of Cicely. They both thought Cicely was as pretty as a movie star.

Ian asked Daphne what the day's Bible verse had been. Daphne said, "Um . . ." and looked down into her lap. She was sitting in the middle, with her legs sticking straight out in front of her and the lawn mower resting across her knees.

"Agatha?" Ian called back, turning onto Charles Street.

Agatha sighed. "As the hart panteth after the water brooks," she said flatly, "so panteth my soul after Thee, O God."

She mumbled the word "God" so, she almost didn't say it at all, but Ian appeared not to notice. "Good for you," he said. "And what did Reverend Emmett talk about?"

Agatha didn't answer, so Thomas spoke up instead. "Juice," he said.

"Juice?"

"How we get juice for the soul and juice for the body, both at once, in Bible camp."

"Well, that's very true," Ian said.

"It's very dumb," Agatha said.

"Pardon?"

"Besides," she said, "isn't 'juice' a bad word?"

"I beg your pardon?"

"It just has that sound to it, somehow, like maybe it could be."

"I don't know what you're talking about," Ian said. They had reached a red light, and he was able to glance over his shoulder at her. "Juice? What?"

"And that pool is full of germs; I think everybody pees in it," Agatha said. "And Sister Audrey makes the sandwiches so far ahead they're all dried out before we get to eat them. And anyhow, what's she doing in a children's camp? A person who'd put a baby in a Dempster Dumpster!"

By now, those words were like some secret joke. Thomas giggled. Ian looked at him in the rearview mirror.

"You're laughing?" he asked.

Thomas got serious.

"You think Sister Audrey is funny?"

A driver behind them honked his horn; the light had turned green. Ian didn't seem to hear. "She's just a kid," he told Thomas. "She's not much older than you are, and had none of your advantages. I can't believe you would find her situation comical."

"Ian, cars are getting mad at us," Agatha said.

Ian sighed and started driving again.

I'm just a kid too, Thomas wanted to tell him. *How would I know what her situation is?*

They took a left turn. Daphne sucked her thumb and slid her curled index finger back and forth across her upper lip, the way she liked to do when she was tired. Thomas kept his eyes wide open so no one would see the tears. He wished he had his grandma. Ian was his favorite person in the world, but when you were sad or sick to your stomach who did you want? Not Ian. Ian had no soft nooks to him. Thomas tipped his head back against the seat and felt his eyes growing cool in the breeze from the window.

On Lang Avenue, with its low white houses and the sprinklers spinning under the trees, Ian parked and got out. He climbed the steps to Cicely's porch, meanwhile taking off his cap. "Ooh," Agatha said. "He's got horrible hat-head." Thomas had never heard the phrase before, but he saw instantly what she meant. All around Ian's shiny brown hair the cap had left a deep groove. "He looks like a goop," Agatha said. That was her way of comforting Thomas, he knew. It didn't really help much, but he tried to smile anyhow.

When Cicely came to the door, she was wearing bell-bottom jeans and a tie-dyed T-shirt. A beaded Indian headband held back her long messy waterfall of curls. First she stood on her toes and gave Ian a kiss. (All three of them watched carefully from the car. For a while now they had been worrying that Cicely didn't like Ian as much as she used to.) Then she waved at them and started down the porch steps. Ian followed, clamping his cap back on.

Daphne took her thumb out of her mouth. "Hi, Cicely!" she called.

"Well, hey, gang," Cicely said. "How we doing?" She opened the door on the passenger side and slid across to the middle of the front seat. The car filled with the moldy smell of the perfume she'd started wearing.

Ian got in on the driver's side and asked, "Have a good day at work?"

"Great," Cicely said. (This summer she worked part-time at a shop where they made leather sandals.) She moved over very close to him and brushed a wood shaving off his shoulder. "How was *your* day?"

"Well, we got a new order," Ian said.

"Right on!"

He pulled into traffic and said, "This woman came all the way from Massachusetts with a blanket box, her great-grandfather's blanket box. Asked if we knew how to make one just like it, using the same methods. Exactly the kind of thing Mr. Brant likes best."

Cicely made a sort of humming noise and nestled in against him.

"Soon as she left Mr. Brant told me, 'Go call those kitchen people.' People who wanted an estimate on their kitchen cabinets. 'Call and cancel,' he said. Cicely hon, stop that, please."

"Stop what?" she asked him, in a smiling voice.

"You know what."

"I'm not doing anything!" she said. She sat up straight. She slid over to her side of the car and set her face toward the window. "Mr. Holiness," she muttered to a fire hydrant.

"Pretty soon we may give up kitchens alto-gether," Ian said, turning down Waverly. He parked at the curb and cut the engine. "We'll build nothing but fine furniture. Custom designs. Old-style joinery."

Cicely wasn't listening. All three of them sitting in back could tell that, just from the way she kept her face turned. But Ian said, "We might hire another worker, too. At least, Mr. Brant's thinking about it. I said, 'Good, hire several, and give me a raise while you're at it,' and he said he might do it. 'I won't be a single man forever,' I told him." Ian glanced over at Cicely when he said that, but Cicely was still looking out the window.

It was amazing, how he could talk on like that without realizing. When even they realized! Even little Daphne, sucking her thumb and watching Cicely with round, anxious eyes!

Thomas all at once felt so angry at Ian that he jumped out of the car in a rush and slammed the door loudly behind him.

Their grandma said they had to change clothes at once, this instant, because Aunt Claudia was arriving at five thirty and they looked as if they'd spent the day rolling in a barnyard. She told Ian to run Daphne a bath, and she said, "Clean shirts for the other two! And clean shorts for Thomas. Hair combed. Faces washed."

But the minute Ian's back was turned, Thomas

followed Agatha up the narrow, steep wooden stairs to the attic. He trailed her into the slanty-ceilinged attic bedroom that was hers and Daphne's, that used to be Aunt Claudia's when she was a girl at home. "Agatha," he said, putting on a fake frown, "do you think we should've bought Aunt Claudia a present? Maybe a card will be too boring."

What he was after, of course, was a glimpse of their mother's jewelry box. He knew Agatha had to open it to return the mustard seed.

"You heard what Grandma said," Agatha told him. "A handmade card means more than anything. What are you in my room for?"

"But she gives *us* presents," Thomas said. He sat on her bed and swung his feet. "Maybe we should've made her something bigger, a picture for her wall or something."

"I mean it, Thomas. You're trespassing in my private room."

"It's Daphne's room, too," Thomas said. "Daphne would be glad to have me here."

"Get out, I tell you."

"Agatha, can't I just watch you put the mustard seed away?"

"No, you can't."

"She wasn't only *your* mama, you know."

"Maybe not," Agatha said, "but you don't keep secrets good."

"I do so. I didn't tell about the jewelry box, did I?"

"You told our father's name, though," Agatha said, screwing up her eyes at him.

"That just slipped out! And anyway, I was little."

"Well, who knows what'll slip out next time?"

"Agatha, I implore you," he said, clasping his hands. "How about I look at the picture and nothing else?"

"You'll get it dirty."

"How about I hold it by the edges, sitting here on the bed? I won't ask to look at anything else, honest. I won't even peek inside the box."

She thought it over. She had taken the mustard seed from her pocket and he could see it glimmering between her fingers, so close he could have touched it.

"Well, okay," she said finally.

"You'll let me?"

"But just for a minute."

She crossed to the closet, which was only more attic—the lowest part of the attic, where the ceiling slanted all the way down. It didn't even have a door to shut. Thomas would have been scared to sleep near so much darkness, but Agatha wasn't scared of anything, and she stepped inside as bold as you please and knelt on the floor. He heard the box's bottom drawer slide open, and then the clink of the mustard seed against other clinky things—maybe the charm bracelet Agatha had let him sleep with once when he was sick, with the tiny scissors charm that could really cut paper and the tiny bicycle charm that could really spin its wheels.

She came back out, holding the picture by one corner. "Don't you dare get a speck of dirt on it," she said. He took it very, very gently between the flat of his hands, the way you'd take an LP record. The crinkly edges felt like little teeth against his palms.

It was a color photograph, with JUN 63 stamped on the border. A tin house trailer with cinder blocks for a doorstep. A pretty woman standing on the cinder blocks—black hair puffing to her shoulders, bright lipstick, ruffled pink dress—holding a scowly baby (him!) in nothing but a diaper, while a smaller, stubbier Agatha wearing a polka-dot playsuit stood alongside and reached up to touch the baby's foot.

If only you could climb into photographs. If only you could take a running jump and land there, deep inside! The frill at his mother's neckline must have made pretzel sounds in his ear. Her bare arms must have stuck to his skin a little in the hot sunshine. His sister must have thought he was cute, back then, and interesting.

It was spooky that he had no memory of that

moment. It was like talking in your sleep, where they tell you in the morning what you said and you ask, "*I* did? *I* said that?" and laugh at your own crazy words as if they'd come from someone else. In fact, he always thought of the baby in the photo as a whole other person—as "he," not "I"—even though he knew better. "Why were you hanging on to his foot?" he asked now.

"I forget," Agatha said, sounding tired.

"You don't remember being there?"

"I remember! I remember everything! Just not why I was doing that with your foot."

"Where was our father?"

"Maybe he was taking the picture."

"You don't know for sure?"

"Of course I do! I know. He was taking our picture."

"Maybe you've forgotten, too," Thomas said. "Maybe these aren't even us."

"Of course they're us. Who else would they be? I remember our trailer and our yellow mailbox, and this dirt road or driveway or something with grass and flowers in the middle. I remember this huge, enormous rainbow and it started in the road and bent all the way over our house."

"What! Really? A rainbow?" Thomas said. He had an amazing thought. He got so excited he slid off the bed, not forgetting to be careful of the picture. "Then, Agatha!" he said. "Listen!

Maybe that's how we could find where we used to live."

"What do you mean?"

"We could ask for the trailer with the rainbow."

She gave him a look. He could see he'd walked into something, but he didn't know what.

"Well, they must have maps of things like that," he said. "Don't they? Maps that show where the really big, really famous rainbows are?"

"Thomas," Agatha said. She rolled her eyes. Clearly it was almost more than she could manage to go on dealing with him. "For gosh sake, Thomas," she said, "rainbows don't just sit around forever. What do you think, it's still there waiting for us? Get yourself a brain someday, Thomas."

Then she took hold of the picture—with her fingers right on the colored part!—and pulled it out of his hands and carried it back to the closet.

"Thomas?" Ian called from the second floor. "Are you cleaned up?"

"Just about."

He would never know as much as Agatha did, Thomas thought while he was clomping down the stairs. He would always be left out of things. People would forever be using words he'd never heard of, or sharing jokes he didn't get the point of, or driving him places they hadn't bothered to tell him about; or maybe (as they claimed) they *had* told him, and he had just forgotten or been too little to understand.

"Last night I dreamed a terrible dream," Aunt Claudia said at dinner. "I think it had something to do with my turning thirty-eight."

She was twisted around in her seat, feeding baked potato to Georgie in his high chair. Over her shoulder she said, "I opened the door to the broom cupboard and this burglar jumped out at me. I kept trying to call for help but all I managed was this pathetic little whimper and then I woke up."

"How does that relate to turning thirty-eight?" her husband asked her.

"Well, it's scary, Macy. Thirty-eight sounds so much like forty. Forty! That's middle-aged."

She didn't look middle-aged. She didn't have gray hair or anything. Her hair was brown like Ian's, cut almost as short, and her face was smooth and tanned. Her clothes weren't middle-aged, either: jeans and a floppy plaid shirt. Whenever Georgie got hungry she would tuck him right under her shirt without unbuttoning it and fiddle with some kind of snaps or hooks inside and then let him nurse. Thomas thought that was fascinating. He hoped it would happen this evening.

"You know what I believe?" she asked now, wiping Georgie's mouth with a corner of her napkin. "I believe what I was trying to do was, teach myself how to scream."

Grandpa said, "Why, hon, I would think you'd already know how."

"I was speaking figuratively, Dad. Here I am, thirty-eight years old and I've never, I don't know, never *said* anything. Everything's so sort of level all the time. Tonight, for instance: here we sit. Nice cheerful chitchat, baseball standings, weather forecast, difficult ages eating in the kitchen . . ."

By "difficult ages," she meant the older children—ten to fifteen, Agatha to Abbie. The "biggies," Grandma called them. The people with exciting things to say. Thomas could hear them even from the dining room. Cindy was telling a story and the others were laughing and Barney was saying, "Wait, you left out the most important part!"

Here in the dining room, there *were* no important parts. Just dull, dull conversation among the grownups while the "littlies" secretly fed their suppers to Beastie under the table. Cicely was holding up a pinwheel biscuit and carefully unwinding it. Ian kept glancing over at her, but she didn't seem to notice.

"Well, Claudia," Grandma said, "would you prefer it if we moaned and groaned and carried on?"

"No, no," Claudia said, "I don't mean that exactly; I mean . . . oh, I don't know. I guess I'm just going through the middle-aged blues."

"Nonsense, you're nowhere near middle-aged," Grandma told her. "What an idea! You're just a slip of a girl still. You still have your youth and your wonderful life and everything to look forward to." She raised her wineglass. Thomas could tell her arthritis was bad tonight because she used both hands. "Happy birthday, sweetheart," she said.

Macy and Grandpa raised their glasses, too, and Cicely set aside the biscuit to raise hers. Ian, who didn't drink, held up his water tumbler. "Happy birthday," they all said.

"Well, thanks," Claudia told them.

She thought a moment, and then she said, "Thank you very much," and smiled around the table and took a sip from her own glass.

The cake was served in the living room, so they could all sing "Happy Birthday" together. But really just the grownups and the little ones sang. The difficult ages seemed to think singing was beneath them, so after the first line Thomas didn't sing either. Then just as Claudia was blowing out the candles, Mrs. Jordan arrived from across the street along with two of the foreigners. The foreigners brought a third foreigner named Bob who apparently used to live with them. Bob greeted Thomas by name but Thomas didn't remember him. "You were only so much high," Bob told him, setting his palm about six inches above the floor. "You wore little, little sneakers and your mother was very nice lady."

"My mother?" Thomas asked. "Did you know her?"

"Of course I knew her. She was very pretty, very kind lady."

Thomas was hoping to hear more, but Mrs. Jordan came over then and started filling Bob in on all the neighborhood news: how Mr. Webb had finally gone to be dried out and the newlyweds had had a baby and Rafe Hamnett's sexy twin daughters were making life a living hell for his girlfriend. Thomas wandered off finally.

His grandma was passing the cake around on her big tole tray. She served the grownups first. She said, "Macy, cake? Jim, cake?" She offered some to Ian, too, but of course he said no. (At church they didn't approve of sugar, as Grandma surely knew by now.) She thinned her lips and passed on. "Jessie? *You'll* have cake."

Ian asked Cicely, "What do you say to a movie after this?"

"Well, I kind of like made plans with some friends from school," Cicely told him.

"Oh."

"Melanie and them from school."

"Okay."

"I'd ask you along except it's, you know, like all just college talk about people you never heard of."

"That's okay," Ian said.

Thomas hooked his fingers into one of Ian's rear pockets. He slid his thumb back and forth across the puckery seam at the top. What did this remind him of? Daphne sucking her thumb, that was it. Curling her index finger across her upper lip. He leaned his head against Ian's side, and Ian put his arm around him. "I should get to bed early anyhow," he was telling Cicely. "Rumor has it tomorrow's another workday."

Now Grandma was offering her tray to the children. She said, "Thomas? Cake?"

"No, thanks."

"No birthday cake?" she asked. She put on a look of surprise.

"Sugar is an artificial stimulant," he reminded her.

He expected her to argue like always, but he didn't expect she'd get angry. Ian was the one she seemed angry with, though. She turned toward Ian sharply and said, "Really, Ian! He's just a little boy!"

"Sure. He's free to make up his own mind," Ian said.

"Free, indeed! It's that church of yours again."

"Excuse me. Mrs. Bedloe?" Cicely said.

"Maybe Thomas is just listening to his body. Processed sugar is a poison, after all. No telling what it does to your body chemistry."

"Well, everybody in this room eats sugar and I don't exactly notice them keeling over," Grandma said.

"Me, now," Cicely said, "I've started using nonpasteurized honey whenever possible and I feel like a whole new person."

"But honey is a stimulant, too," Thomas told her.

Ian said, "Thomas. Hey, sport. Maybe if we just—"

"Do you hear that?" Grandma asked Ian. "Do you hear how he's been brainwashed?"

"Oh, well, I wouldn't—"

"It's not enough that you should fall for it yourself! That you'd obey their half-wit rules and support their maniac minister and scandalize the whole neighborhood by trying to convert the Cahns."

"I wasn't trying to convert them! I was having a theoretical discussion."

"A theoretical discussion, with people who've been Jewish longer than this country's been a nation! Oh, I will never understand. Why, Ian? Why have you turned out this way? Why do you keep doing penance for something that never happened? I *know* it never happened; I *promise*

it never happened. Why do you persist in be-
lieving all that foolishness?"

"Bee, dear heart," Grandpa said.

Now Thomas noticed how still the room had
grown. Maybe Grandma noticed too, because
she stopped talking and two pink spots started
blooming in her cheeks.

"Bee," Grandpa said, "we've got a crew of
hungry kids here wondering if you plan on coming their way."

The others made murmury laughing sounds,
although Thomas didn't see anything so funny.
Then Grandma quirked the corners of her mouth
and raised her chin. "Why! I certainly doo-oo!"
she said musically, and off she sailed with her
cake.

The frosting was caramel. Thomas had
checked earlier. His grandma made the best caramel frosting in Baltimore—rich and deep and
golden, as smooth as butter when it slid across
your tongue.

Daphne went off at nine, kicking up a fuss in
Ian's arms because the cousins were still there,
but Thomas and Agatha got to stay awake till
the last of the guests had said good night—
almost ten thirty, which was way past their normal bedtime.

"Don't forget your baths!" Ian called after them

as they climbed the stairs, but Thomas was too sleepy for a bath and he fell into bed in his underwear, leaving his clothes in a heap on the floor. He shut his eyes and saw turquoise blue, the color of Sister Myra's swimming pool. He heard the clatter of china downstairs, and the rattle of silver, and the slow, dancy radio songs his grandma liked to listen to while she did the dishes. (She would be washing and Ian would be clearing away and drying; she always said the hot water felt so good on her finger joints.) "Where do you want these place mats?" Ian called. Loud announcers' voices interrupted each other in the living room; Grandpa was hunting baseball scores on TV. ". . . never saw Jessie Jordan so gossipy," Grandma said, and someone shouted, "BEEN IN A BATTING SLUMP SINCE MID-JUNE—"

"Could you turn that down?" Grandma called.

Then Thomas must have slept, because the next thing he knew the house was silent and he had a feeling the silence had been going on a long time. There wasn't even a cricket chirping. There wasn't even a faraway truck or a train whistle. The only sounds were those scraps of past voices that float across your mind sometimes when there's nothing else to listen to. "Thank you, Sister Audrey," Reverend Emmett said, and Grandma said, "Why, Ian? Why?"

Thomas should have told her why. He knew

the answer, after all. Or, at least, he thought he did. The answer is, you get to meet in heaven. They'll be waiting for you there if you've been careful to do things right. His mother would be waiting in her frilly pink dress. She would drive her station wagon to the gate and she'd sit there with the motor idling, her elbow resting on the window ledge, and when she caught sight of him her face would light up all happy and she would wave. "Thomas! Over here!" she would call, and if he didn't spot her right away she would honk, and then he would catch sight of her and start running in her direction.

5

PEOPLE WHO DON'T KNOW
THE ANSWERS

After Doug Bedloe retired, he had a little trouble thinking up things to do with himself. This took him by surprise, because he was accustomed to the schoolteacher's lengthy summer vacations and he'd never found it hard to fill them. But retirement, it seemed, was another matter. There wasn't any end to it. Also it was given more significance. Loaf around in summer, Bee would say he deserved his rest. Loaf in winter, she read it as pure laziness. "Don't you have someplace to go?" she asked him. "Lots of men join clubs or something. Couldn't you do Meals on Wheels? Volunteer at the hospital?"

Well, he tried. He approached a group at his

church that worked with disadvantaged youths. Told them he had forty years' experience coaching baseball. They were delighted. First he was supposed to get some training, though—spend three Saturdays learning about the emotional ups and downs of adolescents. The second Saturday, it occurred to him he was tired of adolescents. He'd been dealing with their ups and downs for forty years now, and the fact was, they were shallow.

So then he enrolled in this night course in the modern short story (his daughter's idea). Figured *that* would not be shallow, and short stories were perfect since he never had been what you would call a speed reader. It turned out, though, he didn't have a knack for discussing things. You read a story; it's good or it's bad. What's to discuss? The other people in the class, they could ramble on forever. Halfway through the course, he just stopped attending.

He retreated to the basement, then. He built a toy chest for his youngest grandchild—a pretty decent effort, although Ian (Mr. Artsy-Craftsy) objected to particleboard. Also, carpentry didn't give him quite enough to think about. Left a kind of empty space in his mind that all sorts of bothersome notions could rush in and fill.

Once in a while something needed fixing; that was always welcome. Bee would bring him some household object and he would click his tongue happily and ask her, "What did you *do* to this?"

"I just broke it, Doug, all right?" she would say. "I deliberately went and broke it. I sat up late last night plotting how to break it."

And he would shake his head, feeling gratified and important.

Such occasions didn't arise every day, though, or even every week. Not nearly enough to keep him fully occupied.

It had been assumed all along that he would help out more with the grandkids, once he'd retired. Lord knows help was needed. Daphne was in first grade now but still a holy terror. Even the older two—ten and thirteen—took quite a lot of seeing to. And Bee's arthritis had all but crippled her and Ian was running himself ragged. They talked about getting a woman in a couple of days a week, but what with the cost of things . . . well, money was a bit tight for that. So Doug tried to lend a hand, but he turned out to be kind of a dunderhead. For instance, he saw the kids had tracked mud across the kitchen floor and so he fetched the mop and bucket with the very best of intentions, but next thing he knew Bee was saying, "Doug, I swan, not to sweep first and swabbing all that dirty water around . . ." and Ian said, "Here, Dad, I'll take over." Doug yielded the mop, feeling both miffed and relieved, and put on his jacket and whistled up the dog for a walk.

He and Beastie took long, long walks these days. Not long in distance but in time; Beastie was so old now she could barely creep. Probably she'd have preferred to stay home, but Doug would have felt foolish strolling the streets with no purpose. This gave him something to hang on to—her ancient, cracked leather leash, which sagged between them as she inched down the sidewalk. He could remember when she was a puppy and the leash grew taut as a clothesline every time a squirrel passed.

For no good reason, he pictured what it would look like if Bee were the one walking Beastie. The two of them hunched and arthritic, a matched set. It hurt to think of it. He had often seen such couples—aged widows and their decrepit pets. If he died, Bee would *have* to walk Beastie, at least in the daytime when the kids weren't home. But of course, he was not about to die. He had always kept in shape. His hair might be gray now but it was still there, and he could fit into trousers he'd bought thirty years ago.

A while back, though, their family doctor had told him something unsettling. He'd said, "Know what I hate? When a patient comes in and says, 'Doc, I'm here for a checkup. Next month I hit retirement age and I've planned all these great adventures.' Then sure as shooting, I'll find he's got something terminal. It never fails."

Well, Doug had avoided *that* eventuality. He just hadn't gone for a checkup.

And anyhow, planned no great adventures.

The trouble was, he was short on friends. Why had he never noticed before? It seemed he'd had so many back in high school and college.

If Danny had lived, maybe he would have been a friend.

Although Ian was nice company too, of course.

It was just that Ian seemed less . . . oh, less related to him, somehow. Maybe on account of that born-again business. He was so serious and he never just goofed off the way Danny used to do or sat around shooting the breeze with his dad. Didn't even have a girlfriend anymore; that pretty little Cicely had faded clear out of the picture. She had found someone else, Doug supposed. Not that Ian had ever said so. That was the thing: they didn't talk.

Danny used to talk.

Walking Beastie past the foreigners' house one unseasonably mild day in February, Doug noticed someone lying face down on the roof. Good Lord, what now? They lived the strangest lives over there. This fellow was sprawled parallel to the eaves, poking some wire or electrical cord through an upstairs window. Doug paused to watch. Beastie groaned and thudded to the ground. "Need help?" Doug called.

The foreigner raised his head. In that peremptory way that foreigners sometimes have, he said, "Yes, please to enter the house and accept this wire."

"Oh. Okay," Doug said.

He let Beastie's leash drop. She wasn't going anywhere.

He had been in the foreigners' house several times, because they gave a neighborhood party every Fourth of July. ("Happy your Independence Day," one of them had once said. "Happy *yours*," he'd answered before he thought.) He knew that the window in question belonged to the second-floor bathroom, and so he crossed the hall, which was totally bare of furniture, and climbed the stairs and entered the bathroom. The foreigner's face hung upside down outside the window, his thick black hair standing straight off his head so that he looked astonished. "Here!" he called.

Darned if he hadn't broken a corner out of a pane. Not a neatly drilled hole in the wood but a jagged triangle in the glass itself. A wire poked through—antenna wire, it looked like. Doug pulled on it carefully so as not to abrade it. He reeled it in foot by foot. "Okay," the foreigner said, and his face disappeared.

Doug hadn't thought to wonder how the man had got up on the roof in the first place. All at once he was down again, brushing off his clothes in the bathroom doorway—a good-looking, stocky young fellow in a white shirt and blue jeans. You could always tell foreigners by the way they wore their jeans, so neat and proper with the waist at the actual waistline, and in this man's case even a crease ironed in. Jim, was that his name? No, Jim was from an earlier batch. (The foreigners came and went in rotation, with their M.D.'s or their Ph.D.'s or their engineering degrees.) "Frank?" Doug tried.

"Fred."

They were always so considerate about dropping whatever unpronounceable names they'd been christened with. Or not christened, maybe, but—

"Please to tie the wire about the radiator's paw," Fred told him.

"What is it, anyhow?"

"It is aerial for my shortwave radio."

"Ah."

"I attached it to TV antenna on chimney."

"Is that safe?" Doug asked him.

"Maybe; maybe not," Fred said cheerfully.

Doug wouldn't have worried, except these people seemed prone to disasters. Last summer, while hooking up an intercom, they had set their attic on fire. Doug wasn't sure how an intercom could start a fire exactly. All he knew was, smoke had begun billowing from the little eyebrow window on the roof and then six or seven foreigners had sauntered out of the house and stood in the yard gazing upward, looking interested. Finally Mrs. Jordan had called the fire department. What on earth use would they have for an intercom anyway? she had asked Bee later. But that was how they were, the foreigners: they just loved gadgets.

Fred was walking backwards now, playing out the wire as he headed across the hall. From the looks of things, he planned to let it lie in the middle of the floor where it would ambush every passerby. "You got any staples?" Doug asked, following.

"Excuse me?"

"Staples? U-shaped nails? Electrical staples, insulated," Doug went on, without a hope in this world. "You tack the wire to the baseboard so it doesn't trip folks up."

"Maybe later," Fred said vaguely.

Meanwhile leading the wire directly across the hall and allowing not one inch of slack.

In Fred's bedroom, gold brocade draped an army cot. A bookcase displayed folded T-shirts, boxer shorts, and rolled socks stacked in a pyramid like cannonballs. Doug managed to take all this in because there was nothing else to look at—not a desk or chair or bureau, not a mirror or family photo. A brown plastic radio sat on the windowsill, and Fred inserted the wire into a hole in its side.

"Looks to me like you might've brought the wire in *this* window," Doug told him.

But Fred shrugged and said, "More far to fall."

"Oh," Doug said.

Presumably, Fred was not one of the engineering students.

Fred turned on the radio and music started playing, some Middle Eastern tune without an end or a beginning. He half closed his eyes and nodded his head to the beat.

"Well, I'd better be going," Doug said.

"You know what means these words?" Fred asked. "A young man is telling farewell to his sweetheart, he is saying to her now—"

"Gosh, Beastie must be wondering where I've got to," Doug said. "I'll just see myself out, never mind."

He had thought it would be a relief to escape the music, but after he left—after he returned home, even, and unsnapped Beastie's leash— the tune continued to wind through his head, blurred and wandery and mysteriously exciting.

A couple of days later, the foreigners tried wiring the radio to speakers set strategically around the house. The reason Doug found out about it was, Fred came over to ask what those U-shaped nails were called again. "Staples," Doug told him, standing at the door in his slippers.

"No, no. Staples are for paper," Fred said firmly.

"But the nails are called staples too. See, what you want is . . ." Doug said, and then he said, "Wait here. I think I may have some down in the basement."

So one thing led to another. He found the staples, he went over to help, he stayed for a beer afterward, and before long he was more or less hanging out there. They always had some harebrained project going, something he could assist with or (more often) advise them not to attempt; and because they were students, keeping students' irregular hours, he could generally count on finding at least a couple of them at home. Five were currently living there: Fred, Ray, John, John Two, and Ollie. On weekends more arrived—fellow countrymen studying elsewhere—and some of the original five disappeared. Doug left them alone on weekends. He preferred late weekday afternoons, when the smells of spice and burnt onions had already started rising from Ollie's blackened saucepans in the kitchen and the others lolled in the living room with their beers. The living room was furnished with two webbed aluminum beach lounges, a wrought-iron lawn chair, and a box spring propped on four stacks of faded textbooks. Over the fireplace hung a wrinkled paper poster of a belly dancer drinking a Pepsi. A collapsible metal TV tray held the telephone, and the wall above it was scribbled all over with names and numbers and Middle Eastern curlicues. Doug liked that idea—that a wall could serve as a phone directory. It struck him as very practical. He would squint at the writing until it turned lacy and decorative, and then he'd take another sip of beer.

These people weren't much in the way of drinkers. They appeared to view alcohol as yet another inscrutable American convention, and they would dangle their own beers politely, forgetting them for long minutes; so Doug never had more than one. Then he'd say, "Well, back to the fray," and they would rise to see him off, thanking him once again for whatever he'd done.

At home, by comparison, everything seemed so permanent—the rooms layered over with rugs and upholstered furniture and framed pictures. The grandchildren added layers of their own; the hall was awash in cast-off jackets and schoolbooks. Bee would be in the kitchen starting supper. (How unadorned the Bedloes' suppers smelled! Plain meat, boiled vegetables, baked potatoes.) And if Ian was back from work he'd be occupied with the kids—sorting out whose night it was to set the table, arbitrating their disputes or even taking part in them as if he were a kid himself. Listen to him with Daphne, for instance. She was nagging him to find her green sweater; tomorrow was St. Patrick's Day. "Your green sweater's in the wash," he said, and that should have been the end of it—would have been, if Bee had been in charge. But Daphne pressed on, wheedling. "Please? Please, Ian? They'll make fun of me if I don't wear something green."

"Tell them your eyes are the something green."

"My what? My eyes? But they're blue."

"Well, if anybody points that out, put on this injured look and say, 'Oh. I've always liked to *think* of them as green.' "

"Oh, Ian," Daphne said. "You're such a silly."

He was, Doug reflected. And a sucker besides. For sure enough, later that night he heard the washing machine start churning.

Most days Ian took the car, but Tuesdays he caught the bus to work so Doug could drive Bee to the doctor. She had to go every single week. Doug knew that doctor's waiting room so well by now that he could see it in his dreams. A leggy, wan philodendron plant hung over the vinyl couch. A table was piled with magazines you would have to be desperate to read— densely printed journals devoted to infinitesimal research findings.

Two other doctors shared the office: a dermatologist and an ophthalmologist. One morning Doug saw the ophthalmologist talking with a very attractive young woman at the receptionist's desk. The receptionist must have proposed some time or date, because the young woman shook her head and said, "I'm sorry, I can't make it then."

"Can't make it?" the doctor asked. "This is surgery, not a hair appointment. We're talking about your eyesight!"

"I'm busy that day," the young woman said.

"Miss Wilson, maybe you don't understand. This is the kind of problem you take care of *now*, you take care of *yesterday*. Not next week or next month. I can't state that too strongly."

"Yes, but I happen to be occupied that day," the young woman said.

Then Bee came out of Dr. Plumm's office, and Doug didn't get to hear the end of the conversation. He kept thinking about it, though. What could make a person defer such crucial surgery? She was meeting a lover? But she could always meet him another day. She'd be fired from her job? But no employer was *that* hard-hearted. Nothing Doug came up with was sufficient explanation.

Imagine being so offhand about your eyesight. About your life, was what it amounted to. As if you wouldn't have to endure the consequences forever and ever after.

Wednesday their daughter dropped by to help with the heavier cleaning. She breezed in around lunchtime with a casserole for supper and a pair of stretchy gloves she'd heard would magically ease arthritic fingers. "Ordinary department-store gloves, I saw this last night on the evening news," she told Bee. "You're lucky I got them when I did; I went to Hochschild's. Don't you know there'll be a big rush for them."

"Yes, dear, that was very nice of you," Bee said dutifully. She already owned gloves, medically prescribed, much more official than these were. Still, she put these on and spread her hands out as flat as possible, testing. She was wearing one of Ian's sweatshirts and baggy slacks and slipper-socks. In the gloves, which were the dainty, white, lady's-tea kind, she looked a little bit crazy.

Claudia filled a bucket in the kitchen sink and added a shot of ammonia. "Going to tackle that chandelier," she told them. "I noticed it last week. A *disgrace!*"

Probably it was Ian's housekeeping she was so indignant with—or just time itself, time that had coated each prism with dust. She wasn't thinking how it sounded to waltz into a person's home and announce that it was filthy. Doug cast a sideways glance at Bee to see how she was taking it. Her eyes were teary, but that could have been the ammonia. He waited till Claudia had left the kitchen, sloshing her bucket into the dining room, and then he laid a hand on top of Bee's. "Peculiar, isn't it?" he said. "First you're scolding your children and then all at once they're so smart they're scolding *you*."

Bee smiled, and he saw that they weren't real tears after all. "I suppose," he went on more lightly, "there was some stage when we were equals. I mean while she was on the rise and we were on the downslide. A stage when we were level with each other."

"Well, I must have been on the phone at the time," Bee said, and then she laughed.

Her hand in the glove felt dead to him, like his own hand after he'd slept on it wrong and cut off the circulation.

The foreigners set their car on fire, trying to install a radio. "*I* didn't know radios were flammable," Mrs. Jordan said, watching from the Bedloes' front porch. Doug was a bit surprised himself, but then electronics had never been his strong point. He went over to see if he could help. The car was a Dodge from the late fifties or maybe early sixties, whenever it was that giant fins were all the rage. Once the body had been powder blue but now it was mostly a deep, matte red from rust, and one door was white and one fender turquoise. Whom it belonged to was unclear, since the foreigner who had bought it, second- or third-hand, had long since gone back to his homeland.

John Two and Fred and Ollie were standing around the car in graceful poses, languidly fanning their faces. The smoke appeared to be coming from the dashboard. Doug said, "Fellows? Think we should call the fire department?" but Fred said, "Oh, we dislike to keep disturbing them."

Hoping nothing would explode, Doug reached through the open window on the driver's side and pulled the first wire his fingers touched. Almost immediately the smoke thinned. There was a strong smell of burning rubber, but no real damage—at least none that he could see. It was hard to tell; the front seat was worn to bare springs and the backseat had been removed altogether.

"Maybe we just won't have radio," John Two told Ollie.

"We never had radio before," Fred said.

"We were very contented," John Two said, "and while we traveled we could hear the birds sing."

Doug pictured them traveling through a flat green countryside like the landscape in a child's primer. They would be the kind who set off without filling the gas tank first or checking the tire pressure, he was certain. Chances were they wouldn't even have a road map.

One morning when he came downstairs he found Beastie dead on the kitchen floor, her body not yet stiff. It was a shock, although he should have been prepared for it. She was sixteen years old. He could still remember what she'd looked like when they brought her home— small enough to fit in her own feed dish. That first winter it had snowed and snowed, and she had humped her fat little body ecstatically through the drifts like a Slinky toy, with a dollop of snow icing her nose and snowflakes on her lashes.

He went upstairs to wake Ian. He wanted to get her buried before the children saw her. "Ian," he said. "Son."

Ian's room still looked so boyish. Model airplanes sat on the shelves among autographed baseballs and high-school yearbooks. The bedspread was printed with antique cars. It could have been one of those rooms that's maintained as a shrine after a young person dies.

Danny's room, on the other hand, had been redecorated for Thomas. Not a trace of Danny remained.

"Son?"

"Hmm."

"I need you to help me bury Beastie."

Ian opened his eyes. "Beastie?"

"I found her this morning in the kitchen."

Ian considered a moment and then sat up. When Doug was sure he was awake, he left the room and went downstairs for his jacket.

Beastie had not been a large dog, but she weighed a lot. Doug heaved her onto the doormat and then dragged the mat outside and down the back steps. Thump, thump, thump—it made him wince. The mat left a trail in the sparkling grass. He backed up to the azalea and dropped the corners of the mat and straightened. It was six thirty or so—too early for the neighbors to be about yet. The light was nearly colorless, the traffic noises sparse and distant.

Ian came out with his windbreaker collar turned up. He had both shovels with him. "Good thing the ground's not frozen," Doug told him.

"Right."

"This is probably not even legal, anyhow."

They chipped beneath the sod, trying as best they could not to break it apart, and laid it to one side. A breeze was ruffling Beastie's fur and Doug kept imagining that she could feel it, that she was aware of what they were doing. He made his mind a blank. He set up an alternating rhythm with Ian, hacking through the reddish earth and occasionally ringing against a pebble or a root. In spite of the breeze he started sweating and he stopped to take off his jacket, but Ian kept his on. Ian didn't look hot at all; he looked chilly and pale, with that fine white line around his lips that meant he had his jaw set. For the first time, Doug thought to wonder how this was hitting him. "Guess you'll miss her," he said.

"Yes," Ian said, still digging.

"Beastie's been around since you were . . . what? Eight or so, or not even that."

Ian nodded and bent to toss a rock out of the way.

"We'll let the kids set some kind of marker up," Doug told him. "Plant bulbs or something. Make it pretty."

It was all he could think of to offer.

They ended up cheating a bit on the grave— dug more of an oval than a rectangle, so they had to maneuver to get her into it. She fit best on her side, slightly curled. When Doug saw her velvety snout against the clay, tears came to his eyes. She had always been such an undemanding dog, so accommodating, so adaptable. "Ah, God," he said, and then he looked up and realized Ian was praying. His head was bowed and his lips were moving. Doug hastily bowed his own head. He felt as if Ian were the grownup and he the child. It had been years, maybe all the years of his adulthood, since he had relied so thankfully on someone else's knowledge of what to do.

The two younger children came down with chicken pox—first Daphne and then Thomas. Everybody waited for Agatha to get it too but she must have had it earlier, before they knew her. Daphne was hardly sick at all, but Thomas had a much worse case and one night he woke up delirious. Doug heard his hoarse, startled voice, oddly bright in the darkness—"Don't let them come! Don't let their sharp hooves!"—and then Ian's steady "Thomas, old man. Thomas. Tom-Tom."

In that short-story course, Doug had read a story about an experiment conducted by creatures from outer space. What the creatures wanted to know was, could earthlings form emotional attachments? Or were they merely at the mercy of biology? So they cut a house in half in the middle of the night, and they switched it with another half house in some totally different location. Tossed the two households together like so many game pieces. This woman woke up with a man and some children she'd never laid eyes on before. Naturally she was terribly puzzled and upset, and the others were too, but as it happened the children had some kind of illness, measles or something (maybe even chicken pox, come to think of it), and so of course she did everything she could to make them comfortable. The creatures' conclusion, therefore, was that earthlings didn't discriminate. Their family feelings, so called, were a matter of blind circumstance.

Doug couldn't remember now how the story had ended. Maybe that *was* the end. He couldn't quite recollect.

In the dark, Bee's special white arthritis gloves glowed eerily. She lay on her side, facing him, with the gloves curled beneath her chin. The slightest sound used to wake her when their own three children were little—a cough or even a whimper. Now she slept through everything, and Doug was glad. It was a pity so much rested on Ian, but Ian was young. He had the energy. He hadn't reached the point yet where it just plain didn't seem worth the effort.

Ian invited his parents to a Christian Fellowship Picnic. "To a what?" Doug asked, stalling for time. (Who cared what it was called? It was bound to be something embarrassing.)

"Each of us invites people we'd like to join in fellowship with," Ian said in that deadly earnest way he had. "People who aren't members of our congregation."

"I thought that church of yours didn't believe in twisting folkses' arms."

"It doesn't. We don't. This is only for fellow-ship."

They were watching the evening news—Doug, Bee, and Ian. Now Bee looked away from a skyful of bomber airplanes to say, "I've never understood what people mean by 'fellowship.' "

"Just getting together, Mom. Nothing very mysterious."

"Then why even say it? Why not say 'getting together'?"

Ian didn't take offense. He said, "Reverend Emmett wants us to ask, oh, people we care about and people who wonder what we believe and people who might feel hostile to us."

"We're not hostile!"

"Then maybe you would qualify for one of the other groups," Ian said mildly.

Bee looked at Doug. Doug pulled himself to-gether (he had a sense of struggling toward the surface) and said, "Isn't it sort of early for a picnic? We're still getting frost at night!"

"This is an indoor picnic," Ian told him.

"Then what's the point?"

"Reverend Emmett's mother, Sister Priscilla, has relatives out in the valley who own a horse farm. They're in Jamaica for two weeks and they told her she could stay in the house."

"Did they say she could throw a church picnic in the house?"

"We won't do any harm."

Bee was still looking at Doug. (She wanted him to say no, of course.) The bombers had given way to a moisturizer commercial.

"Well, it's nice of you to think of us, son," Doug said, "but—"

"I've invited Mrs. Jordan, too."

"Mrs. Jordan?"

"Right."

"*Jessie* Jordan?"

"She's always wanting to know what Second Chance is all about."

This put a whole different light on things. How could they refuse when a mere neighbor had accepted? Drat Jessie Jordan, with her lone-woman eagerness to go anywhere she was asked!

And then she had the nerve to make out she was being so daring, so rakish. On the way to Greenspring Valley (for they did end up attending, taking their own car which was easier on Bee's hips than the bus), Mrs. Jordan bounced and burbled like a six-year-old. "Isn't this exciting?" she said. She was dressed as if headed for a Buckingham Palace garden party—cartwheel hat ringed with flowers, swishy silk dress beneath her drab winter coat. "You know, there are so many alternative religions springing up these days," she said. "I worry I'll fall hopelessly behind."

"And wouldn't *that* be a shame," Bee said

sourly. She wore an ordinary gray sweat suit, not her snazzy warm-up suit with the complicated zippers; so her hands must be giving her trouble today. Doug himself was dressed as if for golfing, carefully color-coordinated to compensate for what might be misread as sloppiness on Bee's part. He kept the car close behind Second Chance's rented bus. Sometimes Daphne's little thumbtack of a face bobbed up in the bus's rear window, smiling hugely and mouthing elaborate messages no one could catch. "*What* did she say? What?" Bee asked irritably.

"Can't quite make it out, hon."

They traveled deeper and deeper into country that would be luxurious in the summer but was now a vast network of bare branches lightly tinged with green. Pasturelands extended for miles. The driveway they finally turned into was too long to see to the end, and the white stone house was larger than some hotels. "Oh! Would you look!" Mrs. Jordan cried, clapping her hands.

Doug didn't like to admit it, but he felt easier about Second Chance now that he saw such a substantial piece of property connected to it. He wondered if the relatives were members themselves. Probably not, though.

They parked on the paved circle in front. Passengers poured from the bus—first the children, then the grownups. Doug fancied he could tell the members from the visitors. The members had a dowdy, worn, slumping look; the visitors were dressier and full of determined gaiety.

It occurred to him that Bee could be mistaken for a member.

Carrying baskets, coolers, and Thermos jugs, everyone followed Reverend Emmett's mother up the flagstone walk. They entered the front hall with its slate floor and center staircase, and several people said, "Ooh!"

"Quite a joint," Doug murmured to Bee.

Bee hushed him with a look.

They crossed velvety rugs and gleaming parquet and finally arrived in an enormous sun porch with a long table at its center and modern, high-gloss chairs and lounges set all about. "The conservatory," Reverend Emmett's mother said grandly. She was a small, finicky woman in a matched sweater set and a string of pearls and a pair of chunky jeans that seemed incongruous, downright wrong, as if she'd forgotten to change into the bottom half of her outfit. "Let's spread our picnic," she said. "Emmett, did you bring the tablecloth?"

"I thought you were bringing that."

"Well, never mind. Just put my potato salad here at this end."

Reverend Emmett wore a sporty polo shirt, a tan windbreaker, and black dress trousers. (He and his mother belonged in Daphne's block set, the one where you mismatch heads and legs and torsos.) He put a covered bowl where she directed, and then the others laid out platters of fried chicken, tubs of coleslaw, and loaves of home-baked bread. The table—varnished so heavily that it seemed wet—gradually disappeared. Streaky squares of sunlight from at least a dozen windows warmed the room, and people started shedding their coats and jackets. "Dear Lord in heaven," Reverend Emmett said (catching Doug with one arm half out of a sleeve), "the meal is a bountiful gift from Your hands and the company is more so. We thank You for this joyous celebration. Amen."

It was true there was something joyous in the atmosphere. Everyone converged upon the food, clucking and exclaiming. The children turned wild. Even Agatha, ponderously casual in a ski sweater and stirrup pants, pushed a boy back with shy enthusiasm when he gave her a playful nudge at the punch bowl. The members steered the guests magnanimously toward the choice dishes; they took on a proprietary air as they pointed out particular features of the house. "Notice the leaded panes," they said, as if they themselves were intimately familiar with them. The guests (most as suspicious as Doug and Bee, no doubt) showed signs of thawing. "Why, this is not bad," one silver-haired man said—the father, Doug guessed, of the hippie-type girl at his elbow. Doug had hold of too much dinner now to shake hands, but he nodded at the man and said, "How do. Doug Bedloe."

"Mac McClintock," the man said. "You just visiting?"

"Right."

"His son is Brother Ian," the hippie told her father. "I just think Brother Ian is so faithful," she said to Doug.

"Well . . . thanks."

"My daughter Gracie," Mac said. "Have you met?"

"No, I don't believe we have."

"We've met!" Gracie said. "I'm the one who fetched your grandchildren from school every day when your wife was in the hospital."

"Oh, yes," Doug said. He didn't have the faintest memory of it.

"I fetched the children for Brother Ian and then Brother Ian closed up the rat holes in my apartment."

"Really," Doug said.

"My daughter lives in a slum," Mac told him.

"Now, Daddy."

"She makes less money than I made during the Depression and then she gives it all to this Church of the Second Rate."

"Second Chance! And I do not; I tithe. I don't have to do even that, if I don't want to. It's all in secret; we don't believe in public collection. You act like they're defrauding me or something."

"They're a church, aren't they? A church'll take its people for whatever it can get," Mac said. He glanced at Doug. "Hope that doesn't offend you."

"Me? No, no."

"Want to hear what I hate most about churches? They think they know the answers. I really hate that. It's the people who *don't* know the answers who are going to heaven, I tell you."

"But!" his daughter said. "The minute you say that, you see, you yourself become a person who knows the answers."

Mac gave Doug an exasperated look and chomped into a drumstick.

Bee was sitting on a chaise longue with her legs stretched out, sharing a plate with Daphne. She was the only guest who seemed to have remained outside the gathering. Everyone else was laughing, growing looser, circulating from group to group in a giddy, almost tipsy way. (Although of course there wasn't a bit of alcohol; just that insipid fruit punch.) Reverend Emmett was holding forth on his inspiration for this picnic. "I felt led," he told a circle of women. He had the breathless look of an athlete being interviewed after a triumph. "I was listening to one of our brothers a couple of weeks ago; he said he wished he could share his salvation with his parents except they never would agree to come to services. And all at once I felt led to say, 'Why should it be services? Why not a picnic?' "

The women smiled and nodded and their glasses flashed. (One of them was Jessie Jordan, looking thrilled.) An extremely fat young woman threaded her way through the crowd with a plastic garbage bag, saying, "Plates? Cups? Keep your forks, though. Dessert is on its way."

What could they serve for dessert if they didn't believe in sugar? Fruit salad, it turned out, in little foil dishes. Thomas carried one of the trays around. When he came to Doug he said, "Grandpa? Are you having a good time?"

"Oh, yes."

"Are you making any friends?"

"Certainly," Doug said, and he felt a sudden wrench for the boy's thin, anxious face with its dots of old chicken-pox scars. He took a step closer to Mac McClintock, although they'd run out of small talk some minutes ago.

The women were clearing the table now, debating leftovers.

"It seems a shame to throw all this out."

"Won't you take it home?"

"No, you."

"Law, I couldn't eat it in a month of Sundays."

"We wouldn't want to waste it, though."

Reverend Emmett's mother said, "Mr. Bedloe, we all think so highly of Brother Ian."

"Thank you," Doug said. This was starting to remind him of Parents' Night at elementary school. He swallowed a chunk of canned pineapple, which surely contained sugar, didn't it? "And you must be very proud of *your* son," he added.

"Yes, I am," she said. "I look around me and I see so many people, so many redeemed people, and I think, 'If not for Emmett, what would they be doing?' "

What *would* they be doing? Most would be fine, Doug supposed—his own son among them. Lord, yes. But in all fairness, he supposed this church met a real need for some others. And so he looked around too, following Sister What's-Her-Name's eyes. What he saw, though, was not what he had expected. Instead of the festive throng he had been watching a few minutes ago, he saw a spreading circle of stillness that radiated from the table and extended now even to the children, so that a cluster of little girls in one corner allowed their jack ball to die and the boys gave up their violent ride in the glider. Even Bee seemed galvanized, an orange section poised halfway to her parted lips.

"It's the table," a woman told Reverend Emmett's mother.

"The—?"

"Something's damaged the surface."

Reverend Emmett's mother thrust her way

through the circle of women, actually shoving one aside. Doug craned to see what they were talking about. The table was bare now and even shinier than before; someone had wiped it with a damp cloth. It looked perfect, at first glance, but then when he tilted his head to let the light slant differently he saw that the shine was marred at one end by several distinct, unshiny rings.

"Oh, *no*," Reverend Emmett's mother breathed.

Everyone started speaking at once: "Try mayonnaise."

"Try toothpaste."

"Rub it down with butter."

"Quiet! Please!" Reverend Emmett's mother said. She closed her eyes and pressed both hands to her temples.

Reverend Emmett stood near Doug, peering over the others' heads. (Above the collar of his jaunty polo shirt, his neck looked scrawny and pathetic.) "Perhaps," he said, "if we attempted to—"

"Shut up and let me *think*, Emmett!"

Silence.

"Maybe if I came back tomorrow," she said finally, "with that cunning little man from Marx Antiques, the one who restores old . . . he could strip it and refinish it. Don't you suppose? But the owners are due home Tuesday, and if he has to strip the whole . . . but never mind! I'll tell him to work round the clock! Or I'll ask if . . ."

More silence.

Ian said, "Was it soaped?"

Everyone turned and looked for him. It took a minute to find him; he was standing at the far end of the room.

"Seems to me the finish is some kind of polyurethane," he said, "and if those rings are grease, well, a little soap wouldn't do any harm and it might even—"

"Soap! Yes!" Reverend Emmett's mother said.

She went herself to the kitchen. While she was gone, the fat young woman told Doug, "Brother Ian works with wood every day, you know."

"Yes, I'm his father," Doug said.

She said, "Are you really!"

Reverend Emmett's mother came back. She held a sponge and a bottle of liquid detergent. They parted to let her through and she approached the table and bent over it. Doug was too far away to see what she did next, but he heard the sighs of relief. "Now dry it off," someone suggested.

A woman whipped a paisley scarf from her neck and offered that, and it was accepted.

"Perfect," someone said.

This time when he craned, Doug saw that the rings had vanished.

Right away the congregation started packing, collecting coats and baskets. Maybe they would have anyhow, but Doug thought he detected a sort of letdown in the general mood. People filed out meekly, not glancing back at the house as they left it. (Doug imagined the house thinking, *Goodness, what was all THAT about?*) They crossed the columned front porch with their heads lowered. Doug helped Bee into the car. "Coming?" he asked Mrs. Jordan.

"Oh, I'm going to ride in the bus," she said. She alone seemed undampened. "Wasn't Ian the hero, though!"

"Sure thing," Doug said.

He watched her set off toward the bus with one hand clamping down her cartwheel hat.

Driving home, he made no attempt to stay with the others. He left the bus behind on the Beltway and breezed eastward at a speed well above the legal limit. "So now we've been to a Christian Fellowship Picnic," he told Bee.

"Yes," she said.

"I wonder if it'll become a yearly event."

"Probably," she said.

Then she started talking about Danny. How did she get from the picnic to Danny? No telling. She started kneading the knuckles of her right hand, the hand that looked more swollen, and she said, "Sometimes I have the strangest feeling. I give this start and I think, 'Why!' I think,

'Why, here we are! Just going about our business the same as usual!' And yet so much has changed. Danny is gone, our golden boy, our first baby boy that we were so proud of, and our house is stuffed with someone else's children. You know they *all* are someone else's. You know that! And Ian is a whole different person and Claudia's so bustling now and our lives have turned so makeshift and second-class, so second-string, so second-fiddle, and everything's been lost. Isn't it amazing that we keep on going? That we keep on shopping for clothes and getting hungry and laughing at jokes on TV? When our oldest son is dead and gone and we'll never see him again and our life's in ruins!"

"Now, sweetie," he said.

"We've had such extraordinary troubles," she said, "and somehow they've turned us ordinary. That's what's so hard to figure. We're not a special family anymore."

"Why, sweetie, of course we're special," he said.

"We've turned uncertain. We've turned into worriers."

"Bee, sweetie."

"Isn't it amazing?"

It was astounding, if he thought about it. But he was careful not to.

———

The weather began to grow warmer, and Doug raised all the windows and lugged the summer clothing down from the attic for Bee. Across the street, the foreigners came out in their shirt-sleeves to install an electric garage-door opener they'd ordered from a catalog. Doug found this amusing. A door that opened on its own, for a car that could barely *move* on its own! Of course he kept them company while they worked, but the door in question was solid wood and very heavy, potentially lethal, and he'd just as soon not be standing under it when calamity struck. He stayed several feet away, watching Ollie tee-ter on a kitchen chair as he screwed something to a rafter overhead. Then when Doug got bored he ambled inside with the two who were less mechanically inclined, leaving Ollie and Fred and John Two to carry on. He refused a beer (it was ten in the morning) but accepted a seat by the window, where a light breeze stirred the tat-tered paper shade.

From here the garage was invisible, since it lay even with the front of the house, but he could see Fred standing in the drive with the push-button control in both hands, pressing hard and then harder. Doug grinned. Fred leaned forward, his face a mask of straining muscle, and he bore down on the button with all his might. You didn't have to set eyes on the door to know it wasn't reacting. Meanwhile Ollie walked out to the street and climbed into the car and started the engine, and John Two removed a brick from under the left rear wheel. Optimistic of them; Doug foresaw a good deal more work before the garage would be ready for an occupant. Through the open window he heard the croupy putt-putt as the car turned in and rolled up the drive and sat idling. "In another catalog," John One was saying, "we have seen remarkable invention: automatic yard lights! That illuminate when dark falls! We plan to send away for them immediately."

"I can hardly wait," Doug said, and then he twisted in his chair because he thought he noticed someone emerging from his own house, but it was only shrubbery stirring in the breeze.

He was a touch nearsighted, and the mesh of the window screen seemed more distinct to him than what lay beyond it. What lay beyond it— home—had the blocky, blurred appearance of something worked in needlepoint, each tiny square in the screen filled with a square of color. Not only was there a needlepoint house but also a needlepoint car out front, a needlepoint swing on the porch, a needlepoint bicycle in the yard. His entire little world: a cozy, old-fashioned sampler stitched in place forever.

The best thing about the foreigners, he decided, was how they thought living in America was a story they were reading, or a movie they were watching. It was happening to someone else; it wasn't theirs. Good Lord, not even their names were theirs. Here they spoke lines invented by other people, not genuine language— not the language that simply *is*, with no need for translation. Here they wore blue denim costumes and inhabited a Hollywood set complete with make-believe furniture. But when they went back home, there they'd behave as seriously as anyone. They would fall in love and marry and have children and they'd agonize over their children's problems, and struggle to get ahead, and practice their professions soberly and efficiently. What Doug was witnessing was only a brief holiday from their real lives.

He was pleased by this notion. He thought he'd examine it further later on—consider, say, what happened to those foreigners who ended up *not* going home. The holiday couldn't last forever, could it? Was there a certain moment when the movie set turned solid? But for now, he didn't bother himself with all that. He was happy just to sit here, letting some of their Time Out rub off on him.

Then Ollie turned toward the house and called, "Come see!" and for courtesy's sake, Doug rose and followed Ray and John One to the yard. Other neighbors were here too, he realized. It looked like a party. He joined them and stood squinting in the sunshine, smiling at the foreigners' car which sat half inside the garage and half out like a crumpled beer can, with the door bisecting it neatly across the middle.

6

SAMPLE RAINS

Every Saturday morning, the Church of the Second Chance gathered to perform good works. Sometimes they went to an ailing member's place and helped with the cleaning or the fixing up. Sometimes they went to some stranger. Today—a warm, sunny day in early September—they met at the little house where Reverend Emmett lived with his widowed mother. Reverend Emmett was not a salaried minister. His sole means of support was a part-time counseling job at a private girls' school. So when his house needed painting (as it sorely did now, with the old paint hanging in ribbons off the clapboards), all his flock pitched in to take care of it.

Ian brought the three children, dressed in their

oldest clothes. Thomas and Daphne loved Good Works but Agatha had to be talked into coming. At fifteen she was balky and resentful, given to fits of moody despair. Ian never could decide: should he force her to participate for her own good? Or would that just alienate her further? This morning, though, he'd had an easier time than usual. He suspected her of harboring a certain furtive interest in the details of Reverend Emmett's private life.

The house was a one-story cottage, more gray than white, lying in a modest neighborhood east of York Road. By the time Ian and the children arrived, several members of the congregation were already setting out paint cans and brushes. Mrs. Jordan (Sister Jessie now, but Ian found it hard to switch) was spreading a drop-cloth over the boxwoods, and Reverend Emmett was perched on a ladder wire-brushing the porch overhang. Ian grabbed a ladder of his own and went to take the shutters down. Reverend Emmett's mother came out in high heels and an aqua knit dress and asked if there was any little thing she could do, but they all said no. (What *could* they say? Her cardigan draped her shoulders so genteelly, with the sleeves turned back a precise two inches.)

Partway through the job, someone Ian didn't know was sent to assist him. This was a cadaverously thin man in his thirties with a narrow ribbon of beard like Abraham Lincoln's. Ian glanced at him curiously (their church didn't see many guests), and the man said, "I'm Eli Everjohn. Bertha King's son-in-law; we're visiting from over Caro Mill."

"Ian Bedloe," Ian said.

He could see now who the man's wife must be—the strawberry blonde who did resemble Sister Bertha, come to think of it, scraping clapboards with the children. She seemed much too pretty for such a knobby, gangling husband. This Eli handled tools at a remove. He handled his own *hands* at a remove, as if operating one of those claw arrangements where you try to scoop up prizes. His task was to take the hinges off the shutters and stow them in a bucket, which should have been easy enough; but the screwdriver seemed to confound him and he let it slip so many times that the screw heads were getting mangled. "Tell you what," Ian said, setting down a shutter. "I'll see to this and you can have my job."

"Oh, I couldn't do that!" the man said. "I'm scared of heights."

Heights? The highest shutter was eight feet off the ground. But Ian didn't point that out.

Eli raised one arm to wipe his forehead, waving the screwdriver dangerously close to Ian's face. "At *my* church, we don't mess with such as this," he said. "We visit door to door instead."

"What church is that?"

"Holy House of the Gospel."

"I guess I never heard of it."

"We're much stricter than you-all are," Eli said. "We would never for instance let our women wear the raiment of men."

Ian glanced at Eli's wife. Sure enough, she wore a dress—a rosebudded, country-looking dress that was interfering seriously with her attempts to mount a step stool.

"We don't play cards neither, nor dance, and we're more mindful of the appearance of evil," Eli said. "Why, yesterday my mother-in-law got a prescription filled at a pharmacy that sells liquor! Walked right into a place that sells liquor without a thought for how it might look! And you don't have no missionary outreach, neither."

Ian was starting to feel defensive. He said, "We believe our *lives* are our missionary outreach."

"Now, that's just selfish," Eli said. "To look at someone living in the shadow of eternal damnation and not try and change his ways: that's selfish."

Ian spun on his heel and went to fetch another shutter.

When he came back, though, Eli resumed where he had left off. "And if we did mess with house painting, we'd have prayed beforehand," he said. His screwdriver slashed uselessly across a screw. "We pray before each task. We believe that whatever work we undertake is God's work; I am an arrow shot by God to do His handiwork."

He did look something like an arrow: straight and smooth, a sharp cowlick sticking up on the crown of his head.

"What exactly *is* your work?" Ian asked him, hoping to change the subject.

"I'm a private detective."

This was so unexpected that Ian laughed. Eli scowled. "What's funny about that?" he said.

"Detective?" Ian said. "You mean, like solving murders and mysteries and such?"

"Well, it's more like tailing husbands to motel rooms. But that's the Lord's business too! Believe me."

"If you say so," Ian told him.

"What do you do, brother?"

"I'm a carpenter," Ian said.

"Our Savior was a carpenter."

"Well, yes."

"Nothing to be ashamed of."

"Who said I was ashamed?"

"Those your kids you came with?"

"Yes."

"You look kind of young to have kids that old."

"Really I'm just their uncle," Ian said. "My parents and I take care of them."

"I would've thought you were nothing but a college boy."

"No, no."

"You married?"

"No."

"A bachelor."

"Well, yes. A . . . bachelor," Ian said.

Eli bent over a hinge again. Ian watched for a minute and then turned back to his ladder.

But the next time he brought down a shutter, he said, "So you've never found a missing person, or anything like that."

"Depends on what you call missing," Eli said. "Sure, I've found a few husbands here and there. Usually they're just staying with a girl-friend, though, that everybody except their wives knows the name and address of."

"I see," Ian said.

He leaned the shutter against a sawhorse. He studied it. Not looking at Eli, he said, "Say a person had been missing a long time. Five or six years, say. Maybe seven or eight. Would the trail be too cold for you to follow?"

"What? Naw," Eli said. "Bound to be *some-thing* he left behind. People are so messy. That's been my experience. People leave so much litter wherever they go to."

He rotated one forearm and examined the in-side of his wrist. A dribble of dusty blood ran downward from his palm. "Somebody special you had in mind?" he asked.

"Not really," Ian said.

He brushed a dead leaf from a louver. He cleared his throat. He said, "Those kids I'm taking care of: their father is missing, I guess you could say. The father of the older two."

"Is that so," Eli said. "Ducking his child support, huh?"

"Child support? Oh. Right," Ian said.

"Boy, I hate those child-support guys," Eli said. "Or, no, not hate. Forget hate. The Bible cautions us not to hate. But I . . . pity them, yes, I surely do pity those child-support guys. You'd never get *me* to raise one of them's kids."

"Oh, they're really like my own now," Ian said.

"Even so! Here you are sitting home with three young ones and he's off enjoying his self."

"I don't mind," Ian said.

He didn't want to go into the whole story. In fact, he couldn't remember now why he'd brought it up in the first place.

He was supervising the children's homework at the kitchen table when he heard a wailing sound outdoors. He said, "Was that a baby?"

No one answered. They were too busy arguing. Thomas was telling Daphne that when *he* was in third grade, a plain old wooden pencil had been good enough for him. Daphne had no business, he said, swiping his personal ballpoint pen. Daphne said, "Maybe what *you* wrote in third grade wasn't worth a pen." Then Agatha complained they'd made her lose her train of thought. Thanks to them, she would have to start this whole equation over again.

"Was that a baby crying?" Ian asked.

They barely paused.

"Hey," Thomas said to the others. "Want to hear something disgusting?"

"No, what?"

Ian crossed the kitchen and opened the screen door. It was light enough still so he could make out the clothesline poles and the azalea bushes, and the stockade fence that separated the backyard from the alley.

"In science class, my teacher? Mr. Pratt?" Thomas said. "He stands at the blackboard, he tells us, 'By the time I've finished teaching this lesson, microscopic portions of my mouth will be *all over this room.*' "

"Eeuw!" Daphne and Agatha said.

Just inside the gate, which had not been completely closed in years, sat a minuscule patch of darkness, a denser black than the fence posts. This patch stirred and glinted in some way and uttered another thin wail.

"Kitty-kitty?" Ian called.

He stepped outside, shutting the screen door behind him. Yes, it was definitely a cat. When he approached, it teetered on the brink of leaving but finally stood its ground. He bent to pat its head. He could feel the narrow skull beneath fur so soft that it made almost no impression on his fingertips.

"Where's your owner, little cat?" he asked.

But he thought he knew the answer to that. There wasn't any tag or collar, and when he ran a hand down its body he could count the ribs. It staggered weakly beneath his touch, then braced itself and started purring in a rusty, un-practiced way, pressing its small face into the cup of his palm.

As it happened, the Bedloes had no pets at that particular moment. They had never replaced Beastie, and the latest of their cats had disap-peared a few months ago. So this new little cat had come to the right people. Ian let it spend a few minutes getting used to him, and then he picked it up and carried it back inside the house. It clung to him with needle claws, tense but still conscientiously purring. "See what I found in the alley," he told the children.

"Oh, look!" Daphne cried, slipping out of her chair. "Can I hold it, Ian? Can I keep it?"

"If no one comes to claim it," Ian said, handing it over.

In the light he saw that the cat was black from head to foot, and not much more than half grown. Its eyes had changed to green already but its face was still the triangular, top-heavy face of a kitten. Thomas was lifting its spindly tail to see what sex it was, but the cat objected to that and climbed higher on Daphne's shoulder. "Ouch!" Daphne squawked. "Thomas, quit! See what you made it do?"

"It's a girl, I think," Thomas announced.

"Leave her alone, Thomas!"

"She's not just yours, Daphne," Agatha said. She had risen too and was scratching the cat behind its ears.

"She is so mine! Ian said so! You're mine, mine, mine, you little sweetums," Daphne said, nuzzling the cat's nose with her own. "Oh, what kind of monstrous, mean person would just ditch you and drive off?"

All of a sudden Ian had an image of Agatha, Thomas, and Daphne huddled in a ditch by the side of a road. They were hanging on to each other and their eyes were wide and fearful. And far in the distance, almost out of sight, Ian's car was vanishing around a curve.

But then immediately afterward, he felt such a deep sense of loss that it made his breath catch.

His mother was truly disabled now. Oh, she still hobbled from room to room, she still insisted on standing over the stove and creeping behind the dust mop, but the arthritis had seized up her hands and the finer motions of day-to-day life were beyond her. Folding the laundry, driving the car, buttoning Daphne's dress down the back—all that was left to Ian and his father. And Ian's father was not much help. Any task he began seemed to end in, "How the dickens ... ?" and "Ian, can you come here a minute?" In the old days Claudia had stopped by once or twice a week to see what needed doing, but she had moved to Pittsburgh when Macy found a better job; and first they'd returned for holidays but now they didn't even do that very often.

Meanwhile, these children were a full-time occupation. They were good children, bright children; they did well in school and never got in serious trouble. But even nonserious trouble could consume a great deal of energy, Ian had learned. Agatha, for instance, was suffering all the miseries of adolescence. Every morning she set off for school alone and friendless—the earnest, pale, studious kind of girl Ian had ignored when he himself was her age, but now he cursed those callow high-school kids who couldn't see how special she was, how intelligent and witty and perceptive. Thomas, on the other hand, had too *many* friends. Tall and graceful, his voice already cracking and a shadow darkening his upper lip, he was more interested in socializing than in schoolwork, and one or another of the Bedloes was always having to attend parent-teacher conferences—most often Ian, it seemed.

As for Daphne, she wound through life sparkling at everyone and lowering her long black lashes over stunning blue-black eyes; but any time you crossed her there was hell to pay. She was *fierce*, that Daphne. "I think she had a difficult infancy," Ian was always explaining. "She's really a good kid, believe me. She just feels she's got to fend for herself," he told a teacher. Yet another teacher. At yet another parent-teacher conference. (His second of the year, and school had been in session only ten days.)

Cicely was living out in California now with a folk guitarist. Pig Benson's family had moved away while he was in the army. Andrew was in graduate school at Tulane. And anyhow, the last time Andrew came home it turned out he and Ian didn't have much to talk about. At one point Andrew had referred to the "goddamned holiday traffic," and then reddened and said, "Sorry," so Ian knew he'd heard about Second Chance from someone. And then Ian had to take Daphne for her booster shots, and that was that. Andrew had not suggested getting together again.

Bachelor. What a dashing word. Ian the bachelor. He would live in an apartment all his own. (A bachelor pad.) He'd have friends his own age dropping by to visit. Young women going out with him. And no one trailing behind to ask, "But how about *us*? Who will see to us? Who will find our socks for us and help with our history project?"

At work, he was putting the final touches on a drop-front desk. He was rubbing linseed oil into the wood, while Bert, one of the new men, worked on a bureau across the room.

Their kitchen-cabinet days were over, thank heaven. Now rich young couples from Bolton Hill showed up at Mr. Brant's shop to commission one-of-a-kind furniture: bookcases custom-fitted to Bolton Hill's high ceilings, stand-up desks made to measure, and Shaker-looking benches. Everything was built the old way, with splines and rabbets and lap joints, no nails, no stains or plastic finishes. Orders were backed up a year or more and they'd had to hire three new employees.

You'd think this would delight Mr. Brant, but he remained as morose as always. Or was that only his deafness? No, because whenever his wife dropped by—a much younger woman who'd been deaf from birth, unlike Mr. Brant— she would sign to him with flying fingers, her face lighting up and clouding over to go with what she said; and Ian could see she lived a life as full and talkative as any hearing person's. Mr. Brant would watch her without altering his expression, and then he would make a few signs of his own—clumsy, blunt signs, stiff-thumbed.

Ian wondered how on earth they had courted. What could Mr. Brant have said that would win such a woman's heart? When Mrs. Brant watched his hands, her eyes grew very intent and focused and all the animation left her. Ian had the feeling her husband was somehow dampening her enthusiasm, but maybe it only seemed that way.

One of the new employees was Mrs. Brant's niece, a rosy, bosomy girl named Jeannie who'd dropped out of college to do something more real. (They were seeing a lot of that nowadays.) Jeannie said Mrs. Brant was a regular social butterfly. She said Mrs. Brant had dozens of friends who'd gone to Gallaudet with her, and they would sit around her kitchen talking away a mile a minute, using their special sign language with lots of inside jokes and dirty words; but her husband had come late to sign and could barely manage such basics as "Serve supper" and "Mail letter" (like Tonto, Jeannie said), so of course he was left in the dust. He was neither fish nor fowl, Jeannie said. This made Ian feel fonder of the man. He had long ago given up all hope of befriending him, or of seeing any hint of emotion in that handsome, leathery face; but now he regretted dismissing him so easily. "He must be awfully lonesome," he told Jeannie, "watching his wife enjoy herself with her friends."

"Oh, he doesn't care," Jeannie said. "He just stomps off to his garden. None of us can figure why she married him. Maybe it was sex. I do think he's kind of sexy, don't you?"

Jeannie often talked that way. She made Ian feel uncomfortable. Several times she had suggested they go out together some evening, and although he did find her attractive, with her streaming hair and bouncy peasant blouses, he always gave some excuse.

This afternoon she was helping Bert with his bureau. (She didn't know enough yet to be entrusted with a piece all her own.) Her job was to attach the drawer knobs—perfectly plain beechwood cylinders—but she kept leaving them to come over and talk to Ian. "Pretty," she said of the desk. Then, without a pause, "You like nature, Ian?"

"Nature? Sure."

"Me and some friends are taking a picnic lunch to Loch Raven this Sunday. Want to come?"

"Well, I have church on Sundays," Ian told her.

"Church," she said. She rocked back on the heels of her moccasins. "But how about *after* church?" she said. "We wouldn't be leaving till one or so."

"Oh, uh, there's my nephew and nieces, too,"

Ian said. "I sort of have to keep an eye on them on weekends."

"Why can't their parents do that?"

"Their parents are dead."

"Their grandparents, then," she said, instantly readjusting.

"My mother's got arthritis and my dad is kind of tied up."

"Or the other grandparents! Or other aunts and uncles! Or baby-sitters! Or can't the older ones watch the younger ones? Or maybe you could call the mothers of some of their school friends and see if—"

"It's kind of involved," Ian said. He was surprised at the number of options that could be produced at such short notice. "I guess I'd just better say no," he told her.

"Christ," she said, "what a drag. Why, even chain gangs get their Sundays off."

Then Mr. Brant called, "Jeannie!" He towered over the bureau, glaring in her direction, and she said, "Oops! Gotta go."

She skipped away, a juicy morsel of a girl, and Ian noticed how her long hair swung against the tight-packed seat of her jeans.

He had made it up about the children, of course. They were well past the stage when they needed sitters. But somehow he began to believe his own alibi, and as he watched her he thought, *Right! Even chain gangs*, he thought, *are allowed a little time to themselves*.

Well, no one had ever said this would be easy.

But then why didn't he feel forgiven? Why didn't he, after all these years of penance, feel that God had forgiven him?

The little black cat settled in immediately. She was very polite and clean, with a smell like new woolen yarn, and she tolerated any amount of petting. Daphne named her Honeybunch. Thomas named her Alexandra. Any time one would call her, the other would call louder. "Here, Honeybunch." "No, *Alexandra!* Here, Alexandra, you know who you love best." Agatha stayed out of it. She was abstracted all that weekend, moping because a classmate had thrown a party without inviting her. The reason Ian knew this was that Thomas announced it, cruelly, during Saturday night supper. Agatha had told Thomas he was piggish to chew with his mouth open, and Thomas said, "Well, at least I don't have to buy my clothes in the Chubbette department. At least I'm not so fat that Missy Perkins wouldn't ask me to her slumber party!" Then Agatha threw down her napkin and bolted from the table, and Daphne said, in a satisfied tone, "You're a meanie, Thomas."

"Am not."

"Are so."

"She started it."

"Did not."

"Did so."

"Quit that," Ian said. "Both of you may be excused."

"Why do *I* have to go when he's the one who—"

"You're excused, I said."

They left, grumbling under their breaths as they moved into the living room.

Supper was more or less finished, anyhow. Ian's father had already pushed away his plate and tilted back in his chair, and his mother was merely toying with her dessert. She hadn't taken a bite in the last five minutes; she was deep in one of her blow-by-blow household sagas, and it seemed she would never get around to eating her last half-globe of canned peach.

"So there I was in the basement," she said, "looking at all this water full of let's-not-discuss-it, and the man pulled a kind of zippery tube from his machine and twined it down the . . . ."

Ian started thinking about the comics. It was childish of him, he knew, but one thing he really enjoyed at the end of every day was reading "Peanuts" in the *Evening Sun*. It made a kind of oasis—that tiny, friendly world where everybody was so quaint and earnest and reflective. But what with Good Works, and the weekly grocery trip, and shopping for the kids' new gym shoes, he hadn't had a chance at the paper yet; and now he could hear the others mauling it in the living room. By the time he got hold of it all the pages would be disarranged and crumpled.

"The total bill came to sixty dollars," his mother was saying. "I consider that cheap, in view of what the man had to deal with. When he was done he had me look down the floor drain. Big dark echoey floor drain. 'Hear that?' he said, and I said, 'Hear what?' He said, 'All along the line, your neighbors flushing their toilets. First one here and then one far, far away over there,' he said, 'all connected by this network of pipes.' 'Well, fine,' I said, 'but left to my own devices I believe I could manage to live out my life *not* hearing, thank you very much.' "

In the living room, quarrelsome voices climbed over each other and Ian caught the sound of paper tearing. They were demolishing "Peanuts," he was certain. He sighed.

Suppose, he thought suddenly, his boyhood self was to walk into the scene at this moment. Suppose he was offered a glimpse of how he had turned out: twenty-six years old and still living with his parents, tending someone else's children, obsessed with the evening comics. *Huh?* he'd say. *Why, what has happened here? What has become of me? How in heaven's name did things ever get to this state?*

"Give me one good reason I should have to go to church," Agatha said on Sunday morning. "It's hypocritical to go! I'm not a believer."

"You can go to Grandma and Grandpa's church if you prefer," Ian told her.

"Listen carefully, Ian, I'll only say this one more time: *I am not a believer.*"

He wrapped an elastic around Daphne's ponytail. "How about this," he said. "You attend till you're eighteen, and then you stop. That way, I won't have to feel guilty you didn't get the proper foundation."

"You don't have to feel guilty even now," Agatha told him. "I absolve you, Ian."

He drew back slightly. Absolve?

"Maybe she could go to Mary McQueen," Daphne suggested.

Agatha said, "Mary Our Queen is for Catholics, stupid."

"Agatha, don't call her stupid. Let's get moving. Thomas is already downstairs."

They descended to the living room, Daphne clattering in the patent leather Mary Janes she liked to wear to church. The sound of Sunday morning, Ian thought. He told his parents, "We're off."

"Oh, all right, dear," his mother said. She and his father were reading the paper on the couch.

"Take that business of the fig tree," Agatha

said as she let the front door slam behind her. "Jesus cursing the fig tree."

"Where's Thomas?"

"Here I am," Thomas said from the porch swing.

"Let's go, then."

"Jesus decides he wants figs," Agatha said. "Of course, it's not fig *season*, but Jesus wants figs anyhow. So up he walks to this fig tree, but naturally all he finds is leaves. And what does he do? Puts a curse on the poor little tree."

"No!" Daphne breathed. Evidently she hadn't heard about this before.

"Next thing you know, the tree's withered and died."

"No."

Ian knew that Agatha was just passing through a stage, but even so he minded, a bit. Over the years he had come to view Jesus very personally. The most trite and sentimental Sunday School portrait could send a flash of feeling through him, as if Jesus were . . . oh, one of those older boys he used to admire when he was small, someone he'd watched from a distance and grown to know and love without ever daring to engage in conversation.

Also, Agatha was seeding doubts in the other two.

"Doesn't that seem petty to you?" she was asking Daphne. "I mean, doesn't it seem unreasonable? If *we* behaved like that, we'd be sent to our rooms to think it over."

"Agatha," Ian said, "there's a great deal in the Bible that's simply beyond our understanding."

"Beyond yours, maybe," Agatha said. She told Daphne, "Or Noah's Ark: how about that? God kills off all the sinners in a mammoth rainstorm. 'Gotcha!' he says, and he's enjoying it, you know he is, or otherwise he'd have sent a few sample rains ahead of time so they could mend their ways."

Picture how they must look from outside, Ian thought. A cleaned and pressed little family walking together to church, discussing matters of theology. Perfect.

From outside.

"Or Abraham and Isaac. That one *really* ticks me off. God asks Abraham to kill his own son. And Abraham says, 'Okay.' Can you believe it? And then at the very last minute God says, 'Only testing. Ha-ha.' Boy, I'd like to know what Isaac thought. All the rest of his life, any time his father so much as looked in his direction Isaac would think—"

Ian said, "Agatha, it's very bad manners to criticize other people's religion."

"It's very bad manners to force your own religion on them, too," Agatha told him. "Shoot, it's very *unconstitutional*. To make me go to church when I don't want to."

"Well, you're right," Ian said.

"Huh?"

"You're right, I shouldn't have done it."

By now, they had stopped walking. Agatha peered at him. She said, "So can I leave now?"

"You can leave."

She stood there a moment longer. The other two watched with interest. "Okay," she said finally. "Bye."

"Bye."

She turned and set off toward home.

But without her it seemed so quiet. He missed her firm, opinionated voice and that little trick she had of varying her tone to quote each person's remarks. No matter how imaginary those remarks might be.

"I the Lord thy God am a jealous God," Reverend Emmett read from Exodus, and Ian could almost hear Agatha beside him: "Any time *we* act jealous, people have a fit." He shook the thought away. He bowed lower in his seat, propping his forehead on two fingers. Next to him, Daphne tore a tiny corner off a page of her hymnal and placed it on her tongue. Thomas was sitting behind them with Kenny Larson and his family. A fly was crawling up the front counter.

Reverend Emmett called for a hymn: "Blessed Assurance." The congregation rose to sing, standing shoulder to shoulder. Everyone here was familiar to Ian. Or at least, semifamiliar. (Eli Everjohn and his wife were sitting with Sister Bertha, and Mrs. Jordan had brought her cousin.) "This is my story," they sang, "this is my song . . ." Ian put an arm around Daphne and she nestled against him as she sang, her voice incongruously husky for such a little girl.

The sermon was on the Sugar Rule. Recently a committee had approached Reverend Emmett suggesting that the rule be dropped. It was just so complicated, they said. Face it, they were eating sugar every day of their lives, one way or another. Even peanut butter contained sugar if you bought it from a supermarket. Reverend Emmett had told them he would meditate on the issue and report his conclusions. What he said this morning—pacing behind the counter, running his long fingers through his forelock—was that the Sugar Rule was *supposed* to be complicated. "Like error itself," he said, "sugar creeps in the cracks. You tell yourself you didn't realize, you were subject to circumstance, you forgot to read the list of ingredients and anyhow, it's everywhere and it can't be helped. Isn't that significant? It's not that you'll be damned forever if you take a grain of sugar; nobody says that. Sugar is merely a distraction, not a sin. But I feel it's important to keep the rule because of what it stands for: the need for eternal watchfulness."

The children—those who were listening—sent each other disappointed grimaces, but Ian didn't really care that much. The Sugar Rule was a minor inconvenience, at most. So was the Coffee Rule; so was the Alcohol Rule. The difficult one was the Unmarried Sex Rule. "How can something be right one day and wrong the next?" Cicely had asked him. "And what's done is done, anyway, and can't be undone, right?"

He had said, "If I thought that, I wouldn't be able to go on living." Then he'd told her he wanted them to get married.

"Married!" Cicely had cried. "Married, at our age! I haven't seen the world yet! I haven't had any fun!"

He covered his eyes with his hand.

In his daydreams, he walked into services one morning and found a lovely, golden-haired girl sitting in the row just ahead. She would be so intent on the sermon that she wouldn't even look his way; she had grown up in a religion very much like this one, it turned out, and believed with all her heart. After the Benediction Ian introduced himself, and she looked shy and pleased. They had the most proper courtship, but he could tell she felt the same way he did. They would marry at Second Chance with Reverend Emmett officiating. She would love the three children as much as if they were hers and stay home forever after to tend them. The

Church Maiden, Ian called her in his mind. He never entered this building without scanning the rows for the Church Maiden.

After the sermon came Amending. "Does somebody want to stand up?" Reverend Emmett asked. But standing up was for serious sins, where you confessed to the whole congregation and discussed in public all possible methods of atonement. Evidently none of them had strayed so grievously during this past week. "Well, then," Reverend Emmett said, smiling, "we'll amend in private," and they bowed their heads and whispered their mistakes to themselves. Ian caught snatches of "lied to my husband" and "slapped my daughter" and "drank part of a beer with my boss." "Thursday I stole my sister's new bra and wore it to gym class," Daphne said, startling Ian, but of course he should not have been listening. He averted his face from her and whispered, "I was snappish with the children three different times. Four. And I told Mr. Brant I was sick with the flu when really I just wanted a day off."

Unlike the other denominations Ian knew of, this one had nothing against sinning in your thoughts. To think a sinful thought and not act upon it was to practice righteousness, Reverend Emmett said—almost as much righteousness as not thinking the thought in the first place. Jesus must have been misquoted on that business about committing adultery in your heart. So Ian left unspoken what troubled him the most:

I've been atoning and atoning, and sometimes lately I've hated God for taking so long to forgive me. Some days I feel I'm speaking into a dead telephone. My words are knocking against a blank wall. Nothing comes back to show I've been heard.

"Let it vanish now from our souls, Lord. In Jesus' name, amen," Reverend Emmett said. He looked radiant. Whatever had weighed on his own soul (for his lips had moved with the others', this morning) had obviously been lifted from him.

They sang "Sweet Hour of Prayer," in a tone that struck Ian as lingering and regretful. Then Reverend Emmett gave the Benediction, and they were free to go. Daphne shot off to join a friend. Ian wove his way through the other members' greetings. He answered several inquiries about his mother's arthritis, and politely refused Mrs. Jordan's offer of a ride home. (She drove like a maniac.) Near the door, Eli Everjohn stood awkwardly by in a brilliant blue suit while his wife talked with Sister Myra. "Morning, Brother Eli," Ian said. He started to edge past him, but Eli, who must have been feeling left out, brightened and said, "Why, hey there! Hey!"

"Enjoy the service?" Ian asked.

"Oh, I'm sure your pastor means well," Eli

said. "But forbidding ordinary white sugar, and then allowing your young folks to listen to rock-and-roll music! Seems like to me he's got his priorities mixed up. I don't know that I hold with this Amending business, either. Awful close to Roman Catholic, if you ask me."

"Ah, well, it's a matter of opinion, I guess."

"No, Brother Ian, it is *not* a matter of opinion. Goodness! What a notion."

That more or less finished the conversation, Ian figured. He gave up and raised a hand amiably in farewell. But then he paused and turned back. "Brother Eli?" he said. "I wonder. Do you think you could locate a missing person for me?"

"Why, I'll do my best," Eli told him.

He didn't seem at all surprised by the question. It was Ian who was surprised.

"His name was Tom Dean," he told Eli. "Thomas Dean, Senior. He was married to my sister-in-law before she married my brother, and he's the only one who might be able to tell us who my sister-in-law's family was."

He and Eli sat on the couch in Sister Bertha's living room. No doubt Sister Bertha was wondering what business Ian could possibly have here, but she stayed out of sight, ostentatiously rattling pans in the kitchen and talking to her daughter. Her house was a ranch house with rooms that all flowed together, and Ian distinctly heard her discussing someone named Netta who had suffered a terrible grease fire.

"I don't know where Tom Dean grew up," Ian said, "but sometime in the spring of 'sixty-five he wrote to Lucy from Cheyenne, Wyoming. Or maybe he phoned; I'm not sure. *Somehow* he got in touch, asking her to send him his things."

"How long had they been divorced?" Eli said.

"I don't know. The kids were still small, though. It can't have been too long."

"And what state was this divorce granted in? Maryland? Wyoming? What state of the Union?"

"I don't know that either."

Eli surveyed him mournfully. He had taken off his suit coat and the armpits of his white shirt showed a faint bluish tinge.

"It was only mentioned in passing," Ian said. "You don't discuss your divorce in detail with the family of your new husband. So when my brother died, and then Lucy died, there was no one we could ask. She had left behind the three children and we were hoping some of her relatives could take them, but we didn't know if she had any relatives. We didn't even know her maiden name."

Beyond the plate glass window, Sunday traffic swished along Lake Avenue. Sister Bertha said Netta had escaped unburned and so had her husband and baby and her dear, darling, wonderful, incredible little dog.

"Still," Eli said, "your sister-in-law must have had some kind of document. Some certificate or something, somewhere among her papers."

"She didn't leave any papers. After she died my dad went through her house and he couldn't find a one."

"How about her billfold? Driver's license?"

"She didn't drive."

"Social security card?"

"For Lucy Dean. Period."

"Photos, then. Any photos?"

"None."

"Your family must have photos, though. From after she married your brother."

"We do, but my mother put them away so as not to remind the children."

"Not to remind them? Well, land sakes."

"My mother's kind of . . . she prefers to look on the bright side. But I can find them for you, I'm sure."

"Maybe later on," Eli said. "Okay: let's talk about your sister-in-law's friends. You recall if she had any girlfriends?"

"Not close ones," Ian said. "Just a couple of women she waitressed with, back before she married Danny. One of them we never tracked down, and the other my mother ran into a year or so after Lucy died but she said she really didn't know a thing about her."

"Didn't no one ever *ask* this Lucy anything?"

"It does sound peculiar," Ian said. This was the first time he'd realized exactly how peculiar. He was amazed that they could have been so unaware, so incurious, living all those months alongside another human being.

Eli said, "Tell what was in her desk."

"She didn't have a desk."

"Her topmost bureau drawer, then. Or that ragtag drawer full of string and such in her kitchen."

"All I know is, my dad went through her house and he didn't find anything useful. He talked about how people don't write letters anymore."

"So: no letters."

"And no address book, either. I remember he mentioned that."

"How about her divorce papers? She couldn't have throwed them away."

"Maybe after she remarried she did."

"Well, then, her marriage certificate. Her marriage to your brother."

"Nope."

"You know she would've kept that."

"All I can say is, we didn't find it."

"She must've had a safe deposit box."

"Lucy? I doubt it. And where was the key, then?"

"So you are trying to tell me," Eli said, "that a person manages to get through life without a single solitary piece of paper in her possession."

"Well, I realize it's unusual—"

"It's impossible!"

"Well . . ."

"Had her place been burglarized recently? Did the drawers look like they'd been rifled?"

"Not that I heard of," Ian said.

"Was anybody else living in the house with her?"

"No . . ."

But a dim uneasiness flitted past him, like something you see and yet don't see out of the corner of your eye.

"Anyone suspicious hanging about her?"

"No, no . . ."

But wary, suspicious Agatha pushed into his mind—her closed-off face with the puffy lids that veiled her secret thoughts.

"Now, I don't want you to take this wrong," Eli said, "but you are about the most *unhelpful* client I ever had to deal with."

"I realize that. I'm sorry," Ian said. "I shouldn't have wasted your time."

Eli shook his head, and his cowlick waggled and dipped. God's arrow with no place to go, Ian couldn't help thinking.

Monday noon, he told Mr. Brant he was eating at home today. He drove home and let himself into the house, announcing, "It's me! Forgot my billfold!"

"Oh, hello, dear," his mother called from the kitchen. Then she and his father went on talking, no doubt over their usual lunch of tinned soup and saltine crackers.

He climbed to the second floor and onward, more stealthily, to the attic, to Daphne and Agatha's little room underneath the eaves.

Girls tended to be messier than boys, he thought. (He had noticed that in his college days.) Agatha's bed was heaped with so many books that he wondered how she slept, and Daphne's was a jungle of stuffed animals. He went over to Agatha's bureau, a darkly varnished highboy that had to stand away from the wall a bit so as not to hit the eaves. The top was littered with pencil stubs and used Kleenexes and more books, but the drawers were fairly well organized. He patted each one's contents lightly, alert for something that didn't belong—the rustle of paper or a hard-edged address book. But there was nothing.

He knelt and looked under her bed. Dust balls. He lifted the mattress. Candy-bar wrappers. He shook his head and let the mattress drop. He tried the old fiberboard wardrobe standing at one end of the room and found a rod of clothes, half Daphne's and half Agatha's, packed too tightly together. Shoes and more shoes lay tangled underneath.

He bent to poke his head inside the storage

room that ran under the eaves. In the dimness he made out a dress form, a lampshade, two foot lockers, and a cardboard carton. He crawled further inside and lifted one of the carton's flaps. The musty gray smell reminded him of mice. He dragged the carton toward the door for a closer look: his mother's framed college diploma, a bundle of letters addressed to Miss Beatrice Craig . . . He pushed the carton toward the rear again.

Turning to go, he saw a faded, fabric-covered box on the floor—the kind that stationery sometimes comes in. He flipped up the lid and found a clutter of barrettes and hair ribbons and junk jewelry. Agatha's, no doubt. He let the lid fall shut and crawled on out.

In the bedroom, he paused. He reached back and pulled open the drawer in the box's base.

Right away, he knew he'd hit on something. The contents were so tidy: flattened papers stacked in order of size, and on top of them a few pieces of jewelry, no less junky than those in the main compartment but obviously dating from an earlier time. He pushed the jewelry aside and removed the papers.

A savings booklet from Mercantile Safe Deposit and Trust, showing a balance of $123.08. The title to a Chevrolet owned by Daniel C. Bedloe. A receipt from Morehead TV Repair guaranteeing all replacement parts for thirty days. A marriage certificate for Daniel Craig Bedloe and Lucy Ann Dean. (Ian paused a moment over that one. Was there any remote possibility that Ann could be a last name?) A birth certificate for Daphne Marie Bedloe. A pamphlet of instructions for filing health insurance claims. A birth certificate for Agatha Lynn Dulsimore and then one for Thomas. A receipt for—

Agatha *who?*

Agatha Lynn Dulsimore, born April 4, 1959. Father's full name: Thomas Robert Dulsimore. Mother's maiden name: Lucy Ann Dean. And Thomas Robert Dulsimore, Junior; same parents.

Why, Dean was not Lucy's married name but her maiden name. She must have changed back to Dean after the divorce, and changed her children's names too—at least by implication. All this time, the Bedloes had been hunting a man who didn't exist.

Ian sifted through the few remaining papers— a hazy, unflattering photo of Lucy and the older two children, an auto insurance policy, a recipe for banana bread—but the birth certificates were the only items that told him anything. Both listed the parents' home address as Portia, Maryland. Both carried definite dates, and a doctor's name, and a hospital's name in a town called Marcy, which if Ian recollected right lay not far from Portia, just below the Pennsylvania line. He had enough to track a man down by, provided a person was halfway skilled at tracking.

He slipped the papers inside his shirt and went off to see Eli Everjohn.

"Have some mashed potato, Honeybunch," Daphne said. She held her spoon out to the little cat, who was sitting on Daphne's lap with her front paws folded primly beneath her. First the cat peered into Daphne's eyes, as if checking to make sure she really meant it, and then she leaned forward and lapped daintily. When she was finished, the spoon gleamed. She sat up to wash her face. "Good girl," Daphne said, and she dipped the spoon back in her plate and took a mouthful for herself.

"Ooh, revolting!" Agatha said. "Ian, did you see what she did?"

"What? What'd I do?" Daphne asked.

"You ate from a spoon the cat licked!"

At the other end of the table, Thomas gave an elderly cough. "Well, actually," he said, "the cat's the one who should worry. Mr. Pratt says human spit carries more germs than any other animal's, because humans have these fingers they keep putting in their mouths."

Ian laughed. The others looked at him.

"I was just, ah, thinking," he told them.

They looked away again.

You could never call it a penance, to have to

take care of these three. They were all that gave his life color, and energy, and . . . well, life.

What he would do was, once he got Eli's report he would file it in a drawer someplace. Then when they grew up and started wondering about their origins he would hand it over to them; that was all. He would certainly not use the information himself in any way.

People needed to know their genetic backgrounds—what diseases ran in their families and so forth. Also this would help him apply for guardianship. Social Security. That sort of thing.

He rose and started clearing the table. It was a relief to have all that settled. He was glad he hadn't told anyone what he was doing.

But at work the next day, he did tell someone. He told Jeannie. He was teaching her how to select the right grain of wood and she asked if he'd like to go to a movie that night at the Charles. "I can't," he said.

"What, are movies against your religion?"

"No, it's my turn to car-pool for Brownies."

"Hey," she said. "Ian. How long you going to go on living like this, anyway?"

So he told her about Eli. He didn't know why, exactly. It wasn't as if finding Thomas Dulsimore would change his situation. Maybe he just hoped to prove he wasn't as passive as she supposed. And she did seem gratifyingly interested. When he mentioned the stationery box she said, "Naw!

Go on!" She asked, "What-all was in it?" and she even wanted to know about the jewelry.

"It wasn't the kind of jewelry that would give you any clues," he said. "I honestly didn't pay much attention."

"And the photo?"

"Oh, well, that was . . . well, the detective was glad to see it, of course, so's he'd know more or less what she looked like, but it didn't show a street sign or a license plate or anything like that. Just Lucy."

"Was she pretty?"

"Sure, I guess so."

For some reason, he didn't want to tell her *how* pretty.

Lucy's image swam into his mind—not the real-life version but the version in the snapshot: out of focus, too young, still unformed, nowhere near as finely chiseled as she had seemed later. One hip was slung out gracelessly to support Thomas's weight, and one hand was reaching blurrily to gather Agatha closer. Against all logic (he knew he was being ridiculous), he started resenting Agatha's disloyalty in keeping her mother's likeness. There you are: you give up school, you sacrifice everything for these children, and what do they do? They secretly hoard their mother's photo and cling to her and prefer her. She hadn't even taken proper care of them, willfully dying and leaving them as she did;

but evidently blood motherhood won over everything.

Jeannie said, "I'm really glad to hear you're doing this, Ian."

"Well, it's only so we can get straight," he told her. "I certainly don't plan to hand the three of them over to strangers or anything like that."

"What are you, crazy?" she asked. "You've got a life to live! You can't drag them around with you forever."

"But I'm responsible for them. I worry I'd be, um, sinning, so to speak, to walk away from them."

"You want to know what I think?" Jeannie asked. She leaned forward. Her face seemed sharper now, more pointed. The hollow between her collarbones could have held a teaspoon of salt. "I think you're sinning *not* to walk away," she said.

"How do you figure that?"

"I think we're each allowed one single life to live on this planet. We'll never get another chance in all eternity," she said. "And if you let it go to waste—now, *that* is sinning."

"Yes," he said, "but what if I'm honor-bound to waste it? What if I have an obligation?"

He worried she would make him explain, but she was too caught up in proving her point. "Even then!" she said triumphantly. "You put your regrets behind you. You move on past them. You do not commit the sin of squandering your only life."

"Well, it *sounds* good," he said.

It did sound good. He really had no argument to offer against it.

At Prayer Meeting the following night he looked for Eli Everjohn but didn't find him, or the strawberry blonde either. He spotted Sister Bertha's dark red pompadour and he sat down next to her and asked, "Where's your daughter this evening?"

"She went home."

"Home?"

"Her and Eli both, home to Caro Mill. Eli said to give you a message, though. What was it now he said? He said not to think you had slipped his mind and he would be in touch."

"Thanks," Ian told her.

Then Reverend Emmett announced the opening hymn: "Work for the Night Is Coming."

Every time Ian attended Prayer Meeting, he thought of his first visit here. He remembered how he had felt welcomed by the loving voices of the singers; he remembered the sensation of prayers flowing heavenward. Coming here had saved him, he knew. Without the Church of the Second Chance he would have struggled alone forever, sunk in hopelessness.

So when Prayer Meeting seemed long-winded

or inconsequential, when the petitions had to do with minor health complaints and personal disputes, he controlled his impatience. Tonight he prayed for Brother Kenneth's colon to grow less irritable, for Sister Myra's husband to appreciate her more fully. He listened to a recitation from Sister Nell that seemed not so much a request for prayers as an autobiography. "I learned to stop blaming myself for everything that went wrong," one of her paragraphs went. "I had all the time been blaming myself. But really, you know, when you think about it, mostly it's other people to blame, the godless and the self-centered, and so I said to this gal on my shift, I said, 'Now listen here, Miss Maggie. *You* may think I was the one in charge of the . . .'"

Till Reverend Emmett broke in. "Ah, Sister Nell?"

"What?"

"What would you like us to pray for, exactly?"

"Pray for me to have strength," she said, "in the face of fools and sinners."

Ian prayed for Sister Nell to have strength.

The closing hymn was "Softly and Tenderly," and when they sang, "Come home! Come home!" Ian felt he was the one they were calling.

"Go ye now into the world and bear witness to His teachings," Reverend Emmett said, raising his arms. Almost before his "Amen," people were stirring and preparing to leave. Several spoke to Ian as they passed. "Good to see you, Brother Ian." "How're the kids?" "Coming to paint with us Saturday?" They filed out. Ian hung behind.

Often it seemed to him that this room itself was his source of peace. Even the flicker of the fluorescent lights heartened him, and the faint chemical smell left over from when the place had been a dry cleaner's. He found reasons to loiter, first collecting the hymn pamphlets and then stacking them just so on the counter. He paused at the edges of a conversation between Reverend Emmett and Brother Kenneth, who was offering further details about his colon. He rolled down his shirtsleeves and carefully buttoned his cuffs before, at long last, stepping out the door.

Then behind him, Reverend Emmett said, "Brother Ian? Mind if I walk partway with you?"

Ian felt his shoulders loosen. Possibly, this was what he'd been hoping for all along.

They walked north on York Road through a summerlike night, Reverend Emmett swinging his Bible. He was taller than Ian and took longer strides, although he kept trying to slow down. Occasionally he hummed a few notes beneath his breath—"Softly and Tenderly" again. Ian thought of an evening back in his Boy Scout days, when the scoutmaster (a young, athletic man, a former basketball star) had given him a ride home, filling him with a mixture of joy and self-consciousness. He knew Reverend Emmett merely acted as God's steward, and that for someone who was the church's founder and its sole leader he seemed remarkably unimpressed with his own importance. Still, Ian always felt tongue-tied around him. Tonight he considered discussing the weather but decided that was too mundane, and then when the silence stretched on too long he wished he *had* discussed the weather, but if he brought it up now it would seem strained. So he kept quiet, and it was Reverend Emmett who finally spoke.

"Some Prayer Meetings," he said, "are like cleaning out a closet. Clearing away the dribs and drabs. Necessary, but tedious."

And Ian said, as if making a perfectly apt response: "Is there such a thing as the Devil?"

Reverend Emmett glanced over at him.

"I mean," Ian said, "does someone exist whose purpose is to tempt people into evil? To make them feel torn one way and another so they're not sure which way is right anymore?"

"What is it you're tempted to do, Brother Ian?" Reverend Emmett asked.

Ian swallowed. "I'm wasting my life," he said.

"Excuse me?"

He must have mumbled the words. He raised his chin and said, almost shouting, "I'm wasting the only life I have! I have one single life in this universe and I'm not using it!"

"Well, of course you're using it," Reverend Emmett said calmly.

"I am?"

"This *is* your life," Reverend Emmett said.

They faced each other at an intersection. A woman swerved around them.

"Lean into it, Ian," Reverend Emmett said. Not "Brother Ian," but "Ian." It made what he said sound more direct, more oracular. He said, "View your burden as a gift. It's the theme that has been given you to work with. Accept that, and lean into it. This is the only life you'll have."

Then he clapped Ian on the shoulder, and turned away to cross York Road.

Ian resumed walking. For a while he pondered Reverend Emmett's message, but he didn't find it much help. To tell the truth, the man had disappointed him. And besides, he hadn't answered Ian's question. The question was: Is there such a thing as the Devil?

Ian had been referring to Jeannie, of course—Jeannie sitting forward compellingly, the hollow deepening at the base of her throat as she tempted him from his path. But the face that came to his mind at this moment was not Jeannie's. It was Lucy's. It was the tiny, perfect, heart-shaped face of Lucy Dean.

"Honeybunch has worms," Agatha told Ian.

"How do you know that?"

"You really want me to say?"

"On second thought, never mind," Ian said. "So, what? We have to take her to the vet?"

"I made an appointment: tomorrow afternoon at four."

She and Thomas sat on either side of Ian in the porch swing, enjoying the last of a golden autumn day. Down on the front walk, Daphne was playing hopscotch with the Carter girl and the newlyweds' five-year-old. "You did step on the line, Tracy. You did," she said in her raucous little voice.

Ian said, "Maybe Grandpa could drive you. I could leave the car with him tomorrow and take the bus."

"We like it better when *you* come," Agatha said.

"Well, but I have work."

"Please, Ian," Thomas said. "Grandpa drove us when we went to get her cat shots and he yelled at her for sitting on his foot."

"His accelerator foot," Agatha explained.

"We like it better when you're there, acting in charge," Thomas told him.

Ian looked at him a moment. His mind had drifted elsewhere. "Thomas," he said, "remember that big doll you used to carry around?"

"Oh, well, that was a long time ago," Thomas said.

"Yes, but I was wondering. How come you named her Dulcimer?"

"I don't even know where she is anymore. I don't know why I named her that," Thomas said.

He seemed embarrassed, rather than secretive. And Agatha wasn't listening. You'd think she would suspect; she was the one who'd kept that box hidden away. But she stirred the porch swing dreamily with one foot. "Suppose we got bombed," she said to Ian.

"Pardon?"

He saw the stationery box in his mind: the dust on the lid, the congealed sheaf of papers. She must not have glanced inside for years, he realized. She might even have forgotten it existed.

"Suppose Baltimore got atom-bombed," she was saying. "Know what I'd do?"

"You wouldn't do a thing," Thomas told her. "You'd be dead."

"No, seriously. I've been thinking. I'd break into a supermarket, and I'd settle our family inside. That way we'd have all the supplies we needed. Canned goods and bottled goods, enough to last us forever."

"Well, not forever," Thomas said.

"Long enough to get over the radiation, though."

"Not a chance. Right, Ian?"

Ian said, "Hmm?"

"The radiation would last for years, right?"

"Well, so would the canned goods," Agatha said. "And if we still had electricity—"

"Electricity! Ha!" Thomas said. "Do you ever live in a dream world!"

"Well, even without electricity," Agatha said stubbornly, "we could manage. Nowadays supermarkets sell blankets, even. And socks! And prescription drugs, the bigger places. We could get penicillin and stuff. And some way we'd bring Claudia and them from Pittsburgh, I haven't figured just how, yet—"

"Forget it, Ag," Thomas told her. "That's ten more mouths to feed."

"But we *need* a lot of kids. They're the future generation. And Grandma and Grandpa are the old folks who would teach us how to carry on."

"How about Ian?" Thomas asked.

"How about him?"

"He's not old. And he's not the future generation, either. You have to draw the line somewhere."

"Gee, thanks," Ian said, lazily toeing the swing. But Agatha turned a pensive gaze on him.

"No," she said finally, "Ian comes too. He's the one who keeps us all together."

"The cowpoke of the family, so to speak," Ian told Thomas. But he felt touched. And when his father called from the doorway—"Ian? Telephone"—he rested a palm on Agatha's thick black hair a second as he rose.

The receiver lay next to the phone on the front hall table. He picked it up and said, "Hello?"

"Brother Ian? Wallah," a man said from a distance.

"Pardon?"

"This is Eli Everjohn. Wallah, I said."

"Wallah?"

"Wallah! I found your man."

"You . . . what?"

"Except he's dead," Eli said.

Ian leaned one shoulder against the wall.

"Appears he didn't live much past what your sister-in-law did. Hello? Are you there?"

"I'm here."

"Maybe this is a shock."

"No, that's all right," Ian said.

The shock was not Tom Dulsimore's death but the fact that he had lived at all—that someone else in the world had turned up actual evidence of him.

But Eli started breaking the news all over again, this time more delicately. "I'm sorry to have to tell you that Thomas Dulsimore, Senior has passed away," he said. "Had himself a motorcycle crash back in nineteen sixty-seven."

" 'Sixty-seven," Ian said.

"Seems he was one of those folks that don't hold with helmets."

So Tom Dulsimore was not an option anymore—not even in Ian's fantasies.

"Reason I know is, I phoned his mother. Mrs.
Millet. She'd remarried, is the reason it took me
a while. I told her I was a buddy of Tom's wanting
to get in touch with him. I didn't say no more
though till I got your say-so. Should I go ahead
now and pay her a visit?"

"No, never mind."

"She's bound to know the kids' relatives.
Small-town kind of lady; you could just tell she
would know all about it."

"Maybe I should get her address," Ian said.

"Okay, suit yourself. Mrs. Margie Millet. Forty-
three Orchard Road, Portia, Maryland. You need
to write that down?"

"I have it," Ian said. (He would have it forever,
he felt—chiseled into his brain.) "Thanks, Eli. I
appreciate your help. You know where to send
the bill."

"Aw, it won't amount to much. This one was
easy."

For you, maybe, Ian thought. He told Eli goodbye and hung up.

From the kitchen, his mother called, "Agatha?
Time to set the table!"

"Coming."

Ian met Agatha at the door and stepped past
her onto the porch. She didn't notice a thing.

The evening was several shades darker now,

as if curtain after curtain had fallen in his absence. Thomas was swinging the swing hard enough to make the chains creak, and down on the sidewalk the little girls were still playing hopscotch. Ian paused to watch them. Something about the purposeful planting of small shoes within chalked squares tugged at him. He leaned on the railing and thought, *What does this remind me of? What? What?* Daphne tossed the pebble she used as a marker and it landed in the farthest square so crisply, so ringingly, that the sound seemed thrown back from a sky no higher than a ceiling, cupping all of Waverly Street just a few feet overhead.

"Lucy Ann Dean was as common as dirt," Mrs. Millet said. "I know I shouldn't speak ill of the dead, but there's just no getting around it: she was common."

They were sitting in Mrs. Millet's Pennsylvania Dutch–style breakfast nook, all blue painted wood and cut-out hearts and tulips. (Her house was the kind where the living room waited in reserve for some momentous occasion that never arrived, and Ian had caught no more than a glimpse of its white shag rugs and white upholstery on his journey to the kitchen.) Mrs. Millet slouched across from him, opening a pack of cigarettes. She was younger than he had expected, with a very stiff, very brown hairdo and a hatchet face. Her magenta minidress struck him as outdated, although Ian was not the last word on fashion.

He himself wore a suit and tie, chosen with an eye to looking trustworthy. After all, how did she know he wasn't some knock-and-rob man? He hadn't phoned ahead because he hadn't fully acknowledged he was planning this; he had dressed this morning only for church, he told himself, although he almost never wore a tie to church. After services he had eaten Sunday dinner with his family and then (yawning aloud and stretching in a stagy manner) had announced he was feeling so restless, he thought he might go for a drive. Whereupon he had headed north without consulting a map, relying on the proper road signs to appear or else not, as the case might be. And they did appear. The signs for Portia, the signs for Orchard Road. The giant brass 43 glittering, almost shouting, from the lamppost in front of the redwood cottage. "My name is Ian Bedloe," he had said when she opened the door. "I hope I'm not disturbing you, but I'm Lucy Dean's brother-in-law and I'm trying to locate some of her family."

She hadn't exactly slammed the door in his face, but her expression had frozen over somehow. "Then maybe you better ask *her*," she told him.

"Ask who?"

"Why, Lucy Dean, of course."

"But . . . Lucy's dead," he said.

She stared at him.

"She died a long time ago," he told her.

"Well," she said, "I'd be fibbing if I said I was sorry. I always knew she was up to no good."

He was shamed by the rush of pleasure he felt—the bitter, wicked pleasure of hearing someone else agree with him at long last.

Now she said, "First off, her parents drank." She took a cigarette from her pack and tamped it against the table. "How do you suppose they had that car wreck? Three sheets to the wind, both of them. Then her aunt Alice moved in with her, and she was just plain cracked, if you want my honest opinion. I don't think the two of them had anything to do with each other. It's more like Lucy just raised herself. Well, for that much I give her credit: she'd come out of that run-down shack every morning neat as a pin, every hair in place, every accessory matching, which heaven knows how she did on their little pittance of money . . ."

She stole it, is how. Shoplifted. Not even you know the worst of it.

". . . and she'd sashay off to school all prissy and Miss America with her books held in front of her chest. The boys were fools for her, but my Tommy was the only one she'd look at. You should've seen my Tommy. He was movie-star handsome. He could pass for Tony Curtis, ought to give you some idea. He and Lucy went steady from ninth grade on. Went to every dance and sports event together. Well, excepting Junior Prom. They had a little disagreement the week before Junior Prom and she went with Gary Durbin, but Tommy beat Gary to a pulp next morning and him and Lucy got back together. At their Senior Prom they were King and Queen. I still have the pictures. Tommy wore a tux and he looked good enough to eat. I said, 'Tommy, you could have any girl you wanted,' but then, well, you guessed it."

She lit her cigarette and tilted her head and blew out a long stream of smoke, all the while staring defiantly at Ian. He said, "I did?"

"Lucy went and got herself pregnant."

"Oh."

"I said, 'Tommy, you can't be certain that baby's even yours,' and he said, 'Mom, I know it. I just don't know what on earth I'm going to do,' he told me."

Ian said, "What?" He felt he'd missed something. "You mean it could have been someone else's baby?" he asked.

"Well, who can say?" Mrs. Millet said. "I mean life is all so iffy, right? I said, 'Tommy, *don't* fall for this! You could be anything! You could be a male model, even! Why saddle yourself with a wife and kid?' But Lucy talked him into it. She had him wrapped around her little finger, I tell you. It was the kind of thing that just breaks a mother's heart."

"So . . . but this aunt of hers," Ian said. He seemed to be losing track of the purpose of his visit. "Alice, you say."

"Alice Dean. Well, she had nothing against it. She was delighted to marry Lucy off. Meant she could get back to wherever she came from and her old-maid ways. So Tommy and Lucy set up house in this crummy little trailer over at Blalock's Trailer Park and Tommy started work at Luther's Sports Equipment, but when Lucy told him she was expecting *again*—two babies in three years!—he left her. I don't blame him, either. I do not blame him. He was just a boy! 'When you going to do this, when you going to do that?' she was always asking, but he hadn't had him any kind of life yet! *Naturally* he wanted to roam a bit. She claimed he was irresponsible and she fretted about the least little thing, so of course he stayed away even more and when he did come home they'd fight. Twice the police had to be called. Then thank the Lord, he finally had the sense to leave. Got shed of her and asked for a divorce. And wouldn't you know she hired herself a big-shot city lawyer and sued for child support. Proves what I'd been telling him: all as she was after was his money. Someone to support those kids; by then she'd had the second one and she was always yammering about, 'I can't feed these kids on yard weeds,' and such. I told Tommy, I said, 'She should just go to work, if she needs money so bad.' "

"But then who would watch the children?" Ian asked.

"Lord, you sound just like her. 'Then who would watch the children?' " Mrs. Millet mimicked in a high voice. She flicked her cigarette into a tin ashtray. "She should've got a sitter, of course. That's what I told Tommy. 'And don't expect *me* to sit,' I told him. I never did like other people's children much. So anyhow, Tommy hung around here a whiles but there wasn't all that much for him in Portia, and so finally he hitchhiked to Wyoming. He had in mind to find work there, something glamorous having to do with horses. Well, that didn't quite come through like he had hoped and so of course he couldn't send money first thing, but he was planning to! And then we hear Lucy's run off."

"Run off?"

"Run away with some man. That lawyer that handled her divorce. It was Mr. Blalock called and told me, down at the trailer park. She owed him rent. He said her trailer was empty as last year's bird nest, door flapping open in the wind and everything hauled away that wasn't nailed down. Said her neighbors saw a moving van come to take her belongings. Not a U-Haul; a professional van. The man was loaded, was what they guessed. She must've went with him for the money."

"Went with him where?" Ian asked.

"Why, to Baltimore, but at first we didn't know that. At first we had no idea, and I told Tommy he was better off that way. 'The slate has been wiped clean,' I told him on the phone. 'I do believe we've seen the last of her.' But *then* guess what. She calls him up a few months later. Calls him in Cheyenne. Tells him she's in Baltimore and wants the money he owes her. Oh, I just wish I'd have been on the other end of the line. I'd have hung up on her so fast! But Tommy, I will say, he was a whole lot smarter by then. He says, 'I thought you had yourself some rich guy now,' and she says, 'Oh,' says, 'that didn't work out.' Well, I just bet it didn't work out. I bet the fellow was married, was what. That's the kind of thing you see happen every day. Tommy tells her, 'I can't help *that*, I met somebody here and we're planning on a June wedding. All I got is going for the wedding,' he says. Then he says, 'And anyhow, where's my things? You took every blasted thing I left in that trailer,' he says. 'Stuff I was coming back to fetch someday you packed up and hauled away like it belonged to you.' 'Tommy, I need money,' she says. 'I'm in a awful fix right now.' He says, 'First you send me my things,' and signs off. You see how he'd got wise to her. Oh, she aged him, I tell you. She hardened him. She callused him."

Mrs. Millet stubbed out her cigarette and sat staring into space. Over the stove, a plastic clock in the shape of a cat ticked its long striped tail back and forth.

"It was the winter of 'sixty-seven he had the accident," she said. "Motorcycling on icy roads. His wife called me up and told me. I will never hear the phone ring again as long as I live without going all over cold and sick."

Ian said, "Well, I'm sorry."

But it was only the most detached and courteous kind of sorry. He would never have left the children with such a man, even if the man had been willing.

"Of course, that second wife was pretty no-account herself," Mrs. Millet said.

Ian stood up. (No use staying on for more of this.) He said, "Mrs. Millet, I appreciate your talking to me. I guess what you're saying is, there was only that one aunt."

"That's all as *I* ever heard of," she said.

"And no brothers or sisters, or cousins, or anything like that."

"Not as I know of. Chances are the aunt has passed on too, by this time. Lord, lately it seems the whole world has passed on."

It did seem that way, at times. At times, it really did.

At Prayer Meeting the ghostly smell of dry-cleaning fluid mingled with Mrs. Jordan's cologne. "Pray for me to accept this cross without complaint," Sister Myra said. Accept what cross? Ian hadn't been listening. He bowed his head and felt the silence wrap around him like a clean, cool sheet that you reach for in your sleep halfway through a hot night.

"For our Sister Myra," Reverend Emmett said at last.

"Amen."

"Any other prayers, any other prayers . . ."

In a row toward the rear, Sister Bertha stood up. "I am troubled in my heart for another person tonight," she said. She spoke pointedly to the empty chair in front of her. "I know of someone here who seems to be experiencing a serious difficulty. I was waiting to see if he'd ask for our prayers but so far he hasn't."

He? There were only three men present: Reverend Emmett, Brother Kenneth, and Ian.

"I know," Sister Bertha said, "that this person must be feeling very overworked, very beset with problems, and he's casting about for a solution. But it doesn't seem to occur to him that he could bring it up at Prayer Meeting."

She sat down.

Ian's cheeks felt hot.

Surely private detectives were sworn to se-

crecy, weren't they? Just like lawyers, or doctors. Weren't they?

Reverend Emmett looked uncertain. He said,
"Well . . ." and glanced around at the other worshipers. His eyes did not linger noticeably on
Ian, although of course he must suspect. "Does
this person wish to ask for our prayers?" he said.

No response. Just a few rustles and whispers.

"In that case," Reverend Emmett said, "we
won't intrude. Let us pray, instead, for *all* of us.
For all of us to know that we can bring our problems to God whenever we feel ready to let go
of them."

He raised his arms and the silence fell, as if
he had somehow cast it forth in front of him.

Sister Bertha is a nosy-bones, Ian thought
distinctly. *And I hate that tomato-soup color she
dyes her hair.*

After the Benediction, he was the first one out
the door. He left behind even Mrs. Jordan, who
most likely would want to walk home with him,
and he set off at a brisk, angry pace. So the last
thing he expected to hear was Reverend Emmett calling his name. "Brother Ian!"

Ian stopped and turned.

The man must have run the whole way. He
must have left his flock unattended, his Bible
open on the counter, his church lit up and un-
locked. But he wasn't even breathing hard. He
approached at a saunter, seemingly absorbed

in slipping on a cardigan the same color as the dusk.

"May I tag along?" he asked.

Ian shrugged.

They set off together more slowly.

"Of course, it does come down to whether a person feels ready to let go," Reverend Emmett said in the most conversational tone.

Ian kicked a Dixie cup out of his path.

"Some people prefer to hug their problems to themselves," Reverend Emmett said.

Ian wheeled on him, clenching his fists in his pockets. He said, "*This* is my life? This is all I get? It's so settled! It's so cut and dried! After this there's no changing! I just lean into the burden of those children forever, is that what you're saying?"

"No," Reverend Emmett told him.

"You said that! You said to lean into my burden!"

"But those children will be grown in no time," Reverend Emmett said. "*They* are not the burden I meant. The burden is forgiveness."

"Okay," Ian said. "Fine. How much longer till I'm forgiven?"

"No, no. The burden is that *you* must forgive."

"Me?" Ian said. He stared at Reverend Emmett. "Forgive who?"

"Why, your brother and his wife, of course."

Ian said nothing.

Finally Reverend Emmett asked, "Shall we walk on?"

So they did. They passed a lone man waiting at a bus stop, a shopkeeper locking up his store. Each footstep, Ian felt, led him closer to something important. He was acutely conscious all at once of motion, of flux and possibility. He felt he was an arrow—not an arrow shot by God but an arrow heading toward God, and if it took every bit of this only life he had, he believed that he would get there in the end.

7

ORGANIZED MARRIAGE

It was Agatha who came up with the notion of finding Ian a wife. Agatha was graduating that June; she'd had word she'd been accepted at her first-choice college; she would soon be leaving the family forever. And one night in April she walked into the living room and told the other two, "I'm worried about Ian."

Thomas and Daphne glanced over at her. (There was a commercial on just then, anyhow.) She stood in the doorway with her arms folded, her tortoiseshell glasses propped on top of her head in a purposeful, no-nonsense manner. "Who will keep him company after we're gone?" she asked.

"You're the only one going," Daphne told her. "He's still got me and Thomas."

"Not for long," Agatha said.

Their eyes slid back to the Late Late Movie.

But they knew she had a point. In a sense, Thomas was already gone. He was a freshman in high school now and he had a whole outside existence—a raft of friends and a girlfriend and an extracurricular schedule so full that he was seldom home for supper. As for Daphne, well, their grandma liked to say that Daphne was eleven going on eighty. She dressed like a tiny old Gypsy—muddled layers of clothing, all tatters and gold thread, purchased on her own at thrift shops—and was generally off in the streets somewhere managing very capably.

"Pretty soon all he'll have will be Grandma and Grandpa," Agatha said. "He'll be taking care of them like always and shopping and driving the car and helping with the housework. What kind of life is that? I think he ought to get married."

Now she had their attention.

"And since he doesn't seem to know any women, I think we'll have to find him one."

"Miss Pennington," Daphne said instantly.

"Who?"

"Miss Ariana Pennington, my teacher," Daphne said.

It was just that easy.

Miss Pennington had been teaching fifth grade for only the past two years, so neither Thomas nor Agatha had had her when they were fifth-graders. Thomas knew her by sight, though. Every boy in the neighborhood knew her by sight. Not even the youngest, it seemed, was immune to her hourglass figure or her mane of extravagant curly brown hair. Agatha, on the other hand, had to be shown who it was they were talking about.

So on a Friday afternoon just before the last bell, when Thomas was supposedly in a Leaders of Tomorrow meeting and Agatha had study hall, they met at the old cracked porcelain water fountain behind Poe High and walked the two blocks to the grade school. Almost no other students were out at this hour, but Thomas greeted by name the few who were—those excused early for dental appointments and such. "Thomas!" they said, and, "Yo, man, what you up to?" Agatha merely stalked on, blank-faced. She wore a bulbous down jacket over a skirt that stopped in the middle of her chunky bare knees—not an outfit any of her classmates would have been caught dead in, but then Agatha never concerned herself with appearances. She was supremely indifferent, impervious, striding on without Thomas until he ran to catch up with her.

At Reese Elementary Thomas took the lead,

choosing a side door instead of the main entrance and climbing the stairs two steps at a time. Outside Room 223 he paused, turned toward Agatha, and beckoned.

Through the small window they saw rows of fifth-graders bent over their books. Miss Pennington walked among them, tall and willowy, pausing first at this desk and then at that one to answer questions. You would never take her for a woman of the seventies. In an era when teachers had started wearing pants to work, Miss Pennington wore a silky white blouse and a flaring black skirt cinched tightly at the waist, sheer nylon stockings, and high-heeled patent leather pumps—the sexy, constricting clothes of the fifties. Her hair was shoulder-length and her fingernails were sharp red spears, and her makeup—when she turned as if by instinct and glanced toward the door—was seen to be vivid and expertly applied: deep red lipstick emphasizing her full lips, and plummy rouge and luminous blue eyeshadow. Thomas and Agatha stepped back hastily, out of her line of vision. They looked at each other.

"Well?" Thomas asked.

"She's kind of . . . brightly colored, isn't she?"

"Oh, Agatha, you don't know anything. She's gorgeous! Women are *supposed* to look that way. That's the type guys dream about."

"Oh," Agatha said.

"She's perfect," Thomas told her.

"All right," Agatha said crisply. "Let's get this thing rolling, then."

Daphne told Ian he needed to make an appointment for a parent-teacher conference. "Conference?" Ian said. "*Now* what'd you do?"

"I didn't do anything! How come you always think the worst of me? I just want you to talk to my teacher about my homework."

"What about it?"

"Well, like, are you supposed to help me with it, or let me do it on my own?"

"But I already let you do it on your own. What are you saying, you need help?"

"It might be a good idea."

"Why don't I just go ahead and help, then? We'll set aside a time each evening."

"No, first I think you should ask Miss Pennington," Daphne told him.

He gazed down at her. He and she were doing the supper dishes (she had offered to dry) while the other two sat at the kitchen table, ostensibly studying. Now Agatha said, "It wouldn't hurt to show the teacher you take an interest, Ian."

"Well, of course I take an interest," Ian told her. "Good grief, I'm one of the grade mothers. I baked six dozen cookies for Parents' Night and delivered them in person."

"You never went in for a private conference, though," Daphne said.

"I thought that was an improvement. Your first full year in school I haven't been issued a summons."

"Well, all right," Daphne said sorrowfully. "If you don't want to keep the lines of communication open . . ."

"Keep the what? Lines of what? Well, shoot," Ian said, setting a stack of bowls in the sink. "Fine, I'll go. Are you satisfied?"

Daphne nodded. So did the other two, but Ian had his back to them and he didn't see.

Daphne reported that the parent-teacher conference went very well. "He was wearing that grown-up shirt we bought him for Christmas," she told Thomas and Agatha, "the one he has to iron. He came to school straight from work and he had his wood-chip smell about him. I'm pretty sure she noticed."

"Maybe he should've worn a suit," Thomas said. "Miss Pennington's always so dressy. We don't want her to think he's just a laborer."

"He *is* just a laborer," Daphne said. "What's wrong with that?"

"Yes, but first she should see he's intelligent and all," Thomas said. "Then afterwards she could find out what he does for a living."

"Well, too late now. Anyhow: so I used their

first names in the introductions, just like Agatha told me. I said, 'Ian Bedloe, Ariana Pennington. I believe you-all have met before.' "

"It should have been the other way around," Agatha told her. " 'Ariana Pennington, Ian Bedloe.' "

"Oh, big deal, Agatha. So then they shook hands and Miss Pennington asked Ian what she could do for him. They sat down at two desks in the back of the room and I stood next to Ian."

"You were supposed to leave them on their own."

"I couldn't. They sort of, like, included me. Ian said, 'Daphne, here, wanted me to discuss with you . . .' and all like that."

"Well, I don't guess it matters much at this stage," Thomas told Agatha. "They wouldn't right away start making out or anything."

"Miss Pennington wore her blue scoop-necked dress," Daphne said. "We all just wait for that dress. It's got a lacy kind of petticoat showing underneath, either attached or not attached; we never can make up our minds. And usually she pins this heart-shaped locket pin to her front but not this time, and I was glad. We think there may be a boyfriend's photograph inside."

"You mean she might already have somebody?" Thomas asked, frowning.

"Who cares? Now that she's met Ian."

"She liked him, then," Agatha said.

"She had to like him. He was sitting where the sun hit his hair and turned it almost yellow on top, you know how it does. He kept his cap off and he didn't say anything religious, not once. Miss Pennington kept smiling at him and tipping her head while he talked."

"Gosh, this is going better than we'd hoped," Thomas said.

"And when he called her 'Miss Pennington,' she put her hand on his arm and said, 'Please. Ariana.' "

"Gosh."

"She told him I was one of her very best students and she didn't know why I was concerned about my homework, but she appreciated his coming and she just thought it was so refreshing to see a man involve himself in his children's education."

"She did understand we're not *really* his, didn't she?" Agatha asked. "She knows he's not married, doesn't she?"

"She must, because she had my file opened out in front of her. And besides, Ian told her, 'It's not only me who's involved. Both their grandparents used to be teachers, and they help quite a bit, too.' "

"Well, I wish he hadn't of said that. It's *mostly* him, after all."

Thomas said, "No, this way is better. Now she

doesn't think she'll be totally saddled with kids when she marries him."

"Everyone in my school is going to die of jealousy," Daphne said. "Boy! I can't wait to see DeeDee Hutchins's face, and that stuck-up Lolly Kaplan."

"So get to the end," Agatha told her. "Did you do like we planned about dinner?"

"I did exactly like we planned. When Ian got up to go he said, 'Well, I really do thank you, Miss Pennington—' "

"Not 'Ariana'?"

" 'Miss Pennington,' he said, and I said, 'Me too, thanks; and Ian, can't we ask her to dinner sometime?' "

"That did it," Thomas said. "No way to back out of that."

"Well, he tried. He said, 'Oh, Daph, Miss Pennington has a very busy schedule,' but she said, 'Please, it's Ariana. And I'd love to come.' "

"Goody," Agatha said.

"Except . . . Ian is so backward."

"Backward?"

"He said, 'To tell the truth, our family's not much for entertaining.' "

The other two groaned.

"But Miss Pennington told him, 'Oh, I wouldn't expect a banquet!' and then she laughed and put her hand on his arm again."

"She's nuts about him," Thomas said.

"Except Ian moved his arm away. In fact every time she did it he moved his arm away."

"He's playing hard to get."

That made Daphne and Agatha look more cheerful. Thomas was the social one, after all. He was almost frantically social; he could skate so deftly through any situation. He was the one who knew how the world worked.

On the night Miss Pennington came to dinner, their grandma fixed roast beef. (The Bedloes confined themselves now to foods that didn't require much preparation: roasts and baked chicken and burgers.) She had trouble holding utensils, and so she let Agatha make the gravy. "Pour in a dab of water," she instructed, "and now a dab more . . ."

Thomas was setting the table, arranging the good silver on the place mats their grandma had already spread around. He came to the kitchen with a fistful of forks and said, "How come you've got nine place mats out?"

"Why, how many should we have?" their grandma asked.

"It's only us and Miss Pennington: seven."

"And also Mr. Kitt and the woman from your church," their grandma said. "That comes to nine."

Mr. Kitt needed no explanation; he was the authentic, certified vagrant who'd been more or less adopted by Second Chance last winter. But the woman? "What woman?" Thomas asked.

"Why, I don't know," their grandma said. "Some new member or visitor or something, I guess. You'll have to ask Ian."

The three of them looked at each other. "Rats," Daphne said.

"I'm sure we'll like her," their grandma told them. "Ian said as long as we were going to all this trouble, we might as well invite her. And we've never had Mr. Kitt once; Ian says you're the only people in church who haven't."

"Yes, but . . . rats," Daphne said. "This was supposed to be just Miss Pennington!"

"Oh, don't worry, we won't neglect your precious teacher," their grandma said merrily.

Last week they'd heard a new neighbor ask their grandma how many children she had. They'd listened for her answer: would she say two, or three? What *did* you say when a son had died? But she fooled them; she said, "Only one that's still at home." As if the people who stuck by you were all that counted, as if anybody not present didn't exist.

She probably thought it was fine for Ian to grow old all alone with his parents.

The first to arrive was Mr. Kitt. Mr. Kitt wasn't really a vagrant anymore. He had a job sweeping floors at Brother Simon's place of business and he lived rent-free above Sister Nell's garage. But people at church still traded him proudly back and forth for meals, and he continued to look the part as if he felt it was expected of him. Gray whiskers a quarter-inch long shadowed his pale face, and his clothes always sagged, oddly empty, even when they were the expensive tailored suits handed down from Sister Nell's father-in-law. On his feet he wore red sneakers, the stubby kind that toddlers wear. These made him walk very quietly, so when he followed Daphne into the living room he seemed awed and hesitant. "Oh, my," he said, peering around, "what a family, family type of house."

"Ian's not home from work yet," Daphne told him. The three children had been asked to make conversation while their grandma changed. Thomas said, "Won't you sit down?"

Mr. Kitt settled soundlessly on the front four inches of an armchair. "Last night I ate at Mrs. Stamey's," he told them. (Sister Myra's, he must mean. He refused to go along with the "Sister" and "Brother" custom.) "She served me a porterhouse steak her husband had cooked on the barbecue."

"We're just having roast beef," Agatha said.

"That's okay."

Their grandpa came down the stairs. In the doorway he stopped and said, "Why, hello there! Doug Bedloe."

"George Kitt," Mr. Kitt told him. He rose by degrees and they shook hands. Of the two men, Mr. Kitt was the more dressed up. Their grandpa wore his corduroys and the wrinkled leather slippers that had no heels. "Can I fix you a drink?" he asked Mr. Kitt.

"No, thank you. Drink has been my ruin."

"Ah," their grandpa said. He studied Mr. Kitt a moment. "You must be the fellow from Ian's church."

"I am."

"Well, my wife will be down any minute now. She's just putting on her face."

He took a seat on the couch next to Agatha. Agatha hadn't dressed up either—Agatha never dressed up—but Thomas and Daphne had taken special care. Thomas's heathery pullover matched the blue pinstripe in his shirt, and Daphne wore her favorite outfit: a purple gauze skirt that hung to her ankles and a man's fringed buckskin jacket. She was twisting the silver hoop in one earlobe, a nervous habit she had. One of her crumpled black boots kept jiggling up and down. "Did you remind Ian to come straight from work?" she asked Agatha.

"I reminded him at breakfast."

"I sure hope Miss Pennington doesn't get here before he does."

"Who's Miss Pennington?" their grandpa asked.

"My *teacher*, Grandpa. We *told* you all this."

"Oh. Right."

"My fifth-grade teacher."

"Right."

"Fifth grade?" Mr. Kitt asked, looking anxious. "I detested fifth grade."

"Well, you won't detest Miss Pennington," Daphne told him.

"Fifth grade was long division," Mr. Kitt said. "I used to erase holes in my paper."

"Miss Pennington's super nice and she lets us bring in comic books on Fridays."

The front door opened. "Here he is!" Daphne cried. But the first to enter the living room was a heavyset young woman in a business suit. Ian followed, carrying his lunch pail. He said, "Sorry if we're late."

We? The children looked at each other.

"This is Sister Harriet," Ian said. "She's new at our church. Harriet, this is my father, Doug Bedloe. You know Mr. Kitt, and I guess you've seen Thomas and Daphne at services. Over there is Agatha."

If Sister Harriet had seen them, they had not seen her; or else they'd forgotten. She was extremely forgettable. Her lank beige hair hung down her back, gathered ineptly by a plastic barrette at the nape of her neck. Her face was broad and plain and colorless, and her suit—a straight jacket and a midcalf-length skirt—was made of some cheap fabric without texture. Also she didn't seem to be wearing stockings. Her calves were blue-white, chalky, and her bulging black suede flats were rubbed smooth at the widest part of her feet.

"Oh, Mr. Bedloe," she said, "I'm so pleased to meet you at last. And Mr. Kitt, it's good to see you again." Then she went over to the children. "Thomas, I sat right behind you in church last Sunday. I'm Sister Harriet."

She held out her hand to each of them in turn—a square, mannish hand, with the fingernails trimmed straight across. There was a moment when the only sounds were shuffles and sheepish murmurs. "Um, how do you . . . nice to . . ." Then their grandma arrived. She was always slow on the stairs, gripping the banister heavily as she descended, but she must have guessed this evening that she was needed; for before she'd even entered the living room she was calling out, "Hello, there! Sorry I took so long!" This time the introductions went the way they were supposed to, with everyone talking at once and little compliments exchanged. "Isn't that a lovely pin!" Grandma told Sister Harriet, picking out the one attractive thing about her, and Sister Harriet said it used to be her great-aunt's. Then the doorbell rang and Ian went to admit Miss Pennington.

Miss Pennington looked just right. She was

one of those people who seem to know exactly what to wear for every occasion, and tonight she had not overdressed, as other women might, nor did she make the mistake of shocking them with something excessively informal and off-dutyish. She had on the flowered shirtwaist she had worn all day at school, with a soft flannel blazer added and a double strand of pearls at her throat. The way she moved through the group, greeting everyone so pleasantly, even Mr. Kitt and Sister Harriet, made the children grin at each other. When she came to Daphne, she gave her a little hug. She might as well be family.

The talk before dinner, unfortunately, centered on Sister Harriet. It appeared that Sister Harriet came from a small town near Richmond, and at first she'd found Baltimore a very hard place to make friends in. "The company where I work is as big as my whole town," she said. "At home it was a tiny branch office! Here they have so many employees you just can't hope to get to know them all."

"What company is that?" Miss Pennington asked her.

"Northeastern Life. They handle every type of insurance: not only life but auto, disability—"

"Insurance? But aren't you a nun?"

"Why, no," Sister Harriet said.

Mr. Kitt started laughing. He said, "Ha! That's a good one. Nun! That's a good one."

"It's just what we call each other in church," Sister Harriet told Miss Pennington. "Ian's and my church. We call each other 'Sister' and 'Brother.' But you can say 'Harriet,' if you like."

"Oh, I see," Miss Pennington said.

The three children looked down at their laps. How irksome, that "Ian's and my." As if Ian and Sister Harriet were somehow linked! But Miss Pennington kept her encouraging expression and said, "I imagine church would be an ideal place to make friends."

"It surely is," Sister Harriet told her. And then she had to go on and on about it, how nice and down-home it was, how welcoming, how in some ways it reminded her of the little church she'd grown up in except that there they'd held Prayer Meeting on Tuesdays, not Wednesdays, and they didn't approve of cosmetics and they believed that "gosh" and "darn" were cuss words; but other than that . . .

While Sister Harriet talked, Ian smiled at her. He was sitting on the piano bench with his long, blue-jeaned legs stretched in front of him and his elbows propped on the keyboard lid. One last shaft of sunlight was slanting through the side window, and it struck his face in such a way that the peach fuzz on his cheekbones turned to purest gold. Surely Miss Pennington would have to notice. How could she resist him? He looked dazzling.

At dinner Mr. Kitt offered an account of his entire fifth-grade experience. "I do believe," he said, "that everything that's gone wrong in my life can be directly traced to fifth grade. Before that, I was a roaring success. I had a reputation for smartness. It was me most often who got to clean the erasers or monitor the lunchroom, so much so that it was whispered about by some that I was teacher's pet. Then along comes fifth grade: Miss Pilchner. Lord, I can see her still. Brassy dyed hair curled real tight and short, and this great big squinty fake smile that didn't fool a person under age twenty. First day of school she asks me, 'Where's your ruled paper?' I tell her, 'I like to use unruled.' 'Well!' she says. Says, 'In *my* class, we have no special individuals with their own fancy-shmancy way of doing things.' Right then and there, I knew I'd hit hard times. And I never was a success after that, not then or ever again."

"Oh, Mr. Kitt," Miss Pennington said. "What a pity!"

"Well now, I, on the other hand," their grandpa said from the head of the table, "I was crazy about fifth grade. I had a teacher who looked like a movie star. Looked exactly like Lillian Gish. I planned to marry her."

This was a little too close for comfort; all three children shifted in their chairs. But Miss Pennington merely smiled and turned to Ian. She said, "Ian, I hope *you* have happy memories of fifth grade."

"Hmm? Oh, yes," Ian said without interest. He didn't look up from his plate; he was cutting his meat.

"Did you attend school here in Baltimore?" she asked him.

Her voice was so bendable; it curved toward him, cajoling, entwining. But Ian merely transferred his fork to his right hand, seeming to move farther from her in the process. "Yes," he said shortly, and he took a bite of meat and started chewing. Why was he behaving this way? He was acting like . . . well, like a laborer, in fact.

Finally their grandma spoke up in his place. "Yes, indeedy! He went all twelve years!" she said brightly. "And you know, Miss Pennington—"

"Ariana."

"Ariana, *I* was a teacher, back about a century ago."

"Oh, Ian mentioned that."

"I taught fourth grade in the dark, dark ages."

"Me too," Sister Harriet said suddenly.

Everyone looked at her.

"I taught seventh," she said. "But I wasn't very good at it."

Ian said, "Now, Harriet. I bet you were excellent."

"No," she said. "It's true. I just didn't have the—I don't know. The personality or something."

Well, *that* was for sure. The three children traded amused sidelong glints.

Leaning forward so earnestly that her bolsterlike bosom almost grazed her plate, Sister Harriet said, "Every day I went in was such a struggle, and I had no idea why. Then one night I dreamed this dream. I dreamed I was standing in front of my class explaining conjunctions, but gibberish kept coming out of my mouth. I said, '*Burble*-burble-burble.' The students said, 'Pardon?' I tried again; I said, '*Burble*-burble-burble.' In the dream I couldn't think what had happened, but when I woke up I knew right away. You see, the Lord was trying to tell me something. 'Harriet,' He was saying, 'you don't speak these children's language. You ought to get out of teaching.' And so I did."

"Well, my goodness," their grandma said, sitting back in her chair.

But Ian was regarding Sister Harriet seriously. "I think that was very brave of you," he told her.

She flushed and said, "Oh, well . . ."

"No, really. To admit the whole course of your life was wrong and decide to change it completely."

"That does take courage," Miss Pennington

said. "I agree with Ian." And she sent him a radiant smile that he didn't appear to notice.

Was he blind, or what?

This past Easter, one of the foreigners had dropped by with his younger sister who was visiting from her college. She might have stepped out of the *Arabian Nights*; she was dark and slim and beautiful, with a liquid, demure way of speaking. Twice her brother had made pointed references to her eligibility. "High time she find a husband and settle down, get herself a green card, develop some children," he said, and he told them it was up to him to locate a suitable husband for her, since his family still believed in what he called organized marriage. But Ian hadn't seemed to understand, and later when Daphne asked if he'd thought the sister was pretty he said, "Pretty? Who? Oh. No, I've never cared for women who wear seamed stockings."

They should have known right then that no one would ever meet his qualifications.

"Seconds, anyone?" their grandpa was asking. "Mr. Kitt? Miss Pennington? Ian, more roast beef?"

"I wonder," Ian said, "how many times we dream that kind of dream—something strange and illogical—and fail to realize God is trying to tell us something."

Oh, perfect. Now he was turning all holy on

them. "Ariana," their grandma said hastily, "help yourself to the gravy." But Miss Pennington was watching Ian, and her smile was glazing over the way people's always did when the bald, uncomfortable sound of God's name was uttered in social surroundings.

"It's easier to claim it's something else," Ian said. "Our subconscious, or random brain waves. It's easier to pretend we don't know what God's showing us."

"That is so, so true," Sister Harriet told him.

Miss Pennington's smile seemed made of steel now.

"Damn," Daphne said.

Everybody looked at her. Their grandma said, "Daphne?"

"Well, excuse me," Daphne said, "but I just can't—" And then she sat up straighter and said, "I just can't help thinking about this dream I had a couple of nights ago."

"Oh, tell us," their grandma said, sounding relieved.

"I was standing on a mountaintop," Daphne said. "God was speaking to me from a thundercloud." She looked around at the others— their polite, attentive faces, all prepared to appreciate whatever she had to say. " 'Daphne,' He said—He had this big, deep, rumbling voice. 'Daphne Bedloe, beware of strangers!' "

"And quite right He was, too," their grandma

said briskly, but she seemed less interested now in hearing the rest of it. "Doug, could you send the salad bowl this way?"

" 'Daphne Bedloe, a stranger is going to start hanging around your uncle,' " Daphne bellowed. " 'Somebody fat, not from Baltimore, chasing after your uncle Ian.' "

"Why, *Daphne!*" their grandma said, and she dropped a clump of lettuce on the tablecloth.

Later, Daphne argued that their grandma was the one who'd hurt Sister Harriet's feelings. After all, what had Daphne said that was so terrible? Nothing. She had merely described a dream. It was their grandma who had connected the dream to Sister Harriet. All aghast she'd turned to Sister Harriet and said, "I'm so sorry. I can't imagine what's got into her." Then Sister Harriet, white-lipped, said, "That's okay," and sipped shakily from her water glass, not looking at the others. But she wouldn't have taken it personally if their grandma had not apologized, Daphne said; and Thomas and Agatha agreed. "She's right," Agatha told Ian. "It's not *Daphne's* fault if someone fat was in her dream."

This was after their guests had departed. They had left at the earliest acceptable moment—Miss Pennington reflective, Mr. Kitt bluff and unaware, Sister Harriet declining with surprising firmness Ian's offer to walk her home. As soon as they were gone, the grandparents had turned and climbed the stairs to their bedroom.

"Daphne was only making conversation," Thomas told Ian, but Ian said, "Yeah, sure," in a toneless voice, and then he went into the dining room and started clearing the table.

They followed, humble and overeager. They stacked plates and took them to the kitchen, scraped leftovers into smaller containers, collected pots and pans from the stove while Ian ran a sinkful of hot water. He didn't say a word to them; he seemed to know that all three of them were to blame and not just Daphne.

They couldn't bear it when Ian was mad at them.

And worse than mad: dejected. All his fine plans come to nothing. Oh, what had they done? He looked so forlorn. He stood at the sink so wearily, swabbing the gravy tureen.

Last month he'd brought home a saltcellar shaped like a robot. When you pressed a button in its back it would start walking on two rigid plastic legs, but they hadn't realized that and they hadn't paid it much attention, frankly, when he set it among the supper dishes. He kept asking, "Doesn't anyone need salt? Who wants salt? Shall I just pass the salt?" Finally Agatha said, "Huh? Oh, fine," and he pressed the robot's button and leaned forward, chortling, as it toddled across the table to her. His mouth was perked with glee and his hands were clasped together underneath his chin and he kept darting hopeful glances into their faces, and luckily they'd noticed in time and put on amazed and delighted expressions.

"Dust off the fruitcake, it's Christmas again," he always caroled in December, inventing his own tune as he went along, and on Valentine's Day he left a chocolate heart on each child's breakfast plate before he went off to work, which tended to make them feel a little sad because really all of them—even Daphne—had reached the stage where nonfamily valentines were the only ones that mattered. In fact there were lots of occasions when they felt sad for him. He seemed slightly out of step, so often—his jokes just missing, his churchy language setting strangers' eyes on guard, his clothes inappropriately boyish and plain as if he'd been caught in a time warp. The children loved him and winced for him, both. They kept a weather eye out for other people's reactions to him, and they were constantly prepared to bristle and turn ferocious on his behalf.

One vacation when they were little he took a swim in the ocean and told them to wait on the shore. He swam out beyond the breakers, so far he was only a dot, and the three of them sat down very suddenly on the sand and Daphne started crying. He was leaving them forever and never coming back, it looked like. A man standing ankle-deep told his wife, "That fellow's *gone*," and Daphne cried harder and the other two grew teary as well. But then Ian turned and swam in again. Soon he was striding out of the surf hitching up his trunks and streaming water and shining in the sun, safely theirs after all, solid and reliable and dear.

He lowered a serving bowl into the sink. He swished it back and forth. Daphne said, "Ian? Want for us to take over now?" but he said, "No, thanks." The others sent her sympathetic looks. Never mind. He wasn't the type to carry a grudge. Tomorrow he would view this in a whole new light; he would realize they hadn't meant to cause any harm.

All they had wanted, he would see, was somebody wonderful enough to deserve him.

8

I SHOULD NEVER TELL
YOU ANYTHING

When Reverend Emmett had his heart attack, the Church of the Second Chance was forced to manage without him for most of the month of October. The first Sunday a retired Baptist minister, Dr. Benning, gave the sermon, but Dr. Benning had to leave immediately afterwards for a bus tour of the Sun Belt and so the second Sunday Sister Nell's uncle filled in—a nondenominationalist named Reverend Lewis who kept mixing up his "Thy" and his "Thou." "We beseech Thee to flood Thou blessings upon this Thou congregation," he intoned, and Ian was reminded of the substitute teachers he'd had in grade school who had always seemed just the slightest bit lacking. The sermon was based on

Paul's first letter to Timothy. Many might not realize, Reverend Lewis said, that it was *love* of money, and not money alone, that was held to be the root of all evil. Ian, who had never had much money or much love of money either, held back a yawn. *All* evil? Wasn't that the phrase to examine?

On the third Sunday not even Reverend Lewis was available and they skipped the sermon altogether. They sang a few hymns and then bowed their heads for a closing prayer delivered in an uncertain voice by Brother Simon. "Dear God," Brother Simon said, "please give Reverend Emmett back to us as soon as possible." The fourth Sunday Reverend Emmett returned, gaunter and paler than ever, and preached a message of reassurance. Afterwards, while shaking Ian's hand at the door, he asked if they might have a little talk.

So Ian sent Daphne on home without him and waited at one side, listening to each member inquire after Reverend Emmett's health. When the last of the congregation had departed he followed Reverend Emmett through the door behind the counter, into what passed for an office. Tangled pipes ran overhead and giant bolt holes marred the floor. In the center of the room stood an antique desk and swivel chair that must have come down from Reverend Emmett's family, with two blue velvet armchairs facing them. Reverend Emmett gestured Ian into one armchair but he himself remained on his feet, distractedly running a hand through his hair. As usual, he wore a white shirt without a tie and skinny black trousers. Ian guessed he must be in his mid-forties by now or maybe even older, but he still had that awkward, amateurish air about him, and his Adam's apple jutted above his collar like a half-grown boy's.

"Brother Ian," he said, "while I was in the hospital I did some serious thinking. It's unusual to have a heart attack at my age. It doesn't bode well for the future. I've been thinking I should face the fact that I'm not going to live forever."

Ian opened his mouth to protest, but Reverend Emmett raised a palm. "Oh," he said, "I don't plan on dying tomorrow or anything like that. Still, this kind of thing makes you realize. It's time we discussed my replacement."

"Replacement?" Ian asked.

"Someone who'll take over the church when I'm gone. Someone who might help out before I'm gone, even. Ease my workload."

Ian said, "But—"

But you ARE the church, he wanted to say. Only that sounded blasphemous, and would have distressed Reverend Emmett.

"I believe you ought to start training for the ministry," Reverend Emmett told him.

Ian wondered if he'd heard right.

"You know our congregation is fairly unedu-
cated, by and large," Reverend Emmett said,
finally sitting in the other armchair. "I think most
of them would feel the job was beyond them.
And yet we do want someone who's familiar with
our ways."

"But I'm not educated either," Ian said. "I've
had one semester of college."

"Well, the good thing about this heart attack
is, it serves as advance warning. It gives us a
chance to get you trained. I realize you might
not want to follow my own route—university and
such. I was younger and had more time. You're
what, thirty-four? Still, Lawrence Bible School,
down in Richmond—"

"Richmond! I can't go to Richmond!"

"Why not?"

"I have responsibilities here!"

"But surely those are just about finished
now, aren't they?" Reverend Emmett asked.
"Shouldn't you be thinking ahead now?"

Ian sat forward, clamping his knees. "Reverend Emmett," he said, "Daphne at sixteen is
more trouble than all three of them were at any
other age. Do you know her principal has me
picking her up at school every day? I have to
take off work and pick her up and drive her home
in person. And it has to be me, not my father,
because it turns out my father believes anything

she tells him. Both my parents: they're so far behind the times, they just don't fully comprehend what modern kids can get into. You honestly suppose I could leave her with them and head off to Richmond?"

Reverend Emmett waited till Ian had wound down. Then he said, "What grade is Daphne in in school?"

"She's a junior."

"So two more years," Reverend Emmett said. "Maybe less, if she straightens out before she graduates. And I'm certain that she will straighten out. Daphne's always been a strong person. But even if she doesn't, in two years she'll be on her own. Meanwhile, you can start with a few courses here in Baltimore. Night school. Towson State, or maybe community college."

Ian said, "But also."

"Yes?"

"I mean, shouldn't I hear a *call* to the ministry?"

Reverend Emmett said, "Maybe I'm the call."

Ian blinked.

"And maybe not, of course," Reverend Emmett told him. "But it's always a possibility."

Then he rose and once again shook Ian's hand, with those long, dry fingers so bony they fairly rattled.

When Ian arrived home, Daphne was talking on the kitchen telephone and her grandmother was setting various dishes on the table. Sunday dinner would apparently be leftovers—tiny bowls of cold peas, soggy salad, and reheated stew from a tin. "Cool," Daphne was saying. "We can get together later and study for that Spanish test." Something artificial and showy in her tone made Ian flick a glance at Bee, but Bee missed his point and merely said, "Well? How was church?"

"It was all right."

"Could you tell your father lunch is on?"

He called down to the basement and then beckoned Daphne from the phone. "I gotta go now," she said into the receiver. "My folks are starting brunch."

"Oh, is this brunch?" Ian asked his mother.

She smiled and set a loaf of bread on the table.

Once they were seated Ian said the blessing hurriedly, conscious of his father drumming his fingers on his knees. Then each of them embarked on a different meal. Doug reached for the stew, Ian put together a peanut butter sandwich, and Daphne, who was a vegetarian, dreamily plucked peas from the bowl one by one with her fingers. Bee finished anything the others wouldn't—more a matter of housekeeping than personal taste, Ian thought.

He missed the two older children. Thomas was away at Cornell and Agatha was in her second year of medical school. Most meals now were just this makeshift, often served on only half the table because Daphne's homework covered the other half. And most of their conversations felt disjointed, absentminded, like the scattered bits of talk after the main guests have left the room.

"Me and Gideon are going to study Spanish at his house," Daphne announced into one stretch of silence.

"Gideon and I," her grandmother said.

Ian asked, "Will Gideon's mother be home?"

"Sure."

Ian scrutinized her. Gideon was Daphne's boyfriend, an aloof, chilly type. Evidently his mother, a divorcee, had a boyfriend of her own. She was often out somewhere when Ian stopped by for Daphne.

"Maybe you could study here instead," he told her.

But Daphne said, "I already promised I'd go there." Then she picked up her empty bowl and licked it daintily, like a cat. Everyone noticed but no one objected. You had to select your issues, with someone like Daphne.

It unsettled Ian, sometimes, how much Daphne reminded him of Lucy. She had Lucy's small face and her curly black hair, although it was cut short and ragged. She had her froggy voice. Even in voluminous army fatigues, her slender, fine bones seemed so neatly turned that they might have been produced by a lathe. Her eyes were her own, though: still a dense, navy blue. And her own native scent of vanilla underlay the smells of cigarettes and motor oil and leather.

At the end of the meal Ian's father rose and brought a bowl of instant pudding from the refrigerator. He wiggled it at the others inquiringly, but Bee said, "No, thanks," and Daphne shook her head. "All the more for me, then," Doug said cheerfully, and he sat down and started eating directly from the bowl.

Was it because of the Sugar Rule that Daphne had declined? No, probably not. This was a girl who drank beer in parked cars during lunch hour, according to her principal. But she did continue to go to church every Sunday, singing the hymns lustily and bowing her head during prayers, when most other young people lost interest as soon as they reached their teens. And she flung herself into Good Works with real spirit. Whether she was actually a believer, though, Ian couldn't decide, and something kept him from asking.

There was a knock at the kitchen door, a single, surly thud, and they looked over to find Gideon surveying them through the windowpanes. "Oops! I'm off," Daphne said. No question of inviting Gideon in; he didn't talk to grownups. All they saw of him was the tilt of his sharp face and the curtain of straight blond hair, and then Daphne spun through the door and the two of them were gone. "Daph? Oh, goodness, she'll freeze to death," Bee said.

Ian wished Daphne's freezing to death were the worst he had to worry about.

Doug and Bee went upstairs for their Sunday nap and Ian did the dishes. Scraping the last of the pudding into a smaller container, he thought again about Reverend Emmett's proposal. Bible School! He had a flash of himself packing the car to leave home—participating in the September ritual that he had watched so often from the sidelines. The car stuffed to the ceiling with clothes and LP records, his parents standing by to wave him off. Maybe even a roof rack, with a bike or a stereo lashed on top. Or a butterfly chair like his former roommate's. Provided they still made butterfly chairs.

Over the years he had often wondered whatever had become of his roommate. He had imagined Winston proceeding through school and graduating and finding a job. By now he would be well established, probably in some field involving creative thought and invention. He had probably made a name for himself.

Ian glanced down at the pudding bowl and realized he had been eating each spoonful as he scraped it up. The inside of his mouth felt thick and coated. An unfamiliar sweetness clogged his throat.

At work he was training a new employee, a stocky, bearded black man named Rafael. He was giving his usual speech about the importance of choosing your wood. "Me, I always go for cherry if I can," he said. "It's the friendliest, you could put it. The most obedient."

"Cherry," the man said, nodding.

"It's very nearly *alive*. It changes color over time and it even changes shape and it breathes."

Rafael suddenly squinted at him, as if checking on his sanity.

The shop had seven employees now, not counting the high-school girl who came in afternoons to type and do the paperwork. (And they probably *shouldn't* count her; sometimes her order sheets were so garbled that Ian had to sit down at the typewriter and place his fingers wrongly on the keys so as to figure out what, for instance, she'd meant by "nitrsi.") All around the room various carpenters worked on their separate projects. They murmured companionably among themselves but left Ian alone mostly. He knew they considered him peculiar. A couple of years ago he had made the mistake of trying to talk about Second Chance with Greg, who hap-

pened to be going through some troubles. Forever after that Greg kept his distance and so did
all the others, apparently tipped off. They were
polite but embarrassed, wary. As for Mr. Brant,
he was even less company than usual these
days. It was said that his wife had left him for a
younger man. The one who said it was Mrs.
Brant's niece Jeannie, who didn't work there
anymore but sometimes dropped by to visit. Mr.
Brant himself never mentioned his wife.

Last spring, Mrs. Brant had paused to admire
a bench Ian was sanding and she had softly but
deliberately laid a hand on top of his. Her husband was in his rear office and the others were
taking a break. Mrs. Brant had looked up into
Ian's eyes with an oddly cool expression, as if
this were some kind of test. Ian wasn't completely surprised (several times, women who
knew his religious convictions had started behaving very forwardly, evidently finding him a
challenge), and he dealt with it fairly well, he
thought. He had merely slid his hand out from
under and left her with the sandpaper, pretending he'd mistaken her move for an offer to help.
And of course he had said nothing to her husband. But not two months later Jeannie announced that she was gone, and then Ian
thought maybe he should have said something
after all. "Mr. Brant," he should have said, "it

seems to me your wife is acting lonely." Or, "Wouldn't you and Mrs. Brant like to take a trip together or something?"

But *telling* was what he had promised himself he would never do again.

Oh, there were so many different ways you could go wrong. No wonder he loved woodwork! He showed Rafael the cherrywood nightstand he had finished the day before. The drawer glided smoothly, like satin, without a single hitch.

While the other men took their afternoon break, Ian grabbed his jacket and drove off to fetch Daphne from school. He could manage the round trip in just over twenty minutes when everything went on schedule, but of course it seldom did. Today, for instance, he must have left the shop too early. When he parked in front of the school he found he had several minutes to kill, and even longer if Daphne, as usual, came out late or had to run back in for somethingshe'd forgotten. So he cut the engine and stepped from the car. The air was warm and heavy and windy, as if an autumn storm might be brewing. Behind him, another car pulled up. A freckled woman in slacks got out and said, "What, we're early?"

"So it seems," Ian said. Then, because he felt foolish just standing around with her, he put his hands in his pockets and ambled toward the building. Scudding clouds glared off the second-floor windows—the art-room windows, Ian recalled, and Miss Dunlap's world-history windows, although Miss Dunlap must have retired or even died by now. Two boys in track suits jogged toward him on the sidewalk, separated around him, and jogged on. He wondered if they guessed what he was doing here. ("That's Daphne Bedloe's uncle; she's on suspended suspension and has to go home under guard.") It occurred to him that Daphne would be mortified if anyone she knew caught sight of him. He circled the school, therefore, and kept going. He passed the little snack shop where he and Cicely used to sit all afternoon over a couple of cherry Cokes, and he came to the Methodist church with its stained-glass window full of stern, narrow angels. One of the church's double doors stood open. Almost with-out thinking, he climbed the steps and went inside.

No lights were lit, but his eyes adjusted quickly to the gloom. He made out rows of cushioned pews and a carved wooden pulpit up front, with another stained-glass window high in the wall behind it. This one showed Jesus in a white robe, barefoot, holding His hands palm forward at His sides and gazing down at Ian kindly. Ian slid into a pew and rested his elbows on the pew ahead of him. He looked up into Jesus' face. He said,

Would it be possible for me to have some kind of sign?

Nothing fancy. Just something more definite than Reverend Emmett offering a suggestion.

He waited. He let the silence swell and grow.

But then the school bell rang—an extended jangle that reminded him of those key chains made from tiny metal balls—and his concentration was broken. He sighed and stood up. Anyhow, he had probably been presumptuous to ask.

In the doorway, looking out, he saw the first of the school crowd passing. He saw Gideon with a redheaded girl, his arm slung carelessly around her neck so they kept bumping into each other as they walked.

Gideon?

There was no mistaking that veil of blond hair, though, or the hunched, skulking posture. Almost as if this were Ian's love, not Daphne's, he felt his heart stop. He saw the redhead crane upward for a kiss and he drew his breath in sharply and stepped back into the shadow of the door.

By the time he reached the car, Daphne was waiting in the front seat. The car's interior smelled of breath mints and tobacco. "Where've you *been?*" she squawked as he got in, and he said, "Oh, around." He started the engine and pulled into the crawl of after-school traffic. "No Gideon?" he asked.

"It's his day to go to his dad's."

"Oh."

Daphne slid down in her seat and planted both feet on the dashboard. It appeared she was wearing combat boots—the most battered and scuffed he had ever laid eyes on. He hadn't realized they came that small. Her olive-drab trousers seemed intended for combat too, but the blouse beneath her leather jacket was fragile white gauze with two clusters of silver bells hanging from the ends of the drawstring. Any time she moved, she gave off a faint tinkling sound and the grudging creak of leather. How was it that such an absurd little person managed to touch him so?

He thought of Gideon's blond head next to the coppery, gleaming head of the girl in the crook of his arm.

Daphne, he should say, *there's something I have to tell you.*

But he couldn't.

He pulled up in front of their house and waited for her to get out, staring blankly through the windshield. To his surprise, he felt a kiss on his cheekbone as light as a petal. "Bye," she said, and she slipped away and shut the car door behind her. He could almost believe she knew what he had spared her.

One day last summer, while sitting with Honey-bunch in the veterinarian's waiting room, Ian had noticed a particularly sweet-faced golden re-triever. "Nice dog," he had told the owner, and the owner—a middle-aged woman—had smiled and said, "Yes, I've had a good number in my day, but this one: this is the dog of my life. You know how that is?"

He knew, all right.

Daphne, he felt, was the *child* of his life. He wondered if he would ever love a daughter of his own quite so completely.

It was true the older two were easier. In a sense, he even liked them better. Thomas was so merry and winsome, and Agatha had some-how smoothed the corners off that disconcerting style of hers—the bluntness transformed into calm assurance, the aggressive homeliness into an intriguing, black-and-white handsomeness. He enjoyed them the way he would enjoy long-time best friends who found the same things funny or upsetting and didn't need every last remark explained for them. In fact, you could say they were his *only* friends. But Daphne was the one who tugged at him most deeply.

And Daphne had always relied on him so, had

taken it for granted that he would stand by her no matter what. He still had an acute physical memory of the weight of her infant head resting in the cup of his palm. Even now, sometimes, she would lean against him while they watched TV and artlessly confide her secrets and gossip about her classmates and recount her hair-raising adventures that he had had no inkling of, thank heaven, while she was undergoing them. (She knew the city inside out, and slipped without a thought through neighborhoods that Ian himself avoided.) But if he showed any concern she would say, "I knew I shouldn't have told you! I should never tell you anything!" And when her friends came over she grew visibly remote from him, referring to him as "my uncle" as if he had no name and rolling her eyes when her girl-friends tried to make small talk or (on occasion) flirt with him. When he said he was off to Prayer Meeting, she told her friends he was "speaking metaphorically." When he enforced her curfew, she announced she was running away to live with her mother's people, who—she claimed—were worldly-wise and cosmopolitan and wouldn't *think* of making her return to their mansion at the dot of any set time. Ian had laughed, and then felt a deep, sad ache.

That was what Daphne brought out in him, generally. Laughter and an ache.

Reverend Emmett invited him to supper. "Just the two of us," he said on the phone, "to talk about the matter of your vocation." Ian gulped, but of course he accepted.

Reverend Emmett warned him that he wasn't much of a cook (his mother had died the previous fall) and so Ian asked if he could bring something. "Well," Reverend Emmett said, "you know that cold white sauce that people serve with potato chips?"

"Sauce? You mean dip?"

"It has little bits of dried onion scattered through it."

"You mean onion soup dip?"

"That must be it," Reverend Emmett said. "Mother used to make it whenever we had guests, but I haven't been able to find her recipe. I thought maybe you could ask *your* mother if she might fix it for us."

"Shoot, I'll fix it myself," Ian said. "I'll bring over the ingredients and show you how it's done."

"I'd appreciate that," Reverend Emmett told him.

So Tuesday evening, when Ian rang the doorbell, he was carrying a pint of sour cream and an envelope of the only brand of onion soup mix on the market that didn't contain any sugar. He had washed up after work but (mindful of the sin of superficiality) kept on his everyday clothes, and Reverend Emmett answered the door in jeans and one of his incongruously jaunty polo shirts. "Come in!" he said.

Ian said, "Thanks."

To tell the truth, he felt a bit apprehensive. He worried that Reverend Emmett labored under some false impression of him, for how else to explain his plans for Ian's future?

The living room was small but formal, slightly fussy—the mother's doing, Ian guessed. He had seen it on several occasions but had never gone beyond it, and now he looked about him curiously as he followed Reverend Emmett through a dim, flowered dining room to a kitchen that seemed to have been turned on end and shaken. "I thought I would make us a roast of beef," Reverend Emmett told him, and Ian said, "Sounds good." He wondered how a roast could have required all these pans and utensils. Maybe they'd been used for some side dish. "Would you like an apron to work in?" Reverend Emmett asked.

"It's not that complicated," Ian said. "Just a mixing bowl and a spoon will do."

He emptied the sour cream into the bowl Reverend Emmett brought him and then stirred in the soup mix, with Reverend Emmett hovering over the whole operation. "Why, there's really nothing to it," he said at the end.

"A veritable snap," Ian told him.

"Would you mind very much if we ate this in the kitchen? I'll need to keep an eye on the roast."

"That's fine with me."

They pulled two stools up to the counter, which was puddled with several different colors of liquids, and started on the chips and dip. Reverend Emmett gobbled chips wolfishly, a vein standing out in his temple as he chewed. (Had his doctor not warned him off fats?) He told Ian to call him Emmett. "Oh. All right . . . Emmett," Ian said. But he could force the name out only by imagining a "Reverend" in the gap, and he thought, from the way Reverend Emmett paused at each "Ian," that he was mentally inserting a "Brother."

"The fact is, um . . . Ian, hardly anyone I know calls me just plain Emmett anymore," Reverend Emmett said. "The fact is, this is a lonely profession. Oh, but not for *you*, it wouldn't be. You would be training among our own kind from the start. You would be making your friendships among them, and whoever you marry will know she shouldn't expect a half-timbered rectory and white-glove teas."

"But . . . Emmett," Ian said, "how can I be certain I'm cut out for this? I'm nothing but a carpenter."

"Our Lord was a carpenter," Reverend Emmett reminded him. He rose and went to peer inside the oven.

"Maybe so," Ian said, "but that might have been made a little too much of."

"Excuse me?"

"Well, we don't seem to hear about anything He built, do we? I wish we did. Sometimes when I look at paintings of Him I try to see what kind of muscles He had—whether they're the kind that come from hammering and sawing. I like to think He really did put a few bits of wood together; He didn't just stand around discussing theology with His friends while Joseph built the furniture."

Reverend Emmett set the roast on the counter and cocked his head at him thoughtfully.

"Or camel barns, or whatever it was," Ian said. "I hope I don't sound disrespectful."

"No, no . . . Could you bring in that salad, please?"

"But anyhow," Ian said. He picked up the salad bowl and followed Reverend Emmett into the dining room. "I'm getting off the track here. What I'm trying to say is, I'm not sure someone like me would be able to give people answers. When they had doubts and serious problems and such. All those ups and downs people go through, those little *hells* they go through—I wouldn't know what to tell them."

"But that's what Bible School teaches," Reverend Emmett said.

"It's not enough," Ian said.

They had both taken their seats now at the lace-covered table. Reverend Emmett was brandishing a bone-handled carving set. He paused and looked at Ian.

"I mean," Ian said, "*maybe* it's not enough."

"Well, of course it is," Reverend Emmett told him. "How do you suppose *I* learned? No one is born knowing."

He started slicing the roast. Plainly it was overdone—a charred black knob glued fast to the pan it had been cooked in. "When I began seminary," he said, sawing away manfully, "I had every possible misconception. I thought I was entering upon a career that was stable and comfortable, my father's career—a family business like any other. I envisioned how Father and I would sit together in his study over sherry and ponder obscure interpretations of the New Testament. Finally he would think well of me; he would listen to my opinions. But it didn't happen that way. What happened was I started reading the Bible, really reading it, and by the time I'd finished, my father wasn't speaking to me and my fiancée had left me and all my classmates thought I was some kind of mental case."

He laid down his knife. "Oh, dear," he said, "*that's* not the point I was trying to make."

Ian laughed. Reverend Emmett glanced at him in surprise, and then he laughed too.

"Also, this meat is inedible, isn't it?" he said. "Let's face it, I'm a terrible cook."

"We could always fill up on salad," Ian told him.

"We could, but you know what I'd really like? I'd like to polish off that dip, your onion dip. That was excellent!"

"Let's do it, then," Ian said.

So while he helped himself to the salad, Reverend Emmett went out to the kitchen for the chips and dip. "No," he said, returning, "that wasn't my point at all, believe me. No, my point was . . . well, the ministry is like anything else: a matter of trial and error. I've made so many errors! In the hospital it seemed they all came back to me. I lay on that bed and looked at the ceiling and all my errors came scrolling across those dotted soundproof panels."

"*I've* never seen you make an error."

"Oh, Ian," Reverend Emmett said, shaking his head. He noticed a blob of dip on his finger and reached for a linen napkin. "When I was starting out, my church was going to be perfect," he said. "I figured I was setting up the ideal doctrine. But now I see how inconsistent it is, how riddled with

holes and contradictions. What do I care if someone drinks a cup of coffee? Wouldn't I have done
better to ban TV? And here's the worst, Ian: the
thought of doing that did cross my mind, back
in the beginning. But then I said, no, no. And
never admitted the reason, which was: how
would I get any members, if I didn't let them
watch TV?"

Ian didn't know what to say to that. He supposed it would have been nearly impossible to
get members, come to think of it.

"And then there's tithing," Reverend Emmett
said. "Who am I to tell them they have to give
a tenth of their income? Some of those people
are dirt poor. Not a one of them is wealthy. Now
I see that's why I dispensed with the ritual of
collection. I said, 'Slip your envelopes through
the mail slot, no return address,' because secretly I hoped they *wouldn't* tithe, even when
the heating bill had to come out of my own
pocket; and I didn't want to have to deal with it
if they didn't. I preferred to be looking the other
way. There's so much I've looked away from! I
see everyone has made Second Chance his
own, adapted it to suit his own purposes,
changed the rules to whatever is more conve-
nient, and I pretend not to notice. I know Brother
Kenneth smokes! I can smell it on his clothes,
although I never say so. I know Daphne smokes
too, and also drinks beer, and Sister Jessie has

never given up her evening cocktail, not even the day she joined the church, which rumor has it she celebrated with a split of champagne after services. But I've never so much as mentioned it, because the awful truth is I find I don't mind. I find as I get older that it all seems just sort of . . . endearing, really: this little flock of human beings who came to me first to atone for some sin, most of them, and then relaxed and settled in and entirely forgot about atonement. How long since you've seen someone stand up at Public Amending? And Christmas! Three-quarters of the congregation marks Christmas with trees and Santa Claus, don't you think I know that?"

Ian stirred guiltily.

"But the silliest," Reverend Emmett said, "is the Sugar Rule."

"Oh, well . . ." Ian said.

It wasn't as if this subject hadn't come up before, here and there.

"I knew almost from the start I'd made a mistake on that one. I just didn't know how to get out of it. And truthfully, I never felt sure that I wasn't merely rationalizing, once I'd seen how hard the rule was to follow. But in the hospital I was reading this book Sister Nell brought me. This nutrition book. I was trying to learn how to eat more healthily. Although," he said, waving a hand toward the potato chips, "I may not always act on what I've learned. Well, I came upon a discussion of sugar, and do you know what? It's not a stimulant."

"It's not?"

"It's a tranquilizer."

"It can't be," Ian said.

"It's a tranquilizer. Oh, it gives you energy, all right. *Physical* energy. But as far as the mental effect: it lulls you."

"Well, uh . . ."

"Want to know what *is* a stimulant?"

"What?"

"Milk."

Ian thought about that. He started grinning.

"See?" Reverend Emmett said. He was grinning too. "How could you give answers any more wrong than mine have been, Ian? Why, you could be a better minister with one hand tied behind you!"

"No one could be a better minister," Ian said.

He meant it with all his heart. Reverend Emmett must have realized that, because he sobered and said, "Well, thank you."

"But I'll think about Bible School, um, Emmett."

"Wonderful," Reverend Emmett said. Then he reached for another potato chip. His eyes seemed no longer brown but amber. "Oh," he said, "it would be so wonderful to have somebody working at my side and calling me Emmett!"

And he popped the entire chip into his mouth and chomped down happily.

Bert was telling the new man, Rafael, how Mr. Brant had discovered his wife had left him. "First he claims she's kidnapped," Bert said. "He shows Jeannie the closet: 'See? All her clothes still hanging here. She can't have left on purpose.' 'Uncle,' Jeannie goes. She goes, 'These clothes are her very least favorites. Where's her silk blouse with the poppies on it? Where's her turquoise skirt? These are just the extras,' she goes."

Rafael tut-tutted. He said, "Womens always got so many emergency backups."

"Tell about the neighbor," Greg said, nudging Bert in the ribs.

"Jeannie goes, 'Uncle, your neighbor Mr. Hoffberg is missing too. His wife is just about frantic.' Know what he says? Says, 'Why!' Says, 'Why, it's a *rash* of kidnaps!' "

The three men chuckled. Ian frowned at the bureau he was working on. He should have given Mr. Brant some warning. He wished he had it to do over again.

Unexpectedly, Gideon and the redhead strolled through his memory. Framed by the church's doorway, they kissed, and Ian all at once straightened.

What if that was the sign he had prayed for inside the church?

But if it was, he had no idea what it meant.

The others went for their break and Ian drove off to pick up Daphne. It was a crisp, glittery day, and the leaves were at their brightest. He found the ride so pleasant that when he reached the school, it took him a moment to notice the place was deserted. Not a single car sat out front; not a single student loitered on the grounds. He got out of the car and went to try the main entrance, but it was locked. A janitor pushing a broom down the hall saw him through the glass and came over to open the door. "School's closed," he told Ian. "There's a teachers' meeting. Kids got out at noon."

"Oh. Great," Ian said. "Thanks."

He walked around to the phone booth at one side of the building and called home. "Mom?" he said. "Is Daphne there?"

"Why, no, I thought she was at school."

"They got out at noon today."

"Well, you might try calling the Locklear girl," she said. "Shall I look up her telephone number?"

"Never mind," Ian said.

He wondered how his mother could stay so naive. She must work at it. She still thought the biggest issue confronting a teenaged girl was whether or not to kiss on the first date, and the answer (he'd heard her tell Daphne) was no, no, no. "You have years and years to do all that. You don't want them saying you're cheap."

He drove to Gideon's—a sagging, unpainted house on Greenmount—and parked sloppily and crossed the porch in two strides and rang the doorbell. No one answered, but he sensed a sudden freezing of movement somewhere inside the house. He opened the screen and knocked on the inner door. Shading his eyes, he peered through the windowpane. He saw a threadbare rug, part of a banister, and then Gideon lumbering down the stairs, tucking his shirt into his jeans. For a moment they faced each other through the glass. Gideon yawned. He opened the door and stuck his head out.

"I'd like to speak to Daphne," Ian told him.

Gideon considered. "Okay," he said finally.

He had a burnt, ashy smell, as if his skin were smoldering. And although his shirt was more or less tucked in now, it wasn't buttoned. A slice of his bare chest showed through. "Daph!" he called. "Your uncle's here." He went on facing Ian. Up close, his hair was brittle as broom straw. The color must come from a bottle.

"Ian?" Daphne said. She came clomping down the stairs in her combat boots. Her face looked puckered, the way it did when she first woke up, and her eyes were slits. "What are *you* doing here?" she asked, arriving next to Gideon.

"I might ask you the same," Ian told her.

"We had a half day. I forgot to mention."

"Did you also forget the way home?"

She adjusted an earring.

"Let's go," Ian told her. "I'm running late."

"Can Gideon come?"

"Not this time."

She didn't argue. She tossed Gideon a look, and Gideon gazed back at her expressionlessly. Then she unhooked her leather jacket from the newel post. She shrugged herself into it, slung her knapsack over her shoulder, and followed Ian out to the car.

When they'd been driving a while she said, "You didn't have to be rude to him."

"I wasn't rude. I just want to talk to you alone."

She clutched her knapsack to her chest. Now that she sat so close, he realized she too had that burnt smell. And her lips were swollen and blurry, and a red splotch stretched from her throat to the neckline of her Black Sabbath T-shirt.

"Daph," he said.

She hugged her knapsack tighter.

"Daphne, some things are not what they seem," he said.

"Watch out for that car," she told him.

"I mean some *people* aren't what they seem. People you imagine you'll be with forever, say—"

"That car's edging over the line, Ian."

She meant the dark green Plymouth that was wavering a bit in the right-hand lane just ahead. "No doubt some teenager," Ian grumbled.

"Prejudice, prejudice!" Daphne scolded him. "Nope, it's an old man. See how low his head is? Some white-haired old man just barely peeking over the steering wheel and hanging on for dear life."

Ian said, "What I'm trying to tell you—"

"He's showing off for his girlfriend."

"Girlfriend!"

"See the lady next to him? Probably this hot-and-heavy pickup from the Senior Citizens' Center. He's showing her how in-charge he is, and reliable and steady."

Ian snorted. He applied his brakes and fell behind, allowing the Plymouth more room.

"You think I don't know what I'm up to, don't you," Daphne said.

"Pardon?"

"You think I'm some ninny who wants to do right but keeps goofing. But what you don't see is, I goof on purpose. I'm not like you: King Careful. Mr. Look-Both-Ways. Saint Maybe."

"*Now* look," Ian said. "The Plymouth is slowing down too. Seems he's set on staying with us."

"Mess up, I say!" Daphne crowed. "Fall flat

on your face! Make every mistake you can think
of! Use all the life you've got!"

Ian glanced over at her, but he didn't speak.

"Let's pass," Daphne told him.

"Pass?"

"Speed up and pass. This driver's a turkey."

He obeyed. He whizzed through a yellow light,
leaving the Plymouth behind, while Daphne
rolled down her window and squawked out: "Attention! Attention! Lady in the green car! Your
date's been spotted on an FBI's Most Wanted
poster! I repeat!"

"Honestly, Daphne," Ian said. But he was
smiling.

He turned down Waverly Street, pulled up in
front of the house, and sat there with the engine
running. He said, "Daph?"

"Thanks for the lift," she told him, and she
hopped out.

He watched her cut across the front lawn—
her knapsack bouncing, her ragged hair ruffling.
The sole of one combat boot was working loose,
and at every step she had to swing her left foot
unnaturally high off the ground and stamp down
hard. It gave her a slapdash, rollicking gait. It
made her seem glorious. He was still smiling
when he drove away.

At Prayer Meeting, the church always felt even
smaller and cozier than it did ordinarily. It was

something to do with the darkness closing in around it, Ian supposed. This was especially true tonight, for he was early and the fluorescent lights had not yet been switched on. He made his way through the rows of dimly gleaming metal chairs. He stepped behind the shop counter and tapped on the office door, which showed a thin line of yellow around the edges.

"Come in," Reverend Emmett called.

He was sitting in one of the armchairs with his legs stretched out very long and straight. He was thumbing through a hymn pamphlet. "Why, Ian!" he said, smiling, and he rose to his feet in his loose-strung, jerky manner.

Ian said, "Reverend Emmett—"

He probably could have stopped right there. Reverend Emmett looked so crestfallen, all of a sudden; he must have guessed what Ian was about to say.

"It's not only whether I'd be *able* to give people answers," Ian told him. "It's whether I'd want to. Whether I'd feel right about it."

Reverend Emmett went on waiting, and Ian knew he should explain further. He should tell him about the sign from God. He should say what the sign had finally recalled to him: Lucy rushing home out of breath, laughing and excited, and his own arrogant certitude that he had an obligation to inform his brother. But that would have opened the way for debate. (When is something philosophical acceptance and when is it dumb passivity? When is something a moral decision and when is it scar tissue?) He wasn't up to that. He just said, "I'm sorry."

Reverend Emmett said, "I'm sorry, too."

"I hope we can still be friends," Ian told him.

"Yes, of course," Reverend Emmett said gently.

Out in the main room, Ian lowered himself into a seat and unbuttoned his jacket. His fingers felt weak, as if he'd come through an ordeal. To steady himself, he bowed his head and prayed. He prayed as he almost always did, not forming actual words but picturing instead this spinning green planet safe in the hands of God, with the children and his parents and Ian himself small trusting dots among all the other dots. And the room around him seemed to rustle with prayers from years and years past: *Let me get well* and *Make her love me* and *Forgive what I have done*.

Then Sister Myra arrived with Sister Edna and flipped the light switch, flooding the room with a buzzing glare, and soon afterwards others followed and settled themselves noisily. Ian sat among them, at peace, absorbing the cheery sound of their voices and the gaudy, bold, forthright colors of their clothes.

9

THE FLOODED
SEWING BOX

The spring of 1988 was the wettest anyone could remember. It rained nearly every day in May, and all the storm drains overflowed and the gutters ran like rivers and the Bedloes' roof developed a leak directly above the linen closet. One morning when Daphne went to get a fresh towel she found the whole stack soaked through. Ian called Davidson Roofers, but the man who came said there wasn't a thing he could do till the weather cleared. Even then they'd have a wait, he said, because half the city had sprung leaks in this downpour. So they kept a saucepan on the top closet shelf with a folded cloth in the bottom to muffle the constant drip, drip. Of course they'd moved the linens elsewhere, but still the upstairs hall smelled of something dank and swampy. Ian said it was him. He said he had mildew of the armpits.

Then along came June, dry as a bone. Only one brief shower fell that entire scorching month, and the yard turned brown and the cat lay stretched on the cool kitchen floor as flat as she could make herself. By that time, though, the Bedloes hardly cared; for Bee had awakened one June morning unable to speak, and two days later she was dead.

Agatha and her husband flew in from California. Thomas came down from New York. Claudia and Macy arrived from Pittsburgh with their two youngest, George and Henry; and their oldest, Abbie, drove up from Charleston. The house was not just full but splitting at the seams. Still, Daphne felt oddly lonesome. Late at night she cruised the dark rooms, stepping over sleeping bags, brushing past a snoring shape on the couch, and she thought, *Somebody's missing*. She poured a shot of her grandfather's whiskey and stood drinking it at the kitchen window, and she thought, *It's Grandma*. In all the flurry of arrivals and arrangements, it seemed they had lost track of that.

But after everyone left again, Bee's absence seemed almost a presence. Doug spent hours shut away in his room. Ian grew broody and distant. Daphne was working for a florist at the moment, and after she closed shop she would often just stay on downtown—grab a bite to eat and then maybe hit a few bars with some friends, go home with someone she hardly knew just to keep occupied. Who could have guessed that Bee would leave such a vacancy? Over the past few years she had seemed to be diminishing, fading into the background. It was Ian who'd appeared to be running things. Now Daphne saw that that wasn't the case at all. Or maybe it was like those times you experience a physical ailment—stomach trouble, say, and you think, *Why, I never realized before that the stomach is the center of the body*, and then a headache and you think, *No, wait, it's the head that's the center . . .*

July was as dry as June, and the city started rationing water. You could sprinkle your lawn only between nine at night and nine in the morning. Ian said fine; he just wouldn't sprinkle at all. It just wasn't worth the effort, he said. The grass turned brittle, like paper held close to a candle flame. The hydrangeas wilted and drooped. When Davidson Roofers arrived one morning to hammer overhead, Daphne wondered why they bothered.

Late in August a gentle, pattering rain began one afternoon, and people ran out of their houses and flung open their arms and raised their faces to the sky. Daphne, walking home from the bus stop, thought she knew how plants must feel; her skin received each cool, sweet drop so gratefully. But the rain stopped short ten minutes later as if someone had turned a faucet off, and that was the end of that.

Then summer was over—the hardest summer in history, her grandfather said. (He meant because of Bee's death, of course. He had probably not even noticed the drought.) But fall was not much wetter, or much more cheerful either.

October marked the longest Daphne had ever held a job—one entire year—and the florist gave her a raise. Her friends said now that she was making more money she ought to rent a place of her own. "You're right," she told them. "I'm going to start looking. I know I should. Any day I will." No one could believe she still lived at home with her family.

That Thanksgiving was their first without Bee. It wasn't a holiday Agatha usually returned for— she was an oncologist out in L.A., with a very busy practice—but this time she did, accompanied of course by Stuart. When Daphne came home from work Wednesday evening, she found Agatha washing carrots at the kitchen sink. They kissed, and Agatha said, "We've just got back from the grocery. There wasn't a thing to eat in the fridge."

"Well, no," Daphne said, leaning against a

counter. "We thought we'd have Thanksgiving dinner at a restaurant."

"That's what Grandpa said."

As usual, Agatha wore a tailored white blouse and a navy skirt. She must have a closetful; she dressed like a missionary. Her black hair curled at her jawline in the docile, unremarkable style of those generic women in grade-school textbooks, and her face was uniformly white, as if her skin were thicker than other people's. Heavy, black-rimmed glasses framed her eyes. You could tell she thought prettiness was a waste of time. She could have been pretty—another woman with those looks *would* have been pretty—but she preferred not to be. Probably she disapproved of Daphne's tinkling earrings and Indian gauze tunic; probably even her jeans, which Daphne did have to lie down to get into.

"You know what Grandma always told us," Agatha said. "Only riffraff eat their holiday meals in restaurants."

"Yes, but everything's been so—"

Just then, Stuart came through the back door with a case of mineral water. "Hello, Daphne," he said, setting the case on the counter. He shook her hand formally. Daphne said, "Well, hey there, Stuart," and wondered all over again how her sister had happened to marry such an extremely handsome man. He was tall and muscular and tanned, with close-cut golden curls and eyes like chips of sky, and away from the hospital he wore the sort of casual, elegant clothes you see in ads for ski resorts. Maybe he was Agatha's one self-indulgence, her single nod to the importance of appearance. Or maybe (more likely) she just hadn't noticed. It was possible she was the only woman in all his life who hadn't backed off in confusion at the sight of him, which would also explain why *he* had married *her*. Look at her now, for instance, grumpily stashing his bottles in the refrigerator. "Really, Stu," she said, "you'd think we were staying till Christmas."

"Well, someone will drink it," he told her affably, and he went to hold open the door for Doug, who was hauling in a giant sack of cat food.

Ian arrived from work earlier than usual, and he hugged Agatha hard and pumped Stuart's hand up and down. He was always so pleased to have everyone home. And after supper—mostly sprouts and cruciferous vegetables, Agatha's doing—he announced he'd be skipping Prayer Meeting to meet Thomas's train with them. Ian almost never skipped Prayer Meeting.

He was the one who drove, with his father up front next to him and Daphne in back between Agatha and Stuart, her right arm held stiffly apart from Stuart's suede sleeve. (*She* could not take his looks for granted.) The dark streets slid past, dotted with events: two black men laughingly wrestling at an intersection, an old woman wheeling a shopping cart full of battered dolls. Daphne leaned forward to see everything more clearly, but the others were discussing Agatha's new Saab. So far it was running fine, Agatha said, although the smell of the leather interior kept reminding her of adhesive tape. Agatha probably thought of Baltimore as just another city by now.

At Penn Station all the parking slots were filled, so Ian circled the block while the others went inside. "What's happened to Ian?" Agatha murmured to Daphne as they walked across the lobby.

"Happened?" Daphne asked.

But then their grandfather caught up with them and said, "My, oh, my, I just never can get over what they've done to this place." He always said that. He made them tip their heads back to study the skylight, so airily delicate and aqua-blue above them, and that was what they were doing when Thomas discovered them. "Gawking at the skylight again," he said in Daphne's ear. She wheeled and said, "Thomas!" and kissed his cheek and passed him on to Agatha. Lately he had become so New Yorkish. He wore a short black overcoat that picked up the black of his hair and the olive in his skin, and he carried a natty little black leather overnight bag. But when he bypassed Stuart's outstretched hand to give him a one-armed bear hug, Daphne could see he was still their old Thomas. He had this way of assuming that people would just naturally love him, and so of course they always did.

Now they had to crowd together in the car, and since Daphne was smallest she sat in front between Doug and Ian. As they drove up Charles Street, Thomas told them all about his new project. (He worked for a software company, inventing educational computer games.) None of them could get more than the gist of it, but Ian kept saying, "Mm. Mm*hmm*," looking very tickled and impressed, and Stuart and Agatha asked intelligent-sounding questions. Doug, however, was silent, and when Daphne glanced up at him she found him staring straight ahead with an extra, glassy surface in front of his eyes. He was thinking about Bee, she knew right off. All of the children home again but Bee not there to enjoy them. She reached over and patted his hand. He averted his face and gazed out the side window, but his hand turned upward on his knee and grasped hers. His fingers felt satiny and crumpled, and extremely fragile.

It wasn't till late that night, after Doug and Ian had gone to bed and the others were watching

TV, that Agatha had a chance to ask her question again. "What's happened to Ian?"

"Nothing's happened," Daphne said.

"And Grandpa! And this whole house!"

"I don't know what you're talking about."

"Thomas, you know, don't you?"

Thomas gave a light shrug—his favorite response to any serious question. He was seated on Agatha's other side, flipping channels with the remote control. Stuart lounged on the floor with his back against Agatha's knees. It was after midnight and Daphne was getting sleepy, but she hated to miss out on anything. She said, "How about we all go to bed."

"Bed? In California it's barely nine o'clock," Agatha said.

"Well, *I'm* ready to call it a day," Stuart announced from the floor. "Don't forget, we flew the red-eye."

"I come home and find this place a shambles," Agatha told Daphne. "The grass is stone dead, even the bushes look dead. The front-porch swing is hanging by one chain. The house is such a mess there's no place to set down our bags, and the dishes haven't been done for days and there's nothing to eat in the fridge, nothing in the pantry, not even any cat food for the cat, and when I go up to our room both mattresses are stripped naked and all the sheets are in the

hamper and when I take the sheets to the basement the washing machine doesn't work.
Grandpa told me it's been broken all fall. I asked
him, 'Well, what have you done about it?' and
he said, 'Oh, any time one of us goes out we try
to remember to gather a little something for the
laundromat,' and then he said we're eating our
Thanksgiving dinner in a restaurant. A restaurant! On St. Paul Street!''

"Well, it's not as bad as it looks," Daphne told
her. "There's been a drought, for one thing. I
mean, the grass isn't really our fault. And the
swing is probably fine; it's just that Ian needs to
check the porch ceiling-boards that buckled in
the floods."

But she could hear how lame this was sounding—drought and floods both. And to tell the
truth, she hadn't realized about the mess. She
looked around the living room (newspapers so
outdated they'd turned yellow, dead flowers in
a dusty vase, cat fur from the carpet clinging to
Stuart's corduroys) and she felt ashamed. A
memory swam back to her of her most recent
drop-in visit to the laundromat, during which she
had spotted, on one of the folding tables, a hardened mass of Bedloe plaids that some stranger
had removed from a washing machine and left
to dry in a clump, possibly several days back.

"Also, Ian needs a haircut," Agatha told her.

"He does? But I *gave* him a haircut," Daphne

said. (Ian hated barbershops.) "I gave him one just last—"

Oh, Lord, way last summer. All at once she saw him: the long, limp tendrils drooping over his collar, dull brown mixed with strands of gray, and the worn lines fanning out from his eyes.

"He looks like some eccentric, middle-aged . . . uncle," Agatha said.

"He does not!" Daphne protested, so loudly that Stuart, slumped against Agatha's knees, jolted upright and said, "Huh?" and Thomas raised the volume on the remote control.

"And Grandpa has food stains down his front," Agatha said, "and you've got dirty fingernails."

"Well, I do work in a florist shop," Daphne told her. She darted a glance at her left hand, which rested on the arm of the couch.

"Is it Grandma?" Agatha asked. "But it can't be, can it? I know we all miss her, but Ian's been in charge of the house for ages, hasn't he?"

"It's true we miss her," Daphne said, and just then she heard Bee calling her for supper on a long-ago summer evening. "*Daaph*-ne!"—the two notes floating across the twilight. Surreptitiously, she started cleaning her nails. "But we get along," she said. "We're fine! And no way is Ian middle-aged. He's forty; that's not so old! He's even got this sort of girlfriend. Clara. Have you met Clara? No, I guess not. Woman at our church. She's okay."

"Is she coming for Thanksgiving dinner?"

"Who, Clara?" Daphne asked stupidly. As a matter of fact, she had never given the woman much thought. "Well, no, I don't believe he invited her," she said.

"How about you?"

"How *about* me?"

"Are you seeing anyone special?"

"Oh. No," Daphne said, "I'm between boyfriends at the moment."

"What happened to . . . was it Ron?"

"Rich," Daphne said. "He was getting too serious. I think I'm more the one-night-stand type, if you want the honest truth."

She didn't know why she had this urge to shock, sometimes, when she was talking to Agatha. It wasn't even that effective, for Agatha merely raised her eyebrows and made no comment.

The TV said, "Drop us a postcard stating— female deposits her eggs in—not *thirty*-nine ninety-five, not *twenty*-nine ninety-five, but—"

"Stuart does that too," Agatha told Thomas. "Just hand him a remote control and he turns sort of frantic. It must be hormonal."

"Say what?" Stuart asked, snapping his head up.

"Tomorrow afternoon we clean house," Agatha told Daphne.

"All right," Daphne said meekly.

"We'll have a regular, normal, home-cooked Thanksgiving dinner; I bought an eighteen-pound turkey at the grocery store, and I've invited Mrs. Jordan and the foreigners. Then afterward we'll start cleaning and sorting. Discarding. Do you know Grandma's cosmetics are still on her bureau?"

"Maybe Grandpa likes them there," Daphne suggested.

"Her arthritis pills are still in the medicine cabinet."

"Maybe—"

"Past their expiration date!" Agatha said, as if that settled it.

Stuart said, "Aggie, can't we go to bed now?"

"Now?" Agatha said. She checked her watch. "It's not even nine thirty."

Daphne was so sleepy that the room was misting over, and Thomas had been yawning, but they all settled back obediently and fixed their eyes on the screen.

Thursday afternoon Agatha and Daphne washed all the dishes, even those in the cupboards, and Thomas vacuumed downstairs while Ian tried to reduce the general disorder. Stuart, who turned out to be fairly useless around the house, watched a football game with Doug.

Thursday night at ten they had turkey sandwiches (in California it was seven) and then Agatha dusted the downstairs furniture, Daphne scrubbed the woodwork, and Thomas polished the silver.

Friday Daphne went back to Floral Fantasy, · and by the time she got home the upstairs had been vacuumed and dusted as well and the washing machine repaired and all the laundry done. Bee's little walnut desk in the living room stood bare, its cubbyholes dark as missing teeth; and when Daphne opened the drawers below she found only the essentials: a box of envelopes, a photo album whose six filled pages covered the past twenty-two years, and the document transforming those two strangers, Thomas and Agatha "Dulsimore," into Bedloes and tucking them into Ian's safekeeping along with Daphne herself. This last was so familiar she could have quoted it verbatim, but she scanned it yet again and so did Agatha, breathing audibly over Daphne's left shoulder. "What's disturbing," Agatha told her (not for the first time), "is we don't know a thing about our genetic heritage. What if we're prone to diabetes? Or epilepsy?"

Diplomatically, Daphne refrained from pointing out that she herself did know her heritage, at least on her father's side. She shook her head and put the document back in the drawer.

Saturday Ian went to Good Works, but

Daphne stayed home to continue with the cleaning. "Grandpa," Agatha said, "today we're sorting through Grandma's belongings. Anything you want to keep, you'd better let us know now."

"Oh," he said, and then he said, "Well, her lipstick, maybe. Her perfume bottles."

"Lipstick? Perfume?"

"I like her bureau to have things on top of it. I don't want to see it all blank."

"Couldn't we just put a vase on top?"

"No, we couldn't," her grandfather said firmly.

"Well, all right."

"And I'd like her robe left hanging in her closet."

"All right, Grandpa."

"But you might ship her jewelry to Claudia. Or at least what jewelry is real."

"Well, you're going to have to tell us which is which," Agatha said, for of course they wouldn't know real from Woolworth's.

But later, when they had packed all Bee's limp, sad, powdery-smelling lingerie into the cartons Thomas brought up from the basement, they called for Doug to advise them on the jewelry and he didn't answer. They'd assumed he was watching TV, but when they checked they found only Stuart, channel-hopping rapidly from golf to cartoons to cooking shows. Daphne said, "I bet he's at the foreigners'."

"Honestly," Agatha said.

"The foreigners have a VCR now, did you know? They own every Rita Hayworth movie ever made."

"Run get him, will you?" Agatha asked Thomas.

But Thomas said, "Maybe we should just let him stay there."

"Well, what'll we do about the jewelry?"

"Send Claudia the whole box, for heaven's sake," Daphne said. She told Thomas, "Wrap the whole box for mailing. You'll find paper and string in the pantry."

"But it isn't just the jewelry," Agatha said. "We need him here to answer other questions, too."

"Agatha, will you drop it? He doesn't want to be around for this."

"Well. Sorry," Agatha said stiffly.

They went back upstairs to their grandparents' bedroom, and while Thomas bore the jewelry box off to the pantry Daphne and Agatha started on the cedar chest at the foot of the bed. They had assumed this part would be easy—just sweaters, surely—but underneath lay stacks of moldering photo albums Daphne had never seen before. "Oh, those," Agatha said. "They used to be downstairs in the desk." She picked up a manila envelope and peered inside. Daphne, meanwhile, flipped through the topmost album and found rows of streaky, pale rectangles showing ghostlike human faces with no features but pinhead eyes. "Polaroid, in its earliest days," Agatha explained.

"Well, darn," Daphne said, because the captions were so alluring. *Danny at Bethany Beach, 1963. Lucy with the Crains, 8/65.* Her father, whom she knew only from a boringly boyish sports photo hanging in the living room. Her mother, who was nothing but the curve of a cheek above Daphne's own newborn self on page one of her otherwise empty baby book.

She turned to the albums below. The pictures there were more distinct, but they documented less interesting times. Claudia, thinner and darker, married a plucked-looking Macy in a ridiculous white tuxedo. Doug stood at a lectern holding up a plaque. Claudia and Macy had a baby. Then they had another. People seemed to graduate a lot. Some wore long white robes and mortarboards, some wore black and carried their mortarboards under their arms, and one, labeled *Cousin Louise*, wore just a dress but you could see this was a graduation because of her ribboned diploma and her relatives pressing around. All those relatives attending all those ceremonies, sitting patiently through all those tedious speeches just so they could raise a cheer at the single mention of a loved one's name. It wasn't fair: by the time of Daphne's own graduation, most of those people had vanished and Claudia and Macy had moved out of state.

The family had congealed into smaller knots, wider apart, like soured milk. Their gatherings were puny, their cheers self-conscious and faint.

"Thomas and me with Mama," Agatha said, thrusting a color snapshot at Daphne. "I wonder how *that* got here."

She had pulled it from the manila envelope: a slick, bright square that Daphne took hold of reverently. So. Her mother. A very young woman with two small children, standing in front of a trailer. Probably she and Daphne looked alike— same shade of hair, same shape of face—but this woman seemed so long ago, Daphne couldn't feel related to her. Her dress was too short, her makeup too harsh, her surroundings too tinny and garish. Had she ever cried herself to sleep at night? Laughed till her legs could no longer support her? Fallen into such a rage that she'd pounded the wall with her fists?

Daphne used to ask about her mother all the time, in the old days. She had plagued her sister and brother with questions. They never gave very satisfactory answers, though. Agatha said, "Her hair was black. Her eyes were, I don't know, blue or gray or something." Thomas said, "She was nice. You'd have liked her!" in his brightest tone of voice. But when Daphne asked, "What would I have liked about her?" he just said, "Oh, everything!" and looked away from her. He could be so exasperating, at times. At times she imagined him encased in something plastic, something slick and smooth as a raincoat.

Agatha held out her hand for the snapshot, and Daphne said, "I think I'll keep it."

"Keep it?"

"I'll get it framed."

"What for?" Agatha asked, surprised.

"I'm going to hang it in the living room with the other family pictures."

"In the living room! Well, that's just inappropriate," Agatha told her.

Daphne had a special allergy to the word "inappropriate." A number of teachers had used it during her schooldays. She said, "Don't tell me what's appropriate!"

"What are you so prickly about? I only meant—"

"She has just as much right to be on that wall as Great-Aunt Bess with her hula hoop."

"Yes, of course she does," Agatha said. "Fine! Go ahead." And she passed Daphne the manila envelope. "Here's all the rest of her things."

Daphne shook the envelope into her lap. Certificates. Receipts. A date on one read *2/7/66*. She didn't see any more photos. "Put them away; don't leave them lying around," Agatha said, delving into the chest again. Her voice came back muffled. "We're trying to get organized, remember."

So Daphne took them across the hall to her room. It used to be Thomas's room, and although Thomas had to sleep on the couch now he kept his belongings here during his visits. His toilet articles littered Daphne's bureau and his leather bag spilled clothing onto her floor. Daphne suddenly felt overcome by *objects*. What did she need with these papers, anyhow? Except for the snapshot, they were worthless. And yet she couldn't bear to throw them away.

When she returned to her grandparents' bedroom, she found Agatha looking equally defeated. She was standing in front of Bee's closet, facing a row of heartbreakingly familiar dresses and blouses. Crammed on the shelf overhead were suitcases and hatboxes and a sliding heap of linens—the linens moved last spring from beneath the leaky roof. It showed what this household had descended to that they'd never been moved back, except for those few items in regular use. "What *are* these?" Agatha asked, taking a pinch of a monogrammed guest towel.

"I guess we ought to carry them to the linen closet," Daphne said.

But the linen closet, they discovered, had magically replenished itself. The emptied top shelf now held Doug's shoe-polishing gear and someone's greasy coveralls and the everyday towels not folded but hastily wadded. And the lower shelves, which hadn't been sorted in years, made Agatha say, "Good grief." She gave a listless tug to a crib sheet patterned with ducklings. (How long since they'd needed a crib sheet?) When they heard Thomas on the stairs, she called, "Tom, could you bring up more boxes from the basement?"

She pulled out half a pack of disposable diapers—the old-fashioned kind as stiff and crackly as those paper quilts that line chocolate boxes. From the depths of the closet she drew a baby-sized pillow and said, "Ick," for a rank, moldy smell unfurled from it almost visibly. The leak must have traveled farther than they had suspected. "Throw it out," she told Daphne. Daphne took it between thumb and forefinger and dropped it on top of the diapers. Next Agatha brought forth a bedpan with an inch of rusty water in the bottom—"That too," she said—and a damp, cloth-covered box patterned with faded pink roses. "Is this Grandma's?" she asked. "I don't remember this."

Both of them hovered over it hopefully as she set the box on the floor and lifted the lid, but it was only a sewing box, abandoned so long ago that a waterlogged packet of clothing labels inside bore Claudia's maiden name. There were sodden cards of bias tape and ripply, stretched-out elastic; and underneath those, various rusty implements—scissors, a seam ripper, a leather punch—and tiny cardboard boxes falling apart

with moisture. Clearly nothing here was of interest, so why did they insist on opening each
box? Even Agatha, common-sense Agatha,
pried off a disintegrating cardboard lid to stare
down at a collection of shirt buttons. Everything
swam in brown water. Everything had the dead
brown stink of overcooked broccoli. It was amazing how thorough the rust was. It threaded the
hooks and eyes, it stippled the needles and
straight pins. It choked the revolving wheel of
the leather punch and clogged each and every
one of its hollow, cylindrical teeth.

Daphne thought of the dress form in the attic
storeroom—Bee's figure but with a waist, with a
higher bosom. Once their grandma had been
a happy woman, she supposed. Back before
everything changed.

"Will these be enough?" Thomas asked, arriving with two cartons. But Agatha flapped a
hand without looking. "Shall I pack these things
on the floor?" he asked.

"Oh, don't bother," Agatha told him, and then
she turned and wandered toward the stairs.

"Just *leave* them here?" he asked Daphne.

"Whatever," Daphne said.

In fact they remained there the rest of the day,
obstructing the hall till Daphne finally stuffed
them back in the closet. She piled everything
onto the bottom shelf, and she set the cardboard
cartons inside and closed the door.

"I dreamed this high-school boy was proposing to me," Agatha said at breakfast. "He told me to name a date. He said, 'How about Wednesday? Monday is always busy and Tuesday is always rainy.' I said, 'Wait, I'm . . . wait,' I said. 'I think you ought to know that I'm quite a bit older than you.' Then I woke up, and I laughed out loud. Did you hear me laughing, Stu? I mean, older was the least of it. I should have said, 'Wait, there's another thing, too! It so happens I'm already married.' "

"I dreamed I was going blind," Thomas said. "Everyone said, 'Oh, how awful, we're so sorry for you.' I said, 'Sorry? Why? I've had twenty-six years of perfect vision!' I really meant it, too. I sounded like one of those inspirational stories we used to read in Bible camp."

"I dreamed I was seeing patients," Stuart said. "They all had some kind of rash and I was trying to remember my dermatology. It didn't seem to occur to me to tell them that wasn't my field."

Agatha said, "I'd never go into dermatology."

They were having English muffins and juice— just the four of them, because it was ten thirty and Doug and Ian had eaten breakfast hours ago. Doug was in the dining room laying out a game of solitaire, the soft flip-flip of his cards providing a kind of background rhythm. Ian was moving around the kitchen wiping off counters.

When he passed near Daphne he smiled down at her and said, "What did *you* dream, Daphne?" Something about his crinkled eyes and the kindly attentiveness of his expression made her sad, but she smiled back and said, "Oh, nothing."

"Dermatology's not bad," Stuart was saying. "At least dermatologists don't have night call."

"But it's so superficial," Agatha said.

"You should see Agatha with her patients," Stuart told the others. "She's amazing. She'll say straight out to them, 'What you have can't be cured.' I think they feel relieved to finally hear the truth."

"I say, 'What you have can't be cured *at this particular time*,'" Agatha corrected him. "There's a difference."

Daphne couldn't imagine that either version would be as much of a relief as Stuart supposed.

"Speaking of time," Ian said, draping his dishcloth over the faucet, "when exactly does your plane take off, Ag?"

"Somewhere around noon, I think. Why?"

"Well, I'm wondering about church. If I wanted to go to church I'd have to leave right now."

"Go, then," she told him.

"But if your flight's at noon—"

"Go! Grandpa can drive us."

Ian hesitated. Daphne knew what he was thinking. He was weighing Sunday services, which he never missed if he could help it, against the possibility of hurting Agatha's feelings. And Agatha, with her chin raised defiantly and her glasses flashing an opaque white light, would most definitely have hurt feelings. Daphne knew that if Ian did not. Finally Ian said, "Well, if you're sure . . ." and Agatha snapped, "Absolutely! Go."

He didn't seem to catch her tone. (Or he didn't want to catch it.) He rounded the table to kiss her goodbye. "It's been wonderful having you," he said. She looked away from him. He shook Stuart's hand. "Stuart, I hope you two will come again at Christmas."

"We'll try," Stuart told him, rising. "Thanks for the hospitality."

"You planning on church today, Daphne?"

"I thought I'd ride along to the airport," Daphne said.

"Well, I'll be off, then."

In the dining room, they heard him speaking to Doug. "Guess I'll let you do the airport run, Dad."

"Oh, well," Doug said. "Seems I'm losing here anyway."

"And another thing," Agatha told Daphne. (But what was the first thing? Daphne wondered.) "This business about you not driving is really dumb, Daph."

"Driving?" Daphne asked.

"Here you are, twenty-two years old, and Grandpa has to drive us to the airport. As far as I know you've never even sat behind a steering wheel."

"How did my driving get into this?"

"It's a symptom of a whole lot of other problems, any fool can see that. Why are you still depending on people to chauffeur you around? Why have you never gone away to college? Why are you still living at home when everyone else has long since left?"

"Maybe I *like* living at home, so what's the big deal?" Daphne asked. "This happens to be a perfectly nice place."

"Nobody says it isn't," Agatha said, "but that's not the issue. You've simply reached the stage where you should be on your own. Right, Stuart? Right, Thomas?"

Stuart developed an interest in brushing crumbs off his sweater. Thomas gave one of his shrugs and drank the last of his orange juice. Agatha sighed. "You know," she told Daphne, "in many ways, living in a family is like taking a long, long trip with people you're not very well acquainted with. At first they seem just fine, but after you've traveled a while at close quarters they start grating on your nerves. Their most harmless habits make you want to scream—the way they overuse certain phrases or yawn out

loud—and you just have to get away from them.
You have to leave home."

"Well, I guess I must not have traveled with
them long enough, then," Daphne told her.

"How can you say that? With Ian doddering
about the house calling you his 'Daffy-dill' and
spending every Saturday at Good Works—Good
Works! Good God. I bet half those people don't
even *want* a bunch of holy-molies showing up
to rake their leaves in front of all their neighbors.
And marching off to services come rain or shine;
never mind if his niece is here visiting and will
have to go to the airport on her own—"

"He gets a lot out of those services," Daphne
said. "And Good Works too; it kind of . . . links
you. He doesn't have much else, Agatha."

"Exactly," Agatha told her. "Isn't that my
point? If not for Second Chance he'd have much
more, believe me. That's what religion does to
you. It narrows you and confines you. When I
think of how religion ruined our childhood! All
those things we couldn't do, the Sugar Rule and
the Caffeine Rule. And that pathetic Bible camp,
with poor pitiful Sister Audrey who finally ran off
with a soldier if I'm not mistaken. And Brother
Simon always telling us how God had saved him
for something special when his apartment building burned down, never explaining what God
had against those seven others He didn't save.

And the way we had to say grace in every crummy fast-food joint with everybody gawking—"

"It was a silent grace," Daphne said. "It was the least little possible grace! He always tried to be private about it. And religion never ruined *my* childhood; it made me feel cared for. Or Thomas's either. Thomas still attends church himself. Isn't that so, Thomas? He belongs to a church in New York."

Thomas said, "It's getting on toward eleven, you two. Maybe we should be setting out for the airport."

"Not to change the subject or anything," Daphne told him.

He pretended he hadn't heard. They all stood up, and he said, "Then driving back, you and Grandpa can drop me at the train station. I'll just get my things together. You want me to put my sheets in the hamper, Daph?"

"Are you serious?" Daphne asked. "Those sheets are good for another month yet."

Agatha rolled her eyes and said, "Charming."

"You have no right to talk if you're not here to do the laundry," Daphne told her.

"Which reminds me," Agatha said. She stopped short in the dining room, where their grandfather was collecting his cards. "About the linen closet and such—"

"Don't give it a thought," Daphne said. "Just

go off scot-free to the other side of the continent."

"No, but I was wondering. Isn't there some kind of cleaning service that could sort this place out for us? Not just clean it but organize it, and I could pay."

"There's the Clutter Counselor," Daphne said.

Stuart laughed. Agatha said, "The what?"

"Rita the Clutter Counselor. She lives with this guy I know, Nick Bascomb. Did you ever meet Nick? And she makes her living sorting other people's households and putting them in order."

"Hire her," Agatha said.

"I don't know how much she charges, though."

"Hire her anyway. I'll pay whatever it costs."

"What?" their grandfather spoke up suddenly. "You'd let an outsider go through our closets?"

"It's either that or marry Ian off quick to that Clara person," Agatha told him.

"I'll call Rita this evening," Daphne said.

Rita diCarlo was close to six feet tall—a rangy, sauntering woman in her late twenties with long black hair so frizzy that the braid hanging down her back seemed not so much plaited as clotted. She'd been living with Nick Bascomb for a couple of years now, but Daphne hadn't really got to know her till just last summer when a bunch of them went together to a rock concert at RFK

Stadium. They'd had bleacher tickets that didn't allow them on the field, where all the action was; but Rita, bold as brass, strode down to the field anyway. When an usher tried to stop her she held up her ticket stub and strode on. The usher considered a while and then spun around and called, "Hey! *That* wasn't a field ticket!" By then, though, she was lost in the crowd. Daphne hadn't seen much of her since, but she always remembered that incident—the dash and swagger of it. She thought Rita was entirely capable of yanking their house into shape.

On the phone Rita said she could fit the Bedloes into that coming week, so she dropped by Monday after work to "case the joint," as she put it. Wearing a red-and-black lumber jacket, black jeans, and heavy leather riding boots, she ambled about throwing open cupboards and peering into drawers. She surveyed the basement impassively. She seemed unfazed by the smell in the linen closet. She did not once ask, as Daphne had feared, "What in hell has *hit* here?" She poked her head into Doug's bedroom and, finding him seated empty-handed in his rocker, merely said, "Hmm," and withdrew. This was tactful of her, of course, but Doug's room had urgent need of her services; so Daphne said, "Maybe after Grandpa's gone downstairs . . . ."

"I got the general idea," Rita told her.

"That's where Grandma's closet is and so—"

"Sure. Clothes and stuff. Hatboxes."

"Right."

"I got it."

She climbed the wooden steps to the attic, which had a stuffy, cloistered feeling now that it was no longer in regular use. She bent to look into the storeroom under the eaves. When she plucked one of Bee's letters from a cardboard carton, Daphne felt a pang. "I guess these . . . personal things you'll leave to us," she said, but Rita said, "Not if you want this done right." Then she added, "Don't worry, I don't read your mail. Or only enough to classify it. Stuff like this, for instance: too recent to have historical interest, no postage stamps of value, and the return address is a woman's so we know it's not your grandparents' love letters. I'd say ditch them."

"*Ditch* them?"

Rita turned to look at her. Her face was tanned and square-jawed; her heavy black eyebrows were slightly raised.

"But suppose they told us what young women used to think about," Daphne said. "Politics, or feminism, or things like that."

Rita shook a piece of ivory stationery out of the envelope. Without bothering to unfold it, she read off the phrases that showed themselves: "*. . . tea at Mrs. . . . wore my new flowered . . . self belt with covered buckle . . .*"

"Well," Daphne murmured.

"Ditch them," Rita told her.

They went back downstairs. Daphne felt like a little fairy person following Rita's clopping boots. "What I do," Rita said, "is sort everything into three piles: Keep, Discard, and Query. I make it a practice to query as little as possible. Everything we keep I organize, and what's discarded I haul away; I've got my own truck and two guys to help tote. I charge by the hour, but I generally know ahead of time how long a job will run me. This place, for instance—well, I'll need to sit down and figure it out, but offhand I'd say if I start tomorrow morning, I could be done late Thursday."

"Thursday! That's just three days!"

"Or four at the most. It's a fairly straightforward house, compared to some I've seen."

They were back in the kitchen now. She opened one of the cabinets and gazed meditatively at a collection of empty peanut butter jars.

"It doesn't look so straightforward to *me*," Daphne told her.

"Well, naturally. That's because you live here. You feel guilty getting rid of things. This one old lady I had, she could never throw out a gift. A drawing her son made in nursery school—and that son was sixty years old! A seashell her girlfriend brought from Miami in nineteen twenty—

'I just feel I'd be throwing the *person* out,' she told me. So what I did was, I didn't let her know. Well, of course she knew in a way. What did she suppose was in all those garbage bags? But she never asked, and I never said, and everyone was happy."

She slammed the cabinet door shut. "I've seen houses so full you couldn't walk through them. I've seen closets totally lost—I mean crammed to the gills and closed off, with new stuff piled in front of them so you didn't know they existed."

"Your own apartment must be neat as a pin," Daphne said.

"Not really," Rita told her. "That Nick saves everything. I *would* end up with a pack rat!" She laughed. She hooked a kitchen chair with the toe of her boot, pulled it out from the table, and sat down. "Now," she said, drawing a pencil and a note pad from her breast pocket. The pencil was roughly the size of a cartridge. She licked its tip and started writing. "Six rooms plus basement plus finished attic. Your attic's in pretty good shape, but that basement . . ."

Ian appeared at the back door, lugging a large cardboard box. "Open up!" he called through the glass, and when Daphne obeyed he practically fell inside. Whatever he was carrying must weigh a ton. "Genuine ceramic tiles," he told Daphne, setting the box on the floor. "We're replacing an antique mantel at a house in Fells Point and these were just being thrown out, so—"

"Will you be putting them to use within the next ten days?" Rita asked.

He straightened and said, "Pardon?"

"Ian, this is Rita diCarlo," Daphne said. "My uncle Ian. Rita's here to organize us."

"Oh, yes," Ian said.

"Do you have a specific bathroom in mind that's in need of those tiles within the next ten days?" Rita asked him.

"Well, not exactly, but—"

"Then I suggest you walk them straight back out to the trash can," she said, "or else I'll have to tack them onto my estimate here."

"But these are from Spain," Ian told her. He bent to lift one from the box—a geometric design of turquoise and royal blue. "How could I put something like this in the trash?"

Rita considered him. She didn't give the tile so much as a glance, but Ian continued holding it hopefully in front of his chest like someone displaying his number for a mug shot.

"You see what I have to deal with," Daphne told Rita.

"Yes, I see," Rita said.

Oddly enough, though, Daphne just then noticed how beautiful that tile really was. The design looked kaleidoscopic—almost capable of movement. She couldn't remember now why stripping the house had seemed like such a good idea.

Rita did do an excellent job, as it turned out, but Daphne hardly had time to notice before something new came along for her to think about: Friday afternoon, she was fired.

It wasn't entirely unexpected. Ever since she'd got her raise, she seemed to have lost interest in her work. She had shown up late, left early, and mislaid several orders. The messages people sent with their flowers had begun to depress her. "Well, I think I'll say . . . well, let me see," they would tell her, frowning into space. "Why don't we put . . . Okay! I've got it! 'Congratulations and best wishes.'" Then Daphne would slash *CBW* across the order form. "To the girl of my dreams" was *G/dms*. "Thanks for last night," *Tx/nite*. She felt injured on their behalf— that their most heartfelt sentiments could be considered so routine. And when they were not routine, it was worse: *I am more sorry than I can tell you and you're right not to want to see me again but I'll never forget you as long as I live and I hope you have a wonderful marriage*. "With delivery that comes to twenty-seven eighty," she would say in her blandest tone.

The way Mr. Potoski put it was, she could either leave now or stay on for her two weeks' notice, but she could see he was eager to get rid of her. He already had a new girl lined up. "I'll leave now," Daphne told him, and so at closing time she gathered her few possessions and stuffed them into a paper sack. Then she slipped her jacket on and ducked quietly out the door, avoiding an awkward farewell scene. On the way to the bus stop she found herself composing messages to Mr. Potoski. *Tx/fun: Thanks, it's been fun. TK: Take care.* Not that she had anything against Mr. Potoski personally. She knew this was all her own fault.

Her bus was undergoing some heater problems, and by the time she reached home she was chilled through. Still in her jacket, she went directly to the kitchen and lit the gas beneath the kettle. Ian must be working late this evening. She could hear her grandfather down in the basement, rattling tools and thinking aloud, but she didn't call out to him. Maybe there was some advantage to living alone after all—not dealing with other people, not feeling responsible for other people's happiness. Although that was out of the question, now that she had no salary.

She took a mug from the cupboard, where everything sat in straight rows—eight mugs, eight short glasses, eight tall glasses. The mugs that didn't match and the odd-sized glasses had been sent to Good Works. The cereals that people had tried once and never again had disap-

peared from the shelves. In just three days Rita
had turned this house into a sort of sample kit:
one perfect set of everything. But Daphne hadn't
quite adjusted yet and she felt a little rustle of
panic. She wanted some extras. She wanted
that crowd of cracked, crazed, chipped, handle-
less mugs waiting behind the other mugs on the
off chance they might be needed.

She ladled coffee into the drip pot and then
poured in the boiling water. Coffee was her
weakness. Reverend Emmett said coffee
clouded the senses, coffee stepped between
God and the self; but Daphne had discovered
long ago that coffee *sharpened* the senses, and
she loved to sit through church all elated and
jangly-nerved and keyed to the sound of that
inner voice saying enigmatic things she might
someday figure out when she was wiser: *if not
for you, if not for you, if not for you* and *down
in the meadow where the green grass grows
. . .* She waited daily for caffeine to be declared
illegal, but it seemed the government had not
caught on yet.

She poured the coffee and sat down at the
table with it, warming her hands around the mug.
Now her grandfather's footsteps climbed the
basement stairs and crossed the pantry. Daphne
looked up, but the figure in the doorway was not
her grandfather after all. It was Rita. Daphne
said, "Rita! Aren't you done with us?"

Well, she *was* done. She had finished yesterday afternoon and even presented her staggeringly high bill, which Daphne was going to mail on to Agatha as soon as she figured out where the stamps had been moved to. But here Rita stood, flushed from her climb, looking a bit better put together than usual in a flowing white shirt that bloused above her jeans and a tan suede jacket as soft as washed silk. "Daphne," she said flatly. "I thought you were Ian."

Ah.

Daphne had been through this any number of times. Back in high school, girlfriends of hers showed up unannounced, wearing brand new outfits and carrying their bosoms ostentatiously far in front of them like fruit on a tray. "Oh," they'd say in just such a tone, dull and disappointed. "I thought you were Ian."

But Rita already had somebody, didn't she? She was living with Nick Bascomb. Wasn't she?

"It just occurred to me," Rita said, "that I ought to try once more to sort out your grandpa's workbench. Not that I'd charge any extra, of course. But I didn't feel right allowing it to stay so . . ."

Her voice dwindled away. Daphne, sitting back in her chair and cupping her mug in both hands, watched her with some enjoyment. Rita diCarlo, of all people! Such a tough cookie. Although Daphne could have warned her that she was about as far from Ian's type as a woman could get.

"But it seems your grandpa's sticking to his guns," Rita said finally.

"Yes," Daphne said. She took a sip from her mug.

"So I'll be going, I guess."

"Okay."

In another mood, she might at least have offered coffee. But she had troubles of her own right now, and so she let Rita see herself out.

Daphne started reading the want ads over breakfast every morning. A waste of time. "What *is* this?" she asked her grandfather. "A city where nobody needs anything?"

"Maybe you should try an agency," he said.

When it came to unemployment, he was her best listener. Ian always said, "Oh, something will show up," but her grandfather had been through the Depression and he sympathized from the bottom of his heart every time she was fired. "You might want to think about the Postal Service," he told her now. "Your dad found the Postal Service *very* satisfactory. Security, stability, fringe benefits . . ."

"I do like outdoor exercise," Daphne mused.

"No, no, not a mailman," her grandfather said. "I meant something behind a desk."

She hated desk work. She sighed so hard she rattled her newspaper.

In the afternoons she would take a bus downtown to look in person—"pounding the pavement," she called it, thinking again of her grandfather's Depression days. She gazed in the windows of photographic studios, stationery printers, record shops. A record shop might be fun. She knew everything there was to know about the current groups. However, if customers asked her assistance with something classical like Led Zeppelin or the Doors, she'd be in trouble.

Thomas told her she ought to come to New York. She phoned him just to talk, one evening when she felt low, and he said, "Catch the next train up. Sleep on the couch till you land a job. Angie says so too." (Angie was his girlfriend, who had recently moved in with him although Ian and their grandfather were not supposed to know.) But Daphne couldn't imagine living in a city where everyone came from someplace else, and so she said, "Oh, I guess I'll keep looking here."

One Sunday she even phoned Agatha—not something she did often, since Agatha was hard to reach and also (face it) inclined to criticize. But on this occasion she was a dear. She said, "Daph, what would you think about going to college now? I'd be happy to pay for it. We're making all this money that we're too busy to spend. You wouldn't have to ask Ian for a cent."

"Well, thank you," Daphne said. "That's really nice of you."

She wasn't the school type, to be honest. But it felt good to know both her brother and sister were behind her. Her friends were more callous; they were hunting jobs themselves, many of them, or waitressing or tending bar till they decided what interested them, or heading off to law school just to appear busy. Nobody in her circle seemed to have an actual career.

At the start of her third week without work, her grandfather talked her into going to a place called Same Day Résumé. He'd heard it advertised on the radio; he thought it might help her "present" herself, he said. So Daphne took a bus downtown and spoke to a bored-looking man at an enormous metal desk. The calendar on the wall behind him read TUES 13, which made her nervous because an old boyfriend had once told her that in Cuba, Tuesday the thirteenth was considered unlucky. Shouldn't she just offer some excuse and come back another time? It did seem the man wore a faint sneer as he listened to her qualifications. In fact the whole experience was so demoralizing that as soon as she'd finished answering his questions she walked over to Lexington Market and treated herself to a combination beef-and-bean burrito.

Then she went to a matinee starring Cher, her favorite movie star, and after that she cruised a few thrift shops. She bought two sets of thermal underwear with hardly any stains and a purple cotton tank top for a total of three dollars. By then it was time to collect her résumé, which had miraculously become four pages long. She had only to glance through it, though, to see how it had been padded and embroidered. Also, it cost a fortune. Her grandfather had said he would pay, but even so she resented the cost.

All the good cheer she had built up so carefully over the afternoon began to evaporate, and instead of heading home for supper she stopped at a bar where she and her friends hung out on weekends. It gave off the damp, bitter smell that such places always have before they fill up for the evening, and the low lighting seemed not romantic but bleak. Still, she perched on a cracked vinyl stool and ordered a Miller's, which she drank very fast. Then she ordered another and started reading her résumé. Any four-year-old could see that she hadn't gone past high school, even if she did list an introductory drawing course at the Maryland Institute and a weekend seminar called New Directions for Women.

"Hello, Daphne," someone said.

She turned and found Rita diCarlo settling on the stool next to her, unbuttoning her lumber jacket as she hailed the bartender. "Pabst," she told him. She unwound a wool scarf from her neck and flung her hair back. "You waiting for someone?"

Daphne shook her head.

"Me neither," Rita said.

Daphne could have guessed as much from Rita's shapeless black T-shirt and paint-spattered jeans. Her hair was even scruffier than usual; actual dust balls trailed from the end of her braid.

"I had my least favorite kind of job today," Rita told her. "A divorce. Splitting up a household. Naturally the wife and husband had to be there, so they could offer their opinions." She accepted her beer and blew into the foam. "And they did have opinions, believe me."

"Too many jobs get too personal," Daphne said gloomily.

"Right," Rita said. She was digging through her pockets for something—a Kleenex. She blew her nose with a honking sound.

"Like this florist's I was just fired from," Daphne said. "Everybody's private messages: you have to write them down pretending not to know English. Or when I worked at Camera Carousel—those photos of girls in bikinis and people's awful prom nights. You hand over the envelope with this smile like you never even noticed."

"Look," Rita said. "Did Ian tell you he and I have been seeing each other?"

"You have?" Daphne asked.

"Well, a couple of times. Well, really just once. I guess you wouldn't count when I accidentally on purpose ran into him at the wood shop."

No, Daphne wouldn't count that.

"I went to Brant's Custom Woodworks and ordered myself a bureau," Rita told her.

"I don't believe he mentioned it."

"Do you have any idea how much those things cost?"

"Expensive, huh?" Daphne said.

She glanced again at her résumé. Page two: Previous Employment. Here the facts were not padded but streamlined, for the man had suggested that too long a list made a person look flighty. "What say we strike the framer's," he had said, his sneer growing more pronounced.

"Another example is picture framing," Daphne told Rita. "People bring in these poor little paintings they've done themselves, or their drawings with the mouths erased and redrawn a dozen times and the hands posed out of sight because they can't do hands, and all you say is, 'Let me see now, perhaps a double mat . . .'"

"Then after we talked about my bureau awhile I asked if he'd come look at my apartment," Rita said, "just so he'd have an idea of the scale."

Daphne pulled her eyes away from the résumé. She focused on Rita's face for a moment, and then she said, "Don't you live with Nick Bascomb?"

"Well, I did, but I made him move out," Rita said.

"Oh? When was this?"

"Wednesday," Rita said.

"Wednesday? You mean this Wednesday just past?"

"See," Rita said, "Monday I went to visit Ian at the wood shop, and that night I asked Nick to move out. But I let him stay till Wednesday because he needed time to get his things together."

"Decent of you," Daphne said dryly.

"So then Friday Ian came by and we settled on what size bureau I wanted. I invited him to supper, but he said you-all were expecting him at home."

Daphne tried to remember back to Friday. Had she been there, even? She might have gone out with her usual gang and forgotten supper altogether.

"So when was it you saw him the second time?" she asked Rita.

"Well, that was it. Friday."

"You mean the second time was when he came to measure for your bureau?"

"Well, yes."

Daphne sat back on her stool.

This Rita was so *big*, though. She had that angular, big-boned frame. You'd expect her to be immune.

"Um, Rita," she said. "Ian's kind of . . . hard to pin down, sometimes. Also, I believe he has this sort of girlfriend at his church."

"So what? I had a boyfriend, till last Wednesday," Rita said.

"Yes, but then besides he's very, let's say Christian. Did you know that?"

"What do you think *I* am, Buddhist?"

"He's unusually Christian, though. I mean, look at you! You're sitting here in a bar! Drinking beer! Wearing a Hell Bent for Leather T-shirt!"

Rita glanced down at her shirt. She said, "That's not exactly a sin."

"It is to Ian," Daphne told her. "Or it almost is."

"Daphne," Rita said, "you get to know folks when you rearrange their belongings. Ian's belongings are so simple. They're so plain. He owns six books on how to be a better person. The clothes in his closet smell of nutmeg. And have you ever honestly looked at him? He has this really fine face; it's all straight lines. I thought at first his eyes were brown but then I saw they had a clear yellow light to them like some kind of drink; like cider. And when he talks he's very serious but when he listens to what I say back he starts smiling. He acts so happy to hear me, even when all I'm talking about is drawer knobs. Okay: so he does that to everyone. I don't kid myself! Probably it's part of his religion or something."

"Well, no," Daphne said. She felt touched. She was seeing Ian, all at once, from an outsider's angle. She said, "I didn't mean to drag you down. I was just thinking of back in school when some of my friends had crushes on him. They used to end up so frustrated. They ended up mad at him, almost."

"Well, I can understand that," Rita said. She took a hearty swallow of beer and wiped the foam off her upper lip.

"And he is a good bit older than you," Daphne pointed out.

"So? We're both grownups, aren't we? Anyhow, in some ways it's me who's older. Do you realize he's only slept with two women in all his life?"

"What?" Daphne asked.

"First his high-school sweetheart before he joined the church and then this woman he dated a few years ago, but he felt terrible about that and vowed he wouldn't do it again."

Daphne didn't know which shocked her more: the fact that he'd slept with someone or the fact that he and Rita had discussed it. "Well, how did . . . how did *that* come up?" she asked.

"It came up when I invited him to spend the night," Rita said calmly.

"You didn't!"

"I did," Rita said. "Bartender? Same again." She met Daphne's eyes. "I invited him when he came about the bureau," she said, "but he declined. He was extremely polite."

"I can imagine," Daphne said.

"Then all last weekend I waited to hear from him. I haven't done that since junior high! But he didn't call, and so here I sit, drinking away my sorrows."

He wasn't ever going to call, but Daphne didn't want to be the one to tell her. "Gosh! Look at the time," she said. She asked the bartender, "What do I owe?" and then she made a great to-do over paying, so that when she turned back to say goodbye, it would seem the subject of Ian had entirely slipped her mind.

Agatha and Stuart didn't come home for Christmas. Stuart was on call that weekend. Thomas came, though, and they spent a quiet holiday together, rising late on Christmas morning to exchange their gifts. Ian gave Daphne a key chain that turned into a siren when you pressed a secret button. (He was always after her about the neighborhoods she hung out in.) Her grandfather gave her a ten-dollar bill, the same thing he gave the others. Thomas, the world's most inspired shopper, gave her a special crystal guaranteed to grant steadiness of purpose, and Agatha and Stuart sent a dozen pairs of her favorite brand of black tights. Daphne herself gave everybody houseplants—an arrangement she'd made weeks ago when she still worked at Floral Fantasy.

For Christmas dinner they went to a restaurant. Daphne viewed this as getting away with something. If Agatha had been home, she never would have allowed it. But Agatha might have a point, Daphne thought as they entered the dining room. The owner kept his place open on holidays so that people without families had somewhere to go, and at nearly every table just a single, forlorn person sipped a solitary cocktail. Across the room they saw Mrs. Jordan, which made Daphne feel guilty because if Bee were still alive she would have remembered to invite her. But then Ian and the owner conferred and they added an extra place setting and brought her over to sit with them. Mrs. Jordan was as adventurous and game as ever, although she must be in her eighties by now, and once they'd said grace she livened things up considerably by describing a recent outing she'd taken with the foreigners. It seemed that during that peculiar warm spell back in November, she and three of the foreigners had driven to a marina someplace and rented a sailboat; only none of them had ever sailed before and when they found themselves on open water with a stiff breeze blowing up, the one named Manny had to jump over the side and swim for help. After they were rescued, Mrs. Jordan said, the marina owner had told them they could never take a boat out again. They couldn't even stand on the dock. They couldn't even park on the grounds to admire the view. By now she had them laughing, and she raised a speckled hand and ordered a bottle of champagne—"And you must join us, Ezra," she told the owner—along with a fizzy apple juice for Ian. It turned out to be a very festive meal.

In the evening Claudia and her family telephoned from Pittsburgh, and Agatha from California. Agatha didn't seem as distressed about the restaurant as she might have been. All she said to Daphne was, "Did Ian bring Clara?"

"Clara? No."

Agatha sighed. She said, "Maybe we'll just have to marry *Grandpa* off, instead."

"Actually, that might be easier," Daphne told her.

In January Daphne started working at the wood shop, performing various unskilled tasks like oiling and paste-waxing. She had done this several times before while she was between jobs, and although she would never choose it for a permanent career she found it agreeable enough. She liked the smell of sap and the golden light that the wood gave off, and she enjoyed the easy, stop-and-go conversation among the workmen. It reminded her of kindergarten— everyone absorbed in his own project but throwing forth a remark now and then. Ian didn't join in, though, and whenever he said anything to Daphne she was conscious of the furtive alertness in the rest of the room. Clearly, he was considered an oddity here. It made her feel sorry for him, although he might not even notice.

The Friday before Martin Luther King Day, Agatha and Stuart flew in for the long weekend and Thomas came down from New York. Agatha toured the house from basement to attic, checking the results of the Clutter Counseling. She approved in general but pointed out to Daphne that a sort of overlayer was beginning to sprout on various counters and dressers. "Yes, Rita warned us that might happen," Daphne said. "She offers a quarterly touch-up service but I swore I would do it myself."

Agatha said, "Hmm," and glanced at the cat's flea collar, which for some reason sat on the breadboard. "I wonder how much one of these touch-ups would cost."

"I could probably get a bargain rate," Daphne told her. Shoot, she could probably get it for free, if Rita still had her crush on Ian. But maybe she had recovered by now. Daphne hadn't seen her since that evening in the bar.

Saturday Agatha and Stuart attended an all-day conference on bone marrow transplants, and that night they had dinner with some of their colleagues. This may have been why, on Sunday, they agreed to go to church with the rest of the family. They had barely shown their faces, after all, and tomorrow they would be flying out again. Ian was thrilled, you could tell. He talked his father into coming along too, which ordinarily was next to impossible. Churches ought to *look* like churches, Doug always said. He was sorry, but that was just the way he felt.

It was coat weather, but sunny, and so they went on foot—Doug and Ian, then Thomas and Stuart, with Agatha and Daphne bringing up the rear. As they passed each house on Waverly Street, Agatha inquired about the occupants. "What do you see of the Crains these days? Does Miss Bitz still teach piano?" It wasn't till that moment that Daphne realized how much had changed here. The Crains, no longer newlyweds, had moved to a bigger house after the birth of their third daughter. Miss Bitz had died. Others had gone on to condominiums or retirement communities once their children were grown, and the people who took their places— working couples, often, whose children attended day care—seemed harder to get to know. "All that's left," Daphne said, "are the foreigners and Mrs. Jordan."

"Where *is* Mrs. Jordan? Shouldn't we stop by and pick her up?"

"She has to drive now, on account of her rheumatism."

"This is depressing," Agatha said.

It did seem depressing. Or maybe that was just the season, the thin white light of January; for in spite of the sunshine the neighborhood had a pallid, lifeless look.

The church was barely half full this morning, but there weren't six empty chairs in a row and so they had to separate. The men sat near the front, and Daphne and Agatha sat at the rear next to Sister Nell. Sister Nell leaned across Daphne to say, "Why, Sister Agatha! Isn't this a treat!" Daphne felt a bit jealous; she was never called "Sister" herself. Evidently you had to leave town before you were considered grown.

Two years ago Sister Lula had willed the church her electric organ—the very small kind that salesmen sometimes demonstrate in shopping malls—and Sister Myra was playing "Amazing Grace" while latecomers straggled in. Under cover of the music, Agatha murmured, "Show me which one is Clara."

Daphne looked around. "There," she said, sliding her eyes to the left. Clara sat between her father and her brother—a slim woman in her

mid-thirties with buff-colored hair feathered perfectly, dry skin powdered, tailored suit a careful
orchestration of salmon pink and aqua.

"Why isn't she sitting with Ian?" Agatha
asked.

"Because she's sitting with her father and
brother."

"You know what I mean," Agatha told her. But
just then the music stopped and Reverend Emmett rose from behind the counter to offer the
opening prayer.

He was getting old. It took Agatha's presence
to make Daphne see that. He was one of those
people who hollow as they age, and when he
turned to reach for his Bible his back had a curve
like a beetle's back. But his voice was as strong
as ever. "Proverbs twenty-one: four," he said in
his rich, pure tenor. " 'An high look, and a proud
heart, and the plowing of the wicked, is sin.' "
Then he announced the hymn: "In the Sweet
Bye and Bye."

Daphne loved singing hymns. She had forgotten, though, what a trial it was to sing with
Agatha, who *talked* the words in a monotone
and broke off halfway through to ask, "Where
are the young people? Where are the children?"

Daphne wouldn't answer. She went on
singing.

The sermon had to do with arrogance. Nothing

was more arrogant, Reverend Emmett said, than the pride of the virtuous man, and then he told them a story. "Last week, I called on a brother whose wife had recently died. Some of you may know whom I mean. He was not a member of our church, and had visited only a very few times. Still, I was surprised to see him bring forth a bottle of wine once I was seated. 'Reverend Emmett,' he said, 'you happen to have arrived on my fiftieth anniversary. My wife and I always promised ourselves that when we reached this day, we would open a bottle of wine that we'd saved from our wedding reception. Well, she is no longer here to share it, and I'm hoping very much that you will have a glass to keep me company.' "

Daphne held her breath. Even Agatha looked interested.

"So I did," Reverend Emmett said.

Daphne started breathing again.

"I reflected that the Alcohol Rule is a rule for the self, designed to remove an obstruction between the self and the Lord, but drinking that glass of wine was a gift to another human being and refusing it would have been arrogant. And when I took my leave—well, I'm not proud of this—I had a momentary desire for some sort of mouthwash, in case I met one of our brethren on the way home. But I thought, 'No, this is between me and my God,' and so I walked through the streets joyfully breathing fumes of alcohol."

Agatha fell into a fit of silent laughter. Daphne could feel her shaking; she had a sidelong glimpse of her white face growing pink and convulsed. In disgust, Daphne drew away from her and folded her arms across her chest. She didn't hold with the Alcohol Rule herself, but she almost wished now she did just so she could make a gesture like Reverend Emmett's. In fact, maybe she already had. Couldn't you say that *every* social drink was a gift to another human being? She played with that notion throughout the rest of the sermon, deliberately ignoring Agatha, who kept wiping her eyes with a tissue.

At Amending, Daphne confessed in a low voice that she had spoken rudely to her grandfather. "I told him to quit bugging me about a job," she said, "and I called Ian an old maid, and I said Bert could go to hell when he showed me where I'd skipped on a bookcase." Sister Nell was murmuring something long and involved about a dispute with a neighbor. Agatha said nothing, wouldn't you know. This meant she got to hear everyone else's sins and pass judgment. "Talk about an high look!" Daphne whispered sharply, and then Reverend Emmett said, "Let it vanish now from our souls, Lord. In Jesus' name, amen." After that they stood up to sing "Love Divine, All Loves Excelling."

The Benediction was hardly finished before Agatha was in the aisle, making her way toward Clara as she put her coat on. Daphne followed, but then Brother Simon stopped her to talk and so she arrived at Agatha's side too late to introduce her. "I'm Agatha Bedloe-Simms," Agatha was saying. (Only the rawest newcomer mentioned last names within these walls, but no doubt she wanted to establish her connection to Ian.) "I believe you must be Clara."

"Why, yes," Clara said in her ladylike, modulated voice. "And this is my father, Brother Edwin, and my brother, Brother James."

She was probably making a point, with all those "Brothers," but if so it passed right over Agatha's head. "It's a pleasure to meet you," Agatha told them. "Clara, Ian has talked so much about you."

"Oh! Has he?" Clara asked, and a blush started spreading upward from her Peter Pan collar.

Daphne felt confused. Had he really? Before she could find out, though, Reverend Emmett reached their group. "Sister Agatha," he said, "I'm so glad to see you here."

He gave no sign of recollecting that Agatha had spurned his church for years and insisted on a city hall wedding. And Agatha herself seemed unabashed. "So tell me, Reverend Emmett," she said, "what does a fifty-year-old bottle of wine taste like, anyhow?"

"Oh, it was vinegar," he said cheerfully.

"And don't you think mentioning it to us was another form of mouthwash, so to speak?"

"Ah," he said, smiling. "Something to confess at our next Amending."

He turned to Stuart, who had shown up behind her with Ian. "You must be Agatha's husband," he said.

"Brother Stuart," Stuart announced, with the prideful smirk of someone speaking a foreign language.

There was a bustle of introductions and small talk, and then Reverend Emmett moved off to greet someone else and Agatha whispered to Daphne, "Do we have enough lunch for three extra?"

"Three?" Daphne asked.

"Her father and brother too?"

They didn't, but that wasn't the issue. Daphne said, "Agatha, I really don't think—"

Too late. Agatha turned to Clara and said, "Won't the three of you come home with us for lunch?"

Clara was still blushing. She looked over at Ian. "Oh, we wouldn't want to inconvenience you," she said.

"Right," Ian said. "Maybe some other time." And he took Agatha's arm and propelled her toward the door. Daphne and Clara were left gaping at each other. Daphne said, "Um . . ."

"Well, it was lovely seeing you," Clara said melodiously.

"Yes, well . . . so long, I guess."

Daphne hurried to catch up with the others. Ian still had hold of Agatha, who was looking cross. Outside, when they regrouped—Agatha walking next to Daphne once again—Agatha muttered, "What a dud."

"Who, Clara?"

"Ian."

"Maybe they've had a fight or something," Daphne said.

"More likely they've just withered on the vine," Agatha told her.

Up ahead, Stuart was asking all about the Church of the Second Chance. He wanted to know how sizable a membership it had, when it had been founded, what its tax status was. You could tell he was only making conversation, but Ian answered each question gladly and at length. He said that Second Chance had saved his life. Doug, walking in front with Thomas, coughed and said, "Oh, well, ah . . ." but Ian insisted, "It did, Dad. You know it did."

He told Stuart, "Sometimes I have this insomnia. I fall asleep just fine but then an hour or so later I wake up, and that's when the troublesome thoughts move in. You know? Things I did wrong, things I said wrong, mistakes I want to take back. And I always wonder, 'If I didn't have Someone to turn this all over to, how would I get through this? How do other people get through it?' Because I'm surely not the only one, am I?"

They had reached an intersection now, and they waited on the curb while a spurt of traffic passed. Agatha clutched her coat collar tight and glanced over at Daphne. There was something meaningful in the way she narrowed her eyes. *And you didn't want me to invite a girlfriend for him*, she must be saying.

"You know that clock downstairs that strikes the number of hours," Ian told Stuart. "And then it strikes once at every half hour. So when you hear it striking once, you can't be certain how much of the night you've used up. Is it twelve thirty, or is it one, or is it one thirty? You have to just lie there and wait, and hope with all your heart that next time it will strike two. Or what's worse, some nights it starts striking one, two, three and you say, 'Ah!' And then four, five and you say, 'Can this be? Have I really slept through till dawn?' And then six, seven and you say, 'Oh-oh,' because you can see it's not *that* light out. And sure enough, the clock goes on to twelve, and you brace yourself for another six hours till morning."

The street was clear now and they could have crossed, but instead they stood watching him. It was Agatha who finally spoke. "Oh, Ian," she said. "Oh, damnit. How much longer are you going to be on your own?"

"Why, not long at all," he told her.

They squinted at him in the sunlight.

"I wasn't planning to bring this up yet," he said. "But anyhow. Since you ask. I believe I might be getting married."

Somewhere far off, a car honked.

Agatha said, "Married?"

"At least, we're talking it over."

Stuart said, "Hey, now!" He punched Ian in the shoulder. "Hey, guy. Congratulations!"

"Thanks," Ian said. He was grinning.

"This is you and Clara," Agatha said.

"Who? No, it's Rita," he said. He told Daphne, "You know Rita."

Daphne's mouth dropped open.

"Rita who?" Agatha asked. She tugged Daphne's jacket sleeve. "Who's Rita?"

Their grandfather was the one who answered. "Rita the Clutter Counselor," he said. "Hot dog!"

"But who is she?" Agatha demanded. They started crossing the street, with Ian leading the way. "Have *you* met her, Thomas?"

Thomas said, "Nope." But he was grinning too.

"We've only been going out a month or so," Ian told them. "When I first got to know her I held back, for a while. I was afraid we were too different. But then finally I said, 'I just have to do this,' and I called her up. By the end of that first evening it seemed we'd known each other forever."

"You must have at least suspected," Agatha told Daphne.

"I swear I didn't," Daphne said.

She was in that stunned state of mind where every sound seems unusually distinct. Of course she liked Rita very much, and yet . . . "This is so sudden," she said to Ian. "Shouldn't you go more inch-by-inch?"

He stopped in the middle of the sidewalk and turned. "Look," he said. "I'm forty-one years old. I'm not getting any younger. And you all know my beliefs. You know I can't just . . . live with her or anything. I want to get married."

"Right on!" Stuart cheered.

"Besides which, you're going to love her. Aren't they, Dad?"

"Absolutely," his father said, beaming. "She let me keep my workbench just the way I wanted. She let me keep Bee's lipstick on the bureau."

"She's very tall and slim and beautiful," Ian

told Agatha. "She could easily be Indian. She has beautiful long black hair and she moves in this loose, swinging way, like a dancer."

Daphne looked at him.

As a matter of fact, every word he had said was true.

"There's something honest about her, and just . . . right," he said. "I've never met anyone like her."

Agatha stepped forward, then. She put both hands on his shoulders and kissed his cheek. "Congratulations, Ian," she said.

"Me, too," Daphne said, and she kissed his other cheek, and Thomas clamped his neck in a rough hug. "Mr. Mysterious," he said.

Their grandfather touched Ian's arm shyly. Ian was trying to get the grin off his face.

They started walking again. Agatha asked all about the wedding, and Doug described how Rita admired his baby-food-jar system for sorting screws. But Daphne strolled next to Stuart in silence.

She was thinking about the dream she had dreamed at Thanksgiving. It wasn't so much a dream as a feeling—a wash of intense, deep, perfect love. She had awakened and thought, *For whom?* and realized it was Ian. But it was Ian back in her childhood, when he had seemed the most magnificent person on earth. She hadn't noticed till then how pale and flawed her love had grown since. It had made her want to weep for him, and that was why, at breakfast that day, she had said she hadn't dreamed any dreams at all.

10

RECOVERING FROM THE HEARTS-OF-PALM FLU

She asked if he thought he might ever want children and he said, "Oh, well, maybe some-time." She asked how long he figured they should wait and he said, "A few years, maybe? I don't know."

They'd been married just four months, by then. He could see his answer came as a disappointment.

But why should they rush to change things? Their lives were perfect. Simply watching her— simply sitting at the kitchen table watching her knead a loaf of bread—filled him with content-ment. Her hands were so capable, and she moved with such economy. When she wiped her floury palms on the seat of her jeans, he was struck with admiration for her naturalness.

"I had been wondering about sooner," she told him.

"Well, no need to decide this instant," he said.

He watched her oil a baking pan, working her long, tanned fingers deftly into the corners, and he thought of a teacher he had had in seventh grade. Mrs. Arnett, her name was. Mrs. Arnett had once been his ideal woman—soft curves and sweet perfume and ivory skin. He had found any number of reasons to bicycle past her house. Her front bow window, which was curtained off day and night by cream-colored draperies, had displayed a single, pale blue urn, and somehow that urn had come to represent all his fantasies about marriage. He had imagined Mrs. Arnett greeting her husband at the door each evening, wearing not the bermudas or dull slacks his mother wore but a swirly dress the same shade of blue as the urn; and she would kiss Mr. Arnett full on the lips and lead him inside. Everything would be so focused. No distractions: no TV blaring or telephone ringing or neighbors stopping by.

Certainly no children.

You couldn't say Ian and Rita lived that way, even now. They were still in the house on Waverly Street—partly a matter of economics, partly to keep his father company. (Daphne had a place of her own now.) His father still occupied the master bedroom, and Rita's widowed mother was forever dropping by, and Rita's various aunts and cousins and a whole battalion of woman friends sat permanently around the kitchen table waiting for her to pour coffee. Where would children fit into all this?

"Next birthday, I'll be thirty," Rita told him.

"Thirty's young," Ian said.

Next birthday, Ian would be forty-two.

Forty-two seemed way too old to be thinking of babies.

At the wood shop, one of the workers had a daughter smaller than his own granddaughters. He was on his second wife, a manicurist named LaRue, and LaRue had told him it wasn't fair to deprive her of a family just because he had already had the joy of one. He had reported every detail of their arguments on the subject; and next he'd discussed the pregnancy, which seemed so new and exciting to LaRue and so old to Butch, and finally the baby herself, who cried every evening and interrupted dinner and caused LaRue to smell continually of spit-up milk. Now the baby was two and sometimes came along with her mother to give Butch a ride home after work. She would toddle through the shavings, crowing, and hold out her little arms until he set aside his plane and picked her up.

"Ain't she a doll?" he asked the others. "Ain't she a living doll?" But the sight of his grizzled cheek next to that flower-petal face was disturbing, somehow, and Ian always turned away, smiling falsely, and grew very busy with his tools.

Ian and Rita went to church on foot that next Sunday because the weather was so fine. Besides, Ian liked the ceremony of it: the two of them holding hands as they walked and calling out greetings to various neighbors working in their yards. Rita wore a dress (or at least, a long black T-shirt that hit her above the knees), because she'd grown up at Alameda Baptist and considered jeans unsuitable for church. Her braid was wound in a knot at the nape of her neck. Ian couldn't help noticing the unusually attractive way her hair grew, hugging her temples closely and swooping down over her ears in ripples.

"Did I tell you Mary-Clay went in for her ultrasound?" she asked. "Her doctor said she's having twins."

"Twins! Good grief," he said. A shadow fell over him.

"Two little girls, her doctor thinks. Mary-Clay is just tickled to bits. Girls are easier than boys, she says."

"Rita," Ian said, "neither is easy."

She glanced at him. He hadn't meant to sound so emphatic.

"At least," he said, "not according to my limited experience."

They turned onto York Road. Ahead they could see a cluster of worshipers standing in front of the church, enjoying their last few moments of sunshine before they stepped inside. Rita said, "Well, now that you mention it, your experience *was* limited. Those children weren't your own. You weren't even solely responsible for them!"

"Right," Ian told her. "I had both my parents helping, and still it wasn't easy. A lot of it was just plain boring. Just providing a warm body, just *being* there; anyone could have done it. And then other parts were terrifying. Kids get into so much! They start to matter so much. Some days I felt like a fireman or a lifeguard or something— all that tedium, broken up by little spurts of high drama."

Rita gathered a breath, but by then they'd reached the others. Sister Myra said, "Why, hello, you two!" and kissed them both, even Ian. She had never kissed Ian before he was married. Marriage changed things a good deal, he had learned.

They were the church's only newlyweds at the moment, and almost the only ones ever. Their wedding had taken place at Alameda Baptist, but most of Second Chance had attended and Reverend Emmett had helped officiate, even donning one of Alameda's flowing black pastoral robes so when he raised his arms to pray he had resembled a skinny Stealth bomber. Now they were passed from hand to hand like babies in an old folks' home, with Rita saying those just-right things that women somehow know to say. "Brother Kenneth, how's that sciatica? Why, Sister Denise! You've gone and lightened your hair." Ian was impressed, but also disconcerted. This never seemed to be *his* Rita, who spent her weekdays bluntly informing customers that most of their lifelong treasures belonged in the nearest landfill.

They went inside and took two seats halfway up the aisle. Sister Nell was passing out hymn pamphlets. When Ian opened his he found the top corner of each page torn off as if gnawed by a mouse, and he smiled to himself and looked around for Daphne. (She must have some kind of deficiency, Agatha always said, to eat paper the way she did.) But he didn't see her. The fact was that she attended less and less, now that she lived downtown. Just about all you could count on her for was Good Works on Saturday mornings.

Rita was talking with her neighbor on the other side, Brother Kenneth's son Johnny, who used to be a little pipsqueak of a boy but now was studying for the ministry. Sometimes lately he had assisted with the services. Today, though, Reverend Emmett rose alone to deliver the opening prayer. Rita faced forward obediently and bowed her head, but Ian sensed she wasn't listening. She failed to straighten when Reverend Emmett said, "Amen," and she chewed a thumbnail edgily during the Bible reading. Ian reached over and captured her hand and tucked it into his, and she relaxed against him.

"Thus concludes the reading of the Holy Word," Reverend Emmett said. "We will now sing hymn fourteen."

The little organ wheezed out the first notes and Ian let go of Rita's hand. But she didn't draw away. Instead she looked directly into his face as they stood up, ignoring the hymnal he held before them.

"Listen," she said in a low voice. "I think I might be pregnant."

He had already opened his mouth to start singing. He shut it. The congregation went on without them: "Break Thou the bread of life . . ."

"It wasn't on purpose," she said. And then she whispered, "But I intend to be glad about this, I tell you!"

What could he say?

"Me, too, sweetheart," he said.

They faced front again. Stammering slightly, he found his place and joined the other singers.

That was in July. By September, she was having to leave the waistband of her jeans unsnapped and she wore her loosest work shirts over them. She said she thought she could feel the baby moving now—a little bubble, she said, flitting here and there in a larking sort of way. Ian set a palm on her abdomen but it was still too early for him to feel anything from outside.

She bought a book that showed what the baby looked like week by week, and she and Ian studied it together. A lima bean. A tadpole. Then finally a person but a clumsily constructed one, like something modeled in preschool. They were thinking of Joshua for a boy and Rachel for a girl. Ian tried the names on his tongue to see how they'd work in everyday life. "Oh, and I'd like you to meet my son, Joshua Bedloe . . ." His son! The notion brought forth the most bewildering mixture of feelings: worry and excitement and also, underneath, a pervasive sense of tiredness. He told Rita about everything but the tiredness. That he kept to himself.

Now it seemed the household was completely taken over by women. Rita's batty mother, Bobbeen, spent hours in their kitchen, generally seated not at the table but on it and dangling her high-heeled sandals from her toes. With her crackling, bleached-out fan of hair and snapping gum and staticky barrage of advice, she seemed electric, almost dangerous. "You're insane to go on working when you don't have to, Rita, stark staring insane. Don't you remember what happened to your aunt Dora when *she* kept on? You tell her, Ian. Tell her to quit hauling other folkses' junk when she's four and a half months gone and all her pelvic bones are coming off their hinges." But she didn't actually mean for Ian to say anything; she didn't leave the briefest pause before starting a new train of thought. "I guess you heard about Molly Sidney. Six months along and she phones her doctor, says, 'Feels like somebody's hauling rope out of way down low in my back.' 'Oh,' her doctor says, 'That's normal.' Says, 'Pay it no mind,' and the very next night guess what."

She could recite the most bizarre stories: umbilical cords kinked off like twisted vacuum-cleaner hoses, babies arriving with tails and coats of fur, deluges of blood in the lawn-care aisle at Ace Hardware. If Rita's two married girlfriends were around they would tut-tut. "Hush, now! You'll scare her!" they'd say. But their own stories were nearly as alarming. "I was in labor for thirty-three hours." "Well, they had to tie *me* down on the bed." Serenely, Rita circulated with the coffeepot. Ian retreated to the basement, where his father was repainting the family high chair. "Women!" Ian said. "They're giving me the chills."

"You want to close that door behind you, Ian," his father said. "It was paint fumes caused your cousin Linley's baby to have that little learning problem."

In October Ian started building a cradle of Virginia cherry—a simple slant-sided box without a hood because Rita wanted the baby to be able to see the world. He obtained the materials at no cost but of course he had to contribute his own time, and so he fell into the habit of staying on in the shop after it closed. His metal rasp, zipping down the edge of a rocker slat, said *careen! careen!* Often he seemed to hear the other workers' voices echoing through the empty room. "Drove a spindle wedge too hard and split the goddamn . . ." Bert said clearly, and Mr. Brant asked, "Why the hell you choose a plank with the sapwood showing?" Ian stopped rasping and ran a hand along the slat's edge, trying to gauge the curve. All his years here, he had worked with straight lines. He had deliberately stayed away from the bow-backed chairs and benches that required eye judgment, personal opinion. Now he was surprised at how these two shallow U shapes satisfied his palm.

And all his years here he had failed to understand Mr. Brant's prejudice against nails, his insistence on mortise-and-tenon and dovetails. "You put a drawer together with dovetail, it stays tight a century no matter what the weather," Mr. Brant was fond of saying, and Ian always thought, *A century! Who cares?* It was not that he opposed doing a thing well. Everything that came from his hands was fine and smooth and sturdy. But you could manage that with nails too, for heaven's sake; and if it didn't last forever, why, *he* would not be there to notice. Now, though, he took special pride in the cradle's nearly seamless joints, which would expand and contract in harmony and continue to stay tight through a hundred steamy summers and parched winters.

Early in December Rita and Ian went with Daphne and her new boyfriend, Curt, to a bar downtown that featured pinball machines. Daphne had developed a passion for pinball. Rita was beginning her seventh month and she had lately cut her work hours in half, which left her with too much time on her hands. Any outing at all struck her as preferable to staying home. This was why Ian agreed to go to the bar, even though he didn't drink. And Rita, of course, couldn't drink, and Curt turned out to belong to A.A. So there the three of them sat with their seltzers while Daphne, merrily sloshing her beer, toured the various games. Her favorite, she said, was the one called Black Knight 2000, which she wanted the four of them to try if only the others would give them half a chance. She hoisted herself onto a stool and glowered at the crowd. There were so many people here that Ian couldn't even see what kind of room it was.

Curt was telling Rita about his sister's breech baby. (Did people actively *collect* these tales?) He didn't look like much, in Ian's honest opinion—a bespectacled and bearded type in clothes too determinedly rustic. Also, something unfortunate had happened to his hair. It stuck out all over his head in rigid little cylinders. Ian said, "What . . . ?" He leaned closer to Daphne and said, "What would you call that kind of hairdo, exactly?"

"Do you like it? I did it myself," she said. "You braid dozens and dozens of eentsy braids and dunk them in Elmer's glue to make them last. The only problem is when he jogs."

"Jogs?"

"He claims they bobble against his head and bang his scalp."

Ian snorted, but all at once he felt old. In fact he was very likely the oldest person present. He looked down at the hand encircling his glass—the grainy skin on his knuckles, the gnarled veins in his forearm. How could he have assumed that old people were born that way? That age was an individual trait, like freckles or blond hair, that would never happen to him?

He was older now, he thought with a thud, than Danny had ever managed to become.

Rita was laughing at something Curt had said, unconsciously cradling the bulge of her baby as she leaned back against the bar. Daphne was humming along with the jukebox. "Madonna," she broke off to tell Ian.

"Pardon?"

" 'Like a Prayer.' "

"I beg your pardon?"

"The *song*, Ian."

"Oh."

He took a gulp from his glass. (This seltzer smelled like wet dog.) "So anyhow," he said to Daphne, "where did you and Curt meet?"

"At work," she said.

Daphne had a job now at a place called Trips Unlimited. Ian said, "He's a travel agent?"

"No, no, he came in to reserve a flight. By profession he's an inventor."

"An inventor."

"He's got this one invention: a Leaf Paw. This sort of claw-type contraption you hold in your left hand to scoop up the leaves you're raking. We think it's going to make him rich."

Ian glanced over at Rita, hoping she'd heard. (They often considered the same things funny.)

But Rita was staring fixedly across the room. He followed her eyes and saw a small, pretty girl in a Danzig T-shirt playing the Black Knight 2000 machine. An old friend, maybe? But when he turned back to ask, he realized Rita's stare was unfocused. It was the glazed and inward stare of someone listening to faraway music. He said, "Rita?"

"Excuse me," she said abruptly. She stood and made her way through the crowd, disappearing behind the door marked LADIES.

Ian and Daphne looked at each other. "Think I should go after her?" Daphne asked.

"I'm not sure," he said. "Well, she's probably okay."

Although he was nowhere near as confident as he sounded.

They fell silent. Even Curt seemed to know better than to try and make small talk. Now Ian noticed the noise in this place—the laughter and clinking glassware and the hubbub from the pinball machines, which whanged and burbled and barked instructions in metallic, hollow voices. Everyone was so carefree! Two stools over, a young woman with long hair as dark as Rita's nonchalantly swung her pink-and-turquoise mountain-climbing shoes. A young man in a red jacket and a straight blond ponytail passed her one of the beers he'd just paid for. The jukebox had stopped playing, but some people in a booth were singing "Happy Birthday."

Then Rita was back, white-faced. All three of them stood up. She told Ian, "I'm bleeding."

He swallowed.

Curt was the first to react. He said, "I'll get the check. You three head out to the car," and he dropped a set of keys into Ian's palm.

Ian had forgotten that they'd driven here in Curt's Volvo. "Let's go," he said. He shepherded Rita toward the door. Daphne followed with their wraps. When they reached the sidewalk he stopped to help Rita into her jacket. She shook her head, but he could hear how her teeth were chattering. "Put it on," he told her, and she submitted, allowing him to bully her arms into the sleeves.

Curt caught up with them as Ian was unlocking the car door. "Which hospital?" he asked, sliding behind the wheel, and he started the engine in one smooth motion. He drove as if he'd dealt with such crises often, swooping dexterously from lane to lane and barely slowing for red lights before proceeding through them. Meanwhile Ian held both of Rita's hands in his. Her teeth were still chattering and he wondered if she was in shock.

At the Emergency Room entrance, Curt pulled up behind an ambulance. Ian hustled Rita out of the backseat and took her inside to a woman at a long green counter. "She's bleeding," he told the woman.

"How much?" she asked.

Instantly, he felt reassured. It appeared there were degrees to this; they shouldn't automatically assume the worst. Rita said, "Not a whole lot."

The woman called for a nurse, and Rita was led away while Ian stayed behind to fill out forms. Insurance company, date of birth . . . He answered hurriedly, scrawling across the dotted lines. When he was almost finished, Daphne and Curt came in from parking the car. "They've taken her somewhere," he told them. He asked Daphne, "Do you know her mother's maiden name?"

"Make one up," Daphne said. She looked around at the faded green walls, the elderly black man half asleep on a molded plastic chair. "Not bad," she said. "Usually this place is packed."

How often did she come here, anyway? And Curt, standing behind her, said, "Lord, yes, there've been times I've waited six and seven hours."

"Well, we might have a wait this evening, too," Ian said. "Maybe you should both go home."

"I'm staying," Daphne told him.

"Yes, but," Ian said. He slid the form across

the counter to the woman. He said, "But, um, I'd really *rather* you go. To tell the truth."

He could see she felt hurt. She said, "Oh."

"I just want to . . . concentrate on this. All right?" he asked.

"I could concentrate too," she said.

But Curt touched her sleeve and said, "Come on, Daph. I'm sure he'll call as soon as he has anything to tell you."

When he led her away, Ian felt overwhelmingly grateful. He felt he might even love the boy.

Rita lay on a stretcher in an enclosure formed by white curtains. No one had come to examine her yet, she said, but they'd phoned her doctor. She wore a withered blue hospital gown, and a white sheet covered her legs and rose gently over the mound of her stomach. Ian settled on a stool beside the stretcher. He picked up her hand, which felt warmer now and slightly moist. She curled her fingers tightly around his.

"Remember our wedding night?" she asked him.

"Yes, of course."

"Remember in the hotel? I came out of the bathroom in my nightgown and you were sitting on the edge of the bed, touching two fingers to your forehead. I thought you were nervous about making love."

"Well, I was," he said.

"You were praying."

"Well, that too."

"You were shy about saying your bedtime prayers in front of me and so you pretended you were just sort of thinking."

"I was worried I would look like one of those show-off Christians," he said. "But still I wanted to, um, I felt I ought to—"

"Could you pray now?" she asked him.

"Now?"

"Could you pray for the baby?"

"Honey, I've been praying ever since we left the bar," he said.

Really his prayers had been for Rita. He had fixed her firmly, fiercely to this planet and held her there with all his strength. But he had prayed not only for her health but for her happiness, and so in a sense he supposed you could say that he'd prayed for the baby as well.

She spent one night in the hospital but was released the following morning, still pregnant, with orders to lie flat until her due date. At first this seemed easy. She would do anything, she said, anything at all. She would stand on her head for two months, if it helped her hang on to this baby. But she had always been the athletic, go-getter type, and books didn't interest her and TV made her restless. So every evening when Ian came home from work he found the radio blaring, and Rita on the telephone, and the kitchen bustling with women fixing tidbits to tempt her appetite as if she were a delicate invalid. Which, of course, she wasn't. "I don't care if it takes major surgery!" she'd be shouting into the phone. "You get those moldy old magazines *away* from her!" (She was talking to Dennis or Lionel—one of her poor frazzled assistants.) Her hair flared rebelliously out of its braid and her shirtsleeves hiked up on her arms; nothing could induce her to spend the day in her bathrobe. And constantly she leapt to her feet on one pretext or another, while everybody cried, "Stop! Wait!" holding out their hands as if to catch the infant they imagined she would let drop.

Ian's father, who kept mostly to the basement these days, told Ian this was all a result of a misstep in evolution. "Human beings should never have risen upright," he said. "Now every pregnant woman has gravity working against her. Remember Claudia? Same thing happened to Claudia, back when she was expecting Franny."

"That's true, it did," Ian said. He had forgotten. All at once he saw Lucy in her red bandanna with her hair hanging down her back. "Just, you know, a little bleeding . . ." she informed him in her quaint croak. Lucy had been pregnant herself at the time. She had been pregnant at her wedding, most likely, and only now did Ian stop to think how she must have felt going through those early weeks alone, hiding her symptoms from everyone, trying to figure out some way to manage.

"It won't be real fancy," she said.

And, "Twenty twenty-seven! Great God Almighty!"

She said, "Do you think Danny will mind?"

That evening while he and Rita were playing Scrabble, he rose and wandered over to Lucy's framed photo above the piano. Daphne had hung it there some time ago, but he'd hardly glanced at it since. He lifted it from its hook and held it level in both hands. "I'll trade you two of my vowels for one consonant," Rita said, but Ian went on frowning at Lucy's small, bright face.

Of course, she struck him as preposterously young. That was only to be expected. And everything about her was so dated. That leggy look of the sixties! That childish, Christopher Robin stance grown women used to affect, with their feet planted wide apart and their bare knees braced! She resembled a little tepee on stilts. A paper parasol from a cocktail glass. One of those tiny, peaked Japanese mushrooms with the thready stems.

He was noticing this to gain some distance. Surely he was able to see her clearly now. Wasn't he? Surely he had the perspective, at last, to understand what Lucy's meaning had been in his life.

But Rita said, "Okay, *three* of my vowels. For one lousy consonant. You drive a hard bargain, you devil."

And Ian replaced the picture on its hook, no wiser.

This was going to be the first Christmas of their marriage and Rita had big plans. She sent Daphne on mysterious errands with shopping lists and whispered instructions. She phoned Thomas in New York and Agatha in L.A., making sure they were coming. She drew up a guest list for Christmas dinner: Mrs. Jordan and the foreigners and her mother and Curt. Ian had once mentioned how the Bedloes' holiday meals used to be all hors d'oeuvres, and she decided to revive the practice even though it meant cooking from the living room. For days she lay on the couch with a breadboard across her lap, rolling pinwheels and stamping out fancy shapes of biscuit dough and mincing herbs that Doug obligingly toted back and forth for her. Ian worried she was overdoing, but at least it kept her entertained.

Christmas fell on a Monday that year. Thomas arrived in time for church on Sunday morning, and Daphne met them there, carrying her knapsack because she'd be sleeping over. Agatha and Stuart flew in that afternoon. For the family supper on Christmas Eve they had black-eyed peas and rice. Everybody was puzzled by this (they usually had oyster stew), but Rita explained that black-eyed peas were an ancient custom. Something to do with luck, she said—good luck for the coming year. Almost immediately a sort of click of recognition traveled around the table. Coming year? Then wasn't that *New Year's* Eve? They sent each other secret glances and then applied themselves to their food, smiling. Rita didn't notice a thing. Ian did, though, and he was touched by his family's tact. Lately he'd started valuing such qualities. He had begun to see the importance of manners and gracious gestures; he thought now that his mother's staunch sprightliness had been braver than he had appreciated in his youth. (Last summer, laid up for a week with a wrenched back, he had suddenly wondered how Bee had endured the chronic pain of her arthritis all those years. He suspected that had taken a good deal more strength than the brief, flashy acts of valor you see in the movies.)

"To the cook!" Thomas said, raising his water glass, and they all said, "To Rita!" Rita grinned and raised her own glass. Probably for decades of Christmas Eves to come the Bedloes would be loyally eating black-eyed peas and rice.

It was afterwards, in front of the fire, that Thomas announced his engagement. "You two won't be the newest newlyweds anymore," he told Ian. This wasn't exactly a shock—he'd been dating the same girl for some time now—but they had been hoping he would get over her. They all felt she bossed him around too much. (He kept falling for these managerial types who didn't have any softness to them; they might as well be business partners, Daphne had once complained.) Still, the women hugged him and Doug said, "What do you know!" and Ian suggested they call Angie and welcome her to the family. So they did, lining up in the hall to tell her more or less the same thing in several different ways. While Ian was waiting his turn at the phone he had a sudden memory of Danny presenting Lucy in this very spot. What was it he had said? "I'd like you to meet the woman who's changed my life," he had said, and then as now the family had received the news with the most resolute show of pleasure.

On Christmas morning they opened their presents—most of Ian's and Rita's relating to babies—and then cleared away the gift wrap and started getting ready for the dinner guests. Rita directed from an armchair Ian had dragged into the dining room, except that she kept jumping up to do things herself. Finally Agatha put Stuart in charge of diverting her. "Show her your card tricks, Stu," she said. "Oh, please, no," Rita groaned. Ian and his father fitted all the leaves into the table, and the women added last-minute

touches to the dishes Rita had prepared. Everyone was entranced to find nothing but hors
d'oeuvres. "Look! Artichokes," Doug pointed
out. "Look at this, kids, my favorite: Chesapeake
crab spread. It's just like the old days." Rita
beamed. Stuart told her, "Pick a card. Any card.
Come on, Rita, pay attention."

The current foreigners' names were Manny,
Mike, and Buck. They were the first to arrive—
they always showed up on the dot, not familiar
with Baltimore ways—and Mrs. Jordan followed,
bearing one of her sumptuous black fruitcakes
with the frosting you had to crack through with
a chisel. Then Bobbeen appeared with an old-
fashioned crank-style ice cream freezer, fully
loaded and ready for the ice, and last came Curt,
looking as if he'd just that minute rolled out of
bed. Those who were guests had to have the
hors d'oeuvres explained for them—all but Mrs.
Jordan, of course, who'd been through this year
after year. Mrs. Jordan said, "Why, you've even
made Bee's hearts-of-palm dish!" And later,
once they'd taken their seats and Doug had offered the blessing, she said, "Rita, if Ian's
mother could see what you've done here she
would be so pleased."

"Remember the first time we tasted hearts of
palm?" Agatha asked Thomas.

"Was that when we had the flu?"

"No, no, this was before. You were really little,

and Daphne was just a baby. I don't think she got to try them. But you and I were crazy about them; we polished off the platter. It wasn't till five or six years later we had that flu."

"Ugh! Worst flu of my life," Thomas said.

"Mine too. I couldn't eat a bite for days. But finally I called out, 'Ian, I'm hungry!' Remember, Ian? You were flat on your back—"

"*I* was sick?" Ian asked.

"Everyone was, even Grandma and Grandpa. You said, 'Hungry for what?' And I thought and thought, and the only thing that came to me was hearts of palm."

"So then we all wanted hearts of palm," Thomas told him. "They just sounded so *good*, even though I'd forgotten them and Daphne'd never had them. We said, 'Please, Ian, won't you please bring us hearts of—' "

"I don't remember this," Ian said.

"So you got up and tottered downstairs, holding onto the banister—"

"Put your coat on over your pajamas, stepped into somebody's boots—"

"Drove all the way to the grocery store and brought back hearts of palm."

"I don't remember any of it," Ian said.

They regarded him fondly—all but the foreigners, who were giving the hors d'oeuvres their single-minded attention. "My hero!" Rita told him.

"I said, 'Ian, thank you,'" Agatha went on, "and you said, 'Thank *you*. Until you mentioned them,' you said, 'I didn't realize that's what I'd been wanting all along myself.'"

Stuart said, "Maybe they contained some trace element your bodies knew they needed."

"Well, whatever," Curt said, "these here taste mighty good. You should go into the catering business, Rita."

"Oh, I believe I've got enough to do for the next little bit," she told him. And she patted her abdomen, which Ian's borrowed shirt could barely cover.

Daphne said, "Have you heard? After this baby's born, Rita and I are planning to be partners. Half the time I'll do clutter counseling while she stays home with the baby, half the time I'll stay with the baby while *she* does clutter counseling."

Ian raised his eyebrows. He knew Rita had been considering various strategies, but she hadn't mentioned Daphne. He said, "What about Trips Unlimited?"

"That's not really working out," Daphne told him. "It's too personal."

"A travel agency is personal?"

"Mr. X and Mrs. Y book two flights to Paris and one hotel room, say, and I can't let on I've noticed. Or they cheat on their expense accounts with first-class reservations to—"

No one suggested that this new job would surely be even more personal—that she seemed to *search out* the personal. Finally Curt said, "Well, if you ever get tired of clutter counseling you could always become a scribe."

"Scribe?" Daphne asked, perking up.

"You could rent a stall at Harborplace and offer to write people's letters for them."

Daphne looked perplexed. The only person who laughed was Ian.

There was a little wait before dessert because they had to freeze the ice cream. Bobbeen said, "You realize we don't have a single child here? No one begging to turn the crank for us." But the foreigners, it emerged, would love to turn the crank. They rushed off to the kitchen while Daphne and Agatha cleared the table. Rita stayed seated at Ian's left, debating baby names with Mrs. Jordan. Curt was attempting to break into the fruitcake, and Thomas was telling his grandfather about his latest computer game. The idea was, he said, to show how dislodging one historical event could dislodge a hundred others, even those that seemed unrelated. "Take slavery," he said. "Students would tell the computer that the U.S. has never had slavery, and then they would name some later event. The computer goes, 'Beep!' and a message flashes up on the screen: *Null and void.*"

"But why would that be any fun?" Doug asked.

"Well, it's not supposed to be fun so much as educational."

"I wonder whatever became of Monopoly," Doug said wistfully.

Rita took Ian's hand and placed it palm-down on a spot just beneath her left breast. "Feel," she whispered. A round, blunt knob—a knee or foot or elbow—slid beneath his fingers. It always unnerved him when that happened.

Last week he had signed the papers for Rita's hospital stay. She'd be in just overnight, if everything went as it should. On the first day he was liable for one dependent and on the second, for two. Two? Then he realized: the baby. One person checks in; two check out. It seemed like sleight of hand. He had never noticed before what a truly astonishing arrangement this was.

"So I took a shortcut through a side street," Daphne told him, "or really more of an alley, and it was starting to get dark and I heard these footsteps coming up behind me. Pad-pad, pad-pad: gym-shoe footsteps. Rubber soles. I started walking faster. The footsteps walked faster too. I dug my hand in my bag and pulled out that siren you gave me. Remember that key chain with the siren on it you gave me one Christmas?"

They were heading down to the shop together

to bring home the cradle. Ian was driving Rita's pickup, which had a balky gear shift that was annoying him no end. When the light turned green he had to struggle to get it into first. He said, "Very smart, Daphne. How many times have I warned you not to walk alone at night?"

"I spun around and I pressed the button. The siren went *wow! wow! wow!* and this person just about fell on top of me—this young, stalky black boy wearing great huge enormous white basketball shoes. He was shocked, you could tell. He backed off and sort of goggled at me. He said, 'What the hell, man? You know? What the hell?' And I was standing in front of him with my mouth wide open because I realized I had no idea how to switch the fool thing off. There we were, just looking at each other, and the siren going *wow! wow!* until bit by bit I started giggling. And then finally he kind of like shook his head and stepped around me. So I threw the siren over a fence and walked on, only making sure not to follow him too closely, and way far behind I could still hear *wow, wow, wow . . .*"

"You think it's all a big joke, don't you," Ian said, turning down Chalmer.

"Well, it was, in a way. I mean I wouldn't have been surprised if that boy had said, 'Oh, man, that uncle of yours,' while he was shaking his head. Like we were the old ones and you were the young one. You were the greenhorn."

"At least I won't end up dead in some alley," Ian told her. "What were you doing in that part of town? How come you're always cruising strange neighborhoods?"

"I like newness," Daphne said.

He parked in front of the wood shop.

"I like for things not to be too familiar. I like to go on first dates; I like it when a guy takes me someplace I've never been before, some restaurant or bar, and the waitress calls him by name and the bartender kids him but I'm the stranger, just looking around all interested at this whole new world that's so unknown and untried."

They got out of the truck. (Ian didn't ask how come she still lived in Baltimore, in that case. He was very happy she lived in Baltimore.) He walked around to the rear end to lower the tailgate, and he reached in for the folded blanket he'd brought and spread it across the floorboards.

"If I were a man I'd call up a different woman every night," Daphne said, following him. "I'd like that little thrill of not knowing if she would go out with me."

"Easy for *you* to say," Ian told her.

He didn't have to use his key to get into the shop, which meant Mr. Brant must be working on a weekend again. He ushered Daphne inside and led the way across the dusty linoleum floor, passing a half-assembled desk and the carcass of an armoire. Through the office doorway he glimpsed Mr. Brant bending over the drafting table, and he stepped extra heavily so as to make his presence felt. Mr. Brant raised his head but merely nodded, deadpan.

When they reached the corner that was Ian's work space, he came to a stop. He gestured toward the cradle—straight-edged and shining. "Well?" he said. "What do you think?"

"Oh, Ian, it's beautiful! Rita's going to love it."

"Well, I hope so," he said. He bent to lift it. The honey smell of Wood-Witch paste wax drifted toward him. "You take the other end. Be careful getting it past that desk; I spent a long time on the finish."

They started back through the shop, bearing the cradle between them. Mr. Brant came to the office doorway to watch, but Daphne didn't even glance in his direction. She was still talking about newness. "I'd call some woman I'd just seen across a room or something," she said. "I would *not* say, 'You don't know me, but—' That's such an obvious remark. Why would she need to be informed she doesn't know you, for goodness' sake?"

All at once it seemed time slipped, or jerked,

or fell away beneath Ian's feet. He was fifteen years old and he was rehearsing to ask Cicely Brown to the Freshman Dance. Over and over again he dialed the special number that made his own telephone ring, and Danny picked up the receiver in the kitchen and pretended to be Cicely's mother. "*Yell*-ow," he answered in fulsome, golden tones, and then he'd call, "Cicely, dahling!" and switch to his Cicely voice, squeaky and mincing and cracked across the high notes. "Hello? Oooh! Ian-baby!" By that stage Ian was usually helpless with laughter. But Danny waited tolerantly, and then he led Ian through each step of the conversation. He told Ian it was good to hear from him. He asked how he'd done on the history test. He spent several minutes on the he-said-she-said girls always seemed to think was so important, although in this case it was, "He said mumble-grumble and she said yattata-yattata." Then he left a conspicuous space for Ian to state his business, after which he told him, why, of course; you bet; he'd be thrilled to go to the dance.

Daphne said, "Ian?"

He balanced his end of the cradle on one knee and turned away, blotting his eyes with his jacket sleeve. When he turned back he found Mr. Brant next to him. "Hot," Ian explained. It was January, and cold enough in the shop to see your breath, but Mr. Brant nodded as if he knew all about it and opened the front door for him. Ian and Daphne carried the cradle on out.

Rita started labor in the middle of a working day. Envisioning this moment earlier, Ian had expected it to be nighttime—Rita nudging him awake the way women did on TV—but it was a sunny afternoon in late February when Doreen came to the office door and said, "Ian! Rita's on the phone." The other men glanced up. "Sure you don't want to change your mind, now," one said, grinning. They'd acted much less guarded around him since the news of the baby.

On the phone Rita said she was fine, pains coming every five minutes, no reason to leave the shop yet unless he wanted. By the time he reached home, though (for of course he came immediately), things had speeded up and she said maybe they should think about getting to the hospital. She was striding back and forth in the living room, wearing her usual outfit of leather boots and maternity jeans and one of his chambray shirts. His father paced alongside her, all but wringing his hands. "I've *never* liked this stage, never liked it," he told Ian. "Shouldn't we make her sit down?"

"I'm more comfortable walking," Rita said.

For the last two weeks she had been allowed on her feet again, and Ian often felt she was making up for lost time.

It was the mildest February ever recorded—
not even cool enough for a sweater—and Rita
looked surprised when Ian wanted to bring her
coat to the hospital. "You don't know what the
weather will be like when you come home," he
told her.

She said, "Ian. I'm coming home *tomorrow*."

"Oh, yes."

He seemed to be preparing for a moment far
in the future. It was unthinkable that in twenty-
four hours they'd be back in this house with a
child.

At the hospital they whisked her away while
he dealt with Admissions, and by the time they
allowed him in the labor room she had turned
into a patient. She lay in bed in a coarse white
gown, her forehead beaded with sweat. Every
two minutes or so her face seemed to flatten.
"Are you all right?" he kept asking. "Should I be
doing anything?"

"I'm fine," she said. Her lips were so dry they
looked gathered. The nurse had instructed him
to feed her chips of ice from a plastic bowl on
the nightstand, but when he offered her one she
turned her head away fretfully.

She used to seem so invulnerable. That may
have been why he had married her. He had seen
her as someone who couldn't be harmed, once
upon a time.

It was dark before they wheeled her to the

delivery room. The windowpanes flashed black as Ian walked down the hall beside her stretcher. The delivery room was a chamber of horrors— glaring white light and gleaming tongs and monstrous chrome machines. "You stand by her head, daddy," the doctor told him. "Hold onto mommy's hand." Somehow Rita found it in her to snicker at this, but Ian obeyed grimly, too frightened even to smile. Her hand was damp, and she squeezed his fingers until he felt his bones realigning.

"Any moment now," the doctor announced. Any moment what? Ian kept forgetting their purpose here. He was strained tight, like guitar strings, and all his stomach muscles ached from urging Rita to push. Couldn't women die of this? Yes, certainly they could die. It happened every day. He didn't see what prevented her from simply splitting apart.

"A fine boy," the doctor said, and he held up a slippery, angry, squalling creature trailing coils of telephone cord.

Ian released the breath that must have been trapped in his chest for whole minutes. "It's over, sweetheart," he told Rita. He had to raise his voice to be heard above the racket.

The doctor laid the baby in Rita's outstretched arms and she hugged it to her, cupping its wet black head in one hand. "Hello, Joshua," she said. She seemed to be smiling and weeping both. The baby went on wailing miserably. "So, do you like him?" she said, looking up at Ian.

"Of course," he told her.

It wrenched him that she'd felt the need to ask.

Eventually the baby was carted off somewhere, and Rita sent Ian to make phone calls. In the waiting room he shook quarters from the envelope she had prepared weeks earlier. He called each of the numbers she'd written across the front—first Bobbeen, and then his father, and then Daphne, Thomas, and Stuart (Agatha was still at work), and Rita's two best friends. They all sounded thrilled and amazed, as if they hadn't understood till now that an actual baby would come of this. Bobbeen wanted to drive right over. Ian persuaded her to wait, though. "You can visit her tomorrow," he said. "But stop by early. They're letting her go home right after lunch."

"Modern times!" Bobbeen marveled. "When Rita was born I had to stay a week, and they didn't let Vic in the delivery room, either. You-all are lucky."

It was on Rita's account that he'd asked Bobbeen to wait till morning; he assumed she would be exhausted. But when he went to her room he found her sitting upright, looking ready to spring out of bed. Her hair was combed and she wore her flannel pajamas in place of the hospital gown. "Eight pounds, four and a half ounces," she said. She must be talking about the baby, who wasn't there yet. They kept them in the nursery for the first few hours. "He's got your mouth: those little turns at the corners. And my dad's Italian hair. Oh, I *wish* they'd bring him in."

"Ah, well, you'll have him for the next eighteen years," Ian said.

Eighteen years; merciful heavens.

He sat with her a while, listening to her rattle on, and then he kissed her good night. When he left, she was dialing her mother on the phone.

At home, a single lamp lit the front hall. His father must have gone to bed. It was after ten o'clock, Ian was amazed to see. He trudged up the stairs to his room.

Already Rita's pregnancy seemed so long ago. The pillow laid vertically to ease her backache, the opened copy of *Nine Months Made Easy*, and Doug's pocket watch, borrowed for its second hand—they struck him as faintly pathetic, like souvenirs of some old infatuation.

He sat on the bed to take off his shoes. Then he realized he would never manage to sleep. He was tired, all right, but keyed up. Padding softly in his socks, he went back downstairs to the kitchen and switched on the light. He poured milk into a saucepan and lit a burner, and while he waited for the milk to heat he dialed Reverend Emmett.

"Hello," Reverend Emmett said, sounding wide awake.

"Reverend Emmett, this is Ian. I hope you weren't in bed."

"Goodness, no. What's the news?"

"Well, we have a boy. Joshua. Eight pounds and some."

"Congratulations! How's Sister Rita?"

"She's fine," Ian told him. "It was a very easy birth, she says. To me it didn't look easy, but—"

"Shall I go visit her tomorrow?"

"They're sending her home in the afternoon. Maybe you'd like to come see her here."

"Gladly," Reverend Emmett said. "Why, we haven't had a new baby at church since Sister Myra's granddaughter! I may have forgotten how to hold one."

"You're welcome to brush up on your skills with us," Ian told him.

"God bless you for thinking to call me, Brother Ian," Reverend Emmett said. "I know absolutely that you'll be a good father. Go get some rest now."

"I believe I will," Ian said.

In fact, all at once he felt so sleepy that after he hung up, he turned off the stove and went straight to bed.

He stepped out of his shirt and his jeans and lay down in his underwear, not even bothering to pull the covers over him. He closed his eyes and saw Rita's glowing face and the baby's expression of outrage. He saw Reverend Emmett attempting to hold an infant. *That* would be a sight. It intrigued him to imagine the incongruity—to try and picture Reverend Emmett in this new context, the way he used to try picturing his seventh-grade teacher doing something so mundane as cooking breakfast for her husband.

Apparently, he thought, there were people in this world who simply never came clear. Reverend Emmett, Mr. Brant, the overlapping shifts of foreigners . . . In the end you had to accept that the day would never arrive when you finally understood what they were all about.

For some reason, this made him supremely happy. He pulled the covers around him and said a prayer of thanksgiving and fell headlong into sleep.

"This is proper gift," the foreigner named Buck told Ian. Or Ian *thought* he told him; then a moment later he realized it must have been a question. "This is proper gift?"

He meant the white plastic potty-chair resembling a real toilet, a pink ribbon tied in a bow across the seat like one of those hygienic paper bands in hotel bathrooms. Buck and Manny held it balanced between them on the top porch step. If Ian answered, "No," they seemed ready to spin around and take it home with them. He said, "Of course it's proper. Thank you very much."

"In America, every what you do is proper," Manny said to Buck. They appeared to be resuming some previous argument. "Why you are always so affrighted?"

"Wrong," Buck said. "They *tell* you is proper. Then catch your mistake. Ha!" he cried, startling Ian. "Pink ribbon. For boys should be blue."

"We already have been discussing this," Manny told him severely. "It is no problem." He turned to Ian. "Pink or blue: is all the same to you. Correct?"

"Correct," Ian assured him. "Come on inside."

He stood back, holding open the door, and they carried the potty through the front hall and into the living room. Rita sat in the rocker with a large pillow beneath her. Daphne and Reverend Emmett shared the couch. "This is proper gift," Buck told them. He and Manny set the potty on the floor.

"Well, certainly," Rita said, "and it's exactly what we wanted. Thank you, Buck and Manny."

"Is also from Mike. Mike has been arrested."

"Arrested?"

But before they could get to the bottom of this, Bobbeen called, "Yoo-hoo!" and let herself in. Her heels clattered across the hall and then she appeared in the doorway, wearing an orange pantsuit with a flurry of silk scarf tied artfully at her throat. She held both arms out at her sides; a vinyl purse dangled from one wrist. "Well?" she said. "Where is he? Where'd you put him? Where's that precious little grandbaby?"

"Hi, Ma," Rita said. "You remember Buck and Manny here, and Reverend Emmett."

"Oh! Goodness *yes*, I do," Bobbeen said, directing her squinty grimace solely to Reverend Emmett. He was standing now, looking uncomfortable, and Bobbeen stepped forward to grasp his hands in hers. "Wasn't it Christian of you to take this time from your duties," she said. Ian always suspected her of harboring a romantic interest in Reverend Emmett, but maybe she was just exceptionally devout. "Hey there, Daphne hon," she added over her shoulder. She sat in the center of the couch, pulling Reverend Emmett down beside her. "I can't believe I'm a grandma," she told him. "Isn't it a hoot? I sure don't *feel* like a grandma."

She didn't look like one either, Reverend Emmett was supposed to say, but he just smiled hard and clutched both his kneecaps. Bobbeen studied him a moment. She patted the ends of her hair reflectively and then turned to Rita. "So where's that little sweetie pie?" she asked.

"Ian was just on his way to bring him down," Rita told her.

He was?

Before the foreigners arrived, Reverend Em-

mett and Daphne had been about to follow him
upstairs and peek into the cradle. But now there
were too many of them, Ian supposed, and so
he nodded and left the room. He was a little out
of practice, was the trouble. He wasn't sure he
remembered how to support a newborn's head.

As he started up the stairs he heard Bobbeen
say, "Now tell me, Reverend Emmett, do you-
all hold with christening? Or just what, exactly?"

"We believe christening to be a superficial
convention," Reverend Emmett said.

"Well, of *course* it is," she told him in a
soothing tone.

"Not to say there's anything wrong with it, you
understand. It's just that we don't consider infants capable of . . . but if *your* church favors
christening, why, I certainly—"

"Oh, what do I care about christening?" Bobbeen cried recklessly. "I think it's real holy of
you to cast off the superficial, Reverend."

Ian went into his and Rita's bedroom, where
they were keeping the baby for the first few
nights. It lay facedown in one corner of the cradle
with its knees drawn up to its stomach and its
nose pressed into the sheet. How could it manage to breathe that way? But Ian heard tiny sigh-
ing sounds. Long strands of fine black hair
wisped past the neckband of the flannel gown.
Ian felt a surge of pity for those scrawny,
hunched, defenseless little shoulders.

He knelt beside the cradle and turned the baby over, at the same time gingerly scooping it up so that he held a warm, wrinkled bundle against his chest as he rose. This didn't feel like any eight pounds. It felt like nothing, like thistle-down—a burden so light it seemed almost buoyant; or maybe he was misled by the softness of the flannel. The baby stirred and clutched two miniature handfuls of air but went on sleeping. Ian bore his son gently across the upstairs hall.

"In fact I've been thinking of joining your congregation," Bobbeen was telling Reverend Emmett. "Did Rita happen to mention that?"

"Um, no, she didn't."

"I just feel you-all might have the answers."

"Oh, well, *answers*," Reverend Emmett said. "Actually, Mrs.—"

"Bobbeen."

"Actually, Mrs. Bobbeen . . ."

Ian grinned.

He was halfway down the stairs when he felt a kind of echo effect—a memory just beyond his reach. He paused, and Danny stepped forward to present his firstborn. "Here she is!" he said. But then the moment slid sideways like a phonograph needle skipping a groove, and all at once it was Lucy he was presenting. "I'd like you to meet the woman who's changed my life," he said. His face was very solemn but Lucy was smiling. "Your what?" she seemed to be saying.

"Your, what was that? Oh, your *life*." And she tipped her head and smiled. After all, she might have said, this was an ordinary occurrence. People changed other people's lives every day of the year. There was no call to make such a fuss about it.

A NOTE ABOUT THE AUTHOR

Anne Tyler was born in Minneapolis, Minnesota, in 1941 but grew up in Raleigh, North Carolina. She graduated at nineteen from Duke University, and went on to do graduate work in Russian studies at Columbia University. This is Anne Tyler's twelfth novel; her last novel, *Breathing Lessons*, was awarded the Pulitzer Prize in 1988. She is a member of the American Academy and Institute of Arts and Letters. She and her husband, Taghi Modarressi, live in Baltimore, Maryland.